THE STRAITS OF TREACHERY

RICHARD HOPTON

Allison & Busby Limited
11 Wardour Mews
London W1F 8AN
allisonandbusby.com

First published in Great Britain by Allison & Busby in 2020.
This paperback edition published by Allison & Busby in 2021.

A CIP catalogue record for this book is available from
the British Library.

10 9 8 7 6 5 4 3 2 1

ISBN 978-0-7490-2553-3

Typeset in 11/16 pt Adobe Garamond Pro by
Allison & Busby Ltd

The paper used for this Allison & Busby publication
has been produced from trees that have been legally sourced
from well-managed and credibly certified forests.

Printed and bound by
CPI Group (UK) Ltd, Croydon, CR0 4YY

For Caro

CHAPTER ONE

Punto di Faro, Sicily, 4th September 1810

George Warne, Captain in His Majesty's 27th Regiment of Foot, stood on the beach flicking at strands of seaweed with his cane.

The morning sun was touching the lower slopes of the Calabrian mountains on the other side of the straits, beyond the semi-mythical twin terrors of Scylla and Charybdis. He watched a brace of merchantmen run with the westerly breeze towards the opening of the Straits of Messina, their sails filling as they cut through the indigo waves. They would not be troubled, today at least, by the rock and the whirlpool that had stiffened Odysseus's sinews and wrecked countless mariners, ancient and otherwise. Phoenicians, Greeks, Romans, Arabs, Normans, Venetians had all come to grief here.

As Warne knew, modern scientific observation had established that Charybdis was nothing more than a powerful current, sometimes simply made more hazardous by contrary winds. Scylla was just a rock, albeit a big one; indeed, he could see it – and the castle that sat atop it – with the naked eye. Nevertheless, occasionally, the odd unlucky or incompetent Sicilian fisherman or Calabrian coaster fell foul of these timeless hazards, capsizing in the straits or being driven onto the lee shore. Even the Royal Navy had been known, much to its embarrassment, to get into trouble here.

The real object of Warne's interest was not Scylla or Charybdis or even the navy's occasional difficulties – amusing as it was to tease his naval friends about them – but the French forces on the far, Calabrian shore. Along the coast of Calabria, perched between the mountains and the sea, the French were crouching, waiting to jump across the straits. From where Warne stood on the beach at Punto di Faro, the easternmost point of Sicily, the nearest Frenchman was little more than a mile and three-quarters away.

All along the coast, from Scylla in the west, at about eleven o'clock from where he stood now, to his right, down past San Giovanni to Reggio and beyond, Warne could see the enemy's encampments, his artillery batteries, the thickets of masts above his landing craft. You could follow his infantry formations as they marched along the coastal roads. On a clear day, you could see the French headquarters, with Murat's splendid, tented pavilion in its midst. A couple of days ago Warne had seen three corpses swinging from a gibbet in the French camp. Deserters or spies, no doubt, poor buggers.

The French had been over there for four and a half years now, waiting for the moment to launch their invasion. But that opportunity had never come. The Straits of Messina might only be two miles wide, but it was a very long two miles when defended by strong currents and patrolled by the Royal Navy. And so it had proved.

But recently, the French had been in greater earnest. More troops had arrived. Coasters, landing craft, and fishing smacks had been gathering at Reggio, San Giovanni and other harbours along the coast in large numbers. All this pointed to preparations for an invasion. Warne had no doubt, nor did any man in the British army here, that this was all Murat's doing: Murat the brave, the *beau sabreur*, the greatest cavalryman in Europe, the Emperor's brother-in-law, now King of Naples. At the Battle of Eylau, in the snow, he had led ten thousand horsemen in a charge against the Russians. It is said, Warne recalled with a smile, that he only used two words of command on the battlefield, 'Forward' and 'Charge'.

'Sir!' Warne was jolted from his reverie by his sergeant's friendly Irish brogue. 'Mr Hare to see you in the tower, sir.'

'Very good, Flynn. I'm coming.'

'Get on, Boney, leave it alone,' Warne shouted at his dog who was inquisitively sniffing a dead seabird on the grey, rough sand. As Warne turned to walk back up the beach towards the fort, the spaniel abandoned his trophy and trotted to his master.

Warne, his dog at his heels, skirted around the walls and ditch that defended the seaward side of the tower before passing through the gateway on the landward side. It was a round, squat, solid construction, not unlike the Martello towers which now formed a chain along the south coast of England. It was surrounded by a high wall enclosing several buildings. These were barracks for the men, a cookhouse, stabling, storage and a magazine. As he entered the fort, the sentry came smartly to attention. Warne strode across the courtyard, a couple of chickens flapping and clucking out of his path, and into the tower.

'Ah, George, there you are,' said Hare, looking at Warne. The two men were about the same height, an inch or two short of six foot, and broad-shouldered but George was slimmer, rangier. His hair was blonde, his fair English complexion deeply tanned by the Sicilian sun. His nose was prominent but straight in profile, not aquiline, and his blue eyes deep set, almost hooded, giving him a purposeful, determined look. 'Good morning.'

Hare, like Warne, had been in Sicily since the 27th arrived on the island in 1806. He was a well-liked officer, highly thought of by his superiors. This morning, he looked every inch the British officer in his scarlet tunic with its buff facings at the collar and cuffs, his white breeches and well-polished boots.

'Shall we go up, sir?' suggested Warne.

The two men climbed the steep stairs to the open platform on top of the tower. They walked to the parapet and looked out at the view. Laid out before them were the narrow straits, studded with white sails, with the Mediterranean beyond and the mountains of mainland Italy rearing up behind. On a sunny, late summer morning, it was a spectacular sight.

'George, I've received orders that you are to report to the general at Messina. Sir John Stuart.'

'Do you know why, sir? I hope I'm not in trouble.'

'No. It's some kind of special task, I think, but beyond that I don't know anything.'

'When does he want to see me?'

'At two o'clock this afternoon, in the Citadel.'

A few minutes later Hare departed, down the stairs to the courtyard where he mounted his horse before clip-clopping out through the gateway. George remained on the gun platform gazing at the view, wondering what the general had in store for him. It was not often that a mere captain – and a junior one at that – was summoned to an interview with the commander-in-chief. It must be something important, he decided, rubbing his hand on the cool, rough stone of the parapet before turning towards the door and the stairs.

Three hours later, George was sitting astride his horse trotting along the new military road built by the British between Faro and Messina. It was now very hot; he was sweating profusely in his heavy uniform. This was, Warne knew, the best stretch of road on the entire island, although this was no great compliment as many of them were scarcely better than rocky, potholed paths. He passed the two saltwater lakes at Ganzirri, famous for their fish and shellfish, then the villages of Sant' Agata and Grotto di Pace, hugging the coastal strip. On the landward side, to Warne's right as he trotted along, there were orange and olive groves and terraces of vines clinging to the lower slopes, above which prickly-pear bushes covered the hillside. On Warne's other side was the sea, with the Calabrian shore beyond. Drawn up on the beach were the local fishing boats – *speronari* – while the dark-tanned, bare-legged fishermen in their distinctive red caps repaired their nets or snoozed in the shade. Very sensible, thought Warne enviously, as he rode on towards Messina in the baking sun. He saluted as a party of artillerymen passed in the opposite direction with a limber and horses. Ammunition for the batteries at Faro, no doubt.

Ahead of him, he could see the city of Messina spread out as if on a canvas. To the left was the sickle-shaped spit of land that formed the harbour. At its near end was the fort of San Salvador, its circular bastion guarding the entrance to the harbour. At the other end of the sickle was the low, crouching mass of the Citadel, dominating the wide expanse of the harbour and glowering at the city. In there, somewhere, was General Stuart. Straight ahead was Messina's famous port, since ancient times regarded as the best, safest natural harbour in the Mediterranean. Today it bristled with masts, as vessels of every description, warships, merchantmen, coasters, fishing smacks, oared galleys and so on, came and went, moored and set sail. To the right was Messina herself, sitting in the bowl formed by the hills behind, the red-tiled roofs punctuated by the towers and spires of the city's many churches and monasteries. Warne had been in Messina, on and off, for four and a half years so knew the city well and had grown fond of it. It might be dirty, smelly and half ruined but it had a decided charm.

Soon Warne was passing the monastery of San Salvadore de' Greci and the grand marble gates of San Francesco di Paola. As he got nearer to the city, the bustle of people, animals and vehicles became gradually busier: heavily laden mules, oxen carts, carriages, men on horseback, peasants on foot. Now, within sight of the city walls, he slowed his horse to a walk as he picked his way through the throng. Crossing the *fiumara* di Saddeo – a natural watercourse, dry in summer but often turned into a life-threatening torrent by winter rains or melting snow – he came to the Porta Reale, the gate in the northern flank of the city walls. On his left was the hulking Bastione Reale Basso, which commanded the point where the walls reached the shoreline. To his right the walls – which were about twenty feet high here and crowned with battlements – ran to the west, slightly uphill, away from the sea.

Once through the gate and into the city, he turned his horse's head to the left to go along the seafront. Here, fanned by the breeze off the harbour, it would be cooler than in the city's crowded streets. Messina's Marina was a chaotic, busy place. All along the quay, which extended for over a mile, ships loaded and unloaded their cargoes, fishing boats disgorged their catches and a multitude of other vessels took on water, rations, loaded ballast, spare sails or just sat at their moorings. Men swarmed around the boats, nimbly negotiating flimsy gangplanks, jumping from ship to quayside, scrambling up rigging.

As Warne trotted along the Marina he contemplated for the umpteenth time the damage wrought by the terrible earthquake that had devastated the city in 1783. The seafront had been one of the wonders of Europe. The *Palazzata*, as it was known, had been a long, elegant facade of buildings, in the baroque style with pilasters, pediments and balustrades, sheaved in marble, forming a gentle arc along the harbour. It had been brought crashing down on one terrifying day. Only now, nearly thirty years later, had the rebuilding started. There were still large gaps in the facade and many of the buildings had only one storey. One day, Warne reckoned, it would be a fine sight, but for now it was a building site. The rest of the city had suffered equally badly, but it was here on the waterfront that the damage was still most visible.

By now Warne was more than halfway along the Marina, well beyond the tip of the peninsula, which marked the entrance to the harbour itself. As he passed, he turned to admire the gigantic marble figure of Neptune, gleaming in the sunshine, his right hand raised as if in benediction, his trident clutched firmly in his left. The god of the sea stood on a plinth rising out of a fountain, his head crowned with seaweed as if he had just emerged from the deep. At its foot, in the frothing water, were four seahorses, with fine manes and muscular, fishy tails.

A few minutes later Warne crossed the wide expanse of open ground between the Citadel and the city itself. The Citadel was Messina's fortress, now serving as the British headquarters in Sicily. Built by the Spanish in the late seventeenth century, it had been intended as much to dominate the port and protect the unpopular Spanish viceroys from the populace as to guard the city against attack. It stood on the neck of the narrow spit of land that formed the outer shore of the harbour. It had been designed along the lines laid down by Vauban, Louis XIV's great military engineer: the low, powerful ramparts had five triangular bastions, which formed, in plan, a pentagon. The walls were about thirty feet high and solidly built. On top of each bastion was a wide platform on which were mounted heavy guns; more guns pointed out from embrasures cut in the walls between the bastions. In front of the walls on the city side was a rampart of earth – a glacis – thrown up to afford further protection from any attacker's artillery. Above the gateway, the Union flag fluttered in the breeze.

The sentries snapped to attention as Warne walked his horse across the drawbridge and into the Citadel. Dismounting, he handed the reins to a waiting groom and strode across the wide, dusty courtyard, which formed the centre of the castle towards the low range of buildings housing the general and his staff. He walked in past another sentry. Inside, the stone-flagged room was deliciously cool after the midday heat. Awnings shaded the room from the burning Sicilian sun but even in the dim light he instantly recognised the tall, lithe figure of William Coker.

'Coker, what a surprise to see you. What brings you here?'

Coker, a captain in the 31st Foot, was one of Warne's closest friends in Sicily. They had climbed Etna together two years earlier and often went shooting in the hills above Messina with their dogs.

'I might ask the same question of you,' replied Coker, his suntanned face creasing into a smile. 'I'm here to see the general. It's very secret, you know.'

'I've come to see the general, too. I was ordered to attend only this morning. I wonder what he is about?'

'We'll find out soon enough,' replied Coker. He turned to the clerk who sat at a table towards the back of the room piled high with papers and leather-bound ledgers. 'Mr Rogers, we are here to see the general. Ordered for two o'clock.'

'General Stuart will see you shortly, sir. Please wait over there,' he said, pointing to a high-backed bench against the far wall. Rogers was an Irishman – although this was hardly unusual, Warne's own regiment, the 27th, was recruited exclusively in Ireland – who had been with the army in Sicily since the beginning. He had started as an assistant clerk at headquarters but had worked his way up to his present senior position. Sitting as he did at the centre of things, he knew everyone and everything of any significance to the British army in Sicily. He may have been a clerk in name, but he was an important cog in the machine. Junior officers who called him anything other than 'Mister Rogers' did so at their peril.

A bachelor, he was widely rumoured to have a local mistress who had given him a growing brood of children. The army grapevine had it that they lived in a wing of one of the more obscure royal palaces in Messina, although no one could provide any concrete evidence of this. These rumours had, of course, reached the generals' ears but as Rogers was both hard-working and prodigiously competent, they turned a deaf ear to the gossip. After, all, they reasoned, he's not married and whatever he does in his own time is hardly the army's business, so long as it does not impinge upon his work, which it didn't seem to. Let Rogers get on with his rogering, seemed to be the general view.

As Warne and Coker walked towards the bench, two other officers entered the room from the courtyard.

'Do you know either of them?' Warne whispered to Coker.

'No, but they're in the 44th. Newly arrived, I shouldn't wonder.'

'Yes,' said Warne. He could make out in the dim light the 44th's yellow facings on the two men's tunics. Having announced themselves to the clerk, they approached Warne and Coker.

'Kendall, 44th Foot,' said the taller of the two men, extending his hand. 'I don't believe we've met.'

'No, indeed not,' replied Coker, shaking the proffered hand. 'This is Captain Warne, 27th Foot.'

'And this is Captain Entwhistle, also of the 44th.'

'At your service,' said Warne, inclining his head slightly towards the two new arrivals. Kendall was pink-cheeked with a shock of blonde hair. Entwhistle was darker, shorter and thicker set, with long, spare side whiskers, which only partly disguised a scar on his left cheek. They were about the same age as Warne and Coker. Both were smartly turned out, looking cool and unruffled, their gorgets and buttons brightly polished. They're probably quartered here, thought Warne, so no ride down the coast in the midday sun for them.

As the four officers were introducing each other the door on the far side of the room opened.

'Gentlemen, this way please. The general will see you now.' The voice belonged to a smartly turned-out staff officer in a dark blue uniform, white breeches and gleaming boots with spurs. They followed him through the door into an inner office. There were three desks heaped with papers. On the wall was a large map of Messina, the straits and the near parts of Calabria.

'Are you all ready?' he asked. 'Good. Let's go in, then.' He opened another door and the four young officers followed him, Warne bringing up the rear. On the far side of a large, high-ceilinged, whitewashed room was a long table, with an elaborate silver inkstand. Behind it sat General Sir John Stuart, Commander-in-Chief of the British forces in Sicily, Knight of the Bath, Count of Maida, writing. As they stepped onto the red Turkish carpet, the general replaced his quill in the inkstand and looked up. The staff officer closed the door.

'Gentlemen. Thank you for coming at such short notice.' The general was wearing a scarlet tunic, its buttons arranged in two rows of pairs down the front, and a black stock at the neck, on which hung a gilded medallion on a blue ribbon. He had a gold-tasselled epaulette on each shoulder and a star on his left breast. He looked worn and tired; his grey hair no longer covered the dome of his head, but his eyes flicked alertly around the group standing in a line opposite him on the carpet.

'You have been chosen,' the general began, stiffly, 'for a special duty, one which may, we hope, do much to disrupt the enemy's plans. As we all know, Prince Murat is preparing to invade the island and throw our forces into the sea. We see every day with our own eyes the preparations he is making. It can only be a matter of time before he launches his attack. We must strike at him before he strikes at us.' He paused, adjusting his stock. 'Captain Warne, you will recall the advantages gained by my great victory at Maida four years ago. Attack is the best form of defence. If we can strike at the enemy now, we may be able to disrupt his invasion plans and with the summer coming to an end, this may postpone Murat's ambitions until next year.'

Warne did remember Maida. How could he possibly forget it: the broiling heat, the blinding smoke and ear-splitting noise of the battle, the terror, the exhilaration, the bloodlust?

The general stood up behind his desk before continuing. 'I have asked General Cockburn to command the operation.' At this a man who had been sitting unnoticed at a desk at the back of the room got up and walked across the floor to Stuart's desk. He was about the same height as Stuart with an intelligent, rather quizzical look. His uniform was neat but plain, unadorned by stars, medallions and fussy rows of buttons.

'General Cockburn is newly arrived here and, as you all no doubt know, commands the southern division of our army. Please introduce yourselves to him.' Warne and his three fellow officers – indeed, the whole army – had heard of the general's narrow escape when his ship ran onto the rocks on the approach to Malta in heavy seas on his way to Sicily. He was lucky to be alive.

'Gentlemen,' Cockburn began in a light Irish accent, having acknowledged each officer as he introduced himself. 'I am honoured to be entrusted with this important operation by Sir John. I am sure that you will all do whatever you can to ensure its success. My chief staff officer, Colonel Airey, will explain the plan to you in detail but I propose an attack at night on the enemy's flotilla of landing craft. The object will be to destroy as many of them as we can, thus disrupting the invasion plans.'

A few minutes later, Warne, Coker and the two officers from the 44th were back in the next-door room looking at the large map on the wall as Colonel Airey outlined the operation. George Airey was a man of barely medium height but his high forehead, striking, dark eyes and impeccable turnout gave him a presence which belied his lack of inches. Now in his late forties, his dark, swept-back hair was flecked with grey. The four of them, he explained, would each command a detachment of soldiers, which would be rowed across the straits at night in galleys to where the enemy's flotillas of landing craft were moored. Each raiding party would be allocated a local guide with knowledge of the anchorage. Once there, the men would disembark before casting off, smashing or setting alight as many of the landing craft as possible. Then they would re-embark to return home. 'It'll be plain sailing, gentlemen,' said Airey, breezily.

That, at least, was the plan. But Warne had taken part in several operations across the straits in the four years he had been in Sicily and he was all too aware of how difficult they were. Any force, however small, had to contend with powerful, unpredictable winds and currents before it even got to the enemy. And all this at night, into the bargain. Warne shifted his weight from foot to foot and glanced uneasily at Coker.

'. . . you will be given charges of sulphur, nitre and charcoal, with oily rags, steel and flints to set the boats on fire,' Airey was saying. 'Captain Kendall,' he said, pointing with a stick at the map, 'you will land here, at Scylla.' The other three were allocated targets south, down the Calabrian coast towards Reggio. Entwhistle was to attack at San Giovanni and Coker at Catona. Warne had the southernmost, near Reggio itself.

'Finally, gentlemen, I should warn you that secrecy is vital. If any word of this operation gets to the French, you and your men will be walking into a hornets' nest. I don't need to remind you that Messina is crawling with French spies; any rumour of an attack will be carried straight over there to Murat,' Airey prodded his stick at the boot of Italy on the map, 'before you know it.'

'Sir,' asked Warne, 'we can rely on the loyalty of our own men but what about the crews of the galleys?'

'They won't be told of the targets or the nature of the operation until the last moment,' replied the colonel. 'After that, we'll just have to trust them. They, too, don't forget, will be on the receiving end of the enemy's fire, so it's very much in their interests not to betray the secret. The same applies to the guides, who are all men we know well and have employed in the past. That's all, gentlemen. You will receive my written orders in the morning. Good luck.'

As Warne opened the door into the box, the orchestra was tuning up in the pit below.

'Good evening, George,' said Major Thring. 'How good of you to come. Allow me to present my sister, Emma.'

A young woman in a light blue silk gown stepped forward. Warne noticed at once her lively grey eyes, which seemed to flash even in the operatic penumbra of the theatre. She reminded him, instantly and strikingly, of a Reynolds print he had once seen of a bacchante, lively, adventurous, and touched with a dash of devil-may-care. She'd take the bachelor bastions of British Messina by storm, that was for sure.

'A great pleasure, Miss Thring,' said Warne. 'I have heard much of you from your brother.'

'Oh dear, Robert, I hope you have not been boring Mr Warne with tales of home.'

'Quite the contrary, Miss Thring, I assure you. I gather you speak Italian and French?'

'Too badly, I am afraid.'

'You know Colonel Airey, I think,' said Thring. The colonel was still in the same dark blue uniform he had been wearing when he briefed Warne and his fellow officers earlier in the day.

'Indeed. Good evening, Colonel.'

'Good evening, Mr Warne,' he said, inclining his head gravely.

Once the four of them were seated, Warne looked around the opera house. It was a small theatre, with no more than a dozen boxes, a few rows of stalls and the usual area in front of the stage where people stood to watch the performance. The audience was often rowdy, quick to boo its disapproval and equally quick to shout, clap and whistle its approval. At the moment, they were talking quietly, awaiting the start of the opera. In the candlelight, the little opera house glowed.

In the box opposite was a man in a fine, red embroidered coat, with an extravagant white stock, his thick, dark hair gathered neatly in a bow. Warne recognised him as the Count of Pelorito; they had recently been introduced at a reception. Sitting next to him was a strikingly beautiful woman, her hair piled up on her head, in a cream silk gown. Suspended above her tantalising cleavage, Warne could see an enormous single diamond, glowing yellow in the candlelight. They made a handsome couple.

'Who is that with the count?' Warne asked the colonel. Colonel Airey, following Warne's gaze, leant across.

'That's his mistress, Madame Signotti,' he whispered. 'The count has been most helpful to us in raising the Sicilian Volunteers for the defence of the island. He is a great favourite of the King, who, I am told, rather likes Madame Signotti.'

'His Majesty is a man of excellent taste,' replied George.

'Yes. The count cordially hates the French who have pillaged his estates on the mainland. As a result, unlike many of his fellow countrymen, he will do whatever he can to make their life difficult.'

At that moment the conductor, a stout man in a black coat, waddled into the orchestra pit. The buzz of conversation stilled as he turned to face the audience. He bowed elaborately before turning back to the lectern and raising his baton.

La Serva Padrona was a short, lively opera, a standard in the repertoire here in Messina. Warne had seen it twice before in the four years he had been in Sicily. Written in the early eighteenth century by the Italian composer Giovanni Pergolesi, it comprised an overture and two separate *intermezzi*. Considering, Warne thought, that Pergolesi had died at the tender age of twenty-six, this piece was a remarkably precocious achievement. As the overture skipped joyously along, he looked down into the orchestra pit. Unusually for an opera, the orchestra consisted only of a string quartet; no trumpets and drums tonight. Looking up, he stole a glance across at Emma: she was already wrapped in concentration, staring at the ceiling. As the final chords of the overture faded away, the curtain rose to reveal the bulky figure of Uberto dressing to go out. His fine, dark bass voice filled the theatre as the fat conductor marked time with his baton.

'I greatly enjoyed that,' said Emma as the little open carriage carrying her and the three men pulled away from the opera house. She had covered her shoulders with a woollen shawl against the cooler night air but it was a relief to be out of the hot, stuffy atmosphere of the opera house.

'Me too,' said George. 'I'd never been to an opera before I came to Sicily as it hasn't reached Herefordshire yet, but I took to it from the first. Some of my friends in the regiment tease me for liking it; they call it "Italian warbling" or "foreign shrieking", but I think they are the ones missing out.'

'I've always liked it,' said Colonel Airey as the carriage started to descend the hill. 'When I was in London I used to go whenever I could. Indeed, I saw Herr Mozart's *La Clemenza di Tito* when it was first sung in London four years ago. I was very lucky. What did you think of the evening, Robert?' he asked.

'Oh, I liked it well enough. I think I prefer a good play, but it's fine once in a while.'

Ten minutes later they were sitting at a gate-legged table in Colonel Airey's quarters in the Citadel. The colonel's servant was fussing around the candlelit room, putting supper on the table. There were some thick, juicy tranches of swordfish, with dark welts where they had been cooked on a griddle, and a plate of sweet, ripe tomatoes dressed with olive oil. Airey poured four glasses of white wine.

'This is the kind of thing we've grown accustomed to eating out here, Miss Thring,' he said. 'It's probably not what you're used to at home, but the fish was caught out in the straits this morning, I shouldn't wonder.'

'Yes, sir,' said the servant, 'I bought half a small fish from a fishing boat at the quayside this morning.'

'They must be very big,' said Emma, 'if this is half a small one.'

'They are,' replied her brother. 'I've seen ones six foot long. It's most interesting watching the men catching the swordfish. Sometimes you can watch them fishing through a glass from the ramparts here.'

As they ate, the talk turned to the news from England. Emma, it transpired, had arrived in Sicily only the previous day having stopped at Gibraltar and Malta on the voyage out. She had sailed in an East Indiaman to Gibraltar, before transferring to a ship bound for Alexandria for the remainder of the voyage. She enthused about the sights of Valletta – 'The Knights are so romantic and the Grand Harbour so pretty' – and had enjoyed a boat trip to Gozo but had been less keen on Gibraltar: 'rather dull', she thought.

'Why did you decide to come out to the Mediterranean, Miss Thring?' asked George.

'Well, strange as it may seem, I missed my dear brother whom I hadn't seen for more than four years, and he kept telling me in his letters how nice it is here. Also, with most of the Continent closed to English travellers, opportunities to go abroad have been very limited. Mother was not keen on the idea, but Father said that the voyage is much safer now that the French navy is blockaded in its ports. So when my parents discovered that some friends of theirs, the Reverend and Mrs Allen, were going to Sicily and were happy that I accompany them, that decided it. I am hoping that dear Robert will get some leave while I am here so that we can travel around the island a little. I would love to see Etna and I am interested in visiting the Greek and Roman temples. I have read Mr Brydone's book, which has filled my head with all manner of ideas of things to do while I'm here. Taormina is very pretty, he says.'

'He's right, it is. The Greek theatre there should not be missed. I would be delighted to show you round the sights of Messina, Miss Thring,' offered George, 'although I may be busy for the next couple of days.'

'That would be a great pleasure, Mr Warne,' she replied.

An hour and a half later the party had broken up: Robert Thring had taken his sister back to his lodgings in the city and Airey had gone to bed. George Warne was standing on the ramparts gazing out over the straits, smoking a cigar. To his left the sentry turned smartly, his boots clicking on the paving stones, before pacing slowly back towards the next bastion. The moon was partly obscured by drifting clouds. There was little to see: only the odd light on the far side and one ship, picked out by its lanterns and by the lights in a stern cabin, making its way towards Faro.

Inevitably, George's thoughts turned to the raid. In two days' time he and his men would be waiting, here in the Citadel, to embark, their nerves tightening by the minute. The men would be cleaning their muskets and sharpening their bayonets, chuntering away in their Irish voices, joking and swearing, anything to relieve the nerves. He would be trying to disguise his fears, to remain calm and composed. That was the leader's job. If he couldn't be cool and confident, how could he expect the men to be? It's all going to take place over there, George thought, staring into the darkness over the straits. Who knows what lies in store for me, for the men, for us all?

He also thought about Emma as he stared out into the night. She was bright and intelligent, unlike some of the girls who came out to Sicily from England looking for husbands. Only last month, an officer in his own regiment had got engaged to a girl who'd arrived from England barely a fortnight before. The general opinion in the mess was that he'd live to regret it. Marriage is not for me, thought George, not yet anyway. He thought briefly of Carlotta, the pretty, dark, lithe, young widow from the city into whose bed he had slipped with increasing regularity over the last year or so. But Emma Thring was very pretty too, it could not be denied, and a lively character.

Less appealing was the worry that had been nagging at George rather too much in recent months: his lack of money. Or, to be more specific, his gambling debts. Before he arrived in Sicily, he had never played cards for money but, gradually, over the years the habit had crept up on him. Now he probably played two or three times a month, more in the winter, and his losses had started to grow. Sometimes he won – and won well – but the wins never seemed wholly to offset the steady drain of losses. He owed about a hundred pounds to other men in the card school – some of them brother officers – and another eighty pounds or so to a local money lender. This equated, as he was only too aware, to a year's salary for an infantry captain such as himself. At the moment his creditors seemed happy to wait for their money, but they might soon become restive. What he would do then was anyone's guess. He blew a final plume of smoke into the night air, ground the cigar under his heel and made his way towards the stairs.

Meanwhile, the Thrings' carriage was making its way slowly

through the darkened streets towards Robert's lodgings in a side street off the strada Ferdinanda.

'I hope you enjoyed your first taste of our society here,' said Thring.

'Yes, I did. I thought the opera was charming and the colonel provided a very good supper,' she replied.

'Good. I enjoyed myself, too. What did you think of Mr Warne?' Thring asked his sister.

'He is a very pleasant man and a kind one, too, I'd say, as well as rather dashing,' she replied.

'Yes, he's popular in the regiment and his men would follow him to the Gates of Hell,' said Thring. 'He's also well liked in local society, I understand. He's learnt Italian since he's been here – something not many British officers bother to do, I regret to say, beyond a few words of command – which helps him mix with the locals.'

'So far I find it difficult to understand the Sicilian dialect,' said Emma, 'but I may grow accustomed to it. My Italian was learnt at home from books, and from reading Dante. Mr Warne, I think, speaks as the Sicilians do. Perhaps he could teach me, too.'

'Perhaps he could,' replied her brother, as the carriage pulled up outside his house. 'Here we are, my dear.' He stepped out of the carriage and helped his sister down onto the pavement.

CHAPTER TWO

Punto di Faro, 6th September 1810

It was still early when George Warne mounted his horse outside the stables in the Citadel. The sun had not yet risen above the mountains on the Calabrian side of the straits, but he knew that it was going to be another hot day. It looked as if the attack across the straits was to be carried out tonight. George had already seen Colonel Airey this morning and he had been confident that the weather would hold and that the attack could be pressed home without any further delay. So George was riding up to Faro to assemble his men before marching them back to the Citadel.

George walked his horse through the Citadel's main gate onto the wide expanse of open ground – known locally as Terra Nova – inside the south-eastern angle of the city walls. He skirted the parade ground reaching the water's edge at the Porto Franco. In a minute or two he had joined the Marina. The port was coming alive in the morning sunshine: out in the middle of the harbour a British frigate was taking on water. The barges looked perilously

28

low in the water, weighed down by the heavy casks. On board the frigate George could see an officer standing in the ship's waist supervising the loading of the casks as they were roped up over the side by a couple of burly sailors.

By now George had passed the imposing figure of Neptune and was almost level with Fort Salvador. Then, on sudden impulse, he turned off the waterfront and, one block behind the Marina, joined the strada Ferdinanda. It was just along here that Carlotta lived, in an apartment in one of the big houses on the street. As he passed her house, he looked up at her balcony. The shutters were still closed so she was evidently still in bed. Behind them was her salon and beyond that her bedroom, where he had spent many a rapturous afternoon.

George had been in Sicily for about two years when they met, at a reception given by a local nobleman. He had, luckily, been learning Italian so was able to engage her in conversation. They had got on well and it had not been long before they became lovers. Carlotta had been widowed when her husband, an officer in the Sicilian army and an ardent supporter of the British, drowned in an accident in the straits. He could do things with her that he would never, ever be able to do with a respectable English girl out here in search of a husband. It was also due to her that his command of the Sicilian tongue was as good as it was; she was an inspiring teacher. Imagining her lissom, dark-skinned body sitting astride him, her delicious breasts soft yet weighty against his chest, he shifted in his saddle.

It was still only eight o'clock as George approached the squat tower behind the beach at Faro. He walked his horse through the gateway into the courtyard, where he dismounted. He was

29

immediately greeted by Boney, the spaniel rushing towards his master, jumping up and wagging his tail.

'Good boy, good boy,' said George, bending down to scratch the dog's long, shaggy, brown ears.

'Good morning, sir, how are you? You had a good time in the city?'

George looked up. Stepping out of the guardroom was John O'Connell, a young subaltern – no more than eighteen so far as George knew – who had only been in the regiment for just over a year. He had arrived in Sicily three months previously as an ensign and had recently been promoted lieutenant. He was one of the few officers in this Irish regiment who was himself Irish; the NCOs and the men were almost all Irish, of course. O'Connell had been left in command of the fort during George's absence in Messina.

'Everything been fine, I hope, John, while I've been away?'

'Yes, sir. Last night was quiet, nothing untoward here and nothing happening over the other side that we could see,' replied O'Connell.

'Good. Let's go inside. I'm going to have some breakfast and then I've got something to tell you.'

With Boney at their heels the two men crossed the courtyard and went into the small room that served as the officers' mess in this outpost.

Once George had eaten the plate of eggs and ham brought to him by the soldier-servant who did the mess cooking, he took his cup of coffee and pushed his chair back.

'Now, John, I have been ordered to command a raiding party across the straits. It seems very likely that the attack will happen tonight, so I am going to Grotto when we've finished here to get the men ready.'

'Can I come, too, sir? It would be a great privilege and I'm itching to get at the enemy,' said O'Connell, sitting bolt upright in his chair.

'No, I'm afraid you're needed here,' said George kindly. 'You will be left in charge. All being well, I will be back tomorrow.'

'Very good, sir,' said O'Connell, trying manfully but unsuccessfully to hide his disappointment.

'Now, this is strictly between you and me. There is no need to tell the men here what I'm doing or why I'm not here. The general was most emphatic on the need for secrecy and, as you know, the whole place is heaving with spies. The fewer people who know, the better.' George raised an index finger to his lips. 'Oh, and while I'm away, will you look after Boney for me?'

'Of course, sir. It would be a pleasure.'

Half an hour later George had ridden out of the fort and started down the coast road. Grotto di Paci was a village about halfway towards Messina where, up on a ridge, the British had established a camp. George climbed away from the houses and was soon entering the earthworks, which enclosed the British encampment, home to a company of George's regiment. From here the lookouts had a commanding view of the French positions on the far side of the straits. At the southern end of the earthworks was a battery of four heavy guns pointing menacingly out over the sea. To his left George could just see the big battery at Faro Superiore and two smaller ones in between. This part of the coast was now well defended; the French would be ill-advised to attempt a landing between here and Faro. George dismounted and, handing his horse to the waiting groom, strolled over to the rampart.

As he did so, there was a deep boom, followed by another and then several more. George could see several puffs of smoke across the straits. The French, he knew, had a large battery of heavy guns and big mortars at Torre Cavallo on the Calabrian shore, exactly opposite the tower at Faro, with which they regularly fired at the British. George could see an artillery limber making its way along the coast road to his left. Perhaps this was what the French were firing at. If so, their aim was poor. Two of the shots splashed into the sea, throwing up great spouts of water – those must be the mortar shells – and at least one hit the hillside to George's left cutting a swathe through the prickly pear but otherwise doing little damage. The limber continued unmolested on its way. Sometimes it was more deadly: George had had a friend in the Royal Artillery who had been killed by a single shot fired across the straits from the Torre Cavallo battery. Very unlucky, poor fellow.

George turned and, climbing down off the rampart, walked across the compound to the hut which housed the camp's headquarters. Inside, sitting in a canvas chair, was John Hare, reading a letter. He looked relaxed in his shirtsleeves, with his scarlet tunic hanging over the back of the chair and his sword propped against the table beside him. He was smoking a cigar.

'Ah, George, good morning. This came from the latest packet, which arrived in Messina yesterday,' he said, putting the letter down on the table. 'It's from my dear sister. Did you have any?'

'I'm sure there will be some, sir,' said George, 'as Mother and Father write regularly, but I haven't received them yet.' The arrival of the monthly packet from England with its precious crop of letters from home was always keenly anticipated by the whole army in Sicily.

'So tell me, George, how did your interview with the general go?'

Hare listened carefully as George explained the plan for the raid across the straits, the briefings they had received in the Citadel and the reconnaissance he had carried out the previous day.

'When are you going across?' Hare asked.

'Colonel Airey seems to think that the weather will hold and that we will cross tonight.'

'Well, he's probably right about the weather,' replied Hare. 'I hope he realises that these operations are pretty risky.'

'Colonel Airey is confident that we can carry it out successfully,' replied George. 'And certainly, with the threat of an invasion growing every day, we should try to disrupt Murat's plans, don't you think, sir? And with autumn coming, if we do disrupt his plans now, it may put off any invasion until next year.'

'No, you are right, of course, George, and the colonel is a most competent officer,' said Hare. 'And he couldn't have a better man leading the raid.'

'Thank you, sir.' George smiled. 'I'm here to muster the men I'll take across tonight. I've been ordered to get twenty volunteers for the operation. I'll need a sergeant, too.'

It was mid afternoon by the time George was riding at the head of his men as they marched down the coast road to Messina. The men swung along, two abreast in a column of ten, with Sergeant Fitt alongside, joshing each other and complaining about the heat. Once the company had turned out in the middle of the encampment George had asked for volunteers for a special duty in Messina. The entire company, bar one or two men, had raised their hands. George had then selected twenty of the best volunteers, told them to step forward before ordering Sergeant Fitt to dismiss the parade.

Once he'd done so and the men had dispersed, Fitt sidled up to George. He was a short, wiry man, with the build of a jockey but, as George knew, blessed with enormous strength and reserves of endurance.

'Will you be needing a sergeant on this caper, Mr Warne, sir?' he said, his Irish accent a soft lilt.

'Why, Fitt, do you have an urge to go on a boating trip?' said George with a smile.

'Is that what it is, sir?'

'You'll find out soon enough, but I'd be obliged if you would come with me to keep these scoundrels in order,' replied George.

'Thank you, sir. All this watching and waiting is getting on my nerves.'

Before long the little detachment of His Majesty's 27th Regiment of Foot was marching under the great arch of the Porta Reale into Messina and into some very welcome shade. Now that the troops were in the city itself, it was difficult to maintain a march because the streets were thronging with traffic, carts, the odd coach, and pack animals, to say nothing of people, dogs, chickens and the occasional pig. Reluctantly, George ordered the men to break their step. He didn't like allowing the men to get out of step as it looked unsoldierly, but in the streets of Messina at this time of the day there was little alternative.

As the soldiers passed along the strada Ferdinanda they were greeted by the locals with friendly waves. A pretty girl sitting in a doorway looked up from her sewing and, seeing Michael Hughes, a tall handsome lad from Donegal, blew him a kiss – producing a shower of ribald comments from his pals: 'Is that your fancy girl, then, Mikey?', 'He'll be round later, darlin',' and so on. The British were popular here with much of the population because they kept the French out. The French were hated because of their habit of living off the land. By contrast, where the French troops scavenged and stole, the English army paid for what it took. As a result, the local economy had thrived in the four years the English had been in Sicily: the King's soldiers were allowed a meat ration, a pint of wine and a pound of bread each a day and there were twelve thousand of them in Sicily and thousands more hangers-on and camp followers. Small wonder the locals blew kisses to the redcoats.

Now crossing the Terra Nova, they were marching in step once more as they approached the looming mass of the Citadel. Looking ahead, George saw a column of soldiers – almost exactly the same size as the one behind him now – emerging through the castle's main gate. As the two columns neared each other he soon recognised George Kendall riding at the head of his men. As the two columns drew level, the sergeants barked orders and they both came to a halt.

'Good afternoon,' said George, turning his horse towards Kendall. The two officers walked their horses away from the men.

'You are leaving early, Kendall.'

'Well, Warne, as you know, we are ordered to embark near Faro, which makes sense as we are attacking Scylla. The rest of you are embarking here, I gather.'

'Yes,' replied Warne. 'I have the furthest to go to reach Reggio. The other two have only a short hop across the straits to their targets.'

'I must press on,' said Kendall, shaking the reins at his horse.

'Well, good luck and I'll see you tomorrow,' said George turning his horse back towards his men.

As George's men marched through the gate of the Citadel, he looked back towards the harbour. He could still just see Kendall and his men as they turned onto the Porto Franco before disappearing from view.

Once inside the Citadel, George sent the men to a barrack room where they could lie up until it was time for the operation to get under way. There was no point in allowing the men to wander around the Citadel drawing attention to themselves. It was a long, narrow room, with a fine, ribbed, stone-vaulted ceiling and three windows looking out over the courtyard. Here they could rest out of the sun, clean their muskets, sharpen their bayonets and do all the other things which soldiers do to distract themselves from thinking about the imminent fighting.

'Right men,' said George, 'make yourselves comfortable here for a while. Try to relax. I'll be back to brief you about the operation a bit later. Fitt,' he said, turning to the sergeant, 'I'm leaving you in charge.'

George had a few minutes to kill before he was due to meet Colonel Airey to receive his last-minute orders, so he made his way up onto the Citadel's ramparts. He leant on the warm coping stones of the parapet and gazed out over the sea. With the late-afternoon sun going round to the west, the Calabrian coast seemed very clear and close. He could see the French encampments and batteries; there was a small detachment of infantry making its way down the coastal road; further on was a train of bullock carts inching its way along the same road. There were a few little craft out in the straits, some of them fishing vessels, some coasters. Over to his right a larger merchantman was beating its way up towards the harbour, its white sails bright against the deep blue of the sea. It was, thought George, a peaceful scene.

Further to the right was Reggio where, in a few hours' time, George would be stealing silently into a dark shore. It was, he knew, about seven and a half miles from here to the centre of Reggio, marked by the imposing mass of the *duomo*, too far to make out much with the naked eye. He had been as close in to the target as he dared during yesterday's reconnaissance so had got a good sight of what awaited him and his men tonight – the beach, the anchorage and the menacing battery on the headland – but there was always the unexpected, the mishap to contend with. It was difficult, even with a good telescope, to form an accurate impression from out at sea of the lie of the land; all too often there were folds in the ground and distortions of perspective that concealed important features. He was also acutely aware that his men had not rehearsed a night landing.

In many ways, too, he was looking forward to some action, to some excitement. He'd had a pretty quiet life since the regiment had arrived in Sicily more than four years earlier. There had been the attack on the French position on the mainland, which had resulted in the battle at Maida and the expedition to Ischia the previous year – which had involved almost no fighting. Indeed, they hardly saw the enemy at all. That apart, his military career had consisted of garrison duty, endless parades, route marches and the humdrum routine of a junior officer's existence: worrying about quarters and rations, dealing with the occasional outbreak of ill discipline, checking soldiers' equipment, their feet and so on. How he and his fellow subalterns had grumbled as the months stretched into years. Now, at least, he had something to break the monotony.

As he gazed out across the straits, George's thoughts drifted home, to his parents, his brother and his two sisters. He hadn't seen any of them for the best part of five years. It was difficult, bordering on the impossible – quite apart from the expense of the passage – for junior officers to get home leave. His parents would be older, greyer and slower than when he'd last seen them. One sister, Charlotte, had recently married; no doubt the other, Lizzie, would soon follow. His brother John was following their father into the Church. The comfortable, red-brick rectory under its slate roof, with its log fires and long views over the green, rolling Herefordshire countryside seemed more and more like a childhood dream, an imagined idyll, the longer he spent in Sicily. He devoured the monthly letters from his parents, filled with family news and gossip and those, less frequent, from his brother and sisters, likewise filled with chatter, but their world seemed far away, almost out of reach. He thought, too, of Harriet, his lively, pretty, elfin cousin, whom his family hoped one day he might marry. They had written to each other regularly at first, but with the passing of the years, less so. George felt a sudden pang of guilt for Harriet, remembering the afternoons and nights spent in Carlotta's arms. The sound of hooves from the courtyard below snapped George out of his reverie. It was time to go to the colonel's office.

When he opened the door, he saw that Coker and Entwhistle were already there.

'Sorry I'm late, sir,' said George, hurrying across the room.

'Don't worry. Take a seat.'

George sat down on an upright, wooden chair next to Coker, who smiled in welcome. Entwhistle nodded in his direction.

'The glass is high and steady so it looks as if the weather tonight will be good. Moonset is at about twenty past midnight, gentlemen, so I want you, Warne, and your men to be ready to embark by then at the far end of the Marina, opposite Fort Salvador. I estimate that it will take the galley something approaching two hours to row across to Reggio, perhaps less if it's able to use its sails. It could go more quickly but at a moderate pace it'll make less noise, especially as you get closer to the shore. Is that understood, Captain Warne?'

'Yes, sir.'

'You will have to carry the fire-lighting kit with you when you go. Slow match and quick match, flints and steel, saltpetre, blue lights, oily rags and so on – the kit you'll need for burning the boats – have been assembled by the armourer. That applies to you too,' said Airey, gesturing to Coker and Entwistle. 'He's also provided some small axes for you and made a number of coshes, which you can distribute among your men. They're very useful for knocking out sentries silently. He's also rustled up a handful of naval cutlasses, which are more useful in the kind of close-quarter fighting you'll encounter tonight than your swords.'

The colonel then went through the orders for Coker and Entwistle.

'You both have less distance to travel to your targets than Warne so will set off later from the Marina so that the attacks go in at approximately the same time. You, Captain Coker,' he said, 'have around four and a quarter miles to go to Catona while you, Captain Entwistle, have only around three and three-quarter miles across to San Giovanni. That should take between three-quarters of an hour and an hour in the galleys at a moderate pace. Do you have any questions, gentlemen?'

The three officers looked at each other; Coker raised an eyebrow, almost imperceptibly, and Warne smiled, faintly. Entwhistle remained stony-faced.

'No, sir,' said George. 'Everything is perfectly clear.'

'Good,' said the colonel. 'Does that hold for you two as well?' he said, looking at Coker and Entwhistle.

'Yes, sir,' they said in chorus.

At that moment the door leading to the commander-in-chief's office opened revealing General Cockburn. George and his two fellow officers sprang to their feet. He walked across the room, his boots clicking on the flagstones, and stood beside the colonel. George noticed that he was holding a pair of white gloves in his left hand.

'Gentlemen,' he said, looking at the three officers, 'I wish you good luck and Godspeed tonight. It will be the first attack on the enemy since I assumed command of the southern division of Sir John's army. I know you will all do your best to enhance the high reputation of the division. It is an important operation, which will, we all hope, delay or postpone the invasion that the enemy is so clearly planning. If you succeed, you will have the thanks of the whole army. Good luck.'

His little speech over, the general nodded to Colonel Airey and strode out of the room.

As George opened the door into the barrack room the somnolent buzz of idle chatter fell silent. A cool sea breeze was blowing in through the open windows. The men were lounging around in their shirtsleeves. Some of them were dozing, their heads pillowed on their packs; some were playing cards, others were smoking their pipes. The two Kelly brothers, John and Michael, were sitting cross-legged on the floor playing dice. Sergeant Fitt was sharpening his bayonet for, George suspected, the umpteenth time this afternoon. Fitt was a stickler for his kit and his bayonet was his special pride. As George came into the room, the men struggled to their feet.

'At ease,' said George.

Once the soldiers had formed a rough semicircle facing George, he explained the operation they were embarking on that night. As he talked the men listened intently, as well they might, given that this could be, for any or all of them, their last night on earth.

'It should take the galley about two hours to row across from here to the anchorage we are attacking. We are ordered to leave at about half past midnight once the moon has gone down, so we should be approaching the enemy shore by, say, half past two in the morning. During that time, and especially as we get closer to the mainland, I want complete silence. You all know how even the slightest sound carries across water. And, of course, no smoking. The good news is that you will not have to do any rowing; the galley's crew will do that, poor wretches.' George paused, conscious of his men's eyes boring into him.

'The plan is to surprise the enemy, smash, burn or set adrift as many of his landing craft as we can as quickly as possible before re-embarking. There will be plenty of time once we've landed before the sun starts coming up. To do the job, we have been issued with small axes and a good deal of fire-lighting kit. Now, boys, I am going to divide you into three sections: one to guard the beachhead, one to get the fires going and the other to set about smashing boats by holing them. Do I have any volunteers?'

There was a pause as the men looked at each other. Then one of them put his hand up.

'Yes, Collins?'

'My father is a blacksmith so I'm none too bad with fires, sir.'

'Good. Will anyone volunteer to help him?'

Fitzpatrick and Reynolds – both mates of Collins's – put their hands up.

Then Michael Hughes – the recipient of the blown kiss earlier in the day – put his hand up.

'I'm tall, so perhaps I'd be able to wade in deeper water than the others?' There was a ripple of laughter round the semicircle.

'Yes, thank you, Hughes. You can be in the boat-smashing party. Sergeant,' said George, turning to Fitt, 'I would like you to command the party guarding the beachhead. It is an important job, so please choose six of the steadiest men to join you.'

'Well, sir,' said Fitt, 'Slattery and Hegarty here are among the best marks in the whole battalion for musketry. Byrne, John and O'Brien are none too bad, either.'

'Thank you, Sergeant Fitt. Are there two more volunteers for the guard?'

'I'd be happy to join them, sir.' It was Dai Jones, one of the few Welshmen in this regiment of Irishmen. No one could remember quite how he'd come to join the 27th but he was a popular man in the ranks nevertheless, for his sardonic sense of humour no less than for his fine baritone singing voice, honed in the village chapel.

Before long the twenty men had been divided into the three sections. The armourer and his mate delivered the packages of fire-lighting kit, wrapped in oiled canvas. He also handed over half a dozen small axes, five cutlasses and eight coshes, made from long sausages of tough canvas filled with sand, with a loop for the wrist.

'Right, boys,' said George, 'it's now seven o'clock. It'll be dark in less than an hour. Colonel Airey has arranged for you to eat at eight o'clock. Once you've finished, I suggest you rest here as it'll be a long night. We'll leave the Citadel at around half past eleven to march up to the far end of the Marina where the galleys will be moored. By then, it should all be pretty quiet. Sergeant, I'm going out for an hour, so you're in charge.'

Clapping his hat onto his head, George strode across the courtyard, out of the main gate of the Citadel and across the Terra Nova. In a few minutes he was at the near end of the Marina, which was now crowded with people enjoying the cooler air of early evening. There were couples strolling sedately along, stopping every now and then to greet friends. Men sat in the open doors of their workshops, their day's work done, while their children gambolled on the quayside. People crowded into cafes and ice-shops. Across the straits the ravines and peaks of the Calabrian mountains glowed red in the setting sun. The bells of the city's churches and convents rang out in the evening air. George walked along the water's edge, where the throng was thinner, so he could stretch his legs. He was tempted to make his way to Carlotta's house; the danger ahead had sharpened his desire for her. A final fuck before the storm of battle. No, no, no . . . not now.

George had almost reached the far end of the Marina, across the harbour mouth from Fort Salvador. The light was fading rapidly; the mountains across the straits, which had half an hour earlier been glowing in the dying rays of the sun, were now grey and menacing. He could see the moon, too, partly hidden behind some high, wispy clouds. In the gathering gloom George could make out three galleys moored at the quayside.

The galleys had seventeen oars on each side; down the middle, from stem to stern, was a raised platform about four feet wide. At the stern was a small cabin for the master. There would be plenty of room on board for Fitt and the men. George could see the two long eighteen-pounder guns mounted in the prow of the galley and the two four-pounders in the stern. This firepower would come in very useful if they ran into trouble on the way in or on the way out later. George wanted to step down into the galley – he could see two men in the poop deck cabin – but thought better of it. He was in uniform and in full view of the milling crowds on the Marina. He didn't want to draw attention to himself at this juncture. He turned on his heel and started back to the Citadel.

By the time George had walked back along the port to the Citadel, the twilight had faded into night. Lights could be seen above the Citadel's ramparts; out in the straits, the moon caught the odd vessel in a chalky gleam. It was just as well, thought George, that we're not setting out till after the moon has gone down. Passing through the gate into the Citadel he made his way to the barrack room where his men were whiling away the time.

George opened the door and coughed. Someone had closed the windows so there was now a fug of pipe smoke under the stone-vaulted ceiling. Sergeant Fitt sprang to his feet as George entered the room.

'Get up, you lot,' he shouted, 'the captain's here.' The men scrambled to their feet.

'That's all right, boys. At ease,' said George. 'How was dinner, McLoughlin?'

'It was very fine, sir, thank you. They eat well down here in the Citadel, better than we manage up at Grotto.' McLoughlin, a Dublin boy, had something of a reputation in the regiment as a gourmet. When the regiment had first arrived in Sicily, he was the one who was keenest to try the local dishes. If you wanted to know whether something was likely to be good to eat or not, you asked Barry. He always knew.

'Good,' replied George. 'There's now about three hours until we leave, so I suggest you all try to get a couple of hours' kip. Make sure your kit is in perfect order.' George winked at Sergeant Fitt. 'I'm going to see to a few loose ends and will be back soon after eleven. You're in charge, Sergeant, until I get back.'

With that George clattered out into the courtyard and made his way to the officers' mess. Sometimes it was noisy in there, teeming with officers drinking and dining, but tonight, mercifully, it was deserted. Everyone must be out. George went into the anteroom and sank into a deep leather chair. Stretching his legs out in front of him, he unbuttoned the collar of his tunic, rested his head against the back of the chair and gazed vacantly at the ceiling, looking but seeing nothing. It had been a busy day, made more tiring by the gradual tightening of the nerves as the hours went by. Soon now the time would be upon them. Then his life, the lives of his men, would be in the lap of the gods, riding on momentary chance, brave decision, foolish misjudgement, on the path of a bullet, the arc of a sword or the thrust of a bayonet. He dozed off.

CHAPTER THREE

Messina Harbour, 7th September 1810

The church clocks were striking midnight as the column of British soldiers moved quietly along the quayside. They were wearing boating cloaks, not so much to keep out the chilly night air – it was still a warm evening – as to hide their scarlet uniforms from inquisitive eyes. Their shakos too had been discarded before they left the Citadel. The moon had disappeared below the mountains of Calabria. The water slapped gently against the hulls of the moored boats. The quayside was deserted except for the odd figure hurrying through the darkness. A solitary carriage rumbled towards them before turning towards the strada Ferdinanda. Even the dogs had stopped barking. Messina was settling down for the night.

As the column approached the moored galleys, George could see a faint light in the stern cabin of the nearest one. Earlier in the evening the vessel had been quiet, almost deserted. Now, in the gloom, he could make out the galley's crew sitting silently, hunched over their oars. A figure emerged from the stern cabin and jumped lightly up onto the quayside. It was Lieutenant Younge. Warne had formed a favourable impression of Frank Younge during the reconnaissance trip to Reggio the previous day. He was a bold, young naval officer, who was good company, just the sort for an expedition like this. He was tall, with a weather-beaten face, the result, no doubt, of his years at sea.

'Good evening, Captain Warne,' he said. 'A fine night for it. There's a light breeze up the straits from the south, so we shouldn't give the French any notice of our arrival.' A short, thick-set man with a dark beard jumped up from the galley to join them.

'This is the galley's master, Mr Theopatis,' said Younge, effecting the introductions. 'And this is Captain Warne of the 27th Foot.'

'Yes, I think we've met before, Mr Theopatis,' said George.

'Yes, I have had the honour, Captain Warne,' said Theopatis. His English was surprisingly good, albeit with a heavy Greek accent. He shook George by the hand, crunchingly.

'Where is Mr Davidson?' asked George. Davidson was the young midshipman seconded to Warne's raiding party.

'He's there, in the cabin, with Signor Mazza,' said Younge, pointing. 'We should be getting off soon. Shall we get the men aboard?'

'Quietly as you can there, lads,' said Fitt as the soldiers lowered themselves one by one from the quayside into the galley. The first man aboard was Seamus John, a quiet, reliable fellow, a farm boy from the Pale, the sixth member of the beachhead party. The other men followed, slipping down into the stern of the galley. Once aboard some of them made their way to the galley's central platform, while others gathered round the stern cabin. Fitt passed the oiled canvas packages containing the fire-lighting kit to George before lowering himself into the boat.

'Guard party to the front,' he said, in a hoarse whisper.

'On a boat it's "forward", Sergeant,' said Younge. Even in the gloom, George could see his grin at this gem of landlubberly ignorance.

Soon the soldiers were settled and the master cast off the galley's moorings. The rowers paddled gently to take the galley clear of the other vessels alongside the quay. Soon they were heading towards the dark ramparts of Fort Salvador. As the galley pulled away from the quay, George was standing by the stern post. Staring back through the dark, he could make out a column of troops marching along the Marina towards the two remaining galleys. That would be William Coker arriving to embark his men, or perhaps John Entwhistle. At the same time, he wondered how many unresting, unfriendly eyes were watching the galley make its way out into the straits? Well, he thought to himself, if anyone is watching, whoever they are, they're too late now. We'll be on the other side before they can warn the enemy. He walked gingerly along the deck and ducked into the cabin where the master, Younge and Davidson were standing, talking quietly.

'Once we're out in open water beyond the fort, we'll set course for Reggio,' Younge was saying.

'Will we put up the sail, master?' asked George.

'We will see what the wind is doing when we're out of here,' he replied.

The rowers were still only pulling a half-stroke as the galley nosed its way out of the harbour. On the starboard beam was the black mass of the fort while to port was the odd light in the houses along the Marina. Ahead was the open water of the straits. Once the galley had pulled clear of the fort, Younge, glancing at the binnacle, under its darkened light, gave an order to the helmsman. The galley turned to starboard. The breeze was now almost directly into their faces as they stood around the wheel.

'We're on course for Reggio, Mr Warne. We'll leave the sail down for the time being, with the wind where it is,' said Younge. The master nodded his head in agreement.

As the rowers settled into a steady rhythm, the galley slipped easily through the inky water. By now their eyes were accustomed to the dark; although the moon had set, it was not too black a night under the clear sky. George could just see the puddles made by the oars and a gleaming rim of phosphorescence on the bow wave as the galley pulled ahead with each stroke. He looked back at the lights of Messina receding astern: the jagged peaks above the city showed massy and black against the night sky. The boat was silent apart from the well-timed, rhythmic swoosh of the blades through the water and the long, deep breaths of the rowers, sucking in oxygen. The soldiers were sitting patiently, in the dark, as the little vessel skimmed over the sea. Paolo Mazza, the guide, was standing by the port rail, fiddling absent-mindedly with a piece of rope. George tried to remain calm.

There was little to see as the galley forged steadily on towards the Calabrian coast. The sea was smooth and the breeze barely moderate. In the distance to the south was a ship, well lit up, twinkling in the night. A while later, more than an hour out from Messina, Davidson came into the cabin.

'I think, sir,' he said quietly, leaning in towards Warne and Younge, 'I can just make out the mainland.'

'Right you are, Mr Davidson,' said Younge, stepping out of the cabin. He peered ahead into the night for a while. 'Yes, there it is. How far out do you think we are?'

'I reckon we're a mile to a mile and a half off the coast now, sir, which would give us perhaps fifteen minutes to run to the anchorage.' He grinned in the dark, touching the hilt of his cutlass.

'Sergeant Fitt,' said George quietly, stepping towards the central platform, 'it's not long to go now. Are the men ready? Is the firing kit with the boat party?'

'Yes, sir.'

George then made his way slowly forward along the galley's central platform. To each man he said a few encouraging words, a joke, a pat on the shoulder. Considering what might lie ahead, now just a few minutes away, they were all remarkably calm. They were a brave lot; George knew, he had seen many of them standing cool and proud in a storm of shot and shell at Maida, but landing on an enemy shore in the dark required a different sort of courage.

Halfway along he reached the Kelly brothers, John and Michael.

'D'you think the Frenchies'll be waiting for us, sir?' asked Michael.

'No,' replied George, with a smile, 'they'll be sound asleep.'

'You can hear them snoring from here, sir,' said John, cupping his hand to his ear. His brother laughed. In the prow, squatting next to one of the eighteen-pounders, George spoke softly to the soldiers of the beachhead party. The galley was getting closer to the coast now; the ridges of the mountains stood out clearly against the night sky. George could hear, faintly on the breeze, the waves breaking on the shore. He made his way back to the stern, where Younge and Davidson were standing next to the wheel with the master.

'How far off do you reckon we are now, Mr Davidson?' asked George.

'Maybe half a mile, sir, not much more,' he replied, glancing at the binnacle, 'and we're dead on course.' They could not yet make out the anchorage, the beach or the headland in the dark but that meant that they would likewise still probably be invisible to any watching sentry in the battery.

'It's time to reduce speed, to come in as quietly as we can. Bring the oars to half-stroke, Mr Theopatis, if you please,' said Younge.

The rowers lifted the oars out of the water, letting the galley glide over the water. As she began to lose way, they started rowing again, with shortened strokes.

'We're nearly there, Sergeant. Go forward and join the guard party,' said George.

'Yes, sir.' Fitt saluted before making his way forward to the prow.

Paolo Mazza had positioned himself on the starboard side, from where he was staring intently into the night.

'There's the battery,' he said. He pointed and George, following his finger, could just make out the dark rim of the battery's rampart against the lighter ground in front of it. 'And there,' he continued, turning to the port beam, 'is the breakwater.'

George could see – and hear – the waves breaking gently on its rocks; behind it were the craft they had come to destroy, hulls and masts clustered tightly together.

'Excellent work, Mr Davidson,' said George. 'You've brought us into the bay exactly between the breakwater and the headland.'

Younge came out of the cabin. 'Would you go forward with the line to keep an eye on the depth of the water as we come in?'

'Aye aye, sir.'

The galley was now about two hundred yards from the shore. They'd got this close without being seen but this was the dangerous moment: if they were spotted now, George realised, the battery would open fire and, at that range, even in the dark, there was every chance that the galley might be hit. One hit from a heavy artillery round could well sink this little vessel, killing and maiming on its way. But the distance to the shore was diminishing rapidly and with it the enemy's ability to bring the battery's guns, up on the headland, to bear on the galley.

'Let's go forward,' said George to Mazza. They made their way as quietly as they could along the galley's central platform, stepping past the waiting soldiers.

'We're nearly there now, lads,' George said in a stage whisper as he went down the line. Once they were in the prow, Davidson leant towards George.

'One and a half fathoms, sir.'

Nine feet of water; too deep for the soldiers. The galley continued to glide silently in towards the beach. George could see the beach now, between the dark mass of the headland on the right and the waves at the breakwater to the left. There were a lot of craft pulled up on the beach, above the waterline. It was all very quiet. There was no sign of life in the battery: no lights, no movement, no noise that George could discern. The only sound was the whoosh of the waves on the breakwater and washing up the beach. Even the cicadas were sleeping now.

'One fathom, sir.'

The galley was now about fifty yards from the waterline but even in six feet of water it could, with its shallow draught, go closer still. She nosed slowly on, in towards the darkened shore.

'Half a fathom, sir,' whispered Davidson.

'Fitt,' whispered George, 'now's the time. Hegarty, get the ladder over the side.'

Hegarty lifted the ladder over the side, hooking it onto the rail.

'Off you go, boys,' said George, 'and don't forget to keep your muskets up out of the water.' The first man over the side was Slattery; as he swung his leg over the rail, George gave him a pat on the back. The others followed, climbing down into the water. It came, George could see, to the top of their legs so must be about two and a half or three feet deep. The last man over the side was Fitt.

'Get to the top right-hand end of the beach as quickly as you can and cover the way down from the battery. And don't start shooting until they're good and close.'

'Yes, sir,' replied Fitt as he descended into the water.

As Fitt disappeared over the side, George motioned the rest of his little company forward.

'Off you go, boys. Quietly, now.' One by one, they slipped down the ladder into the water. As the last man was going over the side, George turned to Younge, who had come forward.

'Keep the galley here, Mr Younge, if you please. We'll be back soon. And, Mr Davidson, make sure that the guns,' he touched the barrel of the eighteen-pounder, 'are loaded with grape and ready to fire. We'll likely need them.' With that, George climbed over the side, down the ladder and into the sea. The bottom was sandy and the water surprisingly warm: George waded after his men. He could see that Sergeant Fitt and the beachhead party were already on dry land and heading for the top of the beach.

'Right, boys,' he said, once he'd caught up with his men, 'let's get over to the breakwater anchorage.'

In less than a minute, George and his men were at the anchorage. On the landward side, the boats were either beached or lying in a few inches of water, lashed together.

'Get to it, lads,' said George. 'Take your axes to the bottom of these open vessels. Those larger ones, over there, get to work setting them on fire.' At once the noise of smashing, splintering wood filled the air. There was no disguising their presence now. How long would they have before the garrison in the battery woke up? A couple of minutes? Then it would take them a few minutes to realise what was going on and a few more minutes to be turned out by their officers. In the dark, things might get very confused. George could no longer see Fitt and his men; he hoped his sergeant had found a good defensive position as it couldn't be long now before the French would be racing down the slope of the headland from the battery to attack the intruders.

While these thoughts were swirling round his head, George was attacking the bottoms of the boats with the strength of the possessed: whack, smash . . . there goes another one. One less boat for Murat, twenty fewer Frenchmen coming to Sicily. Smash, whack. Were any fires going yet, George wondered? He couldn't see or smell anything. All around him in the dark the men were smashing and hacking furiously at the boats. They must have damaged thirty or forty by now.

'Don't forget to cut them adrift, too, lads,' said George. He looked up at the battery on the headland: it was still dark, showing no signs of life, although by now the officers must surely have been woken by the noise from the anchorage. He imagined them running round in the semi-darkness, adrenaline suddenly coursing through sleepy limbs, cursing, shouting and sweating, trying to find out what was going on, rousing their men to mount a counter-attack. How was Fitt getting on? He would surely be coming into action very soon now. Hope to God, too, that Davidson has got the guns ready.

Then, above the sounds of axe blows and splintering wood, George heard a noise from his left, up at the landward end of the beach, away from the headland. Looking up he saw, to his horror, a line of soldiers forming up, dark against the dunes at the top of the beach. Could that be Fitt, he wondered momentarily? If so, what the hell was he doing over there? He realised very quickly that it was not Fitt. It was French infantry.

'Boys,' he shouted, 'grab your muskets – we're being attacked.' He pointed up the beach. The soldiers ran, splashing through the shallow water for their muskets, which were stacked like stooks of corn above the waterline. As they retrieved their muskets, the French fired a volley. Fortunately, in the dark, their aim was not good. The shots all went high.

'*Avancez à la baïonette,*' shouted a voice. The line of troops – there were perhaps twenty of them – started coming down the beach at a canter.

'Form a line, boys,' shouted George. 'Steady now. Take aim.' The French soldiers were now about forty yards away. 'Fire.'

The volley crashed out. A thick cloud of smoke obscured George's view but he could hear one or two howls of pain, so some shots had struck home.

'Fix bayonets,' shouted George. The French soldiers were almost upon them but the volley had checked their momentum. George fired his pistol into the advancing French – he saw a man go down – and drew his cutlass. Out of the corner of his eye, he saw Fitzgerald lunge at the leading French soldier with his bayonet. The Frenchman twisted away from its thrust but it caught him in the fleshy part of the thigh. Fitzgerald lunged again. This time, the long blade went straight in the Frenchman's abdomen. He howled with pain and fell to the sand, writhing in agony.

'Well done, lad,' shouted George, slashing down with his cutlass onto the collarbone of a French soldier. He could see that one of the Kelly brothers was down. They were outnumbered here. Where the bloody hell was Fitt? How had these men got past him without being stopped? He hacked again, the cutlass's blade smashing into the barrel of the musket with a clang. He slashed again. This time, it hit the man in the upper arm, almost severing the limb. Blood spurted out as the man screamed in pain. One more down.

There was now the sound of firing coming from the headland end of the beach. Fitt was under attack. George looked up at the battery. He could see lights showing through the embrasures. No doubt the gun crews were getting ready to open fire, but they wouldn't risk firing on the beach – even assuming they could depress the sights sufficiently – while their infantry were still there.

A bugle shrilled from the top of the beach.

'*Retirez, retirez,*' shouted the officer. The enemy turned and soon were running up the beach.

'Don't chase 'em,' shouted George. 'Load and fire, as you will.'

O'Gorman was the first to get off a shot. A Frenchman staggered and fell to the ground, hit in the leg. Others fired, too, a ragged volley but high by the look of it. By now the French had reached the relative safety of the dunes. George was panting from his exertions, pouring sweat. A few yards to his left, Michael Kelly was kneeling on the wet sand, bent over his brother's motionless body. He looked at the wounded French soldiers on the beach: the one Fitzgerald had skewered was lying in a few inches of water, probably dead. The fellow whose arm he'd slashed had made it up to the dunes. Anyway, there was no time to deal with them. They would be seen to by their own side.

'Well done, lads. It's time we got back to the boat. O'Gorman, Reynolds, and the rest of you, go back to the boat now and get aboard. Kelly, I'm afraid you'll have to leave him there. Hughes, you come with me, we're going to see how Sergeant Fitt's getting on.'

George started up the beach, with Hughes following in his wake, avoiding the boats pulled up on the sand. There clearly was a skirmish going on at the top of the beach; George could hear shouting and gunfire. In less than a minute, they were in the dunes.

'Sergeant, where are you?' A shot whistled over George's head.

'Be careful, sir,' said Hughes, ducking.

'I'm here, sir,' came Fitt's reply, a few yards to George's left. He crawled over to where Fitt was crouching behind a large clump of thick, tufty grass. Beside him, firing steadily in the direction of the enemy, was Pat Slattery.

'I think they're mustering for an attack,' said Fitt, breathlessly. 'You can hear the buggers coming down from the battery. They're gathering over there.' He pointed ahead into the darkness. 'I think we've hit some of them, but we'll be outnumbered when they decide to attack. There are at least sixty of them over there, I shouldn't wonder.'

'We must get out of here now,' said George. There was no sense in risking the men's lives in a hopeless fight with a superior enemy. It would be suicidal. They had been sent here to destroy boats but that was no longer possible now that they had lost the advantage of surprise. 'You take the men and get back to the boat. I'll stay here with Hughes and Slattery and try to hold them off for a few minutes. Give me your musket. Go.'

'Yes, sir.' Fitt handed George his musket and ammunition pouch before crawling off.

George loaded the musket and fired in the general direction of the enemy.

'Keep loading and firing, boys. We'll give them two minutes to get back to the boat.'

'Yes, sir,' replied Hughes as he fired. As he did several shots whistled over their head as they crouched in the sand.

'Don't you think we ought to leg it, sir,' said Slattery, 'before they start coming on to us?'

'We'll wait a little longer,' replied George. Fitt must have reached the boat by now. He lifted the musket into his shoulder and fired another round.

'Right, boys, let's go. Keep down.'

The three men started to make their way out of the dunes to the open beach. The enemy fire had slackened. George, Hughes and Slattery were at the edge of the dunes. Down the beach, perhaps sixty yards away, was the boat, dimly visible.

'Run for it,' shouted George. The French were in the dunes now. A shot came uncomfortably close. But running in the dark, the three men did not present an easy target. They were nearly there now – only twenty yards to go. George could see that Younge had turned the boat round. A ladder was hanging from the rail. He could see Davidson and Fitt in the stern, bending over one of the guns. George glanced over his shoulder. The leading enemy soldiers were on the open beach now. They stopped and fired. There was a slamming thud and a groan from George's right. Slattery was hit. He stumbled and fell.

'Are you all right?' George shouted. Hughes was on the ladder now, up and into the boat. George grabbed Slattery and pulled him towards the ladder. A musket ball slammed into the galley's stern; another flicked up the water just to George's left. The French were close now. George put his foot onto the ladder; the galley was starting to move as the oars pulled at the water. Slattery was hit again, pitching sideways into the water where he lay still, face down.

George scrambled into the galley as a shot hit the ladder, smashing a rung. Five seconds earlier that would have been his leg.

'Let's away,' he shouted. 'Mr Davidson, give them a blast of grapeshot.' The French soldiers were running down the beach now, shouting and firing as they went. Several shots thumped woodenly into the galley's hull; one hit the muzzle of the port-side four-pounder, ricocheting away with an alarming zing. Davidson coolly took aim and fired. In the dark, a gout of flame belched from the muzzle of the gun. The grapeshot kicked up a flurry of sand: half a dozen of the pursuing soldiers were swept off their feet. A choking cloud of acrid smoke engulfed the stern. The galley was gathering speed now. The soldiers on the beach steadied themselves before firing at the receding intruders but, in the dark, their aim was not good.

Within a couple of minutes – there was nothing like gunfire to get the rowers working, George thought – the galley was two hundred yards off the beach, well out of musket shot. Now he was more worried about the battery. Surely it would fire at the galley as it went out to sea? All they could do was hope that in the dark the galley would be too small, too difficult a target.

But the shots never came. Perhaps the gun layers had lost their night vision in the battery's lights. Perhaps they just couldn't pick out the little galley in the darkness. Maybe they realised it was a waste of precious shot and powder. For whatever reason, the battery's big guns remained silent.

'Well done, Mr Younge, we showed 'em a clean pair of heels.'

'It was a close-run thing,' he replied. 'The French were practically in the water by the time you came aboard.'

'I've always been a good fox.' George grinned. 'We managed to destroy some of their boats before they interrupted us.'

Now that the action was over, George was aware of how wet and cold he was. His boots and breeches were sodden, while inside his tunic he was damp with sweat from his exertions. He was covered in sand, which rubbed and itched. The sea breeze was very chilly. He shivered and, picking up a boating cloak, fastened it under his chin.

'Sergeant!'

'Yes, sir?' said Fitt.

'What casualties have we suffered?'

'I'm afraid we've lost three killed, sir. Johnny Kelly, Slattery and Byrne. Byrne was hit in the chest just after we reached the dunes. One or two of the lads have got minor injuries but nothing more serious.'

'Thank you, Sergeant. Will you make sure that they are settled? We'll be home soon enough.'

By the time the galley rounded Fort Salvador and entered Messina harbour, dawn was coming up. The sky was beginning to lighten over the Calabrian mountains; the city looked dark, somnolent. George was stiff and cold under his boating cloak. The men were mostly asleep, huddled on the galley's central platform. Younge was standing in the cabin with Davidson; they both looked tired as they watched the master bring the galley into its moorings.

Once the galley was securely alongside, the men disembarked. Fitt formed them up on the quayside: they looked dishevelled in the grey light of dawn. George heaved himself wearily on the quay and faced his men.

'Well done, boys. We didn't get as much time as we'd planned to destroy Murat's boats, but I think we did some damage and let's hope the others managed to make a mess too.'

George noticed that Joe Collins had his right arm in a sling.

'What happened, Collins?'

'It was during the fight on the beach, sir. A Frog got me in the arm with his bayonet, but it's not too bad.'

'Make sure you see the surgeon as soon as you get back to get it cleaned up. Right, Sergeant, to the Citadel.'

As the light came up, the first fishermen began to arrive on the Marina, ready for the day. None of them gave more than a passing glance to the little band of British soldiers winding along the harbour even at this hour of the morning. In a few minutes, George and his men were entering the Citadel. George sent them to the barrack room, to sleep. They could have breakfast and clean up later.

George himself was desperately, achingly, tired but he had to report to Colonel Airey now that he was back. He crossed the courtyard and went into the anteroom next to the staff offices. The sentry clicked to attention as he entered. George strode across the room to the desk, behind which sat Rogers, the chief clerk.

'Good morning, sir,' he said, looking at George's filthy uniform and grimy face. 'I hope you are all right, sir.'

'Yes, Mr Rogers, I'm fine, thank you, nothing a good bath won't get rid of, which is more than can be said for some of the others, I'm afraid. Is the colonel here?'

'Yes. He's expecting you, sir, so go straight in.'

'Good morning, Captain Warne,' said Colonel Airey, rising to his feet behind his desk. 'I'm pleased to see you're in one piece. How are your men?'

'We lost three, sir, and a few are wounded but none seriously, I'm glad to say.'

'I see,' said Airey. 'You look exhausted, Warne, not to mention in need of a bath. Why don't you go off, get some rest, have a bath and breakfast and report back later this morning? Hobhouse, my batman, will see to you.'

'Thank you, sir. And, by the way, any news of the others?'

'Not yet, I regret to say. See you later.'

George climbed the narrow wooden stairs up to Colonel Airey's quarters, where the batman showed him to a cot. He stripped off his uniform and lay down. Within fifteen seconds, he was asleep.

'Wake up, sir.' It was the batman's voice. George stirred sleepily under the blanket.

'What time is it?' he croaked.

'It's just past eleven, sir. The colonel would like to see you at midday. I thought you might like a bath and some breakfast before you report to him, sir.'

'Yes, thank you, Hobhouse.'

The batman had drawn him a bath. George climbed in and lay back, luxuriating in the delicious warmth of the water. He rested his head against the rim of the bath and gazed at the ceiling, idly tracing the length of the stone rib from the corbel at the top of the wall in the corner to the carved boss directly above his head. As he lay there, George began to run through the events of the night. Thank goodness they'd got away relatively unscathed, losing only three men – he made a mental note to speak to Michael Kelly, whose brother had been killed. It could have been a great deal worse. They had managed to put some boats out of action, at least for a while. And the raid would put the French on the alert, mounting extra guards and so on. It was always a good soldier's duty to stir up the enemy, keep him on his toes.

But there was one thing which nagged at George: where did those French soldiers who attacked his party come from? How did they know, so soon after the landing, that they'd be at the anchorage? They couldn't have had time to get down from the battery, avoiding Fitt and his men. So how had they managed to attack them from the far end of the beach? Had the enemy been waiting for them, concealed in the dunes, warned in advance? If so, had the operation been betrayed? Could it have happened? Would it? We'll find out soon enough, George thought. The smell of cooking bacon was wafting through from the next-door room. He grabbed the bar of soap.

As the clock on the mantlepiece in the anteroom chimed midday, George knocked on Colonel Airey's door. Hobhouse had worked miracles with his uniform: the casual onlooker would have no idea that George had worn the same breeches and tunic in a skirmish on a wet beach only a few hours before. He'd mended, almost invisibly, a tear in the left sleeve of his tunic. How had that got there, George wondered? Was it a narrow escape from some terrible, maiming injury during that desperate hand-to-hand fighting? Or had he ripped it clambering back onto the galley? His boots were dry and polished, too.

'Good morning again, Captain Warne,' said the colonel, who was sitting behind the middle of the three desks in the room. The others were unoccupied. 'I trust Hobhouse looked after you?'

'Yes, sir, very well thank you, as you can see.' George raised both his arms from his side.

'Good. Now sit down and tell me what happened. General Cockburn will be in shortly but start away.'

George went through the events of the night, as clearly and concisely as he could. As he spoke, Airey listened in silence, making the occasional note. When George finished, there was a long pause. A bluebottle settled on his knee. George could hear a sergeant-like voice shouting orders outside in the courtyard, followed by the sound of troops coming to attention.

'Warne, you did well.' The colonel paused again, clearing his throat. 'I'm afraid to say that it looks as if the others were not so fortunate. From what I understand – and we haven't got the full story yet, by any means – the other three parties may have had an even warmer reception than you.'

'What do you mean, sir?'

'Well, it seems that Coker walked into a vipers' nest. He has been captured or, perhaps, killed. We don't know yet. I saw Lieutenant Huxtable, who commanded Coker's galley in the attack on the anchorage at Catona, after he got back. He reported that the enemy seemed to react very quickly to their landing and the shore party, or some of it, got cut off. In the dark, it was all very confused. Several of Coker's men – about half of them – did re-embark. When the galley, which was, of course, very close in, started to come under heavy fire, Huxtable took the decision to leave, thus abandoning the remaining men – including Captain Coker himself – on the beach.'

'My God. Do we know anything more about Coker, sir?'

'No, not yet, although if he is a prisoner, we'll find out soon enough.' Airey looked very grim.

'And what of Entwhistle and Kendall, sir?'

'No news of either of them, as yet. In Kendall's case, as he was expected to return to his departure point at Faro, we might not yet have expected to have heard, although,' the colonel slipped his watch from a tunic pocket, 'it is getting a bit late in the day now. As for Entwhistle, he's still not back yet, which does not bode well, I'm afraid.'

At that moment there was a knock on the door and the clerk stepped into the room.

'Sorry to disturb you, sir, but there's a messenger here from Faro with news of Captain Kendall's party.'

'Thank you. Show him in, will you?' said Airey.

Mr Midshipman McLynn came smartly to attention and saluted. He was a tall, slender young man, with a pronounced stoop, the result, no doubt, of life in the Royal Navy's cramped, low-beamed ships. His boots and breeches were covered in dust and his uniform coat bore some gunpowder stains, but he looked otherwise unharmed.

'I have been sent, sir, by Lieutenant Foreman,' he began, sounding slightly overawed by the immaculate, languid colonel of the commander-in-chief's staff, 'to report on the raid on the anchorage at Scylla commanded by the *late* Captain Kendall.'

'The late Captain Kendall?' replied Colonel Airey, shocked.

'Yes, sir,' said McLynn, 'I'm afraid to say that he was killed in the fight at Scylla.'

'Good God,' said Airey. 'Please, Mr McLynn, sit down and tell us what happened, from the beginning.'

McLynn sat down in a chair next to George and began to tell the story of the raid. The galley had set off from the beach at Faro. It had on board Kendall's detachment of infantry from the 44th Foot, twenty-one men, including the sergeant, Foreman, McLynn and the usual complement of rowers. From there it was about three and a half miles to Scylla and the crossing was, as it had been for George further south, easy, with a smooth sea and only a light breeze. All had gone well; as they approached the dark coastline, neither Kendall, his Sicilian guide nor McLynn or Foreman could see anything amiss. The galley came into the beach as quietly as possible and the soldiers began disembarking into the shallow water. At that moment – here McLynn paused as if uncertain how to continue, wiping the sweat from his upper lip with a handkerchief – all hell broke loose on that dark, silent shore. Suddenly, quite without warning, the enemy opened fire on the galley and the disembarking infantry with field guns and muskets.

The effect on Kendall's men, caught between land and sea, and on the galley itself, was devastating. The galley's Sicilian master was killed – his body horribly mutilated and splattered everywhere – by one of the first cannonballs. Several soldiers were killed where they stood in the surf. The galley's wheel was badly damaged and several of the rowers killed in the first salvo. Kendall and Foreman, taken completely by surprise, tried to assess their position. In the dark and the confusion, it was very difficult, McLynn said, to know what to do. They were not there to fight the enemy; they were there to attack his boats. It looked for all the world as if they had walked into a trap. Before they could decide what to do, Kendall was hit by a musket ball in the stomach. He sank to the deck, groaning.

At this point, McLynn said, Foreman decided that the best course was to get back out to sea as quickly as possible. In the dark, noise and confusion, the surviving soldiers were ordered to re-embark, as the rowers began paddling the galley off the beach. As she gathered way, another cannonball smashed into the stern cabin, killing Kendall, who was propped up against it. McLynn stopped and mopped his brow.

'God, what a tale of disaster,' said Airey gloomily. George nodded, aghast. 'Was that it?'

'Well, yes and no, sir,' continued McLynn. 'We were soon, in the dark, out of range of the guns on the shore but it became obvious pretty quickly that the galley was badly damaged and, what's more, short of rowers. Quite a number of them had been killed or wounded and some of the oars themselves smashed by the enemy's fire. The mast, we could see, had been blown away too, so there was no possibility of putting up a sail to help us home. And she was shipping water rapidly.'

'What did Lieutenant Foreman do?' asked Airey, standing up and walking into the middle of the room, his hands clasped behind his back.

'Well, sir, the galley was a hell of a mess, what with the damage to the wheel, the cabin, the mast, and the hull, smashed oars and so on. There were dead and wounded men everywhere, groaning and crying out for help. And, of course, it was pitch-dark, which made it hard to see what was happening. Mr Foreman put some of the soldiers to bailing out the galley, while others did what they could – and it was difficult in the dark – to clear the damaged oars and what remained of the mast and its rigging . . .'

The midshipman's voice tailed off as the door from the inner office opened and General Cockburn entered the room, looking fresh and unconcerned. 'Good morning, Colonel Airey,' he said cheerfully.

'Good morning, sir,' said Airey. 'Mr McLynn here was just telling us what befell Captain Kendall's expedition to Scylla last night.' He paused. 'You should know, sir, that Kendall was killed along with a number of his men and some of the galley's crew.'

'Oh, I am very sorry to hear that,' said Cockburn, his expression clouding. He pulled up a chair and sat down as Airey briefly recounted the story. Cockburn, crossing his legs and adjusting his stock, turned to face the midshipman.

'Carry on, Mr McLynn.'

McLynn coughed nervously. A lowly midshipman reporting directly to a general; his friends would be impressed. A colonel was one thing but a full-blown major-general was quite another. Banishing these thoughts, he continued.

Foreman had displayed great courage and initiative in getting the damaged galley back to Sicily. He had found and plugged the shot holes in the galley's hull; he had reorganised the rowers so that the vessel could be navigated properly – its rudder had been shot away – and had done what he could to help the wounded. While all this was going on, the galley had drifted in the currents. As the dawn came up, Foreman and McLynn could see that they were now some distance to the west of Scylla, along the north coast of Sicily. Eventually, at about eight o'clock in the morning, they brought the galley into Spadafora, a fishing village several miles to the east of Milazzo. McLynn had been dispatched at once to the Citadel on a borrowed horse.

Once McLynn had finished and left the room, Airey recapped the stories of the raids at Reggio and Catona for General Cockburn.

'God,' the general said, 'what a mess. Three of the raids driven off by the enemy before they could inflict much – or indeed any – damage and not a few casualties, I'm afraid to say, with nothing to show for it. Not a good start to my command here. The commander-in-chief will not be impressed.' He glowered at Airey. 'Do we know what's happened to Entwhistle?'

'No, sir, not yet,' replied Airey. 'But as it's now past one o'clock, he should have been back long ago.'

'It doesn't look good, does it, Colonel?' said Cockburn.

'I'm afraid not, sir,' said Airey gloomily.

'We should send a boat out into the straits forthwith to find out what has happened to Entwhistle,' said Cockburn. 'Can you arrange this, Colonel?'

'Yes, sir.'

'Good. And let me know at once when you have some news.' With that the general returned to the inner office, closing the door behind him.

Once the general had left, George glanced across the desk at Airey. He looked immensely weary.

'Do you think, sir,' George began, 'that I should go across to see what's happened to Entwhistle's party?'

'Are you volunteering, Captain Warne?'

'Well, yes, sir,' replied George. 'I'm here, I know the lie of the land over there reasonably well and it needs to be done now.'

'Very well,' replied the colonel. 'Lieutenant Huxtable is still here, I think, so why don't you dig him out and get going? The sooner you're off the better.'

'Yes, sir.' George stood up to leave the room. Before he turned, he paused, uncertainly.

'What is it, Warne?'

'Is it possible, sir,' George began hesitantly, 'that the operations could have been betrayed? Thinking back through the events of last night, I must say I've wondered, and hearing the other two stories reinforces my suspicions. In each case the enemy does seem to have been lying in wait for us to arrive and surprisingly alert for the middle of the night.'

Airey looked quizzically across the desk at George. 'Go on.'

'In our case, the enemy infantry was able to attack from the far end of the beach very soon after we'd landed. They wouldn't have been there in the middle of the night in the normal course of events. In Coker's case – and in Kendall's, too – the enemy also seems to have been waiting for us to arrive. It seems odd, to say the least, sir.'

'Well,' replied Airey thoughtfully, after a long pause, 'I suppose it's possible that some spy or other got news across to the enemy of an impending attack, but it seems unlikely that he could have known the precise timing and location of all four raids, don't you think?'

'Maybe, sir,' said George.

'Isn't it more likely that with the French in a state of alert – which we know they are at the moment – the night sentries at the anchorages had been doubled and ordered to be on their guard? And, we should not forget, it is at least possible that they heard us coming. It was a calm night and those galleys aren't the quietest things afloat. It could be that we were just unlucky, Warne.'

'Very unlucky, in some cases, sir,' said George. Airey looked at him sharply.

'You'd better be off now, Captain Warne. Report back to me the moment you return.'

Two hours later George was leaning against the mast of HM Cutter *Buzzard* as she forged her way across the straits towards San Giovanni. Tucked securely under his arm was a long naval telescope. The breeze had got up since George had returned to Messina earlier in the day. It was now ruffling the tops of the waves and flicking the odd drop of spume into his face as he gazed out towards the Calabrian coast.

The *Buzzard* was Ned Huxtable's ship, cutters being one of the few classes of ship in the Royal Navy which were a lieutenant's command. A ten-gun, single-masted vessel she was rigged fore and aft, which allowed her to lie a point or two closer to the wind than larger, square-rigged ships. As a result, she was a handy vessel, nimble and quick. The *Buzzard* was in immaculate condition, her decks scrubbed, the brass work gleaming and the rigging well maintained. It was obvious even to a landsman like George that Ned Huxtable ran a tight ship.

After a few minutes, Ned Huxtable came ambling along the deck from the stern to join George. They stood in companionable silence, looking at the view. After a while, George broke the silence.

'What did happen to Captain Coker last night?'

'I can't say for sure, I'm afraid.' Huxtable replied in his pronounced Devon burr. 'As you can imagine, it was all very confused in the dark. There was a lot of noise, shouting, gunfire and so on. Captain Coker had been the first man off the galley once we'd reached the beach, but within a minute or so – by which time he and his men were, I reckon, a good way up the beach – the enemy opened fire. There were muskets and at least one field gun, so far as I could tell. The galley was hit almost at once, a couple of times. He'd left four of his men behind as guards but before long we could see some of the French coming down the beach towards us, at least twenty of them.' Huxtable paused, wiping a fleck of watery foam from his cheek.

'It was now obvious that the galley was in serious danger. Captain Coker and I had agreed earlier that if the galley was threatened with capture or destruction I should take her off the beach, regardless of where the landing party was at the time. There was no point, he said, in exposing the galley and its crew to needless danger. After all, he pointed out, if the galley was destroyed or fell into enemy hands, they would all be stranded anyway, if not dead. It was, he said, a positive order.'

'That's typical of William,' said George.

'So I ordered the rowers into action. By the time she'd got under way, the French were in the surf, very close. I didn't want to fire the galley's guns as we pulled off for fear of hitting our own boys in the dark up the beach. But the soldiers in the stern fired as many rounds as they could at the enemy and I saw several of them go down. Within a minute or two we were out of range but, of course, had no idea what was going on on the beach, although we could still hear firing.'

'So you don't really know what happened to William?' asked George.

'No, I'm afraid not.'

'Let's hope to God he's all right. He's a brave man but he's not a fool. It's likely that he and his men would have been surrounded – the men who came for the galley would have been in his rear – so I can only hope that he had the sense to surrender rather than play the hero.'

'Let's hope so,' echoed Huxtable. The two men lapsed into silence.

'There's San Giovanni, Mr Warne,' said Huxtable, pointing over the starboard quarter. 'The anchorage is just to the north, I presume.'

'Yes, that's right. The closer in we go, the better the view we'll get,' said George, opening the telescope. Huxtable gave an order to the man at the tiller, who altered course to take the cutter in towards the anchorage. As the boom swung across, the mainsail flapped before beginning to fill as the *Buzzard* came round onto her new tack. In a few minutes they were less than half a mile off the coast, which stood out clearly in the bright, late afternoon sun. George, steadying the telescope against the rigging, was scanning the anchorage.

'There's what looks like the galley, to the left of the main body of masts and to the right of the rocks. Can you see it?'

'Yes, I think so,' said Huxtable, telescope to his eye. 'Do you see the angle she's at? She's beached, I reckon. It's difficult to be sure from here, but she looks badly damaged. I can't see the full complement of oars and there's no mast.'

'Can we go a bit closer in, Captain, please?'

'We don't want to draw too much attention to ourselves, Mr Warne. The French will be jumpy after last night and there's that battery on the headland over there,' he said, pointing over the port beam.

Then, as if on cue, there was a low, distant boom. Both men looked at the headland: a puff of smoke momentarily obscured the battery before dispersing on the breeze.

'Are they firing at us?' asked George.

'I'd say so,' replied Huxtable. Perhaps fifty yards out to starboard, a plume of water was thrown up by the shot. 'Damn it, that's close enough. There's no point in risking being hit. We won't be able to find out much more about what happened to Entwhistle and the others from out here anyway, and one of those shots would sink this little thing.'

'As you will, Mr Huxtable,' said George. Huxtable shouted

orders to the crew and the boat began to put about. Soon they were standing out from the Calabrian shore, heading back to the safety of Sicily. The French gunners in the battery did not bother to waste ammunition firing at the retreating cutter. It was too small a target.

It was dark by the time George walked into the officers' mess in the Citadel. He had reported to Colonel Airey as soon as he'd arrived back, before checking on Fitt and the men. The colonel had taken the news George had to offer about Entwhistle's fate calmly.

'It only confirms what we'd suspected, I'm afraid to say,' he said.

Now George was sitting with three other officers, none of them from his regiment. In front of him on the table were several bottles of Marsala. He was smoking a cigar as he recounted the story of his raid the previous evening. As two of them were of the 44th Foot, they were keen to know the fate of Entwhistle. George told them. News of Kendall's death had already got around. He was evidently a popular officer, well liked here, despite the fact that he'd only recently arrived in Sicily.

'Entwhistle won't take kindly to being in the hands of the French, a prisoner,' said one of them.

'If he is a prisoner . . .' said George, his voice trailing off.

'Yes, if he is a prisoner.' There was silence round the table as they contemplated the possible death of another fellow officer.

'Ah, here comes our dinner.' The waiter was approaching with a large serving plate on which rested a delicious-looking roast chicken. He placed it in the middle of the table. Warm wafts of herbs and lemon emanated invitingly from the bird.

'Roast fowl,' exclaimed George. 'My favourite and I'm bloody hungry. More wine, anybody?'

He refilled all four glasses and, stubbing out his cigar, waved the empty bottle at the mess orderly who was hovering nearby.

'Another couple of bottles, please, Winch!' George smiled. It was going to be a jolly evening, time to relax after the stresses and strains of recent days.

CHAPTER FOUR

Messina, 8th September 1810

George Warne was riding at the head of his men as they marched back to Grotto di Paci. It was only half past nine in the morning, but it was already hot. They had passed through the city walls at Porta Reale a few minutes before and were now on the coast road. George was not feeling at his liveliest; he was, if the truth be known, hungover. Last night's dinner had gone on longer than it should have done. By the time he flopped into bed he'd drunk far too much Marsala.

Marsala was what British officers here tended to drink. Claret was virtually unobtainable now, thanks to the war, and port, although available, had to be shipped from Portugal. There was the local wine, too, but this, George had decided after considerable exposure, was generally unpalatably rough, although the soldiers were happy enough to drink it in great quantities. Marsala was made in Sicily – in the west of the island, around Trapani – by an enterprising Englishman, John Woodhouse, so was inexpensive and plentiful. But, like port, it was a fortified wine, something George tended to forget as the evening got into its stride. He was now forcibly reminded of its strength by the grey, queasy lethargy that pervaded his body and the dry, stale taste in his mouth. He was also dehydrated and sweaty in the heat. Flies buzzed irritatingly around his face. He swished them away for the umpteenth time. He longed for shade and sleep. The sooner we get to Faro, the better, he thought.

'Fitt,' he barked at his sergeant, 'keep the men going in time there. We want to look like British soldiers, not a bloody rabble.'

'Yes, sir.'

At the same time that George was riding along the coast road from Messina, across the straits John Entwhistle was staring disconsolately out of a small, barred window high inside Scylla castle. From the window he could just make out across the straits the tower of the fort at Faro. He wondered whether George Warne, assuming he had returned in one piece from his raid, was standing on that tower speculating whether he – possibly with his great friend William Coker – was imprisoned in the castle at Scylla.

Captain George bloody Warne, Entwhistle thought angrily, might like to know that his great friend William Coker was alive and well – apart from a broken collarbone – and lying on a truckle bed across the room, dozing. He hadn't really taken to Warne on the few occasions they'd met during the preparations for yesterday's raids. He'd struck Entwhistle as a bit too pleased with himself, with a touch too much of the cultivated, gentlemanly insouciance which so irritated him in many British officers. Why did they all have to pretend that war was simply a day's hunting in uniform? It was, or should be, a serious business. And all those officer-like airs and graces; you'd have thought he was the son of an earl at the very least, whereas in fact, Entwhistle had heard, his father was a country clergyman. Nor was the 27th Foot exactly the Guards, a very ordinary, bog-Irish line regiment, where commissions were considerably cheaper than in the more fashionable regiments. The 44th might not be the smartest regiment in the British army but it was at least English.

As Entwhistle stared resentfully out of the window, he began to replay in his mind's eye the events of the night before last. He and his men had reached the galley's berth on the quayside not long after Warne's raiding party had set off. Indeed, as he stood on the quay, he could just see Warne's galley edging its way out to sea, past the looming shadows of Fort Salvador. The crossing towards San Giovanni had been uneventful in good conditions. As they came into San Giovanni, he had heard gunfire from further up the coast. He had wondered at the time, and still wondered, whether it came from Scylla and was the result of Kendall's attack. What had happened to George Kendall, he wondered? It was difficult to get any news while locked up in this dreary cell.

Anyway, as the galley nosed inshore, all had seemed quiet. Entwhistle had mustered his troops in the galley's prow, ready to scramble ashore as soon as they could. In the dark they could make out the masts of the boats they had come to attack, over to the right. Entwhistle ordered the men to disembark and was soon leading a party of ten of them up the beach. Meanwhile, Sergeant Warwick led the rest of the men to the anchorage to start attacking the boats. The two naval officers, Lieutenant Edwards, commanding, and his midshipman, Doyne, remained with the galley.

Entwhistle and his men quickly reached the dunes but before they could establish a defensive position – their job was to protect the wrecking party for as long as possible – they came under attack. Soon afterwards, Entwhistle heard firing – including field artillery, it seemed – from behind, down on the waterline, near the galley. In the dark it became very confused; the enemy seemed to be all around them. Entwhistle knew that at least five of his men had been killed. That left five against an unknown – and presumably much larger – number of the enemy. Suddenly, there was a lull in the firing. A voice from down the beach, in Entwhistle's rear, shouted in heavily accented English:

'Your boat is destroyed . . . you 'ave no escape. Surrender now. It is 'opeless to fight.'

'We're surrounded, sir, and there's only three of us left unwounded,' said the private kneeling next to him in the dunes. 'There's no sense in fighting on alone.'

Entwhistle thought rapidly. Smith was right, of course; it would be a senseless sacrifice. But the shame, the dishonour to the regiment and the army, and to his name. What would his fellow officers think? But his overriding responsibility was to his men.

'All right,' he shouted in the direction of the voice down the beach, 'we surrender. Send me your officer. Cease fire, boys.' And with that, it was all over.

Later on, talking to Lieutenant Edwards – poor Doyne had been killed, which was a pity as he was a pleasant lad, promising, too – as they sat in the dark watched over by guards, Entwhistle found out what had happened to the galley. Somehow – Edwards wasn't sure how – the galley had become stranded shortly after Entwhistle had left. Perhaps she had come in to the beach too quickly; perhaps, in the dark, they had overestimated the depth of the water – although Edwards had positioned a man forward with a line – but the result was a terrible, long, grinding crunch as the galley's hull embedded itself in the wet sand. Edwards had tried frantically to get the rowers to pull the galley off, but in vain. She quickly came under attack from a field gun and infantry – this was when Doyne was killed – and, very soon, the French had surrounded the vessel. Edwards, in a hopeless position, stranded on the beach, his command already badly damaged, surrendered rather than inflict death and mutilation on the remainder of his crew.

Entwhistle had ordered the men of the wrecking party to surrender rather than fight a pointless battle against a vastly superior enemy. All the British soldiers on the beach and the rowers from the galley were rounded up and forced to sit on the damp sand, under the watchful eye of a handful of French soldiers. Entwhistle did the rounds of his men, establishing that twelve of the twenty who had set off from Messina had been killed. Three others were wounded, to varying degrees, Entwhistle himself was unharmed and Sergeant Warwick was still brimming with fight. Once the sun had risen, they were ordered to form up to march the few miles along the coast to the castle at Scylla. The rowers remained at San Giovanni. Entwhistle didn't want to contemplate the fate that awaited them as prisoners of war pressed into service in a French or Neapolitan galley.

As the little column of men wound its way along the coastal road, Entwhistle had time to enjoy the magnificent view of the northern tip of Sicily laid out before him in the glory of a late-summer morning. The low sun sparkled on the water, illuminating the fluffy pink and apricot clouds on the horizon. Before they rounded the headland to the north of San Giovanni, he could see Messina laid out beneath the mountains. Once they had passed the headland, the point of Faro was directly ahead, no more than a couple of miles across the straits. Entwhistle could see the squat tower of the fort sitting just behind the flat apron of beach. In the straits, two merchantmen were forging towards Messina, their sails tight in the breeze.

It was only five miles from San Giovanni to Scylla but as the exhausted, wounded men made slow progress it was nearly ten o'clock by the time they marched into Scylla. The town was dominated by the castle, which sat in a dramatic position atop the celebrated rock, the lair from which the mythical sea monster terrorised passing mariners. There had been a castle on the rock since the Dark Ages, testament to the strategic importance of its position overlooking the straits. Above it, the French tricolour fluttered in the breeze.

Beneath the castle, squeezed into the narrow coastal strip between the sea and the higher ground, was the town of Scylla. Beyond the castle, curving away towards the headland, was a shingly beach crowded with fishing boats hauled up above the waterline. As they entered the town, Entwhistle hoped that he might get some clues about what had befallen Kendall and his men. He had a passing glimpse of the beach, in the gaps between the houses, but it left him none the wiser.

When the column marched into the castle, the commandant, an immaculately turned-out French officer, came to meet it. He was a tall, fair man, with an impressive walrus moustache and pale blue eyes. He spoke good English, rather to Entwhistle's surprise.

'May I introduce myself?' he said, stepping towards Entwhistle. 'Jules Lafite, major in the Imperial Army.'

'Captain John Entwhistle, of His Majesty's 44th Foot.'

'I will do my best to look after you now that you are under my orders as a prisoner of war. Your men will be given quarters in the stables. You have a room in the castle itself. It has a fine view out over the straits. On a clear day you may be able to see your English friends in Sicily.' He laughed. 'And,' he continued, 'you will find that you have company there to keep you entertained. *À plus tard, monsieur.*' With that Lafite saluted Entwhistle before walking briskly away.

A few minutes later, Entwhistle was escorted up a narrow, spiral staircase in the keep of the castle. On the third floor they came to a door, which the guard unlocked. Inside, standing by the window, was William Coker, his left arm in a sling. Entwhistle entered the room and the door shut behind him. They heard the key turn in the lock.

'Well, well, well, what a surprise to see you here!' exclaimed Coker.

That had been yesterday morning. Entwhistle and Coker had, of course, immediately exchanged news, but neither of them knew what had happened to Kendall or, of course, to Warne.

'God, what a shambles,' said Entwhistle, after hearing Coker's account of his capture. His collarbone had been broken by a blow from a cutlass; he had been very lucky that the wound was not a great deal worse. 'Not your fault, of course,' Entwhistle added, hurriedly. 'You did all you could. But it does sound remarkably like what happened to me, don't you think?'

'There are some similarities, I agree,' said Coker. 'I'm beginning to wonder whether the Frogs were waiting for us.'

After a while the two men fell silent. They had no idea what the future held for them; they just had to wait. During the afternoon, they dozed, stared out of the little window and fretted. At least in here, behind the castle's massive, ancient walls, it was relatively cool. In the early evening, a meal of fish and beans was brought to them, with a bottle of rough local white wine. The rest of the evening and the night passed very slowly.

It was now morning. In the Citadel, George Warne was waking up with a sore head and a dry mouth. In Scylla, Entwhistle and Coker had been awake for some time when the door opened. It was breakfast – two slices of bread each and some quite palatable coffee – brought by an orderly in a dirty white apron. Behind him was a soldier, musket in hand.

The two men munched their way through the bread, drank the coffee and chatted desultorily. After a while Entwhistle stood up and crossed the room – it was all of four paces – to open the window. A waft of sea breeze entered the room and with it a low-pitched, muffled roar.

'That's the water in the caves at the foot of the rock, I think,' said Coker. 'The ancients believed it was the monster in his lair.'

'If that's what you thought it was, it must have been quite frightening if you were being driven towards the rock in a high sea.'

'I suppose so, but I don't think very much scared Odysseus,' replied Coker.

At that moment the door was unlocked, opening to reveal two soldiers in French uniform, one a sergeant.

'*Vite, messieurs, vite*,' said the sergeant, before giving his instructions in rapid French. '*Allez-y, allez-y*. Major Lafite is waiting for you.'

'It sounds to me,' said Coker, 'as if we're being taken to see Murat.'

'That'll be interesting,' replied Entwhistle.

Murat's headquarters were not far along the coast from Scylla, on the ridge above Punta di Pezzo. Coker and Entwhistle knew what to expect as the camp could be seen easily from across the straits in Sicily. On the plain of Melia, below the ridge, a large number of tents were pitched in orderly rows; seen from Sicily, they resembled white studs on the dun-coloured ground. Seen close up, they were altogether larger and more spacious, thronged with men cooking, chatting, smoking, relaxing in the sun, snoozing in the shade. Above them, on the ridge, was Murat's pavilion, flanked by an enormous French tricolour and his army's regimental eagles. The tented pavilion was a grand structure, with an imposing entrance beneath a large Imperial eagle, draped in swooping swags of bullion tassels; glancing inside, Coker could see elaborate furniture, tapestries hanging on the walls and carpets on the floor. Murat may be in the field, he thought, but he keeps himself well. Over to the right, Entwhistle noticed the tall gibbet.

'Let's hope we don't end up there,' he whispered to Coker, who smiled grimly.

The two British officers and their escort halted on the wide expanse of baked earth, which doubled as a parade ground in front of Murat's pavilion.

'*Attendez un moment, messieurs, s'il vous plaît,*' said Major Lafite, who had escorted the two English officers to Murat's camp. He strode towards the pavilion's entrance and disappeared. A few minutes later he re-emerged.

'*Venez ici, tout de suite, messieurs,*' he shouted.

Coker and Entwhistle started towards the pavilion, the guards following behind. In the entrance, under the Imperial eagle, they paused next to Lafite.

'The King will see us now,' he said. '*Suivez-moi.*' He led Entwhistle and Coker past the two sentries into the pavilion's loggia and from there they entered a room furnished as a study. To one side was a fine mahogany desk with a tooled leather top, its frieze decorated with rams' masks complete with curly horns. Some campaign desk, Coker said to himself. On an easel behind the desk was a portrait of the Emperor, looking purposeful in a plain uniform. It was, Coker supposed, a protestation of loyalty, although if the gossip was to be believed, Murat and Napoleon, despite being old comrades-in-arms and brothers-in-law – Murat was married to the Emperor's sister, Caroline – were these days barely on speaking terms.

As the two British officers were looking around the empty room, the door behind the desk opened, and a young staff lieutenant swept into the room.

'*Le Roi,*' he announced grandly, stepping aside.

As Joachim Murat, King of the Two Sicilies, walked into the small canvas-walled study, Lafite bowed deeply. Coker and Entwhistle looked at each other fleetingly before bowing – albeit not so deeply – in their turn. A hot stab of pain shot through Coker's left shoulder as he did so, causing him to wince.

The King was a fine figure of a man, at forty-three in the prime of life. Although of no more than medium height, his bearing and poise commanded attention. He may have been the son of a provincial innkeeper from the depths of central France, but he had an undeniably regal air. Here was a leader, a man accustomed to deference and unquestioning obedience. His hair was a tousled mass of dark curls and he had luxuriantly bushy side whiskers, but the eye was drawn to his magnificent uniform. The Napoleonic establishment set great store by uniforms as an outward and visible sign of power, a symbolism Murat embraced wholeheartedly. Today he was kitted out as a general in the Neapolitan army, as he was fully entitled to be. He wore a close-fitting dark blue tunic with gold frogging across the chest, a crimson collar and cuffs edged with gold embroidery, and heavy gold epaulettes. His breeches were also dark blue with a broad gold side-stripe up the leg, his hussar boots edged with gold trim and tassel. It was quite a sight, the magnificence of the uniform somewhat at odds, Entwhistle thought, with the widely known incompetence and lack of backbone of Neapolitan generals.

As Murat entered the room he put his hat – a magnificent confection of cockaded gold lace and feathers – down on the desk.

'So, gentlemen,' he began in the twanging accent of the south-west of France, 'you attempted to disrupt my plans to invade Sicily. You know that His Imperial Majesty,' he pointed at the portrait behind the desk, 'places a high priority on reuniting the two halves of my kingdom. *Traduisez, s'il vous plaît, monsieur,*' he nodded to Major Lafite. 'What the Emperor desires, the Emperor gets. General Stuart should know that by now.'

Murat paused as he sat down in the chair behind the desk, stretching his legs out in front of him. There were no chairs for Lafite or for Coker and Entwhistle. The young staff lieutenant stood stiffly to attention behind the King.

'You will be disappointed,' he continued, 'to hear that your general's attacks two nights ago were not successful. None of the four attacks achieved anything at all, beyond some slight, temporary damage to a few transport vessels. This will be quickly repaired. Nor were the attacks pressed home with the vigour that any general is entitled to expect. Perhaps the British soldier is losing his fighting spirit.'

Coker and Entwhistle looked at each other.

'Your attacks, gentlemen, at San Giovanni and Catone did not, I think you would agree, achieve what you might have hoped. The other two, at Reggio and at Scylla, were even less successful. The force attacking at Reggio ran back out to sea at the first sign of opposition. Hardly a shot was fired, my officers tell me. The force attacking at Scylla showed scarcely more resolution. If this is how General Stuart's army fights now, I shall be in Sicily whenever I want. *Comme ça.*' He snapped his fingers loudly. 'I just have to say the word.'

The interview with Murat had lasted only a few minutes more before the young lieutenant coughed discreetly and bent over to whisper in the King's ear.

'Thank you, Lafite,' said Murat. 'Please make sure that our British guests are comfortable. Goodbye, gentlemen.' The interview was over.

Neither Coker nor Entwhistle said anything to each other

during the journey back to Scylla, although Coker could see that Entwhistle was boiling with anger. Once they were back in their cell, the door securely locked behind them, Entwhistle exploded.

'That bloody coward, Warne, scarpered at the first whiff of trouble. So much for all his fine pretences.'

'Do you really believe what the King said, John? It doesn't sound like George to me,' said Coker.

'Why would he make it up?' snapped Entwhistle.

'Why not?' said Coker.

'At least we didn't go down without a fight. I lost a dozen men at least, and so did you. Bloody Warne and his Irish bog rats just buggered off to safety the moment they realised the enemy was alive and kicking.'

'That's a bit harsh, John. And we've only got the enemy's word for it. If I were you, I'd wait and see what you can find out when we get back to Sicily.'

'If we get back to Sicily,' replied Entwhistle.

'Oh, I expect we'll be exchanged before too long,' said Coker.

'Let's hope so.'

That evening – eight or so hours after William Coker and John Entwhistle had been summoned before Murat – George Warne was once again entering Messina. He was on his way to visit Carlotta, his mistress. He had not seen her for nearly a week, as the preparations for the raid had consumed so much of his time. A note had been waiting for him at Faro, when he'd got back that morning. *Come to me this evening & I will surprise you. C.*

He'd had some duties to attend to, not least composing the official report on his raid for Colonel Airey. By the time he had finished the draft he was feeling very sleepy – the Marsala's revenge – so had a siesta. George had, in four years in Sicily, come rather to like the local habit of having a siesta in hot weather and – although it was frowned upon by the more straight-laced British as the first step on the slippery slope to continental decadence – took one whenever his military duties allowed.

He had woken refreshed and shouted for his servant, Callaghan, who drew a bath and, once he had finished, stropped a razor to shave George. George then got dressed in dark blue breeches and a white silk shirt, tied a clean stock neatly round his neck and took the green lightweight coat which Callaghan held out for him. He picked up his sword and buckled it round his waist: better not to venture out unarmed, as the Sicilian *banditti* had a ferocious reputation. George knew of several incidents in which British officers had been attacked by bandits, although it was more likely to happen in the wilder, less populated parts of the island. Down in the courtyard, George collected his horse, ruffled Boney's ears and set off for Messina.

It was early evening as George walked his horse through the thronging crowds on the strada Ferdinanda. The glaring sun was mellowing into the gentler glow of evening, the fierce heat of the day fading into balmy warmth. Soon he came to the large, rather grand house in which Carlotta had her apartment. George handed his horse's reins to the son of the man who kept the shop next door. For a couple of small coins, the boy would look after his horse as long as he was inside.

'Good evening, Signor Warne,' said the boy's father, winking knowingly. 'Enjoy yourself.'

Glancing up, George could see that the shutters and windows were open. He clattered up the short flight of stone steps from the pavement, pushed open the heavy, embossed front door and went in. Inside, in the cool half-light, was an elegantly cantilevered stone staircase. George bounded up, two at a time, and knocked on the door on the landing. After a few moments it opened.

Inside was Carlotta, wearing a long white silk dressing gown, loosely tied at the waist.

'My darling, my Giorgio,' she said, opening her arms to him. George took two steps into the room, closing the door behind him with his foot. 'I've missed you so.' She spoke the Sicilian dialect; it was how they communicated now.

'I've missed you, too, *cara*,' said George, holding her tightly. He could feel her wonderful, firm, voluptuous body moulding into him beneath the dressing gown. They kissed, their tongues snaking round each other, slowly, sensuously, then more urgently.

'What's the surprise?' asked George.

'You cheeky man, you couldn't wait, could you?' she replied playfully.

'Well, what is it?'

'This,' Carlotta replied. She stepped back out of George's arms, untied the cord at her waist and opened the dressing gown. Underneath she was completely naked. She took George's hand.

'Come with me, my darling.' As she led him across the salon towards the bedroom, the sounds of the street floated up through the open windows. The bedroom door closed gently behind them.

Sometime later, Carlotta and George were sitting at the table in the salon drinking white wine from tall-stemmed glasses. It was now dark outside, so Carlotta had closed the shutters in front of the open windows and lit half a dozen candles.

'I was so worried about you, *amore*,' she said. 'I'd heard rumours that some attacks against the French were planned and, when I didn't hear from you, I thought you might have been ordered to carry them out. I feared the worst. But you are safe, my Giorgio.' She stroked his cheek.

George told her the story of his raid. He told her about the unexpected appearance of the French infantry on the beach. He told her about the hand-to-hand fight with them and about the brief but desperate attempts to keep the enemy at bay while his men re-embarked. He told her about the chase down the beach to the galley and about poor Slattery, killed almost as he reached safety, and about the other men who didn't make it, Kelly and Byrne. He also told her what he knew about the other attacks. When he had finished, George took a long draught of wine and refilled his glass. In the silence, one of the candles guttered noisily.

'I am beginning to think,' he said reflectively, 'that the enemy was waiting for us.'

'How could that be? Were the attacks betrayed? Was it not all very secret?' asked Carlotta, shocked.

'Well, yes, but the coincidences are too great to ignore, don't you think?'

'Yes, it does seem odd. Have you raised your suspicions with your superiors?'

'I've told Colonel Airey what I think, but he's not convinced.'

'Are you going to do anything about it?' she asked.

'Well, I think I should, if only for the sake of the men who were killed. I have an idea, too.'

'What's that?'

'You, Carlotta, my sweet.'

'Me?'

'Yes, you,' said George, bending over to kiss her. 'Your family is well connected, you know a lot of important people, you could make some enquiries, very discreetly, without raising any suspicions. After all, very soon the news of the attacks will be public knowledge and everyone will be talking about them. Rumours will be flying all over the city,' George waved his hand expansively, 'so you'll hear all sorts of things. What do you think?'

'Well, I suppose it wouldn't do any harm to keep my ears and eyes open.'

'Now, that's what I like to hear,' said George, pulling her onto his lap.

While George and Carlotta were making love on the mahogany four-poster bed in the house on the strada Ferdinanda, just a few streets away Robert Thring was preparing to welcome a dozen guests to his lodgings.

'I have organised, very much at the last minute, my dear,' he had announced to his sister Emma that morning, 'a small party to welcome you to Sicily. I've invited some fellow officers and one or two Sicilians. I hope you will find them agreeable.'

'I am sure,' she replied, 'it will be a most interesting evening. And,' she added, 'it will give me an opportunity to practise my Italian.'

The major's lodgings occupied the *piano nobile* of a house on a side street off the Corso, Messina's second great thoroughfare, a few minutes' walk inland from the harbour and the strada Ferdinanda. The reception was being held in the large, rectangular, high-ceilinged salon, with three tall windows, which looked out over the street below. The gilded carving of the ceiling loomed in semi-darkness above the luminous, flickering glow of the three candelabra. At one end of the room were two buffet tables, draped in crisp linen, on which stood wine coolers brimming with bottles, serving dishes piled high with ices and a large cake. The rest of the room had been cleared of furniture and rugs, leaving only a wide expanse of polished floorboards. Emma and her brother stood in the middle, waiting for the guests to arrive, while the two footmen – servants from the officers' mess in the Citadel, borrowed for the occasion – stood by the door, each holding a salver laden with glasses.

Within a quarter of an hour, most of the guests had arrived. Robert introduced his sister to each new arrival. Now she was deep in conversation with two young officers: one, Lieutenant Wilkins, was from Robert's regiment, the 27th; the other, Lieutenant Younge, had taken George Warne and his men over to Reggio two days previously. Robert Thring was talking to Major Campbell, a Scots officer in the Royal Artillery who had been in Sicily for two or three years. A tall, handsome, well-liked officer, he had a reputation for dash and gallantry.

'Major Thring,' he was saying, 'may I introduce my wife, Clare, who has recently arrived in Sicily?'

'A pleasure, Mrs Campbell,' said Thring, inclining his head. Mrs Campbell, was a short, very stout woman whose face was disappearing into a mask of blubber. She and her husband were an ill-matched pair. Mrs Campbell had come to Sicily to do some sightseeing, although she did not seem too enthusiastic about Messina.

'It's very dilapidated, and rather dirty and smelly, Major, don't you find?' she said, dismissively.

'Well, Mrs Campbell, I suppose I've come to like it over the years. It has a certain charm and there are some fine things to see here. How are you proposing to travel around the island?'

'Major Campbell,' she said, pointing her fan in the direction of her husband, 'says that I could travel by mule, but I think a litter might be easier. What do you think?' Mrs Campbell did not look the type who might relish tackling the dreadful Sicilian roads on a mule. Indeed, Thring thought to himself, the poor mule might find carrying Mrs Campbell around Sicily hard work.

'You might consider travelling by sea, especially if you intend to visit Taormina, Mount Etna, Catania and Syracuse. It's quicker and a great deal more comfortable than going by land, if somewhat more expensive. Major Campbell and I engaged a felucca for our expedition to climb Etna two years ago.'

After about ten minutes, a hand touched Thring's sleeve. It was Fabrizio Falcone, a local lawyer and landowner, who was well known to many of the more senior officers of the British garrison. A worldly, cultivated man, he had been a great help to the British since they had been in Messina.

'Signor Thring, could I have a word with you?' He spoke good but heavily accented English.

'Of course, Signor Falcone,' said Thring. With some relief he excused himself from the Campbells and joined Falcone.

'A nice evening,' said Falcone, 'very kind of you, Major.'

'It is to introduce my sister, Emma, to the important people in Messina, *signore*,' said Thring, smiling at Falcone. 'She's just arrived from England.'

'Ah, you must introduce me,' replied Falcone, taking a sip of his wine. 'But first, there is something I would like to ask you.'

'Do, please.'

'I have heard rumours of some raids across the straits against the French,' said Falcone quietly. 'I hear that they were not successful, that many men were killed, and that Murat is saying that the British fled like sheep. He is telling people that Sicily is his for the taking. This is worrying as the French are cruel and greedy and will not be kind to those who have helped the English.'

'Well, my friend, as you know,' the major replied, 'I am not privy to the secrets of our generals but I do know that some raids across the straits took place two nights ago. I know little of the details at the moment, but I will hear more in the coming days. How many men were killed, or how great a failure the raids were, I cannot tell you.' Thring smiled. 'And as for the King of Naples' boasting, all I can say is that you must have spies in very high places.'

'Well, you know us Sicilian lawyers, *signore*,' replied Falcone with a grin.

'Yes, I do. Now come and meet my sister, *signore*.' He took Falcone's arm and guided him across the room towards Emma.

As the two men crossed the floor Emma was still talking to Wilkins and Younge. Wilkins was a gentle, mild-mannered young man, more suited, Thring thought, to being a clergyman or a schoolmaster than an army officer, but he had taken to military ways and traditions with all the zeal of the convert. Wilkins was fiercely proud of the regiment and had quietly delighted in his recent promotion.

'Mr Wilkins was telling me about the Spanish castle at Milazzo,' said Emma as the two older men joined them. 'It sounds quite wonderful, with its long promontory out into the sea. Have you been there, Robert?'

'Yes, I know it well as I was quartered there for more than a year when I first arrived here. Some of the Spanish parts are charming and it commands a fine view along the coast and out to sea. Strolling among the vineyards on the promontory is a pleasant way to pass an hour or two. Now, my dear, allow me to introduce Signor Falcone. He is a very important man in these parts and a great friend of England.'

Falcone took Emma's hand and bent to kiss it. Wilkins looked a little put out as he watched this display of Latin gallantry, Thring thought, although he was trying not to show it.

'*Gran' piacere*,' said Falcone. 'I understand from Major Thring that you have only just arrived in our island.'

As Emma replied, Thring turned towards Wilkins and Younge, who was the first to speak.

'It is a great pleasure to make your sister's acquaintance, sir. As you know, young ladies of good family so rarely come to Sicily.'

'I know, but she was determined to make the journey,' replied Robert, 'and I hope I can show her the sights while she is here.'

'I have offered, sir, to show your sister the *duomo* and the other important sights of Messina tomorrow,' said Wilkins, 'if she is free.'

'Perhaps, Wilkins,' interrupted Younge, 'we could escort Miss Thring around the city together. Then she would get the benefit of both your knowledge and mine. Two is better than one, don't you agree?'

'Why don't we see what Miss Thring has to say to that proposal?' said Wilkins.

'Yes, why not?' said Thring. The last thing he wanted was two young officers vying for his sister's affections. That way lay trouble for all concerned.

Half an hour later, Robert and Emma were standing at the middle window gazing out over the darkened street. The smells of the city wafted up in the warm evening air. All the guests had departed; behind them, the two servants were clearing up the remains of the party.

'What did you make of Mr Wilkins and Mr Younge?' asked Robert. 'They seemed delighted to make your acquaintance.'

'They both seemed pleasant young gentlemen, eager to please,' said Emma. Even in the low light Robert could see that his sister was blushing at this line of questioning. She had until recently lived a closeted life in the nursery and the schoolroom. This trip to Sicily was her first adventure into the wider world.

'Mr Younge was telling us amusing stories about life at sea, especially about a voyage his ship made to the West Indies. It all sounded so exciting.'

'Yes, my dear, I'm sure it did. Was he telling you about sea monsters and pirates?' asked her brother, smiling.

'No, Robert, more about smugglers, hurricanes and yellow fever,' replied Emma reprovingly. 'I am no longer the child I was when you left England, you know.'

'No, no, I know,' said Robert apologetically. 'How did you find Signor Falcone?'

'He seemed very much the man of business, a man of influence, but unlike many such people, not boastful or too full of himself.'

'He's certainly a man with high-placed friends and someone who has fingers in many pies, but he's always been friendly to me.'

The conversation tailed off. As they stood in the darkened window, Robert thought about the raids, about what Falcone had said about them and decided he must warn his superiors that the locals were worried about a French invasion. It was not good for British prestige that they should doubt their ability to protect them from the French.

The servants had left. The salon, lit by a single candle, was now almost dark. He was on duty in the morning. It was time for bed.

'Come on,' he said to Emma, 'it's late. Let's close up.'

CHAPTER FIVE

Messina, 9th September 1810

As George woke up the light was creeping round the edges of the shutters. Nestled into his back was Carlotta, warm, loving. Outside the city's bells were ringing from chapels, churches and monasteries, summoning the citizens of Messina to Mass.

'Damn it,' said George, suddenly wide awake, 'it's Sunday. It must be nearly eight o'clock by now. I should be at Faro.'

He had overslept after the exertions of the last few days. Kissing Carlotta, he leapt out of bed and began pulling on his clothes. As he left the bedroom, George picked up his sword and made for the front door. The gilt clock on the mantlepiece in the salon showed ten to eight.

'See you soon, my Giorgio,' Carlotta shouted after him. 'Write to me.'

'I'll come as soon as I can, my darling.'

He galloped down the stairs two at a time and ran out into the street. It was a bright morning, with the promise of another bakingly hot day. The boy who had taken his horse last night was sitting on the steps of his father's shop next door, playing with a kitten.

'My horse, and quickly please, I'm in a hurry.'

'*Si signore, si signore*,' said the boy, disappearing into an alley beside the shop. The kitten rubbed itself against George's ankle, curling its tail round his leg.

In less than a minute the boy was back, leading George's horse.

'Here you are, sir,' said the boy in the Sicilian dialect. 'I've looked after him myself.'

'Thank you very much,' replied George, handing the boy a brass coin. It was worth one *grano*, or rather less than a penny, but he seemed pleased enough. He held the bridle as George jumped into the saddle. The horse whinnied as George turned his head towards the Porta Reale and Faro.

It was about eight and a half miles to Faro from the centre of Messina, as George knew well. With luck he should be back at the fort by nine, in time to change into uniform before the Sunday parade. To be late would be a breach of discipline and a bad example to the men. Once through the Porta Reale, he flicked the reins at his horse, who broke into a trot.

George trotted along the coast road towards Faro grinning as he thought about the previous evening. Carlotta had been *very* pleased to see him – and he her. He sometimes thought about marrying her: the language barrier had crumbled away almost to nothing; they got on admirably, and as a lover, well, what more could a man want? What's more, he knew of at least two British officers who had recently married Sicilian girls. As Messina dropped behind him, George thought of Carlotta having a bath, brushing out her long, dark hair and getting dressed. To his right, across the straits, the morning sun was slanting onto the peaks of the Calabrian mountains but the shoreline, a thousand and more feet below, was still in deep shadow.

During their conversation the previous evening, Carlotta had agreed to engineer a meeting with the Count of Pelorito – a friend and patron of her late husband who had supported her financially after his untimely death – to find out what he knew about the raids across the straits. She knew that the count, a religiously observant man, invariably attended Mass in the *duomo*, so would meet him there, ostensibly by chance, after the service. The count was a man of influence, who knew everyone; little escaped his eyes and ears. If the raids had been betrayed, George was confident that the count would know about it, or at least have heard something. The question was, would he open up to Carlotta?

These questions were still swirling round in George's head as he arrived at Faro. Slowing from a trot to a walk, he entered the fort's courtyard and dismounted. He was relieved to see that the garrison had not yet mustered for the Sunday parade. He had avoided making a fool of himself in front of the men, but only by a short head.

The moment George swung down from the saddle, he was greeted by a delighted Boney, all wagging tail and bounce. George bent down to stroke the spaniel's head, whereupon he promptly rolled onto his back, imploring George to tickle his tummy.

'Good morning, sir.' It was John O'Connell, whom George had left in charge in his absence. He was immaculately turned out: even the colonel, who was a stickler in such matters, would have been satisfied with Lieutenant O'Connell this morning. The lapels of his short scarlet coat were buttoned back in the approved fashion, revealing the 27th's pale buff facings. His gorget was brightly polished and his sword hanging exactly to the prescribed length – the colonel had a particular dislike of the practice affected by some officers of slinging their belts so low that their swords trailed along the ground, mimicking the cavalry fashion. His white breeches were spotless, his half-boots gleaming and the crimson sash tied neatly around his waist.

'Good morning, John,' replied George. 'All well here?'

'Yes, sir. The guard noticed a couple of boats acting oddly at dusk last night out in the straits. I thought of going after them but by the time we'd got a boat ready it was dark and there seemed little point in going out as we'd never have found 'em.'

'You made the right decision, John. They were probably only fishermen. I've been out into the straits so many times after some boat or other, only to stop them and discover that they are bona fide fishermen with a British licence to prove it.'

'Oh, and sir, there's a message for you from the Citadel. Arrived late yesterday evening.'

O'Connell produced a letter from his coat pocket and handed it to George, who tore it open and read it. It was very brief.

After a moment, George looked up. 'Colonel Airey wants to see me at the Citadel at noon. Let me go and get into my uniform before we parade, then I'll have to be off again.'

Later that morning George entered the Citadel, the sentries snapping to attention as he did so. Now that his horse was at a walk, Boney was alongside but for much of the ride down the coast the spaniel had been behind, running to keep up. After an eight-mile run in the heat, he was now sitting down, panting wildly, ears back, head up, flanks heaving. As George dismounted, the dog jumped into one of the stone horse troughs, where he wallowed happily in the cool water. Looking around, George could not see a groom so led his horse into the shade to tether him.

As he did so, he heard a commotion from the direction of the guardhouse inside the main gate. Looking up, he saw one of the Citadel's assistant provost marshals, a tough-looking, burly sergeant; with him were two soldiers and a man pinioned between them. It was Michael Kelly, whose brother, John, had been killed in Friday's raid on Reggio. George hurriedly tethered his horse and strode across the courtyard. Kelly was swearing loudly and foully at the provost marshal and his men. It was obvious that he was very drunk, even in the middle of the morning. His uniform was dirty and torn, missing several buttons. His shako had long since disappeared. He'd also lost one of his boots. He had a nasty-looking gash on his forehead.

'What do we have here, Sergeant?' asked George. The provost marshal and his assistants were responsible for policing the soldiers when they were out in Messina.

'I've just arrested him in the city, sir. He was threatening a man with a bayonet, demanding money for wine. There were reports of a brawl with some sailors in a tavern, too. He's also, sir, as you can see, being difficult now.' Kelly was struggling to free himself from the grip of the two soldiers on either side of him.

George sighed. Drunkenness was a perennial problem in the British garrison here. Even the best soldiers, when they went into Messina, frequently got stinking drunk. Wine was plentiful and cheap, an irresistible temptation to the soldiers and all too often they made the most of it. It was a rare Sunday morning when the provost marshals had no drunken miscreants to deal with.

'Lock him up, please, Sergeant, and let him sleep it off. And would you send for the surgeon to clean up that cut,' George said. 'Kelly, go quietly with the provost marshal. I'll come and see you later.'

'Come on, son, off we go,' said the sergeant as the two men heaved Kelly into the guardhouse.

Oh dear, thought George, this was going to be an awkward case. Kelly had breached army discipline; soldiers could not be allowed to career drunkenly around Messina, threatening the locals with bayonets, demanding money. This kind of behaviour had to be punished. The problem was that the punishments were serious: a brutal flogging at best but, possibly, in a case like this, the death penalty. On the other hand, in mitigation, Kelly was a good soldier, one of the best in the company, with an excellent record, normally reliable, steady and loyal. He had fought well in the desperate scrap on the beach. George liked him and he was popular in the ranks. No doubt the death of his brother during Friday's raid had something to do with this fit of drunkenness. But it would be difficult to sway a court martial to mercy.

George had an hour to kill before his appointment with Colonel Airey so he strolled across the courtyard to the officers' mess. The monthly mail from England had arrived on Wednesday but George had not yet collected his letters – if there were any. The mail was brought to Sicily from Falmouth in small, fast vessels, known as Post Office packets. Generally, it took about six weeks for letters from home to arrive, but it could be much longer, if bad weather or enemy action intervened. The monthly packet was, naturally, eagerly awaited by every man in the army here for news of spouses, of children, of family. It was the only link with home.

The mess orderly was putting bottles into the wine coolers when George entered.

'Good morning, Winch,' said George. Abel Winch was a young man but as his pronounced stoop, flat feet and poor eyesight made him unfit for active duties, he had been found a job as an orderly, waiting on the officers. One of his most important duties was collecting and distributing the officers' letters. 'Are there any letters for me from last week's packet?'

'Yes, Captain Warne, I think there are, sir,' he replied. He shuffled off, returning a few minutes later with two letters.

'Thank you,' said George. Holding the two letters he left the mess and made his way up onto the ramparts, calling Boney as he went. The dog jumped out of the horse trough, shook himself vigorously and trotted over to join his master. Walking round to one of the bastions overlooking the straits, George settled himself on the warm, rounded breech of a gun and inspected the envelopes. The first one was from his parents, addressed in his father's precise hand. The other was from his cousin Harriet. There had been a time, during his early years in Sicily, when the mere sight of Harriet's distinctive, looping handwriting would have set his heart a-flutter. Since then, George recognised, the passage of time had conspired with distance and separation to dilute, if not extinguish altogether, any romantic sentiments he may have had towards her. Nor, it had to be admitted, had his entanglement with Carlotta done anything to sharpen his longing for Harriet. He broke the seal of her letter and started to read.

My dear George, it began,
I find this a most difficult letter to write but I would like you

to know that I am engaged to be married. Mr Scott, who is the vicar at Bisley in the county of Gloucester, proposed to me last week and I have accepted him. Papa & Mama are delighted as Mr Scott is a man of good family and gentle disposition, devoted to his parishioners and to the Church. We are to be married in October. With God's grace, I am sure I shall be very happy.

Harriet continued with a paragraph or two of family news before signing herself 'Your affectionate cousin'.

George put the letter down on the breech of the gun and looked out over the battlements. Two or three years ago, this letter would have been a bombshell, which would have plunged him into a deep gloom for weeks. Now, he realised, he could read the news with, more or less, complete equanimity. Nevertheless, he wondered why the lively, fun-loving, mischievous Harriet he had known had decided to marry a stuffy clergyman: 'devoted to his parishioners and to the Church' indeed! And how old, he wondered, was the estimable Revd Mr Scott? He'd have to write to Harriet to congratulate her on her forthcoming marriage.

The other letter, from his father, was full of news of family and friends and of local goings-on in Herefordshire. His father reported on the harvest, which had been imminent when he wrote in mid July, and on the long-running saga of the church tower, which had been badly damaged in a winter storm. There was news of a great ball given by a local landowner and of various picnics and other events. Enclosed with his father's letter was one from his mother. She gave George news of Charlotte and Lizzie, his sisters, and of his brother, John. Charlotte was expecting a baby so, she said, 'my little boy will soon be an uncle'. She also referred to Harriet's forthcoming marriage: 'Mr Scott, who is a man of middling years . . .' So she's marrying a man twice her age, thought George. Well, good luck to her. She'll be a nursemaid rather than a wife before too long, he thought, spitefully.

Reading his parents' letters always made George wistful. He enjoyed his life in Sicily but he longed to see his family, his friends and the fields and woods of Herefordshire once more. He'd been away for nearly five years now, and with no end to the war in sight, how much longer might he be here? Nor was there much prospect of obtaining home leave.

Then George, banishing these thoughts, stood up, stuffed the two letters into his pocket, and descended the stairs to the courtyard from where he made his way to Colonel Airey's office. The clerks' room was quiet; even Mr Rogers took Sunday off. As he entered, the colonel looked up from his papers and replaced his pen in the inkstand.

'Good morning, George. Good of you to come in on a Sunday. Sit down.' He paused, looking intently at George, before continuing. 'I've been considering what you said the other day about the possibility that Friday's raids were betrayed. I am inclined to agree that the fact that all four raids ran into apparently well-organised defences in the middle of the night almost as soon as they landed cannot be a coincidence or simply bad luck. It seems at least possible that the enemy had some warning of the attacks.'

'I agree, sir,' replied George. 'Surely the enemy couldn't have organised such an effective defence against all four raids in the middle of the night without warning? One perhaps, two possibly, but not all four.'

'So the question is,' Airey continued, 'how did the enemy get wind of our plans? How did the secret get out?'

'We all know that Messina is full of enemy spies,' said George. 'Do you think that the masters of the galleys could have betrayed the operation, or one of their poor, unfortunate crew?'

'It's possible, of course, but hardly likely, as by doing so they would be deliberately putting themselves in the line of fire.'

They lapsed into silence. A bluebottle buzzed around the room, before landing on the ceiling. Outside, a horse was clip-clopping across the courtyard.

Colonel Airey was the first to break the silence. 'It seems that Murat was piqued by our attacks on his anchorages, so much so that he's already taken his revenge.'

'What do you mean, sir?' asked George.

'Last night a party of about twenty-five French soldiers came ashore on the outskirts of Messina, near that big church just outside the walls on the way to Faro,' Airey waggled his fingers in the air, 'what's it called?'

'San Francesco di Paola, sir,' replied George.

'Yes, that's the one. Anyway, it seems they landed, overwhelmed the men in the guardhouse, tied them up, ran the French tricolour up the flagpole and pushed off home.'

'Bloody cheek!' said George. 'But there was nothing awry when I rode past this morning, just before eleven.'

'No. It was all over by then. The alarm was raised at first light when some sharp-eyed sentry noticed the tricolour fluttering over the guardhouse. A party went down there at once and found the postern gate open and three men bound, gagged and chained to the wall inside. On the lookout platform the fourth member of the garrison was found dead, his throat cut. God knows how they managed to scale the wall without attracting the attention of the men inside. Apparently, before they left, the French soldiers told the men that they were grenadiers of Murat's Guards and that the King had personally ordered the operation.'

'Do you think it's revenge for our attacks, sir? Murat showing he can land his men on our side of the straits whenever he wants? That what we can do, he can do?'

'It looks rather like it, doesn't it? Sir John won't be pleased when I tell him, if he hasn't heard already,' replied the colonel. He paused, turning over some papers on his desk. 'I've spoken to Major Thring this morning.'

'Oh yes, sir?' said George.

'He came to me with some worrying information.' Airey looked at George. 'He told me that he'd spoken last night to a prominent local figure who asked him about Friday's raids. This fellow told Major Thring that he'd heard the raids had been a disaster for us with heavy casualties and that our men had turned tail without a fight at the first sign of resistance. He says that the city is rife with rumours.'

'That's outrageous,' said George, angrily.

'Yes, I know, but, according to Major Thring, he went on to say that Murat is now boasting that he can invade Sicily whenever he wishes. This fellow also told Thring that these rumours are frightening people in Messina, who fear the French. And, incidentally, if news of Murat's little demonstration last night gets out, these people will be even more alarmed. Those who have helped us since we've been here can expect little sympathy from Murat and his friends. That was why the major came to me. He was concerned that our reputation among the Sicilians could be damaged by these rumours.'

'I suppose he's right,' said George. 'Who is this fellow, sir?'

'I might as well tell you, I suppose, but you will be discreet, I trust, George? I know you have,' and here the colonel paused, clearing his throat, 'friends in the city.'

'Of course, sir.' George shifted in his chair. 'You can rely on me.'

'Good. He's called Falcone. He's an important lawyer in Messina and a landowner with estates in this part of the island. I've only met him once or twice but I do know that he's been a great help to us over the years in various ways. I also know that he's well thought of by many of our senior officers here. I'd be inclined to trust him. Have you ever come across him?' asked Airey, looking George straight in the eye.

'No, sir, I haven't had the pleasure.'

'Anyway, George, I must tell you why I got you here this morning.' He paused, smoothing the sleeve of his blue tunic. 'This business with Falcone only confirms my suspicions that something's afoot. I'm not saying that I think the raids were definitely betrayed, just that there's enough evidence to justify looking into the matter.'

'I agree, sir,' replied George. 'But where do I come into it?'

The colonel paused. 'George, I'm asking you to help me.'

'I'll do what I can, sir,' replied George.

'Good. I'd like you to see if you can, very discreetly, make some enquiries in the city, to find out whether the raids were betrayed or not and who was behind it.'

'If someone did betray the operations, they're hardly going to tell a British officer, are they, sir?'

'No, but you do have better connections among the locals than most of our officers, and you speak the lingo, which helps. I'm not asking for the answers, just a few clues, the odd lead, at this stage. Ask around, keep your ear to the ground, see what you come up with and report back to me, no one else. By all means use initiative but be discreet.'

'Of course, sir. What about my regimental duties? I am in command of the fort at Faro.'

'Yes, I've arranged with your colonel for you to take a week's leave to start with. The garrison will be told that you've gone on a trip to Taormina, a bit of well-deserved rest. I suggest you stay with your, er, friend in the city. Wear ordinary clothes and you'd better leave that dog of yours at Faro.' He glanced at Boney, who was lying at George's feet. 'We don't want you drawing attention to yourself, do we?'

'No, sir, we don't.'

George wondered whether he should tell the colonel that Carlotta was already investigating the rumours. Indeed, she might be speaking to the Count of Pelorito at this very moment. He decided against it.

'Before you go, George, I should warn you that this is a murky, dangerous business. It is a game being played for very big stakes by, we suspect, some of the highest in the kingdom.'

George stiffened in his chair. He had heard the rumours, of course, about Queen Maria Carolina's dislike of the British and the various plots that supposedly centred on her, but rumours swirled around all armies and the British in Sicily were no exception. Was Colonel Airey about to tell him the full story?

'Suffice it to say, George, that we have grounds for believing that the Queen is in touch, secretly of course, with the Emperor in Paris. It seems that she uses her granddaughter, the Empress, as the conduit. Her plotting is aimed at regaining the mainland portion of her husband's kingdom. The situation is further complicated by the fact that Murat and the Emperor, despite being old comrades-in-arms and, indeed, brothers-in-law, are now barely on speaking terms.'

He paused and, standing up, walked towards the door.

'Just remember, George,' he said quietly, 'spies aren't treated like officers. There's no parole in comfortable quarters with the prospect of an exchange in due course for someone caught spying, more likely a stiletto between the shoulder blades in a dark alley. It's a brutal business, so be careful.'

With that Colonel Airey opened the door. George walked into the outer office towards the courtyard and the midday sun, his mind swirling. He had passed into a new life. He was no longer an infantry officer; he was a spy.

While George was sitting in Colonel Airey's office in the Citadel, across the Straits of Messina, high in the keep of the castle at Scylla, William Coker and John Entwhistle were dozing. They were allowed an hour's exercise in the castle courtyard twice a day, morning and afternoon. Major Lafite had promised that they would be given access to the garrison's library but, as neither of them could read French well, that might not do much to alleviate the boredom. Meanwhile, time hung heavy on their hands.

The sound of footsteps on the stone stairs outside the room brought Coker and Entwhistle back to the present. The lock turned and the door opened to reveal two soldiers.

'*Allez-y, messieurs,*' one of them said, making a gesture with his hand indicating walking.

'It's time for our walk,' said Entwhistle. Coker nodded.

Soon the two men were walking round the perimeter of the castle's courtyard, in the blazing midday heat, moving from sun to shade and out again as they went. It took about three and a half minutes to complete a circuit at a steady pace. As they walked round, they discussed the possibility of making an escape. Their guards stood in the shade, watching as the Englishmen lapped the courtyard.

'What chance, d'you think, we'd have of making a dash for it?' asked Entwhistle. From their present position they could see directly out under the arch of the castle's main gate, to the town beyond.

'Well, I can see two sentries there,' replied Coker. 'We could probably get past them if we moved quickly, but would they be able to hit us before we were out of range?'

'They'd only get one shot each at us, and it's not easy to hit a man who is sprinting away from you, particularly if you're taken by surprise.'

'No,' said Coker pensively. 'But if we did make it, what would we do then? Every Frog in Calabria would be looking for us. They'd trawl the town inch by inch so we'd have to get out into the country and lie low until we could find a friendly fisherman to take us back to Sicily.'

'Maybe.'

They lapsed into silence as ahead, standing outside the gatehouse guardroom, was the dapper figure of Major Jules Lafite, their gaoler.

'Good morning, gentlemen,' he said stiffly in English. 'I hope you are well?'

'As well as can be expected in the circumstances, Major,' replied Coker.

'Good. I have been commanded by the King himself,' he continued, 'to inform you that last night a small party of grenadiers from his personal guard landed in Sicily and captured one of your forts. The garrison surrendered without firing a shot. The grenadiers ran up the tricolour on the fort's flagstaff before leaving. They didn't suffer a single casualty. It is proof, I think you will agree, that we can take Sicily whenever the King desires. Britain may have the Royal Navy, but your army has lost the will to fight. Good day, *messieurs*.' With that, Lafite turned on his heel and strode off towards the gate.

As he did so, the two guards emerged from the shadows.

'*Votre promenade est terminé, messieurs*,' said the taller of the two, pointing towards the keep with his musket.

It was early evening. The light was fading as George sat in the window of Carlotta's salon overlooking the strada Ferdinanda. The bustle of traffic, of people, of animals and children, of hawkers and beggars, was beginning to subside. The devout citizens of Messina were emerging from vespers, singly, in pairs and in small clusters, clutching their rosaries and missals. As he gazed out of the window, George thought back over the events of the day.

Colonel Airey now appeared as much more than a mere staff officer, the efficient administrator who did the generals' bidding, reducing their plans to logical, written orders. He was, clearly, the British army's spymaster in Sicily, the puppeteer whose strings controlled any number of agents, informers and spies, who knew their shady underworld, its deceits, its plots and its dangers. More to the point, why had he accepted the colonel's invitation to join this world? He had no experience of its ways and no training in its methods; he was an infantry officer, not a spy. He preferred to see his enemy, to confront him, rather than creep around in the shadows. But, for all that, it was exciting, a welcome change from the drudgery of garrison duty at Faro.

The rest of the day George had spent riding between Faro and Messina, collecting his clothes and other belongings and making arrangements for his week's 'leave'. George Warne, Captain in His Majesty's 27th Regiment of Foot, had been left behind in the little fort at Faro. It was George Warne, the spy, who was refilling his glass with white wine from the decanter on the table.

A few minutes later Carlotta glided across the salon's parquet floor and sat down at the table. She had just returned from calling on relations around Messina.

'So, my darling,' said George, pouring her a glass of wine, 'tell me what happened at Mass this morning.' He spoke in the Sicilian dialect.

'I sat near the back of the church so that I could keep an eye on the congregation. Before too long I saw the count, in a stall to one side.' She paused, taking a sip of her wine. 'After the service in the crush to leave the *duomo*, I managed, accidentally on purpose, to bump into him.'

'And how was he?'

'He seemed pleased to see me. We left the *duomo* together and he suggested that we walk a little, so we strolled out onto the Marina. We talked about my family, about friends and a little about the political situation. Eventually, I plucked up the courage to ask him about the rumours concerning the raids. He looked at me curiously, wondering why I should be interested in such matters. Then he said, "Why don't you get him to come and see me?"'

'He knows about me, does he?' said George.

'It seems so, my Giorgio, but he knows most things that go on here. Anyway, he's agreed to see you tomorrow at five o'clock at his house.'

'Stakes, gentlemen.'

Arthur Broderick shuffled the pack before dealing five cards to each player. George watched as he flicked the cards from the top of the pack with practised ease into six small piles on the green baize.

'Hearts are trumps,' announced Broderick, as he turned the top card before placing the remainder of the pack on the table. George picked up his cards.

'Damn it,' he said to himself, 'another lousy bloody hand.' So far this evening the cards had not run for George and he was already sitting on a considerable loss.

The six men sitting around the table in their shirtsleeves belonged to a disparate group, which met regularly to gamble at cards. They were mostly English, although they were frequently joined by a number of locals, including an aristocratic landowner, a prominent government official and a senior customs officer. Tonight, to George's left, sat John Egan, the Messina representative of a London bank, then Elias Rodger, an elderly naval lieutenant; beyond him was Josiah Cunningham, a major in the Royal Artillery, then Broderick, a captain in the 44th Foot, and lastly, on George's right, Richard Shipman, a wine merchant. Tonight they had gathered in Major Cunningham's apartment in a house on a side street between the Corso and the strada Ferdinanda, behind the Piazza del Duomo. On a side table were glasses and several decanters of wine.

They often played *vingt-et-un* or, if there was a group that could be divided into fours, whist, but tonight they were playing loo, a game in which a winning hand was a flush, five cards of the same suit. A player holding a flush, broadly speaking, won the hand and collected the pot made up of the other players' stakes. There were refinements revolving around the knave of clubs – always referred to as 'Pam' – and if no player claimed a flush then the hand was played trick by trick. Any player who failed to win a trick had to pay a second stake by way of penalty into the pool. This was known as being 'looed'.

Shipman, on the dealer's left, discarded two cards, picking up two more from the top of the pack, before closing his hand and, frowning almost imperceptibly, placing his cards face down on the table. George had been dealt two low clubs, the ten of spades and the queen and three of diamonds. Should he throw his hand in now or carry on, and risk being 'looed' for the fourth time this evening? On the other hand, if he changed some of his cards there was a chance that he might pick up a better hand and start recouping some of his losses. He paused, aware of the others round the table looking at him.

'I'll have three,' said George. Discarding the spade and the two low clubs, he picked up three new cards from the pack. They were all diamonds: the seven, the nine and the knave. Good God, thought George, a bloody flush, and a decent one, too. As nonchalantly as he could, he folded his hand and put the cards down on the table.

To his left, John Egan put his cards on the table.

'I'm out.'

Elias Rodger was sitting bolt upright in his seat, his cards face down on the table in front of him.

'I'm in,' he said softly. He must have a good hand if he's not changing any cards, thought George.

'One,' said Josiah Cunningham, discarding a card and picking another up from the pack.

'I'm taking four,' said Broderick. He's hoping for the best, thought George. Normally, Broderick was a steady, conservative player who bided his time, waiting for the good hand.

'Right, gentlemen,' said Broderick, folding his cards together, 'do we have a flush?' He looked at Shipman, who shook his head.

'George?'

'Yes, Arthur, as it happens, I do.' He put the five cards down in a row on the table. 'Diamonds to the queen.'

'I've got a flush,' said Rodger. George stiffened in his seat. 'But, regrettably, it doesn't beat Warne's.' He fanned his cards out and put them down on the table. 'Spades but only to the nine.'

'Well done, Elias,' said Cunningham, 'but I'm out.'

'No flush for me, either, and no sign of Pam,' said Broderick.

George breathed a sigh of relief. At last, he'd won a hand. Rodger kept his stake but George won the rest of the pot. He'd stemmed the tide. Perhaps now he would start winning and make some money. It was Shipman to deal.

CHAPTER SIX

Messina, 10th September 1810

The fishing smack was forging out into the straits, the breeze filling her brown, patched sails and ruffling the surface of the water. Emma Thring stood at the stern rail, wearing a boating cloak fastened at the collar over her dress, watching as Messina receded into the protective embrace of the mountains. It was a beautiful, late-summer morning; the sun sparkled on the waves and lit the tops of the mountains looming above the Calabrian shore. Ahead, dotted across the blue expanse, she could see a handful of tall-masted vessels. It was these boats they had come to watch chasing and catching the magnificent swordfish that inhabited these waters. Her only worry was the boat's motion on the choppy swell. She had survived the passage from England without suffering too badly from seasickness – even in the notorious Bay of Biscay – but she was unsure how she would react to the sharper movements of this smaller vessel. She gripped the stern rail more tightly and looked determinedly at the horizon.

In the waist of the boat, at the foot of the mast, stood the three men who were escorting her on this trip, laughing as they talked. Nearest to her was Peter Wilkins, his light brown hair tied neatly in a knot. In the middle was Frank Younge, the tallest of the three, towering over Wilkins. He, as the naval officer, was in charge of today's excursion. She had met both of them at her brother's reception two evenings ago. Beyond him was George Warne, not quite as tall as Younge but broader shouldered and every bit as suntanned. It was George, a friend of her brother Robert's, who had suggested the excursion.

'I've got a bit of leave this week, Miss Thring,' George had said, when Emma and her brother had met him in the courtyard of the Citadel the previous afternoon. 'So why don't we go out tomorrow morning to see if we can find the boats catching swordfish? It's quite a sight, seeing how they do it.'

'That would be most interesting, Captain Warne,' replied Emma, looking at her brother, as if for confirmation.

'How's your sailing, George?' asked Robert Thring.

'None too good, I regret to say,' replied Warne, 'but I'll see if I can get Lieutenant Younge to take us out. He's competent and, I think,' he looked at Emma, 'you know him.'

She nodded.

'If you're getting Lieutenant Younge along, perhaps you could ask Peter Wilkins to join you, as he kindly offered to take Emma sightseeing in Messina.'

'I'll see what I can do,' promised George.

'I'm glad to see that the French don't seem to be shooting this morning, Frank,' said George. Over the summer, the French

121

artillery had fired across the straits at the British positions more or less daily.

'They probably wouldn't bother shooting at a fishing smack,' replied Younge.

'Thank goodness for that,' said Wilkins, running his fingers through his hair.

'Why don't you two go aft and join Miss Thring? I'll see to trimming the sail. And, George, keep an eye out for the fishing boats.'

'Frank,' called George, pointing, 'is that one there, out to larboard?'

'Yes, it looks like it.' He gave an order to the helmsman and the boat changed course, swinging closer to the wind. After a few minutes, Emma and the two men at the stern rail could make out the fishing boat, which was anchored against the current. It was an ungainly-looking craft: a long, low hull with two booms laid across it supporting a tall mast, far too tall, it appeared, for the size of the vessel. About four feet from the top of the mast was a platform; on it stood a man. It looked dangerously precarious as the boat rocked on the swell.

'What's that man doing up there, Mr Warne?' asked Emma.

'He's looking out for fish. From there he can see a long way and, I think, to quite a depth. You see the small rowing boat alongside?'

'Yes,' replied Emma.

'You'll see that when the fellow up the mast spots a fish, the rowing boat will go off in pursuit of it.'

Suddenly, there was a commotion aboard the fishing vessel, the lookout shouting and pointing, as the smaller boat began rowing towards the watching English. It too had a mast amidships and, although lower than the one in the main boat, there was a platform for the lookout. In the bow stood a man holding a long, barbed spear attached to a line. He was bare-chested, burnt dark by the Sicilian sun.

'When they're within range of the fish, he'll throw the spear and start to play it. It can go on for an hour or more. Often another boat comes out from the shore to take over the line so that this boat can concentrate on spearing another fish.'

As they watched, the rowing boat zigzagged across the water, following the shouted instructions from the lookout. It was only about a hundred yards away when the man in the bow suddenly raised his arm and hurled the spear into the water. The lookout shouted loudly.

The line attached to the spear began whipping out over the bows, so rapidly that at one point the harpoonist nearly lost his footing.

'The fish is going very deep,' said Emma. 'Look how much line he's taking with him.'

'Probably forty or fifty fathoms, I shouldn't wonder,' said George.

Suddenly, the line over the bow went slack; immediately, the oarsmen stopped rowing and stood up on their benches as the lookout shouted from his platform.

'It's stopped pulling out and may come to the surface and they fear it might attack the boat,' said George. 'They can easily drive their swords through the planking of the boat, which could cause a nasty injury to the oarsmen.'

'How big are the fishes' swords?' asked Emma.

'I've seen one which was nearly four feet long and four inches broad at the top, Miss Thring,' volunteered Wilkins.

Then the line tightened again, jerking the boat away from the spectators. The oarsmen, seated once more, set their blades against the direction of the fish's pull.

'They're playing him now. In the end they'll exhaust him and he'll come to the surface. When he does, they'll finish him off.'

Within a minute or two the swordfish was swimming with the current, which was strong in these waters. With the double pull of fish and current, the four oarsmen were fighting hard – the muscular effort was visible to the watching English two hundred yards away – to stop themselves being pulled far out to sea.

'It must be a hard life for these men,' said Emma, watching the straining oarsmen.

'Yes,' replied Younge, who had joined them in the stern, 'it is. The best time of the year for catching the fish is the summer, June and July, when it's very hot and, as you can see, it's tough and sometimes dangerous work.'

'Do they sell the fish for a lot of money when they get into Messina?' asked Emma.

'Well,' replied George, 'the big ones can weigh upwards of one hundred and fifty pounds and the meat fetches five pence a pound, so that can add up. On top of that, a crew could, on a very good day, catch five or six fish. On the other hand, they could come away empty-handed. But half the profits from the fishing go to the coastal landowners, who own the fish.'

'Look, Miss Thring,' said Wilkins, pointing at the fishing boat. He had been feeling rather left out of the conversation and was keen to join in. 'It looks as if the fish has come up to the surface.'

It had. The swordfish, exhausted and weakened by loss of blood, had surrendered. The man in the bow was pulling it in, the spear protruding from its side above the water. Once it was alongside, he picked another spear up from the bottom of the boat and stabbed, hard and two-handed, down into the fish. He then shortened the line to tow the carcass back to the bigger boat. Here, the big, black and silvery fish with its menacing sword was heaved aboard, its skin glistening in the sun. Even from this distance Emma could see the blood splashing onto the fishermen as they struggled to get the slippery deadweight out of the water.

Younge gave an order to the helmsman who took the vessel smartly about. She was now running with the wind so would fly across the waves back to Messina. The ungainly fishing boat, with its booms, odd lookout's mast, and tough, sharp-eyed crew, was now falling astern fast.

'Well, Miss Thring,' said Younge, 'I'm glad we managed to put on a show for you. It doesn't always happen, quite often one can come out here and sail around for ages without seeing a catch, so we've been lucky this morning.'

'I must say, it's all most interesting, quite unlike any fishing I've ever seen before, very different from how Papa catches his little trout in the river at home.'

'Shall we go to the bow, Miss Thring?' asked Younge. 'It's quite safe and from there you'll get a splendid view of the city as we come in. You see things about a place from the sea which you would never notice from the land.'

'I would like that very much, Mr Younge,' replied Emma.

'Good. Come with me, then.' Frank held out his right arm for Emma. As they started towards the bow, Frank said, turning to George and Wilkins at the stern rail, 'There's not really room enough for more than two people in the bow and it may be Miss Thring's only chance. I hope you don't mind.'

George didn't mind at all. He'd seen Messina from the sea many times in the four years he'd been stationed here and would, no doubt, see it again. But he could see that Peter Wilkins did, a dark shadow passing briefly across his face – irritation? jealously? slighted pride? – as the two made their way, arm in arm, towards the bow.

'Very interesting,' said Wilkins, conversationally, 'how those fellows catch the fish. The man who throws the spear must be devilish good at it. It can't be easy.' He was trying, rather obviously, to make light of the situation, but George was not fooled.

As they chatted about local fishing practices, George could see that Wilkins was keeping an eye on Younge and Emma, who were by now standing next to each other in the bow beneath the bowed jib, taut against the breeze. Younge was, thanks to his sea legs, standing up straight, his right hand resting gently on the bow rail; Emma was holding the rail more intently, in both hands; her hair had come loose in the breeze, the sun lit up her face. From afar, they looked easy in each other's company. Younge was talking, perhaps telling some story of naval derring-do, while Emma listened intently. After a minute or two, she laughed, leaning in, slightly but perceptibly, towards him. At that moment, George noticed, Wilkins frowned.

By now, as the boat came closer, Messina was beginning to reveal her secrets. On the port bow was the lowering mass of the Citadel, its great bastions seemingly propping up the southern flank of the city. To the north, opening up on the starboard bow, was Messina herself, between the protective crescent enclosing the harbour and the mountains that enveloped the city on the inland side. The *duomo* was clearly visible, its white facade shining in the light, as were a number of other spires and towers, above the mass of tiled roofs, red, orange and pink in the morning sun.

As George stood at the stern rail taking in the view of the city, his thoughts turned to the previous evening's cards. It had been a disaster. The diamond flush, far from being the start of a winning streak, had turned out to be an isolated success. From that point on, he had hardly won a farthing and by the end of the evening he was heavily down. Once the totting up had been done, he owed Arthur Broderick forty-eight pounds – more than three months' pay – on top of the fifteen pounds he already owed him. He'd been a bloody fool. In all – George did some rapid mental arithmetic – his debts amounted to around two hundred and thirty pounds, or about fifteen months' pay. What the hell was he going to do if Broderick and the others pressed him for payment? The local moneylender in particular was unlikely to be patient or forgiving once he started asking for his money back. What he might do to enforce his debt did not bear thinking about.

The boat was now beyond the Citadel, level with the lighthouse. Younge had returned from the bow and was preparing to take them into the harbour under the ramparts of Fort Salvador. Emma was now back at the stern rail, looking up at the battlements high above her head. As the boat tacked to port to round the point of the fort, another small vessel, of a similar type, was making its way out to sea. They were steering towards each other, so close that for a moment it looked as if they might collide.

'Ahoy there! To starboard!' bellowed Younge, as he realised the imminent danger. The helmsman, alert, turned the tiller to port, bringing the boat a few yards inside the course of the other vessel. Luckily, even in the lee of the ramparts, she had sufficient way on her to make the sudden alteration in course necessary to avoid a collision.

'By God, that was a close-run thing,' exclaimed George.

'Bloody idiot,' said Younge. 'He wasn't looking where he was going.'

Nevertheless, the two small vessels passed very close to one another, only a few yards apart. As they drew level, Younge looked across the narrow gap to the other boat. There, unmistakably, sitting in a canvas chair by the stern rail, was Fabrizio Falcone. He was wearing a dark coat with lace cuffs and two rows of silver buttons. His black hair was tied neatly at the collar in a bow and on his feet was a pair of buckled court shoes. He looked every inch the wealthy lawyer and landowner he was.

As the two vessels passed, he was engrossed in reading a letter. Disturbed by Younge's hail, he looked up but, once the collision had been avoided, having loudly and volubly chided his crew, he returned to his letter. By the time Younge had realised who it was, the two vessels were moving apart, his into harbour, the other out to sea. But it was definitely Falcone sitting in the canvas chair on the other boat, quite definitely. After all, Younge had been introduced to him at Major Thring's *soirée* only two days earlier. What, Younge wondered, was he doing going out into the straits on a fishing boat on a Monday morning? Whatever else Signor Falcone was doing, he was not going fishing.

It was two o'clock in the afternoon by the time George strode through the gate of the Citadel. It was a hot day but inside it was like a crucible, its walls concentrating the heat of the sun while at the same time blocking the breeze off the sea. Within a minute of entering the castle, George was mopping his brow. The Citadel was comatose, prostrated by lethargy. Even the dust seemed to have given in to the heat. In the half-light of the stables, George could see a groom stretched out on a hay net. Next door, one of the armourer's mates was snoozing in the shade of the awning in front of the workshop, propped up between two barrels.

He had come to see Colonel Airey so made his way, as he had done so frequently of late, to the entrance of the large, stone-flagged clerks' office at the side of the courtyard. George saluted the sentry and walked across the room to the desk. Rogers looked up from his papers, peering over the spectacles on the end of his nose. On either side of him, leather-bound ledgers were piled up, a defensive parapet against a world that was only too eager to disrupt his ordered universe of accounts, indentures and returns, all laid out in a neat, black italic hand.

'Is the colonel in, Mr Rogers?'

'Yes, sir. He's free, so why don't you go straight in?'

Colonel Airey was sitting behind his desk, his legs swung to one side with his feet up on a footstool, reading a dispatch from a pile of papers on his lap.

'Ah, George. Do sit down.' He gestured towards the chair across the desk from him.

'Thank you, sir.'

George had decided that he should tell Colonel Airey about his meeting with the Count of Pelorito. After all, the colonel was now his commanding officer. However, he had also decided to gloss over the fact that it was Carlotta who had made contact with the count in the first place.

'Very good, George,' said Airey, when George told him. 'When are you seeing him?'

'At five o'clock this afternoon, sir.'

'That's very quick work.' He paused, picking up the sheaf of papers on his lap and putting them on the desk. 'Where?'

'He's asked me to come to his house.'

'Well, I suppose that's better than meeting him in a public place. And, if you're lucky, Madame Signotti may be there. You'll like her.' He paused, sitting upright in his chair. 'What are you going to ask him?'

George then explained his plan. While he spoke, the colonel listened carefully and, at the end, nodded approvingly.

'And there is one other thing, sir.'

'Oh, yes?'

'Well, sir, this morning Frank Younge and I took Lieutenant Wilkins and Miss Thring out into the straits to watch the boats catching swordfish. I thought it would be an interesting thing for Miss Thring to see.'

'Did you see a fish being taken?'

'Yes, practically under our noses, which was very exciting for Miss Thring.'

'Good. It's always nice to be able to put on a show for our visitors,' laughed the colonel. 'It's good for our reputation back home.'

'But there is a point to this, sir. As we were coming back into harbour we passed – indeed, we nearly collided with – a small boat on its way out.' George paused.

'And . . .'

'And guess who was on the boat?'

'Who?'

'Our friend Signor Falcone, sir. As you know, I've never met him, but Frank Younge was introduced to him the other day at Major Thring's reception and is absolutely sure that it was Falcone on the boat. As the boats passed each other, they were very close, no more than a few yards away, so he had a good sighting.'

'What do you think he was doing?' asked the colonel.

'Well, it didn't seem to us as if he was going fishing. He was wearing buckled shoes and a dress coat. When we passed, he was sitting in a chair, reading letters.'

Colonel Airey stared at the ceiling, deep in thought.

'That's interesting, George. We know that Falcone has business interests of some sort or another on the mainland, which give him an excuse to go back and forth across the straits quite regularly. Presumably, this is what he was doing this morning. However, I am not alone in wondering whether he is perhaps closer to the French than he would like us to think. He always seems very helpful and friendly to us – witness his conversation with Major Thring the other night – but could it be that he's playing a bigger game?' He left the question hanging in the air.

Then, with a sudden determination, Colonel Airey stood up from his chair.

'Come, George, I've got something to show you. You might find it amusing.'

'What is it, sir?'

'Wait and see,' said Airey.

With that he picked up his hat, clapped it onto his head and headed towards the door.

Leaving the cool, dim-lit office they plunged into the somnolent heat and the fierce, bright sunlight, which threw sharp-edged shadows round the southern rim of the courtyard. God, it was hot, thought George. They climbed the steps to the ramparts, walking round to the north-east bastion. Here, beside a cannon's smooth, metallic rump, a pale canvas awning had been set up; under it stood a large brass telescope on a hinged, wooden stand. Alongside was a high stool. George looked quizzically at Colonel Airey.

'All in good time, George,' said the colonel, teasingly. Taking off his hat, he stepped under the awning and perched on the stool. As George watched, Airey swung the telescope round so that it was pointing out to sea, in the rough direction of Scylla. He lowered his head to the eyepiece and began to scan the far shore of Calabria. After about a minute, he suddenly stood up.

'There, got it! Have a look at that, George,' said the colonel, stepping back.

George sat on the stool and squinted into the telescope's eyepiece. Once he had got used to the telescope, he could see Murat's tented pavilion, on the ridge above Punta di Pezzo. With the afternoon sun now illuminating the Calabrian shore, the scene was picked out in sharp relief. He could make out the huge Imperial eagle surmounting the entrance to the pavilion and a large tricolour fluttering to the left. He stood up.

'That's quite a sight, sir. Even at this distance, it's pretty distinct.'

'We set the thing up this morning, and at noon Sir John, General Cockburn and one or two others came up to have a look.' Colonel Airey looked at George. 'And do you know what they saw?'

George shook his head.

'They could see Murat himself, in front of his tent, surrounded by his staff. He seemed to be holding a map or chart in one hand and a spyglass in the other. According to Sir John, he was gesticulating towards Faro. Sir John is convinced that this is strong evidence that an invasion is coming soon.' He paused. 'And I'm not sure that I don't agree.'

George looked out over the straits towards Calabria and thought of the hundreds of little craft nestled into anchorages all along the coast, of the enemy's regiments, straining at the leash, of Murat the *beau sabreur*, Murat the bold, his ambition and his vanity. And, if the French were coming, they'd have to come soon, before the weather broke.

'Yes,' said George meditatively. 'D'you know, I think you might be right, sir.'

It was a few minutes to five that afternoon as George strolled south along the strada Ferdinanda. It was Messina's main thoroughfare: grand houses painted in bright colours – whites, pale greens, yellows, pinks and blues – and with large balconies lining both sides of the street. This was where the great and the good lived. As the city shook itself from its siesta, the streets were coming alive with people going about their business, on foot, in carriages, carts and on horseback. He was on his way to the appointment Carlotta had arranged for him with the Count of Pelorito. Normally, George would have been striding along at a brisk military pace, but now he was walking deliberately slowly, partly to ensure he didn't arrive in a sweat and partly because he didn't want to arrive early. It was important to maintain his dignity in the eyes of this Sicilian nobleman.

He had spent the last two hours or so since returning from the Citadel composing himself for what was likely to be an important interview. Although the count was known to be favourably inclined to the British and hostile to the French, George nevertheless had to be careful. In the Sicily of 1810, there were many conflicting loyalties: to the British, to the French, to the King and Queen and, of course, to the bedrock of self-interest. With the prevailing uncertainty – the French poised to invade the island, the British deeply embroiled in Spain and Portugal, and the King and Queen determined to reunite their kingdom and reassert their authority – any sensible man would be tempted to hedge his bets. It was unwise and dangerous – perhaps even deadly – to be too trusting of anyone.

At the southern end of the strada Ferdinanda, next to the little *piazza* dominated by the ancient church of the Annunziata dei Catalani, George forked right into the strada Candines. It was quieter than the strada Ferdinanda but paved in the same big, square slabs of black lava. The count's *palazzo* was halfway along on the right-hand side. It was an imposing building in the baroque style, dating, George supposed, from the early eighteenth century. At street level the facade was heavily rusticated; in the middle was a large arched doorway, its outsized keystone decorated with a mask. The first floor had eight tall windows, with fine scrolled pediments; the two middle windows gave onto a wide balcony with an elaborate wrought-iron balustrade overlooking the street. Attached to the balustrade was a row of flower baskets, a blaze of colour against the black-painted iron. Above the second, attic floor was a decorated frieze and cornice topped with carved urns. In front of the house stood an open carriage, with a curlicue

'*P*' cypher painted in green and picked out in gold on its side. The coachman dozed on the seat while the horse, a handsome bay, flicked his tail at the flies that buzzed around him. George crossed the street and rapped on the great wooden door.

Nothing happened until, after a minute or so, George heard footsteps inside. Then the great door swung slowly open to reveal a young footman in green livery with a powdered wig.

'Capitano Warne,' he said in the local dialect, 'come in, please, the count is expecting you.'

George walked through the door, which the footman pushed closed behind him. Once in the half-light of the marbled hall, he motioned George towards the stone staircase leading up to the *piano nobile*. At the top of the stairs were three sets of double doors; the footman opened the right-hand pair with a flourish.

'Capitano Warne, *eccellenza*,' he announced as Warne entered the room. It was a square, high-ceilinged, panelled room with an ornately patterned parquet floor and an elaborate plaster ceiling. On the wall facing the doors were two tall mirrors above a pair of demilune pier-tables. On the right, the two windows overlooking the street were closed but on the other side of the room the two windows over the central courtyard were wide open. The count, resplendent in a yellow coat and dark blue breeches, was standing in front of one of these windows when George entered the room.

'My dear Captain Warne,' said the count, moving smoothly across the polished parquet, his hand outstretched, to greet George. 'How good of you to come.'

His English was good, albeit with a strong accent. The count, who was, George guessed, aged about forty, was a large, barrel-chested, powerful-looking man with a jutting chin and beaky nose. His thick, black hair was neatly gathered by a velvet bow in a short ponytail. His dark, alert eyes appraised George.

'It is very good of you to see me, sir.'

'It's a pleasure, Signor Warne. I have always been fond of *la bellissima* Signora Fanelli so I'm only too happy to oblige her. And, you and I, we have met before, have we not?'

'Yes, sir, we have. At a reception given by General Perini a couple of weeks ago.'

'I noticed you with Colonel Airey and a very pretty young woman at the opera last week, *signore*. Do you like opera?'

'Yes, I do. Since I've been here, I've been to quite a number of performances and I enjoyed *La Serva Padrona* last week. Do you go often?'

'Yes,' replied the count. 'Madame Signotti likes it very much.'

The count guided George with an outstretched arm across the room towards the windows.

'Come, would you like a glass of wine? It's one of my favourites, from my estate on the slopes of Mount Etna, one of the most famous wines in all of Sicily. I have it brought here from the vineyard in barrels on a boat and then it rests here in the cellar.' The count went over to the pier-table, on which was a tray with a decanter and two glasses.

The two men stood by one of the windows overlooking the central courtyard. In the middle of the courtyard, in a huge square, wooden tub, was a lemon tree, its branches thick with plump, lustrous fruit. Vines were trained around the walls, their big bunches of ripe grapes hanging invitingly down.

'Those are the best sweet grapes I know,' he said. 'And now they are perfect. I will get some sent up later.'

'I look forward to that, sir.' George sipped his glass of wine. It was, as the count had promised, delicious: cool, dry and fruity.

'So, *signore*, what is it that you wish to ask me?'

George composed himself for a moment.

'Well, sir,' he started, 'I'm sure you know that Sir John Stuart launched some raids across the straits last week to attack and destroy as many of the boats intended to carry the French across to Sicily as possible.' The count nodded. 'I commanded one of them, the one ordered to attack the anchorage just up the coast from Reggio.' George paused, taking a mouthful of wine.

'To cut a long story short, all four raids ran into very stiff defence at four different anchorages in the middle of the night. The raids were really rather a failure: I don't think we did much damage but we lost quite a number of men. Two of the commanding officers are still missing and the other's dead.'

'I see,' said the count, staring out of the window.

'Thinking about it, I've come to the conclusion that perhaps the raids were betrayed. It all seems too much of a coincidence. I've told Colonel Airey and he admits now there may be something in it, although to start with he was not convinced. The question is, who could have betrayed the plans? Not many people on our side knew of them until the last minute. The men were not told until the afternoon, by which time they were confined to the Citadel. It's possible that someone in the galley crews passed news of the plans to the French, but as Colonel Airey pointed out, that seems unlikely as they would have been deliberately putting themselves in great danger. Which leaves the possibility that an enemy spy somehow got hold of the plans and managed to get the information to the French before the raids took place. This would explain why the enemy, at the dead of night, was waiting for us.'

'Yes,' said the count thoughtfully. 'I can see why you think the plans might have been betrayed. Let's have some more wine.'

'As you know,' he continued, once he had poured more wine, 'the French have a lot of spies here. There are many people who prefer the French to the King and Queen, who are happy to take their money. There are also many people who try – how do you say it? – to keep in with both sides. No one knows who is going to come out on top, so it's sensible to keep a foot in both camps. If this involves passing a little information to the French in exchange for some money, then who cares?' He paused. 'But, Signor Warne, what do you want from me?'

George hesitated for a moment, unsure how far he should take the count into his confidence.

'Well, sir, I have been ordered by Colonel Airey to investigate whether the plans for the raids were betrayed by enemy spies, to see if I can find any evidence that they were.'

'Go on.'

'And I thought you might be willing to help. You're an important man. Very little of what goes on in Messina passes you by, and I know that you've been helpful to us in the past.'

'I have good reason to dislike the French,' said the count with a smile.

Dusk was falling now and lights were coming on in the windows round the courtyard as the servants lit the candles. The count clapped his hands. A footman appeared almost instantly and busied himself with lighting the sconces around the wall.

'I have, Signor Warne, other matters to attend to now, I am

afraid. I will think about what you have said to me and I will send you a note.'

'There is one last thing, sir,' said George.

'Yes, Signor Warne,' said the count. 'What is it?'

'I was out in the straits in a boat this morning, taking a young lady from England to watch the fishermen at work. As we were coming back into harbour we passed another boat and on it was Signor Falcone. It seemed odd that he should be out on a fishing boat on a Monday morning.'

The count stood in silence for what seemed an age before replying.

'Signor Falcone is a man of many parts. He has business interests on the mainland and, I believe, he goes to Calabria frequently. That is probably what he was doing when you saw him this morning. I won't say more than that I have always wondered where his loyalties lie.' The count turned to look at George.

'If I were Colonel Airey,' he continued, 'I'd be tempted to find out a little bit more about Fabrizio Falcone. But be careful, he is not a man to cross. He can be very violent. Now, Signor Warne, I really must be going.'

CHAPTER SEVEN

Messina, 11th September 1810

George Warne was bored; his legs were stiff and his backside ached. He'd been sitting on a stone step at the side of the Piazza dei Quattro Cavallucci for the last two hours. On his lap was his cover, an artist's sketchbook. Artists were a common sight in Sicily, sketching churches, palaces and fountains in the cities and the island's picturesque landscapes and Classical remains out in the countryside, so he did not attract a second glance from the passers-by. A drawing – shamingly amateurish to George's eye – of the fountains after which the piazza was named was slowly taking shape. In fact, the fountains were well worth drawing: carved in marble, they stood against the pier between the Corso and one of its cross-streets, depicting plump Cupids astride muscular seahorses splashing vigorously through the waters. For an artist more accomplished than George, they would have made an alluring subject.

But the intrepid Cupids and their marble steeds were only George's cover; the reason he was sitting in this piazza at the northern end of the Corso was that it was an ideal spot from which to keep an eye on the comings and goings of Fabrizio Falcone's offices. George had seen Signor Falcone arrive at around nine o'clock but since then there had been nothing to report: no clients this morning, so far at any rate. George had adopted what he hoped was a suitably artistic disguise for his vigil: a scruffy, patched old coat with tarnished brass buttons, a battered, wide-brimmed black hat, pulled well down over his forehead, a big wooden box of pencils, crayons and chalks and, of course, the sketchbook.

On leaving the Count of Pelorito's house the previous evening, George had gone straight to the Citadel to report to Colonel Airey. Once George had given his account of the meeting, the colonel suggested that it might be a good idea to watch Falcone's office to see if he had any untoward visitors.

So George had walked from Carlotta's house to the northern end of the Corso, arriving before eight o'clock so that he would be in position in good time for the start of the working day. He chose a vantage point in the piazza that commanded a view of the entrance to the building – a large, mildly baroque town house, the facade rusticated at ground-floor level with fluted Ionic columns above – which housed the lawyer's offices. From his position, he could see the windows on the first floor of the building. Indeed, just now, he had seen Falcone himself at one of the windows, looking out into the street.

Nobody came or went from the building until, just as the clock of the nearby church chimed half past eleven, a young man wearing a dark coat with a prominent white stock and black breeches hurried out of the door of the building. Tucked under his arm was a leather portfolio. He turned south along the Corso, soon disappearing from George's view in the throng. Who was that, George wondered? Falcone's assistant? A client? Or someone unconnected with Falcone? Whoever it was, George hadn't seen him enter the building this morning so either he'd arrived before George was in position, or he lived in the building or, and this was more worrying, there was another entrance that George could not see. He stood up, stretching his legs. It was going to be a long day.

George had been sketching desultorily for the best part of another couple of hours – the horses were taking some sort of shape now – when Falcone himself emerged from his office. With him was another man, of approximately the same age, but taller and thinner than the thick-set Falcone. As he was not wearing a hat, George could see that he had blonde hair, not common among Sicilians. They crossed the Corso towards George before walking down a side street that led towards the Marina and the port. The two men passed within five yards of George, without giving him a sideways glance, so he got a good look at both of them. More importantly, they were close enough to George that he could hear them talking. Deep in conversation, they were speaking French.

Well, thought George, they're off for lunch now so I've got at least two hours to myself. Taking his hat off to ruffle his hair, he leant back against the wall, stretching his legs out in front of him. It hadn't been an entirely wasted morning, he reflected. Hearing Falcone speaking French with someone who didn't look obviously Sicilian was an interesting development. Now that the coast was clear, George decided that he should investigate the rear of the building. Closing the wooden box, he gathered it and the sketchbook up under his arm and ambled off across the piazza.

He took a side street off the Corso opposite where he had been sitting. It ran uphill in the direction of the Rocca Guelfonia, one of the craggy outcrops that dominated the landward side of the city. After a few yards, seeing an alley to the left between two houses, George crossed the street. It was narrower, meaner, altogether dirtier and smellier than the mews George had seen behind the grand town houses in London. He knew that Falcone's building was the third one along from the junction of the Corso and the side street. All the buildings that backed onto this alley had doors leading out into it. Looking round to make sure that no one was looking, George cautiously tried the third one along. The handle turned but it was locked. He pushed at the door but there was no give. Well, at least he now knew that the building had a back door. The question was, had the two unidentified men he had seen leaving the building come in this way? Or had they been inside all along?

Deciding to investigate further, George left the alley and retracing his steps to the Corso made his way, with all the nonchalance he could muster, to the front door of Falcone's building. He would go into the building to see what he could find. If he came across anyone – and it wouldn't be Falcone himself – he would simply claim that he was looking for someone but, he was so sorry, he'd got the wrong address. He turned the handle and pushed. The heavy door opened, moving smoothly on its hinges as it went.

Inside it was dark after the bright sunshine in the street. George pushed the door shut and stood still to allow his eyes to adjust to the gloom. After a minute or so a big, rectangular space began to resolve itself into a whitewashed, vaulted ceiling and cobbled floor. In the middle, a stone staircase led up to the first floor. To one side George could see a small, two-wheeled carriage, similar to an English curricle, propped up on its shafts. Against one of the walls wooden packing cases were stacked head high. It was eerily quiet after the bustle of the street, which was now barely audible through the thick walls and solid door. George climbed the stairs, trying to make as little noise as possible but his boots rasped on the stone treads, each step amplified by the echo of the vaulted ceiling. As he did so, he remembered his father taking him to visit a friend of his at his chambers in the Temple: he recalled the scurrying clerks and stately barristers, the piles of papers, depositions, statements, briefs, the shelves of books, the panelled rooms and coal fires. That, George's young mind had decided, was what a lawyer's office was like. This place did not fit the bill at all. It was more like a warehouse.

On the landing at the top of the stairs two doors confronted George. Thinking quickly, he chose the right-hand one as it had been in the windows to the right that he had seen Falcone earlier. He paused in front of the door, his fingers on the handle. Suddenly, he could feel his heart pumping in his chest and a nervous prickle of sweat in his armpits. If Falcone caught him here, God knows what he might do to him. Then he knocked on the door and opened it.

At the same moment that George was entering Signor Falcone's office, half a mile across Messina, Peter Wilkins was explaining the facade of the *duomo* to Emma Thring.

'. . . it's said to be one of the oldest examples of Norman

architecture in Sicily, about the same age as the Tower of London. It's been damaged quite a lot over the years, especially by the terrible earthquake of 1783, but much of the original detail has survived. Shall we go and have a look at the main doorway?'

'Yes, Mr Wilkins,' said Emma, twirling her parasol, 'I would like that.'

As they walked across the piazza towards the *duomo*, Wilkins pointed at the great arch over the central door.

'It strikes me that the elaborate carving surrounding the door is quite at odds with the plain aspect of the rest of the facade. What do you think, Miss Thring?'

'I rather like the contrast between the decoration of the door and the simplicity of the rest of the building. After all, it would be too much if the whole thing were covered in carving. One wouldn't know where to look, would one, Mr Wilkins?'

By now she was examining the carvings depicting naked boys climbing, picking grapes, catching birds and monkeys and generally larking about. Wilkins coughed.

'Shall we look at the famous Orion fountain now, Miss Thring?'

'Yes, in a moment. I like these carvings. Look at the naughty little monkeys.'

As they wandered off towards the fountain – a striking confection of white marble nymphs, reclining, bearded water carriers and *putti* – Emma looked at Wilkins from beneath her parasol. He was a kind, sweet man but a touch too earnest. She thought, fleetingly, of Frank Younge, of how he'd made her laugh yesterday, of his languorous charm and easy manner.

'Now, Miss Thring,' continued Wilkins, 'the Orion fountain is one of Messina's best-known landmarks, executed by the Florentine sculptor Montorsoli in the middle of the sixteenth century . . .'

As the door swung open George stepped into the room. Closing the door behind him, he looked around: the room was empty. There were two other doors, both open, leading out of the room, one to his left and one on the opposite wall. Quickly, he checked to see that the rooms beyond were empty. They were.

Falcone's office was a large, square, high-ceilinged room with two tall windows overlooking the Corso. In the middle was a table, heaped with papers tied in bundles. The far wall, on either side of the door, was lined with bookcases up to the level of the picture rail. Between the windows hung a full-length portrait of a man in lawyer's subfusc: Falcone's father, George wondered briefly? To George's right, against the wall, was a bureau, its writing-top down and strewn with papers.

It struck George forcibly as odd, uncomfortable, to be in here, in someone else's office, as an intruder. If he was discovered there would be no escape. He'd be cornered. But this was no time to worry about that, he thought: just see what you can find and get out as quickly as possible. He was conscious of a tightness in his midriff, a sure sign of nerves. Calm down, he told himself. Pulling up a chair, he started with the bureau. The papers on the writing-top seemed, so far as George could tell in a glance, to concern clients' legal business: property disputes, family wrangles and wills, the daily fare of any lawyer's practice.

He closed the writing-top and opened the bureau's drawers, one by one. The top drawer contained fresh sheets of paper, a sheaf of uncut quills and two bottles of ink. The stationery drawer. In the second drawer were two fat, leather-bound ledgers. George lifted one of them out onto his knees. As he opened it, the dry, acrid smell of dust and flaky leather wafted up. Inside were page after page of figures, money paid, money received, going back many years. The accounts, thought George, replacing the ledger in the drawer and pushing it shut. Nothing so far.

As George opened the bottom drawer he caught his breath: inside was an iron strongbox, with a handle on its lid, about a foot long, six inches wide and four inches deep. He lifted it out and placed it on the floor; it was heavy and, George quickly realised, locked. He rifled through the little drawers in the top of the bureau, hoping he might find the key but found only a pile of Falcone's calling cards. He shook the box, but it made no noise beyond a soft, padded shifting. It's full of coins, gold or silver, he thought – too heavy for anything else. But they were in pouches, which is why they weren't clinking when he shook the box. Apart from three bundles of dusty papers, there was nothing else in the bottom drawer.

George considered his options. There was, evidently, a great deal of money in the strongbox, enough, one might have thought, to be worth depositing in a bank. On the other hand, if depositing the money was likely to raise suspicion, then it might be better for a prominent citizen like Falcone to keep it under lock and key here. If the money were French, then Falcone would, at the very least, have some explaining to do. Nor did George think it likely that he'd find any better evidence of Falcone's complicity in plotting with the enemy. It would take hours to search the bookshelves thoroughly, let alone look through all those papers on the table in the middle of the room. It was also unlikely that he would have another opportunity to get in here again.

So, he decided, he would attempt to force the lid of the strongbox. If he found French gold inside, then Falcone would be a marked man; if not, well, at least he'd tried. Either way, George reflected, an attempt to break the strongbox open would make his visit look like a run-of-the-mill burglary, rather than anything more sinister. Opening his wooden box, he picked out his penknife – essential for sharpening pencils and crayons – and knelt on the floor.

George inserted the blade of the knife – fortunately, it was a sturdy implement – under the lid next to the lock and pushed firmly down. At first, nothing happened so George began to jiggle the knife around and apply more pressure to the lid. Then, suddenly, the lock gave way and the box sprung open.

'Haha!' exclaimed George.

Inside, snugly packed in two rows, were eight plump, blue leather pouches, each one tied at the top with a leather lace. George leant forward and picked one up. It was heavy in his hand; it must weigh at least two pounds. He untied the fastening at the neck of the pouch and looked in: gold coins. He tipped the coins out onto the floor. There must be fifty or sixty in this pouch alone, he thought; with eight pouches, maybe five hundred in all. That was a lot of money, even for a prosperous lawyer like Falcone, and in gold, too. He picked up one of the coins; it bore the head of the Emperor. These were *napoleons*, gold twenty-franc pieces, the expression in solid bullion of the wealth and power of the French Empire, Bonaparte's answer to the British sovereign. Now, thought George, we know exactly why Signor Falcone keeps going to the mainland. The question was, for what were the French paying Falcone so handsomely?

But that, George realised, was for another time. Now, he had to get out of here, and quickly. He couldn't risk being caught red-handed by Falcone. Hastily, he grabbed two of the *napoleons*, shoving them into his pocket as evidence. He then opened two more pouches, tipping the coins onto the floor. Seeing the gold *napoleons*, George was forcibly reminded of his gambling debts, of the impossibility of paying them off out of his salary, of the hopelessness of trying to play his way back into profit. Here, out of the blue, was a chance, if not to clear them altogether, at least to reduce them significantly. He thought of the moneylender's polite yet mildly threatening note, delivered to the Citadel the other day.

It would, he realised, be theft, and theft while on duty as an officer holding the King's commission. If caught, he would be cashiered. On the other hand, if his debts became too pressing, he might be forced to resign his commission anyway, with all the dishonour and humiliation that that would entail. Theft it might be, but Falcone had almost certainly acquired the money nefariously and from the enemy. With your eyes half-closed, George reasoned, the *napoleons* could be regarded as legitimate booty of war. Needs must. He scooped up a handful of the gold coins before tipping them into his wooden box where they slipped down among the pencils.

Lifting one of the bundles of papers out of the bottom drawer, he cut the ribbon holding them together and scattered them around. That would have to do; there was quite a mess on the floor, so with any luck Falcone might think it was a casual burglary that went wrong. George took one of Falcone's calling cards and, gathering up his box and sketching book, left the room, closing the door behind him. He went down the stairs, swung the great door open and, as calmly as he could, avoiding the temptation to look around, stepped out into the bright sunlight and bustle of the Corso. Breathing a sigh of relief, he closed the door behind him, turned right towards the Citadel and was soon lost in the crowds.

What George failed to notice as he strode off, in the deep shadows on the far side of the street, was a man keeping watch on the building.

It was late afternoon by the time George knocked on the door of Colonel Airey's office in the Citadel. The colonel was sitting at his desk in shirtsleeves, his habitual dark blue tunic hanging on the back of his chair.

'I apologise for my state of *déshabillé*, George,' he said. 'It's poor form, I know, and sets a bad example, but the generals are away and it's damned hot in here. What have you got for me?'

'This, sir.' He put his hand into his pocket and placed the two gold coins, side by side, on the leather top of the colonel's desk.

Airey picked one of them up and examined it between thumb and forefinger.

'Good God!' he exclaimed, feeling the weight of the coin. 'Gold *napoleons*. Don't tell me you found them lying in the gutter.' He looked quizzically at George. 'I won't believe you.'

'No, sir, I didn't.'

'So where did you find them, then?'

'Well, sir, it's a long story,' replied George.

'Tell me.'

George gave an account of his vigil outside Falcone's office, of the few comings and goings he had seen and of his exploration of the rear of the building. When he had finished, he paused, weighing one of the gold *napoleons* in his palm.

'And?' said Airey.

'Once the coast was clear, I decided it was too good an opportunity to miss to have a look round Falcone's office. So I went into the building and found my way to his office. There was no one in, so I started going through the contents of his bureau. In the bottom drawer I found a strongbox, with these coins and several hundred more in it.'

'Was it locked?' asked Airey.

'Yes, sir. I had to force it.'

'I see,' said Airey. There was a long pause while he stared into space, stroking his chin. 'So you, a holder of His Majesty's commission, have committed a burglary at the office of one of Messina's most prominent lawyers, a man who is, moreover, a good friend of England.'

'I suppose you could put it like that, sir,' said George. His earlier feeling of quiet satisfaction at having achieved something tangible in his very first operation as an intelligence officer was evaporating rapidly.

'Yes, you bloody well could put it like that, Captain Warne, and I will,' said Airey. There was an edge of anger in his voice now. 'What the hell did you think you were doing? I told you to use initiative, yes, but I didn't, in my wildest dreams, imagine that you'd take this to mean that you could break into people's offices, rummage through their possessions and force their strongboxes.'

He stood up and walked to the far side of the room.

'Particularly when the person in question is one of Messina's most important lawyers. My God, George, this could turn very bad if Falcone realises who's responsible, and it'll be my neck on the block.' He made a cutting motion with his outstretched palm. 'Sir John, who sets great store by good relations with the locals here, especially the prominent ones, will take a very dim view of all this, if he finds out.' Colonel Airey leant against the wall.

'And another thing, Captain Warne.' The anger in his voice had given way to weariness. 'Do you imagine for a moment that Signor Falcone will think that the break-in was a simple burglary? Won't he wonder why the thief, any self-respecting thief, having found the hoard of gold coins, didn't take them all?'

'Well, yes, I suppose he might, sir, but I couldn't have taken them all with me, even if I wanted to, but I needed evidence of the French gold. I only took two coins in the hope that when he comes to clear up the mess, he might not realise that there is any money missing.' George hoped that this lie sounded convincing.

'Even if he does think that – and, for what it's worth, I don't think he will, I'd bet a penny to a pound that he knows *exactly* how much money was in that box – won't he wonder even more what the burglar was after?'

There was silence while both men contemplated the prospect of professional disgrace, social shame and penury. The only noise was the clanging of hammer on metal from the armourer's workshop across the courtyard. Was he, George wondered, beating out an axe for his neck?

'I'm sorry, sir,' said George after a while. 'I should have thought through the consequences of my plan, but I didn't. It seemed a good opportunity to find out if Signor Falcone was spying for the enemy.' He decided against pointing out that his little adventure had, in fact, come up with some valuable evidence. Better to keep quiet. 'I went too far, sir, and I apologise. I hope you don't get into trouble as a result.'

'I'll cope with that if and when it happens.' Airey walked back across the room to his desk, where he picked up one of the gold *napoleons*, lobbing it gently from hand to hand.

'For all its reckless stupidity, your burglary has produced some useful evidence. I won't let my anger at what you've done blind me to this fact. The question we should be asking ourselves, George, is how has Signor Falcone come by all this French gold?' He paused. 'Add the money to the fact that you heard him speaking French to a man who didn't look obviously Sicilian and, suddenly, our friend doesn't look quite so friendly, does he?'

'No, he doesn't,' said George.

'Add to that the fact that we know he crosses over to the mainland regularly and, possibly, we have a traitor on our hands. What do you think?'

'Well, sir, Falcone probably has the connections here to acquire intelligence that would be useful to the French, he certainly has the opportunity to feed it to them, and it looks as if he's already reaped the rewards. So he could be our man.'

'Very good, George, you're a quick learner,' said the colonel, smiling. 'So what do you think we should do about our Signor Falcone?'

'Watch him as closely as we can, sir, and make every effort to find more evidence against him. The count didn't seem at all convinced of Falcone's loyalty to us. I could try to see if I could get anything more out of him, sir.'

'Yes, you could, but tread carefully. He's a very influential, powerful man and you don't want to get on the wrong side of him,' warned Airey. 'Treat him with great respect, George.'

'Of course, sir,' replied George.

'That'll be all, George. I've got work to do,' said Airey, looking at the pile of papers on his desk. 'Keep me informed and don't be tempted to commit any more burglaries,' he said with heavy emphasis and a smile in George's direction.

As George made his way out of Airey's office he felt a surge of relief flood through him. This affair was by no means over yet – there was still the small matter of his theft of the *napoleons* and his lie to the colonel, which may well come back to haunt him – but perhaps the worst had passed. He'd been very stupid and very lucky. He'd have to be more careful in future.

It was about two hours after George had ambled off along the Corso feigning innocence that Falcone returned to his office. He was alone; his fair-haired companion had left. They had lunched at Falcone's house as it was too risky for the pair of them to be seen eating together in public. Maria, Falcone's housekeeper, had served them big, juicy slices of grilled lamb with ripe, sweet tomatoes and a green salad followed by a lemon *granita*, washed down with a flask of white wine from the famous vineyards on the peninsula at Milazzo.

As Falcone approached, he glanced across the street for the man he had posted to keep watch on the building. He was still there, patiently in the shadows, leaning against the wall. Falcone caught his eye and, with a barely perceptible movement of the head, signalled to follow him inside. Falcone pushed open the heavy door to the building and climbed the stairs. He opened the door into his office and, looking in, swore softly.

He didn't immediately start clearing up the mess of scattered documents and coins on the floor. For a minute or two he stood and stared, deep in thought. Whoever had been here had not been interested in the money; that much was abundantly clear from the large number of coins left all over the floor. The thief had gone to the trouble of forcing the strongbox but had then left the money behind. Very strange. He'd find out in due course how many of the gold *napoleons* had been stolen. More difficult was establishing which, if any, documents had been taken. It seemed, at first glance, that the intruder had concentrated on the bureau; all three of its drawers had been left open but the piles of papers on the central table appeared undisturbed. There were no especially important papers in the bureau, so far as he could remember.

At that moment the man who had been watching the building came heavily up the stairs and entered the room. A big man running to fat, he was wheezing as he came in. He was Falcone's oldest retainer, utterly loyal and reliable, if sometimes lacking in imagination, but with a well-developed sadistic streak, a dab hand with stiletto or knife. He was ruthlessly efficient when ordered to deal with his boss's enemies.

'Ah, Luigi,' said Falcone, in the Sicilian dialect. 'So, tell me which mother-fucker did this?'

'Well, *signore*, I hadn't been in position long when I noticed a fellow sitting in the shadows at the side of Quattro Cavallucci. At first, I thought he was just another artist, drawing the fountain – you see them the whole time here. But I kept an eye on him and became suspicious because he didn't seem to be doing much drawing. I wanted to get closer to him to get a glimpse of his sketching book but it would have been too obvious.' He paused to mop his brow on his sleeve.

'Go on,' said Falcone, impatiently.

'Anyway, almost the moment you left the building, he packed up his things and disappeared off up the side street towards the Rocca. I was tempted to follow him, but your orders were to keep watch here so I let him go. I needn't have worried, though, because, less than five minutes later, he reappeared from the side street, walked to the front and let himself in. About ten minutes later, he came out of the building and disappeared off down the Corso.'

'Why didn't you follow him in?'

'Because, *signore*, you told me on no account to leave my post. And there might have been others coming to join him.'

'Yes, Luigi, all right,' said Falcone wearily. If you wanted initiative in an underling, Luigi was not your man. 'Was he carrying anything when he came out?'

'No, *signore*, he wasn't, apart from his sketching book and the box.'

'What did he look like?'

'He was tall, well-built but not fat. Scruffily dressed. Fair-skinned, I'd say, but tanned. Big nose. He was wearing a hat which was pulled down, so it was difficult to see his face, but his hair was blonde.'

'Could he have been English?'

Luigi thought for a moment, scratching his stubbly jaw.

'Yes, *signore*, I think he could have been. He didn't look very Sicilian, too blonde and a little too tall, maybe.'

* * *

As dusk fell over Messina, Frank Younge was leaning on the stern rail of His Majesty's sloop *Sprite*, moored out in the middle of the harbour. As the wind had dropped, it was a still, balmy evening. The lights in the gap-toothed line of houses along the Marina were now shining brightly in the velvety gloom.

Younge had been invited to dine on the *Sprite* by Commander Plumb and had, a few minutes ago, been rowed out to her in what passed for a captain's barge – in fact a small rowing boat with one burly seaman at the oars. He had sat in the stern of the boat looking admiringly at the *Sprite*. She was an eighteen-gun, quarterdecked ship-sloop, a type which had only been introduced into the Royal Navy at the beginning of the French wars. A three-masted, square-rigged ship, she mounted a powerful armament of eighteen thirty-two-pounder carronades on her main deck with a further six eighteen-pounder carronades on her quarterdeck and forecastle. Fore and aft, she carried a long six-pounder chaser. This gave her, Younge knew, a broadside twice as heavy as that of a thirty-two-gun frigate of double her tonnage. She was a formidable weapon of war and a dream command for an ambitious young officer. One day, perhaps, he too would stand on the quarterdeck of a ship like the *Sprite*, bold in the face of the enemy, calculating, making decisions, giving orders. One day, one day.

David Plumb had been, before his promotion, a senior lieutenant, a good few years older than Younge, but despite the age difference the two men had been friends since serving in the same frigate in the Channel Fleet before Trafalgar. His sloop was now part of the Mediterranean Fleet but as she was frequently detached on cruising duties, Plumb was able to put into Messina every so often. On this occasion, he had arrived yesterday and had immediately invited Younge to dinner.

'Frank, my dear fellow.'

Younge turned round to see Plumb emerging from the companionway. He strode across the deck, his arm extended, and shook Younge heartily by the hand.

'How very good to see you. Are you well?' boomed Plumb, a man of medium height with the beginnings of a paunch beneath his waistcoat, a florid complexion and thinning hair.

'Very well, thank you, David. And how have you been on your travels around the Med?'

'I was in Malta last week and,' he lowered his voice – not, thought Frank, that anyone would be listening – 'once I've taken on water and a few supplies here, I'm off to Port Mahon.'

'You should stay a few days here,' said Frank. 'I could arrange some shooting up in the hills for you or you could try what passes for hunting here.'

'Sadly, I have the commander-in-chief's immediate orders for Port Mahon and, as you know, he is not a man to be kept waiting.' He peered into the gloom. 'I've invited Midshipman Davidson to join us this evening. Do you know him?'

'Yes, oddly enough. He accompanied me on a jaunt to Reggio last week.'

'I've never met him,' said Plumb, 'but I knew his uncle well when he commanded the *Alnwick* on blockade duty in the Channel Fleet, so when I heard that the boy was in Messina I thought I'd ask him for dinner.' He paused. 'And here he comes.'

As he spoke, the ship's boat, a lantern glowing in her bow, glided towards the *Sprite*, coming alongside at the bottom of the rope ladder hanging from the main deck. A moment later, Davidson swung over the rail and down onto the deck.

'Welcome aboard, Mr Davidson,' said Plumb. 'I believe you know Lieutenant Younge.'

'Indeed I do, sir.' He looked at Frank. 'Good evening, Mr Younge.'

'Right, gentlemen, as it's almost dark now, shall we go to my cabin? I'm sure Protheroe's got dinner ready by now and I'm damned thirsty.'

In a sloop, the captain's cabin was tiny. A gate-legged table, four chairs, a cot and Plumb's sea chest almost filled the entire space. The low beams meant that any man of six foot or taller would develop a permanent stoop.

'Mind your head, Frank!' said Plumb – who was only five foot seven – as they entered the room.

As *Sprite* was at anchor in harbour, Protheroe, the steward, had laid the table with Plumb's silver, an elegant candelabrum and two flat-bottomed cut-glass ship's decanters. Plumb had, Younge remembered, captured a valuable prize soon after he had been appointed to the *Sprite*. The silver and crystal had been paid for, no doubt, out of his share of the prize money. Through the open stern window Younge could hear water slapping gently against the ship's counter; in the distance, the sounds of the city drifted across the harbour.

Once the three men were seated, Plumb poured them each a glass of wine and they began discussing the prospects for a French invasion.

'By all accounts,' said Frank, 'the Emperor is pressing Murat to get moving. We all know how much he hates the Bourbons of Naples, how keen he is to see them toppled off their thrones.'

'Well, he'll have to get going before the autumn storms begin,' said Plumb, twiddling the stem of his glass, 'which suggests that if an invasion is coming, it'll be in the next couple of weeks.'

'I agree,' said Younge and Davidson, almost in chorus, nodding.

At that point, Protheroe came into the cabin with two serving dishes. The delicious aroma of grilled fish filled the air.

'Swordfish, sir, fresh from the market today,' said the steward, 'and lovely ripe tomatoes.'

He placed the dish of sliced tomatoes in the middle of the table and began serving the juicy fish steaks, striped with dark weals from the grill, to the three men.

Gradually, as the wine slipped down – Plumb was a generous host and regularly refilled his guests' glasses – the talk turned to naval gossip and the goings-on in the garrison. After a while, Younge found himself telling the others about Emma Thring.

'She arrived here last week to visit her brother, Major Thring of the 27th. She's a lively girl and, I must admit, very pretty. I took her out yesterday to watch the fishermen in the straits, which I think she enjoyed.'

For the next few minutes, Younge endured some good-natured ribbing from Plumb and, to a lesser extent, Davidson about Miss Thring. He fiddled with his glass and hoped that he had managed to avoid blushing.

It was nearly midnight by the time the party broke up. Frank Younge was full of that benevolent humour that follows a good dinner in excellent company with lots of wine. Plumb had produced a couple of bottles of port, acquired on a recent visit to Lisbon. As Frank swung his leg over the side to climb down into the boat to be rowed ashore he very nearly missed, in the dark, his footing on the rope ladder. That would have been embarrassing, to have fallen into the harbour in full view of the watch. He was, he realised, decidedly tipsy. He went very deliberately down the ladder towards the little boat on the black water.

As Frank descended the rope ladder his host leant over the rail above his head.

'Goodnight and thank you for coming. Let me know how you get on with the delectable Miss Thring, will you?'

I may keep that to myself, thought Frank, but he said: 'Of course, and thank you again for dinner.'

The boat pulled away from the side of the *Sprite*. As they passed under the stern of a British frigate Frank could hear the muffled sound of merriment through the windows of the captain's cabin. The rest of the harbour was quiet and dark. The water lapped gently at the bottom of the harbour steps.

CHAPTER EIGHT

Messina, 12th September 1810

The church clocks were striking half past seven but the Corso was already thick with traffic. George was back in the Piazza dei Quattro Cavallucci to resume his observation of Fabrizio Falcone's office, playing the indigent, itinerant artist drawing the piazza's splendid fountains. This would, he hoped, continue to provide cover for his presence here. In his scruffy coat and battered hat, clutching his box of pencils – no longer carrying its hoard of gold *napoleons*, now hidden in Carlotta's apartment – and his sketchbook, he scarcely stood out in the crowded street. George settled down on the cool paving stones of the steps at the edge of the piazza, the leather-bound sketch book on his knees.

The previous evening, one of the Count of Pelorito's footmen – discreetly not in livery – had delivered the promised note to Carlotta's apartment. Addressed to George, it was in French.

'J'ai quelque chose à vous dire au sujet de notre ami au bateau. Venez demain soir à 7 heures.'

It was signed, simply, '*P*'. Once he had read the note, George lit it with a candle and let it burn away to ash.

George was agog to know what the count had unearthed about Signor Falcone but he would have to wait, to sit out the hours here, watching the lawyer's office. He looked at the drawing in front of him, sighed, and began to rework one of the seahorses, attempting to correct its misshapen neck.

George had been sketching and watching for about an hour when he saw Signor Falcone stride up to the front door of the building. Wearing a scarlet coat, he appeared vigorous and alert, ready for whatever the day held for him. He did not pause or look round – why should he? – but produced a large key from his pocket, unlocked the door and went inside. That might be the last I see of him for a while, thought George. It had been Colonel Airey's idea that George should continue his vigil outside Falcone's office.

'After all, now that you've put a stick into the wasps' nest, you might as well wait to see what happens. You never know what might turn up. It's certainly worth another couple of days of watching and waiting, I'd say.'

'Yes, sir,' George had dutifully agreed.

Once Falcone had disappeared behind the great studded door into the building, George looked around him. The Corso was crowded with people and traffic: men walking to work, women on their way to market, liveried servants, hawkers, children, idlers, beggars, a platoon of the local militia, marching out of step. Over there, on the pavement in front of one of the fountains, stood two young blades, immaculate in silk coats, buckled shoes and tricorn hats, in animated conversation, somehow removed from the urban clamour all around them. They didn't look, thought George, as if they were discussing business; more likely they were boasting about their sporting prowess or gossiping about their latest conquests. The street itself was a seething flood of city life: pedestrians, men on horseback, carts, mules and donkeys uncomplaining under spreading loads, the occasional carriage, its whip-flicking driver impatiently clearing a passage through the crowd, a sedan chair making its stately way among the throng, the odd mangey dog, an aged priest bent over his walking stick, a couple of chickens pecking jerkily in the gutter, men labouring under weighty parcels, a peasant pushing a small handcart laden with lemons, a prim posse of nuns, a pair of young boys rolling a barrel. Just beyond the piazza, in the Corso, was a barber's shop; outside, sitting in the chair, was an elderly man, his face extravagantly lathered, being shaved. Content that in all this activity he would blend into the background, George turned back to his sketchbook.

On the other side of the piazza, through the noise and bustle, Falcone's stooge, Luigi, was also keeping watch. He was standing behind a fruit stall, chatting to the owner, a friend, while he kept an eye on George. In the inside pocket of his tatty coat was a sharp-bladed knife.

By mid morning the sun had moved round, advancing the shadow of the buildings towards George. He would be glad of the shade come the heat of the day. George was pleased with his reworking of the seahorse's neck and head. Practice makes perfect: the beast now looked altogether more convincing. 'Mr Stubbs', he said to himself, 'you might have had a little competition.' He briefly imagined himself as an equestrian painter, summoned to grand houses to paint their owners' favourite steeds and loafing around Newmarket touting for commissions.

While indulging this pleasant fantasy, George was gazing across the piazza in the direction of Falcone's office. Suddenly, he noticed a large, stout man with a lumbering gait, in a dark coat, approach the door of Falcone's building from the other direction. He turned, opened the heavy door and went inside. Who's he? wondered George. He didn't look as if he might be one of Falcone's clients but, on the other hand, one could never tell. His lack of a hat, his obviously unshaven cheeks – clearly visible from across the piazza – and his old, dowdy coat marked him out as a servant, a coachman, perhaps, a gardener or general factotum.

What George had failed to notice was that a few minutes earlier, the tall, heavy man standing behind the fruit stall across the piazza had replaced the orange he had been rolling in his hand on its pile, touched his friend on the arm and wandered off into the throng. Once he had left the fruit stall, Luigi turned right into a side street. From there he walked up to the next street on the right, crossed into it and went to the end. Then he turned right and quickly right again. He was now back on the Corso, fifty yards or so to the far side of Falcone's office from where George was sitting. He could now enter the building without the observer, whoever he was, thinking anything other than that he had walked up the Corso from the city centre.

Having stumped heavily up the stairs, Luigi knocked on the office door – which George had opened so apprehensively the previous day – and went in without waiting for a reply. Fabrizio Falcone was sitting at the bureau, in shirtsleeves, his coat hanging over the back of the chair. As Luigi entered the room, he looked up from his papers.

'Well, Luigi,' he said, replacing his quill in the inkstand, 'what do you have for me this morning?'

'He's there again, *signore*,' replied Luigi, 'outside, more or less where he was yesterday, watching the door.'

'Are you sure it's the same fellow?'

'*Si, si, signore*. Definitely the same man. I've had him in my sights for at least two hours. There can be no doubt.'

'You'd better point him out to me then,' said Falcone, standing up from his chair and walking towards the window. The two men crossed the room to the right-hand window from which they had a commanding view of the piazza and the Corso on either side of it.

'There he is, *signore*,' said Luigi. He pointed towards the figure sitting on the stone steps in the edge of the shadow at the side of the piazza.

Falcone followed his man's finger. From this distance and angle, it was difficult to make out much. He could see the sketchbook and the box but the man's features were obscured by the wide-brimmed hat pulled well down over his forehead.

'So you're sure, Luigi, that this is the man who broke in here yesterday?'

'Yes, *signore*, as sure as I can be.'

'Right then, in that case, I am going down to the street to get a better view of our light-fingered friend. I can't see him properly from up here.'

'May I make a suggestion, *signore*?'

'Yes, Luigi, what?'

'He almost certainly saw you arrive here this morning, so perhaps you might cover up your coat before you go out into the street.'

'A good idea, Luigi. We wouldn't want our friend getting nervous, would we? Fetch my riding cape, please.'

Leaving his distinctive scarlet coat over the back of the chair, Falcone took the dark cape and draped it over his shoulders, fastening the chain under his chin. He picked up a floppy-brimmed hat from the table, put it on and turned to face Luigi.

'So, what do you think?'

'I'd hardly recognise you, *signore*,' replied Luigi, grinning.

'Good, good. You stay here and keep an eye on him from the window but don't show yourself too obviously.'

With that Falcone left the room and clattered down the stairs before making his way out through the back door into the alley. From there he walked up to the side street and stopped. Looking towards the Corso, he could see a deep doorway on the left from which he might have a good view of the piazza and the waiting, watching stranger. Strolling across the street, Falcone stepped into the shady porch and turned to face out towards the Corso and the piazza.

Falcone stood in the doorway for about fifteen minutes before deciding it was a waste of time. It was a poor vantage point. There was too much traffic in the Corso for him to get a decent view of his adversary who was, for good measure, now completely in shadow. The fellow's wide-brimmed hat made any positive identification uncertain. He could see, as Luigi had told him yesterday, that the man was blonde, that his skin was darkened by the sun and that he had a beaky nose. So far as he could judge, the man was tall, perhaps around six foot, but it was difficult to gauge his height accurately while he was sitting down. Falcone toyed with the idea of moving closer but dismissed it. He didn't want to be recognised. He slipped out of the doorway and returned to the alley. Back in his office, he took off the cloak, threw it on the table and tossed the hat to Luigi.

'That was a waste of time, Luigi. I couldn't get a proper view of him, but I think he's English. I want you to keep an eye on him all day and when he leaves follow him, discreetly, you understand, wherever he goes. Is that clear?' It was always as well to make sure that any instructions given to Luigi were as clear as could be.

'Si, si, signore,' said Luigi.

'Good. And report back to me this evening if you can or tomorrow, first thing. I'll cover him until you're in position. Off you go.'

Falcone returned to the window and looked out. There, across the piazza, was the man, quietly watching, his sketchbook on his lap, pretending to draw the fountains. What, he wondered, was he after? As Falcone looked down, the Englishman raised his pencil in front of his eyes, as if assessing the proportions of the fountains. He's a better actor than a spy, thought Falcone, with a laugh. Looking to the left, he could now see Luigi emerging from the side street and skirting round the piazza towards the fruit stall. Once he was ensconced behind it, Falcone went back to the bureau and sat down.

Peter Wilkins was sitting at a writing table in the officers' mess in the Citadel. It was the end of the morning so he had finished his duties for the time being: he had paraded the platoon at seven o'clock, inspected the men, dealt with the day's defaulters – an incident of drunkenness, an allegation of fighting and several cases of lost or poorly maintained kit – and filled in the daily returns. The men were fit – thankfully, the garrison was now free of the ophthalmia, which had been such a curse over the last few months – and seemed in good spirits. At a table on the far side of the room, Abel Winch, the orderly, was trimming the wicks of the candles.

He now had a few minutes of peace and quiet before the mess began to fill up to finish the letter he had been writing to his brother in England in spare moments over the last week. His brother, David, was the clever one of the family. Thanks to the connections of an uncle, he had been found a place as a clerk – a 'writer', as they were known – with the East India Company. At present he was labouring away in the bowels of John Company's grand headquarters in Leadenhall Street in the City of London but had high hopes of a transfer to Calcutta. Once there, David was sure, with hard work and good luck, he would make his name and his fortune.

Wilkins unfolded the letter – it was headed 'The Citadel, Messina, 7th Sept. 1810' – and skimmed through the paragraphs he had already written: news about the war in the Mediterranean, the odd detail of his life in Sicily, snippets of garrison gossip and army rumour, rejoinders to matters raised in David's letters to him and so on. All pretty mundane stuff, Wilkins thought, but then, by and large, life here wasn't all that exciting. There was one thing, though, which his brother might like to hear about. He dipped his pen into the inkwell and started writing.

'Since I began this letter I have been introduced to a very spirited – and very attractive – girl. She is lately arrived in Sicily from England to see the wondrous antiquities this island has in such profusion. Her name is Emma; she is the sister of our Major Thring, who was kind enough to introduce me to her at an assembly he gave four nights ago. Her eyes are like dark moonstones and her face the colour of peaches and soft roses. Her smile lights up the darkest day. I and two other fellows took her out the other day into the straits to watch the fishermen catching swordfish. I confess, brother dear, that I am smitten. There are already other bees buzzing around the pot, but I will do my best to press my suit. What say you to a sister-in-law?'

With that, Wilkins signed off 'Yr affect. brother, P. Wilkins', placed the letter in another sheet of paper, which he then folded, sealed with a blob of green wax and addressed.

'Winch,' Wilkins called. 'Would you be kind enough to make sure this gets into tonight's packet before it closes?'

'Yes, sir, by all means,' said Winch, as he took the letters and bowed slightly to Wilkins before shuffling off across the room.

George continued his vigil opposite Falcone's office as Messina went about its business in front of him. His drawing of the fountains was definitely improving: another couple of days and it would be approaching the passably good, George thought. But two more days sitting here was not an inviting prospect. By early afternoon, he was hungry so delved into his haversack for the picnic lunch Colonel Airey's servant had rustled up for him: two slices of cured ham, a hunk of bread, a piece of local cheese and a flask of red wine.

As he was munching the bread and cheese, he heard a rumble of thunder. In Sicily in late summer thunderstorms were frequent and often spectacular. They freshened the sultry atmosphere, laid the dust and cleared the air, leaving the Calabrian mountains washed in tints of light and dark blue. If this rumble presaged a full-blown storm, George knew he would get very wet indeed. Glancing behind him, he saw a large porch in which he could shelter from the rain but still keep watch on Falcone.

Within a minute of the opening rumble, it began to get darker; soon, the first, fat drops of rain were falling on the paving stones. George hurriedly closed his sketchbook, packed away his pencils and, tossing the last crumbs of his bread to a nearby pigeon, sauntered to the shelter of the porch. As he slipped into the porch, there was a second, much louder, crack of thunder from directly overhead. With it, the rain started in earnest: the big, lazy raindrops were now a pelting stream, bouncing off the paving stones, forming gushing, eddying currents in the gutters of the Corso. Passers-by dived gratefully into the porch beside George, cursing and shaking the water off themselves; out in the street, those whose loads or animals prevented them from running for cover plodded on, suddenly drenched.

Then, as quickly as it had arrived, the storm passed. Within a few minutes, the sun was shining once more, making the wet pavements steam. The other people sheltering in the porch looked up enquiringly at the sky and, one by one, sure that the storm was over, continued on their way. Soon, George was alone again in the porch, clutching his sketchbook and box but it wouldn't be long before the steps had dried out and he could return to his lookout position.

It was at about half past five – the church clocks had just chimed the half hour – that Falcone, resplendent in his scarlet coat, appeared, locking the heavy door behind him and setting off on foot along the Corso. That's him gone for the day, thought George, but he decided that he would stay put until it was time to make his way to the Count of Pelorito's house for their seven o'clock rendezvous. The Corso was busier again now that siesta time was over; there were lots of children chasing each other around and playing games while their elders sat around in groups, talking. The last hour of the day passed slowly. George had had enough of sketching the fountains; after two days, his drawings were as good as they were ever going to be and his backside was stiff and sore after hours of sitting on the hard paving stones.

The light was starting to fade as George walked along the Corso towards the count's *palazzo* in the strada Candines. Cutting through the Piazza del Duomo, he passed the Orion fountain, its waters cascading playfully from the upper bowls into the pool below. Even at this time of the evening, people were congregating around the fountain, talking and laughing. A minute later George walked past the facade of the church of the Annunziata dei Catalani. He looked up.

It was, he had been told, one of the oldest churches in Messina. Even to his untutored eye, the rounded, almost horseshoe-shaped arches suggested the Norman or Romanesque style. Its name, George supposed, derived from one of the several periods of Spanish occupation of the city since the Middle Ages. As he turned into the strada Candines he wondered, as he often did, at the number of different civilisations that had passed through Sicily, leaving their mark on the island: the Phoenicians, the Greeks, the Romans, the

Arabs, the Normans, the Venetians, the Angevins, and the Spanish. We, the British, are only the last in a long line of self-important visitors; what will our monument be, he wondered? The Greeks left their magnificent temples, the Normans their castles, their churches and their mosaics, the Spanish some elegant streets and fine houses. Will we be remembered for our roadbuilding? Or perhaps, just for having kept the French out.

Fifty yards behind George, loitering in the shadows, was Falcone's man, the loyal Luigi. Obeying his master's orders, he had waited patiently until George packed up for the day, then followed him, at a safe distance, from the Piazza dei Quattro Cavallucci along the Corso and into the strada Candines. Now, he was knocking on the door of a large, grand-looking house halfway along on the right-hand side. After a moment or two, the door opened and the Englishman disappeared inside.

'*Buona sera, signore*,' said the liveried footman who opened the door to George. 'Follow me, please, sir.' He climbed the stone staircase before opening the left-hand set of double doors on the landing with a flourish. This was the library – stocked, George could see, with several thousand books; beyond it was the count's study.

The count was sitting behind his desk. The small, panelled room was lit by a pool of yellow candlelight, which cast strange, flickering shadows on the ceiling. As George entered the room, the count stood up. He looked, briefly curious, at George's scruffy attire but said nothing.

'Good evening, Capitano Warne. I am glad you received my note. Do please sit down.' He waved George to the chair on the other side of the desk.

'Thank you for seeing me so quickly, sir.'

'Well,' the count said, in Italian, 'I haven't yet spoken to all my sources, but I did come up with one interesting snippet – rather by chance – which I thought you should hear.'

'Yes, sir?'

'Well, *Capitano*, I have it on good authority – the man in question is both observant and reliable, I know, from many years of dealing with him – that yesterday our friend Signor Falcone met a French intelligence officer here in Messina.'

George leant forward in his chair, thinking of his sighting of Falcone and the tall, fair-haired stranger conversing in French the previous day, and was about to speak but the count raised his hand.

'Let me finish, *signore*.' He paused, twiddling his quill. 'My source says that our friend's visitor is a middle-ranking officer attached to Murat's headquarters at Punta di Pezzo, named Armand Jardel.'

'That's extraordinary, sir,' said George, who could contain himself no longer. 'Yesterday I watched Signor Falcone's office all day and at lunchtime, I saw him leave with a tall, fair-haired man. They passed so close to me that I could hear them speaking French. Could the man I saw with Falcone yesterday be Armand Jardel?' The count's impassive expression fractured for a second.

'*Buon Dio*.' He paused. 'I think it is very likely that they are one and the same. My source tells me that Monsieur Jardel is tall and blonde.'

George felt a surge of excitement and relief; Falcone was clearly up to something. Perhaps this would revive Colonel Airey's faith in him.

'And what's more,' the count continued, 'my man tells me that Monsieur Jardel came over from the mainland in the morning and returned in the afternoon.'

'So a day trip. What else do we know about Armand Jardel, sir?'

'I gather he has served in Calabria for several years, running spies here and helping to fight the insurgents on the mainland. It seems that he has quite a network of informants.'

George wondered whether to tell the count what he found during his visit to Falcone's office but decided against it, for the time being. He would tell the colonel the count's news first. Then they could decide what to do next.

'Thank you very much, sir,' said George, rising from his chair. 'I will pass your information to Colonel Airey at once. He will be very grateful for all your help, I know.'

'I am glad to be able to help, *Capitano*. We live in difficult and dangerous times. Please send my greetings to the good Colonel Airey.' With that, the count rapped loudly on his desk. Immediately, the door opened and a footman stepped into the room.

'See Capitano Warne out, please.'

As George left the room, the count picked up his quill and returned to his papers.

A minute later George stepped out into the street as the count's footman closed the door behind him. As it was now half past seven, it was almost dark and the lights were shining in the grand houses that lined the strada Ferdinanda. The flowerpots hanging from the balconies had been watered at sundown and were dripping onto the pavement. From one of the open windows, the sound of laughter drifted down as he passed; from another the notes of a piano and a violin floated mellifluously out on the evening air, a soothing caress in the dusk. As he passed beneath another open balcony, he could hear raised voices inside, a man and a woman.

Ambling along the street, George turned over in his mind what the count had told him. If the count's source was sound, then it looked as if Falcone was up to no good. Moreover, his sighting of the lawyer with the tall, blonde French stranger appeared to corroborate the source's claim. It was a significant revelation that Falcone, far from being a trusted ally of the British was, at the very least, playing a double game for which he was being handsomely rewarded by the French. His protestations of friendship could be taken with a large pinch of salt from now on. On the other hand, none of this proved conclusively that the raids had been betrayed, let alone by Falcone. If Falcone had got wind of the plans for the raids, how had he done so? He must have a man in the Citadel. How else, thought George, could he have acquired the necessary detailed knowledge about the plans?

He began to run through in his head who knew about the plans. The generals and Colonel Airey? No, it was unthinkable that they would betray plans to the enemy, putting the lives of their men and their own reputations at risk. Could one of his fellow raid commanders have betrayed the plans? Coker definitely not. He didn't know either Kendall or Entwhistle at all well, but it was equally unthinkable, wasn't it, that a British officer would betray his own side to the enemy? The same applied, George thought, to the naval officers who led the raids in. In poor Kendall's case, if he had done so, he'd paid a high price for it. And, George suddenly remembered, the same might still be true of Coker and Entwhistle, for all he knew. The sergeants and the men were beyond suspicion, not least because they were confined to barracks before they were told of the intended targets.

A more likely suspect was one of the Sicilian galley captains who took the raiding parties across the straits. But he had already canvassed this possibility with Colonel Airey who considered it unlikely. They were not necessarily the most reliable or loyal of men – and one or two of them were notoriously venal – but by betraying the raids they would be placing themselves and their crews in mortal danger.

That left the worrying possibility that there was an enemy spy inside the Citadel. Could it be that one of the mess waiters or one of the clerks employed on the generals' staff was the source of the intelligence? Abel Winch, the mess orderly, was in a position to overhear any number of conversations between officers during dinner and, moreover, he was responsible for collecting, distributing and dispatching all the officers' letters. Or could it be one of the officers' servants? Or even a rogue officer? Well, thought George, anyone with a grudge against the King, the army, a particular general, or the country as a whole might be persuaded to pass intelligence to the enemy, especially if well paid to do so. Anyone from a disaffected Irishman to the son of a merchant bankrupted by the war might be willing to take French gold. Or, indeed, money might be the sole motive: there were lots of men in the army – as George himself was only too painfully aware – with heavy gambling debts, extravagant habits and demanding wives.

George had now reached the building in which Carlotta lived. The man who owned the ironmongery on the ground floor was putting up the shutters as George arrived.

'*Buona sera, signore,*' said George. 'How are you?'

'Very well, thank you, *signore*. Signora Fanelli is at home,' he replied, pointing in the direction of the first-floor windows.

George opened the front door and went in, pushing it shut behind him.

As he did so, Luigi, who had followed George at a discreet distance along the strada Ferdinanda from the count's house, eased into the shadow of the building opposite Carlotta's apartment. He settled against the outsized, rusticated stones of the wall, rubbed his bristly chin with the back of his hand and looked up at the building across the street.

The first floor had three tall windows, the middle one of which was open, giving onto a small balcony. Inside the candles had been lit, giving Luigi a good view of the high-ceilinged interior. As he watched, a dark-haired woman walked across the room before disappearing from view. Very soon she reappeared, closely followed by a tall, blonde-haired man.

'That's him, all right,' said Luigi to himself, fingering the knife in his inside pocket. He watched as the man and the woman turned to each other and began to kiss.

After a minute or so the couple parted and began to close the shutters.

'And that,' thought Luigi, 'is that.'

Once the shutters were closed and the windows stared blankly over the street, Luigi crossed to where the ironmonger was sitting on the steps quietly smoking a pipe. The two men had a brief conversation.

It was ten o'clock before Luigi decided he could abandon his post; Signor Falcone had been very insistent that he should follow the intruder all day. But now he, whoever he was, was clearly settled in for the night. And Luigi was very hungry. It was time to report what he'd seen to his master.

It took Luigi only a few minutes to walk to Falcone's house, which was on a piazza near the *duomo*. Knocking on the door, he was let in and shown up to his employer's study, a small panelled room with an elaborate, gilded, scalloped cornice. Falcone was sitting at his desk in his shirtsleeves, surrounded by heaps of papers. On a side table next to his chair was a half-empty decanter of red wine and a glass. He looked tired.

'Luigi,' he said, looking up, 'you're a good man. Thank you for coming to see me so late. Now, what do you have to tell me?'

Luigi began to recount events since the late afternoon.

'Very interesting,' said Falcone, ruminatively, at one point. 'So he called on our good friend the Count of Pelorito, did he? I wonder what they discussed? Church affairs? The price of olive oil? Madame Signotti's cleavage?' He laughed.

Luigi then described the visit to the house in the strada Ferdinanda and what he saw through the windows before the shutters were closed.

'And, *signore*, I discovered from the fellow who runs the shop on the ground floor who lives there.'

'Oh, yes?'

'Signora Fanelli, a young widow.'

'Thank you *very* much, Luigi. Good work. Now go off, have something to eat and get some sleep. There is much to do tomorrow so be ready at six, please.'

Falcone poured himself another glass of wine as Luigi closed the door, sat back in his chair and stared at the ceiling.

So our friend, whoever he is, he mused, is screwing the widow Fanelli. Is he, indeed? Well, in that case, it wouldn't be difficult to find out *exactly* who he is. Falcone raised the glass to his lips triumphantly and drank.

Once they had closed the shutters, Carlotta and George ate supper at a round table in the salon. They then sat in the candlelight, drinking wine, discussing the day's events. George told her briefly of his long vigil outside Falcone's office and then, in much greater detail, about his interview with the count. They discussed Falcone, speculating about the motives for his duplicity.

'I've been told,' said Carlotta, 'that he has a good reputation as a lawyer and that he makes a good living at it. His contacts with the British,' at this point she leant towards George and kissed him on the cheek, 'have given his practice a boost, too, I gather.'

'So, why's he spying for the French? Does he need the money for some reason we don't know about? Does he want to see the back of us and welcome the French to Sicily? If so, he's mad. The French will strip the island bare, they're like a swarm of locusts. They never pay for anything – that's half the trouble on the mainland, the cause of the peasants' endless violence against Murat's armies.'

'I think, *Giorgio mio*, that he's more likely to be trying to keep in with both sides, as a lot of people here are. It's an insurance policy.'

'Oh, yes?' said George quizzically, looking at Carlotta. 'And what about you? Are you trying to keep in with both sides?'

She glanced at him, coquettishly: 'What do you think, my darling?'

'I think you're Murat's mistress, just waiting patiently for the great man to step across the straits, chase this pathetic British garrison back onto its ships before sweeping you up in his arms.' He laughed.

'You silly man,' she said, smiling. 'Not everyone thinks that the British are bound to win the war, you know. Yes, your navy is strong, but your allies have been defeated by the Emperor many times. All of Europe now dances to his tune. The English armies in Spain are fighting a long war with no end in sight, it seems. Lord Wellesley has won battles, for sure, but the French have huge armies in Spain and are full of fight. So you see, my *Giorgio*, that the view from here is not as clear as it might be from your Horse Guards. Men like Falcone see no harm in keeping their lines open to both sides.'

'Especially, I dare say,' George added, with an arched eyebrow, 'if they can make good money doing so.' He poured them both some more wine.

As Luigi was making his way wearily out of his master's study, across Messina in the officers' mess at the Citadel the evening was starting to get boisterous. The mess consisted of three rooms: an anteroom, well supplied with deep armchairs, a dining room and a moderately stocked library in which the garrison's more thoughtful officers could while away the hours between duties. The three rooms had flagged stone floors strewn with Turkish carpets, high, ribbed, vaulted stone ceilings and mullioned windows, which looked out over the Citadel's inner courtyard.

On some evenings, there were only a handful of officers in the mess; tonight, however, the rooms were busy, buzzing with conversation and warm, despite the sea breeze coming in through the open windows. The crowd consisted mainly of young subalterns from the garrison's various regiments, leavened with a handful of junior naval officers.

Peter Wilkins was dining with two other officers, one from his own regiment, the 27th. They had finished dinner – an excellent joint of mutton – and were now eating lemon *granita*. They had already had several bottles of Marsala but Winch, the mess orderly, was approaching with two more bottles. Wilkins, flushed in the heat, his tongue loosened by the wine, was telling his companions about Emma Thring and the outing to watch the fishermen in the straits.

'She's a very pretty girl, and spirited with it.'

'In that case, I'd be surprised if you had the field to yourself,' said one of his companions, Charles Parsons. Parsons, a large, red-faced man, with bushy side whiskers, now a captain in the 27th, was a few years older than Wilkins, but they had become firm friends since Wilkins joined the regiment. 'Most of the good 'uns get snapped up pretty quickly when they come out here. Not everyone has Warne's good fortune in finding himself a local berth. I'd get on with it, if I were you, my dear Wilkins. Here's to Cupid and his arrows!' He raised his glass and drained it, setting it down on the table with a bang.

The other member of the threesome, Lieutenant Hay of the 31st Foot, picked up one of the new bottles of Marsala and refilled their glasses. He and Wilkins had forged a close bond during the voyage out to Sicily on the same ship. He raised his glass.

'To the lovely Emma, the future Mrs Wilkins!'

'Hear, hear,' said Parsons as they all drank the toast.

Wilkins, feeling that he ought to reply to his friends' good wishes, refilled the glasses again.

'To the fair Miss Thring,' he offered.

'Fair, and a good deal besides, I'll wager,' said Parsons with a guffaw, before draining his glass.

Wilkins shifted awkwardly in his chair and blushed.

On the other side of the room four naval officers were having dinner. Three of them had made up the party which had assembled aboard the *Sprite* the previous evening: Frank Younge, David Plumb and Robert Davidson. The fourth was Ned Huxtable, who had commanded the galley taking William Coker's raiding party across the straits to Catona. Younge had an arrangement that allowed him to dine in the Citadel's mess and he was returning David Plumb's hospitality.

'It's a bit rough and ready here, being the army,' Younge had said with a grin as he and his friends arrived at the table. 'As you can see, no silver candlesticks for us! For that you have to dine with the navy but the food's usually pretty decent, although I'm afraid the cellar here doesn't run to the excellent port you gave us last night.'

'Don't worry, Frank,' Plumb had said as he settled into his chair. 'It's kind of you to invite us all.'

They had dined well, eating some swordfish and a succulent roast chicken followed by figs and a local cheese. Now the table had been cleared, leaving the four men to their wine. They had already drunk five bottles of a Sicilian red recommended by Younge, who preferred it to Marsala. He ordered some more.

Younge had been feeling grey and tired for much of the day, the result of his overindulgence aboard the *Sprite* the previous evening. It was fortunate that he had not had a busy day. Now, with a good dinner and a few glasses of wine inside him, he was beginning to return to form.

'So, gentlemen,' said Plumb, now in expansive mood, pushing back his chair and stretching out his legs, 'I think we should hear more from Frank here about the delectable Miss Thring. He was uncharacteristically coy last night, you'll remember, Mr Davidson.' Plumb winked at Huxtable. Davidson nodded, smiling.

Frank Younge made a show of reluctance – reminding his friends of the convention of avoiding contentious subjects such as shop talk, women and politics in the mess – but was soon cajoled into it. He tried to be as *dégagé* as possible; it was important, after all, to maintain one's dignity in front of one's fellow officers. No one wanted to appear like an eager young pup. After a few minutes of friendly banter, the conversation moved on. The wine, too, kept coming.

It was over an hour later when Younge and his friends got up to leave. By now, it was stuffily hot in the mess and the atmosphere was raucous: most of the officers were well lubricated. Many of them had loosed their stocks and discarded their coats; there was revelry in the air, but the mood could all too easily become belligerent, given the amount of wine that had been consumed. Frank Younge was, if the truth be known, feeling rather tight, in the sort of mood when he could do or say more or less anything. David Plumb's face had, he noticed, turned an alarming shade of puce but he seemed, otherwise, to be sober enough. He must have hollow legs, thought Frank. The young midshipman, Davidson, had contrived to drink rather less than the rest of them. He was a canny lad, no doubt of that; he would go far. Huxtable, for his part, was mildly drunk, loquacious but far from reeling around.

As Younge's little group made its way to the dining room door they passed Wilkins, Parsons and Hay at their table. They, too, were coming to the end of dinner. There were several empty bottles on their table. Parsons was telling a joke, to much ribald laughter from his two companions.

As Younge and his friends passed the table, Parsons looked up.

'Ah, Wilkins,' he said, nodding his head towards Younge, 'is that not your rival for the favours of Miss Thring I see before me?'

'Indeed, it is, sir,' replied Younge, overhearing Parsons's remark. As he spoke, he stopped and executed an elaborate mock bow. 'And,' he continued, looking directly at Wilkins, 'may the better man win the prize.'

'To the victor the spoils, Mr Younge,' said Wilkins.

'May the King's Navy show itself the true defender of our . . . our fair maidens.'

Parsons stood up.

'Are you implying, sir, that the army does not do its duty?'

'No sir,' replied Younge, flushed, 'but I'm sure that Mr Wilkins will get the reply he deserves from Miss Thring.' He paused. 'And we all know what that will be.'

'How dare you, sir,' replied Wilkins, standing up, suddenly emboldened. 'Miss Thring knows her own mind and will, I don't doubt, speak it truly.'

'No gentleman can know a lady's mind, Mr Wilkins,' said Younge. 'Yet you say you do.'

By now a number of men sitting at neighbouring tables, sensing a row, had turned and were listening to the exchanges.

'I think my friend Wilkins deserves an apology, Mr Younge,' said Parsons, trying to retrieve the situation.

'No. I've not said anything for which an apology is owed. None but the brave deserve the fair, Mr Wilkins.'

'Are you suggesting that I am not worthy of the King's commission?'

'No, but have you stood in line under hot fire from the enemy?' There was an angry edge to his voice now.

'I am not a coward, sir.'

'Come on, Frank,' said Plumb, putting his hand in Younge's shoulder, 'I think it's time to be going.'

'We'll see about that when Murat comes across the straits with his men,' said Younge, sneeringly, looking Wilkins in the eye. 'That'll sort out the men from the boys.'

The room was now hushed; all conversation had ceased as everyone tried to hear what was passing between the two men.

'In that case, I demand satisfaction,' said Wilkins in a quiet, firm voice, taking a step towards Younge.

'You shall have it, Mr Wilkins, you shall have it,' said Younge, turning on his heel and striding from the room.

CHAPTER NINE

Messina, 13th September 1810

Earlier, there had been a full moon. Under a cloudless sky, its light had cast deep shadows across Messina's streets and squares, picking out the spires and campaniles of the churches and the high cornices and roofs of the grand houses, mimicking the sun in black and silver, as the city slept.

By the time Luigi left *casa* Falcone the moon had long since set and the dawn was coming up. As he walked along the strada Ferdinanda, the city was starting to stir: there were a few figures walking through the empty streets, domestic servants, perhaps, on their way to work or to buy fish from the morning boats unloading their catch at the Marina or the first shopkeepers opening up for another day. An old man led a mule slowly along the street, its unshod hooves clicking on the stones. A dog sniffed speculatively in the gutter. Over to the left, a cockerel was tuning up to greet the new day. While he was chomping through his breakfast – a chunk of warm bread and a cup of coffee – Luigi had received his instructions from his master. Falcone, even at this early hour dressed and reading a sheaf of papers, had told him to return to Signora Fanelli's house to keep watch. He should follow the blonde man wherever he went during the day.

Arriving outside the house, Luigi leant against the wall on the other side of the street. The sea fret drifting in from the straits was damp and chilly. Luigi folded his arms, hunched into his coat and settled down to watch and wait.

A few hundred yards away, in his billet in one of the buildings along the *Palazzata*, a stone's throw from the statue of Neptune, Frank Younge had woken up. His head ached mildly; his mouth tasted dry and stale: the second hangover in as many days. As he belched, a powerfully alcoholic geyser of last night's wine filled his throat. He lay in the darkened room staring at the ceiling for a moment. Then he remembered the previous evening.

Suddenly, it all came flooding back: the excessive drinking, the pointless verbal jousting with Wilkins, the flushed faces of the other men in the mess egging them on, the needless posturing and aggression. He and Wilkins had nothing against each other, for God's sake, apart from a passing interest in the same girl, certainly nothing remotely serious enough to have got them into this appalling mess. Wilkins had challenged him to a duel but, in the circumstances, last night, in the mess, in front of half the officers in Sicily, he had given him little alternative. What an idiot I've been, what a fucking idiot, he thought. And I might pay for it with my life. For all I know, Wilkins may be a crack shot who can hit a sovereign at fifty paces. Fuck, fuck, fuck. Perhaps Plumb could smooth things over. He rolled over and buried his head in the pillow.

By the time Frank Younge woke up, across the harbour in a room high in the south-west bastion of the Citadel, Peter Wilkins had been sitting at a table for over an hour trying to read. Open in front of him was *The Lay of the Last Minstrel*.

> *Can piety the discord heal*
> *Or staunch the death feud's enmity?*
> *Can Christian lore, can patriotic zeal*
> *Can love of blessed charity?*

Worthy sentiments, Wilkins was prepared to admit, but Scott's flowing cadences and rhythms failed to provide much comfort in his present predicament. There was plenty of patriotic zeal in the army, but piety, Christian lore and blessed charity were in shorter supply, nor were they likely to come to his rescue now. He'd spent much of the last hour staring blankly out of the narrow window into the night. Coming into view now below him as the dawn rose was the wide expanse of the parade ground with the city walls beyond. In the distance the dark ochre roofs of the suburbs squatted between the sea and the mountains rising behind.

Why, in God's name, had he challenged Frank Younge to a duel? It was madness, stark, staring, raving madness. What had he been thinking? What on earth had possessed him? He'd never even held a duelling pistol, let alone fired one. Younge was probably a dead-eyed veteran of countless duels, cool and steady of hand. He thought of the injuries a pistol ball could inflict and the agony of the surgeon's knife or saw.

The stupid thing was that Wilkins didn't really even know how he was expected to behave in a duel. He didn't know the form. Last night, he'd reacted – as now, in the cold light of early morning he realised, in the way he imagined that officers were supposed to react – by challenging the other man to a duel. He didn't believe in the whole process for a moment. Of course, no officer or gentleman could afford to lose face in the eyes of his fellows, but shooting at each other to prevent it was ridiculous. Wilkins had heard too many stories of ruined careers, grieving widows and fatherless children to be fooled by any notions of the glamour and courage of the gentleman duellist defending his precious honour. It was a cruel, sordid and vicious custom, a bully's charter. Was there any way out of this mess? God, I've been a fool, he thought, thumping the table in anger.

Charles Parsons was wedged into the stern of the *Sprite*'s gig. With the bo'sun pulling lustily at the oars, the little boat sped across the harbour. Parsons, who was a big, bulky man, felt perilously close to the water in the gig; the sooner they were on the *Sprite*'s solid wooden decks, the better. It was a glorious morning now; the surface of the water, gently ruffled by the breeze, was reflecting the sunlight at a million shimmering angles, all at once, all the time.

Parsons was going to the *Sprite* as Peter Wilkins's second to meet David Plumb, Frank Younge's second. Wilkins had asked him to act as his second within a minute or so of his very public spat with Younge the previous evening. Parsons had not fought a duel himself, but he had been second to an officer in his regiment who had been challenged following an accusation of cheating at cards. That was in Milazzo a couple of years ago. The two combatants had exchanged shots in a vineyard on the promontory beyond the castle but, thank God, no one had been wounded. Honour had been satisfied but no damage done.

Parsons was acutely aware of the importance of seconds; they were umpires, mediators and cornermen rolled into one. They were responsible for ensuring that the etiquette governing duelling was scrupulously observed. Without the protocols, this supposedly gentlemanly and honourable quadrille would descend rapidly into straightforward murder. It was up to the seconds to do their best to resolve the argument between the principals without resort to violence. If this was not possible, then it was their responsibility to ensure that the duel was properly and fairly conducted. All experienced duellists knew that if the case ended up in court it was vital to be able to tell the jury that the rules had been followed to the letter. It was, after all, only a couple of years since Major Alexander Campbell had been hanged for killing his opponent, the luckless Captain Boyd of the 21st Foot, in a savage duel, which, quite clearly, had not been conducted according to the etiquette. In the end, the major's fate was sealed when the Prince Regent declined to grant him a pardon. That case had been the talking point of the army for months – even penetrating as far as Sicily – and had been a sharp reminder to many officers of the importance, if a duel was unavoidable, of making sure that it was properly conducted.

The gig was coming alongside the *Sprite*, bumping gently against her hull. The bo'sun shipped his oars and held the boat steady while Parsons scrambled in an ungainly fashion up and over her side. There, waiting for him on the main deck, was the solid figure of David Plumb, resplendent in his uniform. He was wearing his dark blue undress coat, tailored in the latest fashion with a roll collar, cutaway front and short, square-cut tails. The two rows of brass buttons shone brightly in the sun although he was not wearing, Parsons noticed, his commander's epaulette.

'Welcome aboard, Captain Parsons,' he said rather formally, stepping forward, hand outstretched. 'It's a great pity that a very jolly evening was ruined by that unpleasant business at the end.' He emphasised the words 'unpleasant business' to leave no doubt as to what he thought of the affair. 'Come,' said Plumb, extending his arm. The two men walked across the spotless white planks to the quarterdeck. Perched high above them, up the mizzen mast, was a group of sailors repairing the rigging, their larking and chatter just audible as it drifted down on the breeze.

'I agree, Mr Plumb, and I think we should do all we can as seconds to call a halt to this farce.'

Plumb and Parsons stood in silence against the quarterdeck rail, looking out over the harbour towards Fort Salvador. Eventually, Parsons spoke, measuring his words carefully.

'The difficulty we have in getting Wilkins and Younge to settle their differences – slight as it seems to me they are – is that the row was so public. They will both feel that with so many witnesses among their brother officers it would difficult, even humiliating, for either of them to back down.'

'Yes,' replied Plumb, 'I agree and you know as well as I do that all too often agreeing to resolve a dispute after a challenge has been made is seen as an act of cowardice in itself and no officer could countenance *that*.'

Half an hour later Charles Parsons was in the gig being rowed back to the quayside. As the bo'sun pulled on the oars, Parsons turned what had been said over in his mind. He and Commander Plumb had agreed that they must persuade Wilkins and Younge to settle their argument peacefully. They agreed that it was absurd that two English officers should fight each other when the enemy was poised to invade the island. They also decided to tell them that the affair would gravely embarrass Miss Thring and her brother who was, lest they forget, a senior officer in Wilkins's own regiment. News of the duel would inevitably come to Sir John Stuart's attention, who would be furious that his officers were fighting each other rather than the French. It could ruin a man's career, they should hint. Wilkins and Younge should be forcibly reminded that the whole episode had arisen from a trivial, drunken spat. It was hardly a great matter of honour, for which to risk life and limb.

'Let's give ourselves twenty-four hours to talk sense into them,' said Parsons.

'Good idea. I'll see Mr Younge later this morning. Why don't you come back this evening at six? I hope I'll have some news for you by then.'

At about the same time that Charles Parsons was being rowed back to the Marina, Fabrizio Falcone was returning to his office. He had been paying a call on an old friend, a fellow lawyer who was a fount of knowledge about everyone and everything in Messina. There was nothing he did not know. Falcone had had only one question for him: did he know the identity of Signora Fanelli's lover? He had teased Falcone gently before answering. 'So, my dear fellow, why are you so interested in who *la bella signora* is screwing? Do you fancy a bit of it yourself and want to find out what the competition consists of?' Falcone mumbled something unconvincing about a friend wanting to know. The lawyer nodded, knowingly.

'I believe that he's a British officer, a captain called George Warne. He and Signora Fanelli have been lovers for a while, I understand. Capitano Warne has been in Sicily since the British first arrived, speaks Italian and has a number of friends in the city. Most of the British officers keep themselves to themselves but he is not one of them.'

Falcone thanked his friend profusely.

Back in his chambers, Falcone stood looking out of the window, watching the ebb and flow of the traffic in the Corso, while he considered the implications of the news he had just received. So a serving British officer had been responsible for burgling his office. It was inconceivable that he would do such a thing without authority from above, so the question was, what were the British after? Clearly not the money – only sixteen of the hundreds of gold *napoleons* in the strongbox had been taken. It was unlikely that they were interested in his legal practice. Were they perhaps looking for evidence that he was in touch with the French? He knew that the British were aware that there were French spies in Messina, but how could they have connected him to this? What was the significance of Warne's visit to the Count of Pelorito? What, if anything, should he do with this information? Perhaps he should try to frighten off the English *capitano*; Luigi would be only too happy to oblige. He watched a bullock cart lumber along the Corso, laden with firewood. The white bullock swished his tail at the flies, which buzzed around him. Fabrizio Falcone was deep in thought.

* * *

Peter Wilkins and Charles Parsons were standing on the Citadel's south-east bastion looking out over the Straits of Messina. It was a warm, sunny morning and the straits were already busy. There were a number of fishing boats, a handful of merchantmen, and one British man-o'-war, its white ensign just visible to the naked eye. Two of the merchantmen were beating up against the westerly breeze towards Faro, tacking in time with each other like a pair of dancers performing an elaborate *pas de deux*.

Parsons had come straight to the Citadel after he had been put ashore at the Marina. He had found Peter Wilkins in his quarters. He looked dreadful, tired and haggard.

'Didn't sleep too well, I'm afraid.'

'No, I'm not surprised,' replied Parsons with a smile.

Once they were up on the bastion, Wilkins's spirits seemed to recover. He straightened his back and squared his shoulders. A smile of sorts returned to his face. It was as if the anger, anxiety, remorse and fear, which had settled on him during his lonely, guilt-ridden vigil in the small hours, were suddenly lifted by the light and the tangy sea air.

'So what should I do, Charles?' he asked. 'And by the way, it's very sporting of you to agree to be my second.'

'It's the least I could do. Brother officer in trouble, the honour of the regiment and so on,' replied Parsons, putting his hand on Wilkins's shoulder. 'The least I could do.' He looked at Wilkins before continuing. 'You're going to have to prepare yourself to fight, I'm afraid to say.'

'It'll be pistols at dawn, I suppose?'

'Yes, I should think so. Nobody fights with swords these days, they went out of fashion years ago, like wigs. It's not always clear who has the choice of weapons. Some say that it should be the man who was challenged while others insist that the choice lies with the man who has been wronged, in this case, you. But, either way, Plumb and I will probably settle on pistols.'

'But I've never held a duelling pistol, let alone fired one.'

'No, but we might be able to fire a few practice rounds if I can lay my hands on a case of pistols.'

'Is there any chance that the duel could be avoided, Charles, without damaging my standing as an officer? After all, the spat was *very* public.'

'Well, that depends—'

'On what?' Wilkins interrupted.

'On whether Lieutenant Younge is willing to offer you a reasonable apology for his slight on your character.'

'And what are the chances of that?'

'Well, I don't know Younge at all, but I do know that the navy thoroughly disapproves of its officers fighting duels. I also know that his second, David Plumb, is keen to avoid it. He'll try to persuade him to offer an apology. And you would be well advised to accept any apology he might offer. Fighting duels is not a good way for junior officers to ingratiate themselves with their superiors.'

'Yes, I know that,' said Wilkins, momentarily gloomy again. His military career could be stopped in its tracks almost before it had begun by a stupid, drunken argument, which was not even his fault. 'Where would it take place, do you think?'

'We'll find some secluded spot not too far from the city.'

'And when would we meet, Charles?'

'Well, as you know, the early morning is the traditional time for these affairs, and it has the advantage that the duel can take place before too many people are up and about. After all, we wouldn't want anyone catching us in the act, now would we? And, I'd say, the sooner we got the whole damn'd business over and done with, the better. So maybe tomorrow or the day after.'

Wilkins gazed out over the straits. So this time tomorrow, he thought, he might be wounded or a murderer. It was hard to know which was worse: the unspeakable agony of the surgeon's table or the prospect of the gallows. Or he might be dead, with a pistol ball lodged in his chest.

'What happens next?' he asked.

'You carry on with whatever duties you have but keep your head down. Whatever you do, don't speak to Younge if you run into him. And don't discuss the affair with anyone else, even if you're asked. Just keep quiet.' Wilkins nodded. 'I'm seeing Plumb at six, so I'll come back here as soon as I'm ashore.'

With that Parsons turned away and walked towards the steps that led down to the courtyard. Wilkins leant against the warm stonework of the bastion and looked out to sea. The two merchantmen had reached the narrow point of the straits at Faro and were now setting a course north up the coast of Italy. He wondered vaguely where they were heading: Naples? Rome? Or even further north, to Pisa or Genoa. Or maybe they were bound for Sardinia or Corsica.

It was nine o'clock as George Warne made his way from the Porto Franco across the Terra Nova parade ground to the entrance of the Citadel. He had a spring in his step as he and Carlotta had started the day in the best possible fashion. He smiled at the memory of her lithe, dark, inviting body straddling him, her sure, arousing touch, and her natural, confident sensuousness. Afterwards, he had wallowed in the hip bath reading yesterday's newspaper. Now, smartly dressed in his favourite green coat and white breeches – a welcome change after the scruffy artist's disguise he'd been wearing for the last couple of days – he was on his way to report to Colonel Airey on last night's meeting with the Count of Pelorito.

At this hour of the morning the Citadel was buzzing with activity. In the stables, the grooms were busy with the horses while the stable boys mucked out the loose boxes and filled the mangers with hay. The farrier was shoeing a horse, a fine bay. The armourer was watching one of his underlings sharpen an officer's sword on the whetted stone wheel. High up on the walls above the courtyard, George could see the sentries pacing their sections, evenly, back and forth.

He strode up to the desk at the far end of the cool, flagstoned anteroom. There, as usual, behind his protective barricade of ledgers, was the bent, bespectacled figure of the chief clerk carefully annotating a file.

'Morning, Mr Rogers,' said George cheerily. 'Is Colonel Airey ready to see me?'

'Yes, sir, go straight in. He's waiting for you.'

George knocked on the door of Airey's office and went in without waiting for a reply. Colonel Airey was sitting at his desk wearing a scarlet infantry tunic instead of the dark blue uniform he generally favoured. The top two buttons were undone and folded back to reveal the yellowish-buff facings of his regiment, the 62nd, and a black stock, neatly tied. As George went into the room, Airey looked up from his papers.

'Good morning, George. I hope you have something interesting for me,' said Airey, smoothing down his dark, greying hair with his left hand.

'Yes, sir, for once I do,' said George. 'The count came up trumps yesterday.'

'Sit down and tell me all.' He motioned George to a chair.

George ran the colonel quickly through the events of the previous day, recounting the comings and goings from Falcone's office. He then told Airey what the count had revealed about Falcone's contact, the French spymaster Armand Jardel. When George had finished, Airey pushed back his chair, stood up and walked across the room, his hands clasped behind his back, deep in thought. For a couple of minutes there was silence, broken only by the sound of the colonel's footsteps. Then he asked:

'Do you believe him, George?'

'I see no reason not to, sir,' he replied.

'But it might suit the count to place the blame for the betrayals at Signor Falcone's door, might it not?'

'Yes,' conceded George, 'it might, sir, but taken with the evidence of the coins found in Falcone's office and the fact that I heard Falcone speaking French with someone fitting the description offered by the count's source, it becomes more convincing, I'd say.'

Airey listened intently, rubbing his nose against his index finger.

'And, sir, don't forget that I hadn't told the count about Falcone and the blonde stranger. And he still doesn't know, at least from our side, about the business in Falcone's office earlier in the week.'

Airey sat down in his chair and leant forward over his desk towards George.

'So, if we believe what the count tells us, what are we going to do about it?' asked Airey.

'Well, sir, if he's responsible for passing our plans to the enemy, he cannot have got the information on his own. He must have spies in here somewhere, in the Citadel.' Airey raised an eyebrow, but George continued. 'I think we need to keep watching Falcone to see where he goes and who he sees, sir, in the hope that he'll lead us to his sources.'

'I agree, George,' said Airey, 'and I know just the man for the job.' He laughed.

'I'll have to dream up a new disguise, sir. I can't go on drawing those bloody fountains, it'll drive me mad.'

It was early afternoon by the time Commander Plumb was rowed ashore to see Frank Younge. It was bakingly hot in the little open boat; Plumb was already sweating in his heavy uniform coat. He ran a finger around the inside of his stock and dabbed his forehead with a handkerchief. Most sensible people, he thought to himself, have gone inside to eat lunch and doze. The quayside, bustling with activity during the morning, had now lapsed into its afternoon somnolence. Even the scavenging street dogs who continually snarled and snapped over the discarded fish were asleep in the shade.

The gig deposited Plumb on the quay in front of the imposing marble statue of Neptune. He crossed the waterfront into one of the streets running between the blocks of the *Palazzata* towards the strada Ferdinanda. It was in this side street that Frank Younge had his lodgings. The building was one of the few blocks of the *Palazzata* which had survived the catastrophic earthquake of 1783 relatively unscathed. Where some blocks had been completely flattened, this one had survived with the loss of a few sections of cornice and some cracks in the masonry.

He went in through the open door and climbed the narrow wooden staircase. There were only three short flights of stairs up to Younge's rooms in the attic, but by the time he reached the top landing, Plumb was out of breath. He paused before knocking on the door.

'Ah, Mr Plumb, how good of you to come. I got your note. Come in.'

The room was low-ceilinged and untidy. Beyond, through a door, was a bedroom. Being up under the eaves, it was uncomfortably warm, too. Plumb could smell, in the confined space, the acid whiff of stale wine on Younge's breath.

'Well,' Plumb began, 'I saw Captain Parsons this morning.'

'Oh, yes, and what did he have to say on Wilkins's behalf?'

'Not very much, but he and I are agreed that you and Wilkins should settle your dispute without fighting.'

'You mean,' replied Younge, tartly, 'that you want me to apologise to him.' There was a slight, tired, resentful flicker of anger in his eyes.

'In a word, yes,' said Plumb. He then rehearsed the reasons why an apology was the right course of action in this instance. When he had finished, there was a long silence. Younge walked across the room – it was no more than three or four paces – and looked out of the little window. On the building opposite a pigeon perched on a section of cracked cornice, preening itself.

'How long do I have to decide?' asked Younge eventually.

'Well, if the duel is to go ahead it would be best it were done quickly – tomorrow or the following day – and I'm seeing Captain Parsons this evening at six.'

'I'll think it over and let you know by then.'

'Good. You can send a note out to the *Sprite* by boat from anywhere along the Marina.'

At about the same time as Frank Younge and David Plumb were discussing the duel, Peter Wilkins and Charles Parsons were riding through the Porta Chiara, the nearest gate in Messina's walls to the Citadel. Since he had left Wilkins earlier that morning, Parsons had borrowed a pair of duelling pistols from a brother officer. They were magnificent and expensive weapons, made by the famous London gunsmith Robert Wogdon. The polished mahogany case was stowed in Parsons's saddlebag while the two men rode out of the city to a secluded spot where Wilkins could fire a few practice shots. It was not, Parsons knew, considered good form to practise prior to a duel but, as Wilkins had never even picked up a duelling pistol, let alone fired one, it seemed the prudent thing to do. Duelling pistols were sophisticated weapons that took some getting used to. For one thing, they had extremely sensitive hair triggers, which could easily result in disaster in inexperienced hands; if a duellist accidentally discharged his weapon early, he would leave himself at his opponent's mercy.

Once they had passed through the Porta Chiara, the houses and streets of Messina gave way to market gardens and orchards, the trees heavy with fruit. Here and there were the *zenia*, the ancient, wooden cartwheel-like devices for raising water from the wells to irrigate the crops. To their right were Messina's suburbs, a cluster of houses outside the city's walls. To their left was the sea and the mainland beyond.

'We'll ride down the coast towards the village of Mili,' said Parsons, as they walked their horses through the orchards. 'We should be able to find a secluded spot there where you can fire a few practice shots away from prying eyes.' He shook the reins at his horse, which broke into a trot. After about two miles they passed a large orange grove, which ran down to the shoreline; there were no houses in the immediate vicinity.

'Come on, this'll do,' Parsons announced, turning off the road into the trees. They walked their horses into the middle of the grove before dismounting and tethering them to a branch of an orange tree. Parsons took the case of pistols from the saddlebag and, putting it on the ground, unlocked the lid. Inside, the two pistols lay in their baize-lined compartments, beautiful instruments of death, with chasing on the silver mounts of the stock and body of the gun. The barrels were octagonal, burnished to a steely-blue. Also in the case, each in its prescribed place, were a powder horn, miniature ramrods for loading the pistols, wadding and a supply of lead ball ammunition.

Peter Wilkins picked up one of the pistols and weighed it in his hand. He stood up and raised the gun slowly to his eyeline, as if preparing to fire.

'How does that look?' he asked.

'Very impressive. I'd be quaking in my boots if I were facing you. Now let's load and get shooting. We haven't got all day.' Parsons took the pistol from Wilkins and loaded it, carefully pouring the powder into the muzzle, followed by the shot and the wadding, tamping the charge down with the miniature ramrod. He then flicked up the cover of the priming pan, checked to see that the touchhole was clear before pouring in a small amount of gunpowder and closing the cover. Then, without cocking the hammer, he gently laid the pistol back on the case.

'Right,' he said, 'let's set up a target on that tree over there.' Parsons walked over to an orange tree and tied a strip of white cotton eighteen inches wide to the trunk at about five feet above the ground. He then measured out fifteen paces back from the tree.

'Right,' he said, 'that'll do. The target represents, more or less, your opponent's chest, which is where you should be aiming, if you want to kill him. You should stand side on, like this, so that you present a smaller target.'

Wilkins took up his position and Parsons handed him the pistol before withdrawing a few paces to one side.

'Right, Peter, cock the gun.' Wilkins eased back the hammer, which held the knapped shard of flint. 'Now hold it up with your arm extended and then lower your forearm until the pistol is in your eyeline. And when you're ready, fire.'

Wilkins looked along the barrel towards the small pimple sight and beyond to the midpoint of the white strip of material tied around the tree. He squeezed the trigger.

There was a flash as the flint sparked the powder in the pan, then, after a split-second delay, the main charge exploded with a great crash and a gout of flame, visible even in the bright afternoon sun, as Wilkins's arm jerked up. A cloud of grey, acrid powder smoke eddied in the breeze while all around them birds rose from the orange trees, flapping and chattering in alarm.

'I think you've missed. Shooting high is a common mistake

with these weapons, particularly when you are not used to them. But another few shots and you'll be fine. After all, you shoot game well enough, so you should be all right.'

Parsons walked over to the tree.

'Yes, you missed the target but took off a few leaves and an orange,' he said, pointing down with a laugh. 'So a couple of feet high and a foot or so wide. Let's try again.'

An hour later, the two men were walking their horses back into the city through the Porta Chiara.

'Well, Peter,' said Parsons, 'I think you should acquit yourself well enough if it comes to a duel.' Wilkins had fired a further seven practice rounds at the target on the tree, scoring four hits with only one misfire, a flash in the pan.

'Let's hope so,' said Wilkins, trying to sound confident.

'I asked him earlier to consider making an apology to Lieutenant Wilkins,' Plumb was telling Charles Parsons as they stood on the *Sprite*'s quarterdeck in the evening sunshine.

'And what did he say?'

'He said he'd think about it and let me know by this evening, but I haven't heard from him as yet.' Plumb paused. 'But I think we might be about to hear,' he said, pointing towards the quay. 'That gig there is heading our way, I'd say.'

A few minutes later the gig hove to under the *Sprite*'s starboard rail.

'Mr Sutcliffe,' Plumb called to the bo'sun who was standing at the foot of the main mast, 'would you be so kind as to see what this boat wants?'

'Aye aye, sir,' he replied, crossing the deck to the rail.

There was a brief flurry of conversation – Sutcliffe spoke some Italian, having served in the Mediterranean Fleet for ten years – before the bo'sun approached the quarterdeck holding a letter.

'It's for you, sir,' he added, almost superfluously.

'Thank you, Mr Sutcliffe,' said Plumb, breaking the seal with his forefinger and unfolding the sheet. He then glanced at the note before passing it to Parsons.

Dear Plumb, it read, *I have decided that I cannot make an apology to Lieutenant Wilkins. The matter will have to take its course. Please believe me when I say that I have come to this conclusion only after long and earnest consideration. It is not something I have decided lightly. I remain, sir, your respectful friend, F. Younge.*

'I hoped he'd see sense,' said Plumb, gloomily.

'Do you think there's any chance he could be persuaded to change his mind?'

'No, I doubt it. He wasn't too happy about making an apology when I saw him earlier this afternoon and he hasn't changed his mind. The difficulty is that it was all so bloody public. Too many men saw what happened.'

'Yes.' Parsons paused, turning to look out over the rail. He could see the gig forging back across the harbour; it had already nearly reached the quayside. 'So I suppose we've got no option but to fight?'

'No. What do you suggest?'

'I know a place that would suit well enough: an orange grove a couple of miles outside the city.'

'Pistols?' asked Plumb.

'I'd have thought so, unless your man has any objection.'

'I shouldn't imagine he has.'

'Pistols it is, then. I've already taken the precaution of borrowing a pair.' Plumb looked at him, momentarily suspicious. 'Shall we meet outside the Porta Chiara at six o'clock in the morning, the day after tomorrow, Saturday?'

'Yes, that's fine. I'll get a message to Mr Younge to that effect. And I'll bring the ship's surgeon with me, just in case he's needed, God help us. If anything crops up tomorrow, you know where to find me.' The two men walked across the deck to the rail.

'Thank you, Captain,' said Parsons, 'that's all for the moment. Good evening to you.'

Parsons lowered himself down the *Sprite*'s side into the waiting launch.

David Plumb stood by the rail watching the little rowing boat as it picked its way past a seventy-four-gun ship of the line, a frigate, a pair of Royal Navy cutters and innumerable merchantmen and fishing boats towards the Marina.

'God, what a mess,' he said quietly to himself.

Dusk was falling as Warne walked along the Corso on his way to Carlotta's apartment. He had spent much of the day watching Signor Falcone's office. Despite what he had jokingly said to Colonel Airey about continuing to draw the horses and their Cupid jockeys splashing through the fountains of the Piazza dei Quattro Cavallucci, he had been obliged to persist with the cover in the absence of any other plausible reason for him to spend all day in the piazza. Airey had promised, however, to make alternative arrangements for keeping watch on Falcone.

In the event, it had been largely a blank day. He had taken up position too late to see Falcone arrive in the morning but saw him leave in the late afternoon. At about midday, the tall, stout retainer in the brown coat who he'd seen on previous days had appeared and gone inside. He left mid afternoon. And that was the sum of George's observations for the day. Intelligence work, he was beginning to think, might not be quite the distraction he had hoped from the routines of regimental soldiering.

He turned left off the Corso into one of the side streets that led down to strada Ferdinanda. These streets were narrower than the main thoroughfares, little more than alleyways, darker in the fading light and less busy. This particular street was almost deserted as George turned into it. He had walked about fifteen yards when he became aware of footsteps coming up quickly behind him. He turned to see two men in the gloaming. One of them – he looked young, wirily built, with, George could see, black, irregular teeth – holding a club, was almost on him, perhaps two yards away. George threw down the sketchbook and the box as he turned to face his attacker, the pencils and chalks cascading out over the stones.

The man swung the club hard, diagonally down towards George's left shoulder. George sidestepped the blow, kicking viciously at the man's shins as he did so. The impact threw the Sicilian off balance for a fraction of a second, just long enough for George to punch him hard in the ribs. He doubled up with a grunt, staggering backwards. Before he could raise the club again George threw another punch at his assailant, smacking into his jaw and knocking him backwards onto the paving stones. The other man, bigger-framed and heavier, was still a little way behind his mate but George had no intention of giving him any opportunity to attack. God knows what he might be armed with, a stiletto or worse. He turned and sprinted off down the dark alley, out onto the broader, lighter, busier strada Ferdinanda.

Panting and sweating from the brief, furious fight, he turned to look back up the alley. There was no one coming after him; the bigger man had given up the chase and black-teeth was picking himself up. Catching his breath, George wondered whether to wait and go back for the sketch pad and the box of chalks. No, let them have 'em, he thought, with a wry grin. They, whoever they were, might even enjoy his drawings. It was only as he set off along the strada Ferdinanda that he realised he'd lost his hat in the scuffle. Well, he thought, if that's the worst of it, I've got off lightly.

Five minutes later, George was sitting at the table in Carlotta's apartment as she fussed around him.

'Oh, *Giorgio mio*, what happened?' He recounted the story.

'Do you think it was connected with your work for the army?' Carlotta asked.

'I don't think so. It was just two ruffians in an alleyway, one younger one with a club and an older one who stood off a bit. Perhaps they thought the sketchbook and box I was carrying was worth stealing. Muggings are two a penny in Messina, after all.' While he was speaking, George wondered whether the attack was connected to the money he owed the local moneylender, but said nothing.

'Yes, I suppose they are, *caro*,' replied Carlotta.

Back in the alley, the older man was berating the younger one.

'You useless prick, you didn't even hit him! You told me you'd give the Englishman a good hiding but he put you on the floor and got clean away.'

'I think I got him on the arm. He was very quick and hit me hard.' Tenderly, he rubbed his jaw. 'I don't think it's broken but it's very sore.'

'Serves you right,' said Luigi. 'My master will not be pleased.' He was not looking forward to reporting the debacle to Signor Falcone. The other man grunted. 'Come on, now, pick up that book and the box and we'll be off.'

As they were turning to go, Luigi noticed the black, wide-brimmed hat, which George had been wearing, lying in the gutter.

'Pick that up, please,' said Luigi. 'At least we'll have something to show *il capo*.'

'My arm is damn'd sore,' remarked George, gingerly touching his left bicep. 'That little rat must have hit me with his club, although I didn't feel it at the time.' In fact, there was already a nasty-looking bruise on George's arm; by tomorrow it would be quite a sight.

'I'll look after it, darling,' said Carlotta, kissing him playfully on the cheek.

'I can't wait, *carissima*,' said George.

George and Carlotta had eaten a supper of cold chicken and tomatoes, washed down with a carafe of white wine. The rich aroma of coffee was now wafting from the tall, silver pot that Carlotta had just placed on the table. She poured two cups and brought them over to George and sat down on the chaise longue next to him.

'I'm beginning to think,' he said, 'that the larger of the two men who attacked me, the one who held back, rings a bell. The light wasn't good, and I didn't have much time, but he looked familiar, somehow.'

'What did he look like?'

'Well,' replied George, 'he was a big man, rather older than the fellow with the club, I'd guess. He was wearing a dark coat and a hat, but that doesn't narrow the field much.' He paused, sipping his coffee. 'It was his outline and gait that looked familiar, I think. He's a big, tall man, stout, who walks in a lumbering, rolling way. It's as if I've seen him before somewhere but, for the moment, I can't think where.'

'Perhaps it will come to you,' said Carlotta, 'maybe when you least expect it.'

'Yes, let's hope you're right,' replied George, putting his coffee cup on the floor and pulling Carlotta gently towards him. 'Now, we have some more important business.'

'Are you sure you're up to it after your fight earlier?' She looked up at him, teasingly.

'Well, there's only one way to find out, isn't there?'

They kissed, their tongues flicking against each other softly at first, then more pressingly. Carlotta ran her fingers across George's lap.

'I think you'll be all right,' she whispered.

CHAPTER TEN

Messina, 14th September 1810

The raised ground-floor window was not perfect but it did allow George to sit in comfort, out of the sun, while keeping watch on Fabrizio Falcone's chambers. It also, thank God, excused him the pretence of drawing the horses and fountains of the Piazza dei Quattro Cavallucci. He was relieved to be able to shed his artistic cover. At first, he had enjoyed sketching the horses and the plump cherubs, but the pleasure had palled in the face of mounting evidence of a lack of artistic talent. And, of course, now he'd lost the sketchbook. He had gone back to the alley this morning on the off chance that it might still be lying in the gutter but it was nowhere to be seen.

A friend of the colonel's – a Royal Artillery officer – rented these rooms and had been prevailed upon to let George use them during the day. They were a few yards down the Corso from Falcone's building but offered a reasonable, if oblique, view of the lawyer's front door. He was confident that he would be able to keep an eye on Falcone's comings and goings during the day. He settled back in his chair behind the open window, his face hidden in the shadow.

Outside, in the bright morning sun, the street was alive with people and traffic of every description. Messina was going about its business. And there, George noticed with a start, was Falcone. He was dressed soberly in lawyer's subfusc; no scarlet coat today. George watched as Falcone made his way along the crowded street towards his office. At one point, a cabriolet mounted the pavement almost hitting Falcone as it swerved to avoid a cart. There was a brief altercation before the driver, perched high above the pavement, sped off. A moment later, Falcone disappeared into his building, closing the door behind him.

At about the same time as George was settling in for the day's vigil, William Coker and John Entwhistle were eating breakfast in their cell in the castle at Scylla. They had been prisoners for a week now, a fact confirmed by the accumulated scratches on the windowsill, one for each day, which Entwhistle had been making every morning with a piece of broken tile. Since the excitement of the interview with Murat, their days had settled into a mind-numbing routine: breakfast, doze, exercise; lunch, doze, exercise; doze, supper, doze. After a week continuously in each other's company with little external stimulation they were running out of topics of conversation. On the second day, Major Lafite had sent them a pack of cards – French cards with '*Roi*', '*Dame*' and '*Valet*' for 'King', 'Queen' and 'Jack' – so they had played whist for a few hours. On the fourth day Coker – who had a smattering of schoolboy French – had asked to be taken to the castle library, returning with a copy of Molière's play *L'Avare*.

'It'll improve my French,' he told Entwhistle, holding the book up, 'and, who knows, I might even enjoy it.'

'What's it about?' Entwhistle had asked a couple of hours later.

'A miser and his family, I think,' replied Coker.

'Oh, that doesn't sound much fun.'

What conversation they did have was concerned with the failure of the raids and the likelihood or otherwise of their being exchanged. Entwhistle continued to vent his spleen about what he saw – based solely on what Murat had told them – as George Warne's failure to press home his attack and his precipitate retreat. To begin with Coker reminded Entwhistle that they only had the enemy's word for this, but increasingly he simply ignored his sallies.

They continued intermittently to discuss escaping from the castle during their period of exercise but never seriously. For one thing, they noticed that the guard at the castle gates had been doubled – clearly, they speculated with amusement, they were regarded as likely escapers – and Coker's broken collarbone incapacitated him for the time being. There was little for it but to do what they could to keep their spirits up and wait.

Emma Thring was sitting at the breakfast table in her brother's lodgings. She was reading *The Times*, dating from the first week of August, one of the London newspapers which had arrived with the latest mail packet from England. It was now a week since she had arrived in Sicily and she was greatly enjoying herself. She'd been taken round most of the major sights of Messina; she had been on a boat trip to watch the fishermen out in the straits.

The plans for her tour of the island with Robert were now well advanced; they hoped to be departing for Taormina and Etna next week if Robert could get leave. She had been to the opera and had met a number of English and Sicilian notables at various receptions and dinners, as well as quite a few of the younger officers serving in the British garrison.

Emma's youthful good looks and vivacious personality had created a stir among the bachelor officers in Messina. She had enjoyed being the centre of the attention of a crowd of mostly eligible, good-looking young officers. However, the previous evening, at a reception given by one of her brother's fellow officers, she had heard a disturbing rumour. Fat Mrs Campbell – whom she barely knew – had bustled up to tell her about the spat between Peter Wilkins and Frank Younge.

'I just thought I ought to warn you, my dear,' said Mrs Campbell, fanning herself after the exertion of crossing the room, 'that you are in danger of becoming the subject of gossip.' Emma looked surprised but before she could speak, Clare Campbell continued. 'I have it on good authority,' she said, her dewlaps quivering with the excitement of this juicy morsel, 'that you were the subject of an argument between two young gentlemen.'

'And who are these two gentlemen, Mrs Campbell?' asked Emma, doing her best to remain calm.

'Mr Wilkins of your brother's regiment and Lieutenant Younge of the Royal Navy. Mr Younge has challenged Mr Wilkins to a duel; it is to be fought tomorrow afternoon, with swords, a delightfully old-fashioned touch, if I may say so, Miss Thring.'

Later, Emma had asked her brother whether he had heard any talk of this incident.

'No, my dear, I haven't but I didn't go to the Citadel today so might well have missed it. I will see what I can find out when I go in tomorrow. I'm taking the early parade tomorrow and will have breakfast in the mess afterwards so I should be able to get to the bottom of it then.'

'I do hope it's not true, Robert,' said Emma. 'It would be dreadfully shaming, and I would hate to think that two young men, both so charming in their own way, could be putting themselves in mortal danger on my account.'

Emma was still at the breakfast table glancing at the newspaper when Robert arrived back from the Citadel. As he walked into the room, he loosened his stock and unbuttoned his tunic.

'It's hot out there,' he exclaimed.

'Robert, did you manage to find out what happened between Mr Wilkins and Mr Younge? Was Mrs Campbell speaking the truth?'

'It seems that she was, at least in part.'

'How dreadful, Robert, how dreadful.'

'I am told by someone who saw what happened that there was an argument between Wilkins and Younge during which your name was mentioned, but that the challenge arose from an imputation of cowardice on Lieutenant Wilkins.'

'Oh, how ghastly. How shall I ever again hold my head up in public here?' Robert put his hand on his sister's shoulder.

'Don't worry, my dear, I know you didn't do anything to provoke this affair.' He paused. 'Mrs Campbell was, however, wrong when she told you that it was Mr Younge who challenged Mr Wilkins; it was the other way round.'

'But Mr Wilkins seemed such a mild-mannered man, not the peppery, duelling type at all.'

'Quite. Nor,' her brother continued, 'is it to be fought this afternoon or with swords. I understand that it'll be pistols tomorrow morning.' By now Emma was visibly distressed.

'What am I to do?' she asked plaintively.

'Well, my dear,' replied Robert, 'there's not much we can do, I'm afraid. We have to let these things run their course.' He paused. 'But as I am free for the rest of the day, why don't we make a trip out of town up to the point at Faro? It's not too far and there are some pretty villages on the way and the views across to the mainland are spectacular. What do you say?'

'I think that sounds a lovely idea. It'll take my mind off things. I'll go and get ready.'

Peter Wilkins was strolling across the great expanse of the parade ground towards the Citadel's gatehouse. Although it was not yet eight o'clock, the morning parade had already been dismissed and the sergeant major was marching the men back into the Citadel. The company was in commendably good order, well turned-out and in high spirits. The colonel would be pleased although, no doubt, he would pretend not to be. Every subaltern in the regiment knew that there was no imperfection of kit or uniform too small to evade the colonel's eye. Still, it was a beautiful morning, full of promise, the parade had gone well and Wilkins was looking forward to some breakfast.

As he walked through the gate into the Citadel, the duty sergeant came out of the guardroom and, jumping to attention, saluted.

'Mr Wilkins, sir, there's a message for you.' He handed Wilkins a folded note.

'Thank you, Sergeant,' said Wilkins, taking the note. As he walked into the courtyard he broke the seal but glancing down curiously at the sheet came to an abrupt halt.

Please report at your earliest convenience to the Adjutant-General.

God, thought Wilkins, alarmed, what the hell is this all about? Few junior subalterns are summoned personally to see the Adjutant-General. Nor did he summon young officers to discuss the weather: the AG, as he was universally known, was in charge of army discipline. Wilkins tried to calm himself, breathing deeply: in through the mouth and out through the nose, once, twice, three times.

The Adjutant-General of the British army in Sicily was Major-General James Campbell. He had occupied the post since the original expeditionary force had arrived in the Mediterranean in 1805. Earlier in his career he had served with distinction in America and in India. In the five years he had been Adjutant-General in Sicily, Campbell had earned the confidence and respect of the whole army.

Well, thought Wilkins, the note does say 'at your earliest convenience' so I'd better go now. At least I'll get it – whatever 'it' is – over with before breakfast. He folded the note and walked slowly towards the range of low buildings that housed the army's staff. In the large, stone-flagged hall Rogers, the chief clerk, was already hard at work.

'I'm here to see the Adjutant-General, Mr Rogers.'

'Yes, Mr Wilkins,' said Rogers, adding, ominously, 'he's waiting for you.' He pointed to the door.

'I'll go straight in, then,' said Wilkins. Before knocking, Wilkins stopped momentarily to compose himself.

'Come in.'

The Adjutant-General was alone, sitting at his desk reading a letter. Wilkins could see the gold tooling on the green leather desktop. On the near side, he noticed, it was bright and well formed but on the far side, where the general sat, it was faded and rubbed. It was odd what one notices at such moments, thought Wilkins fleetingly.

'Good morning, Lieutenant Wilkins,' said Campbell. He had a deep, mellifluous voice, with a faint Scottish accent. 'Thank you for coming in at such short notice.' Wilkins stood to attention.

James Campbell was a handsome man in his late forties, with a full head of gently curly hair. He was wearing a scarlet tunic with a black stock and a white cravat. His tunic buttons, Wilkins could see, bore Scottish saltires. His big brown eyes, aquiline nose and full, almost pouting lips could, in other circumstances, have given him a mildly libidinous air. But this morning he was wholly businesslike, almost curt.

'I gather,' he began, 'that you challenged an officer of His Majesty's Navy, Lieutenant Younge, to a duel two evenings ago.' Christ, thought Wilkins, so that's what this is about.

'Yes, sir, that's true,' said Wilkins, doing his best to keep his voice steady.

'And are arrangements in hand for the two of you to meet?'

'Yes, sir. Our seconds are arranging matters.'

'Who is your second?'

'Captain Parsons, sir, of my regiment.'

'I see,' said Campbell, pausing. 'Your duel will not take

219

place, Lieutenant Wilkins. This is an order and any failure to obey it will bring the full rigour of military discipline down on your head. I do not need to tell you what that will entail. Your commanding officer has been informed and is in complete agreement. Do I make myself clear?'

'Yes, sir,' said Wilkins.

'The naval officer commanding here at Messina is giving similar orders to Lieutenant Younge.'

'Yes, sir.'

'Nor should Captain Parsons be in any doubt as to the consequences for his career should he persist in this irresponsible course.'

'Yes, sir.'

'Good day to you, Lieutenant Wilkins.'

'Thank you, sir, and good morning.' Wilkins saluted stiffly, turned and left the room closing the door softly behind him. General Campbell sighed as he sat back in his chair.

Peter Wilkins marched straight past Rogers without saying a word and out into the courtyard. Rogers looked up from his ledger but seeing the rapidly receding Wilkins said nothing and returned to his work with a raised eyebrow. Wilkins crossed the courtyard and climbed the steps up to the ramparts. Once up, he went over to the parapet of the nearest bastion and tried to compose himself.

I suppose it was inevitable, he thought, given the number of his fellow officers who had witnessed the contretemps between himself and Younge, that it would become public knowledge. It was also inevitable that once the authorities knew of the proposed duel, they would do their damnedest to stop it taking place. For all that, he was now in a very difficult position. On the one hand, he had explicit orders from a very senior officer forbidding the duel. On the other, his challenge to Younge had set the well-oiled machinery of the duel in motion. It would be difficult to avoid fighting now without a severe loss of face among his fellow officers. His reputation would be tarnished, possibly permanently. Men would whisper that he funked facing Younge, that he'd let the authorities know so that they'd act to stop the duel, that he was a coward. But if he ignored the AG's order and fought the duel, he was risking his entire military career. He would be court-martialled and sent home in disgrace. And then there was Parsons to consider. It would be hard on him to land him in trouble with the AG through a pig-headed desire to fight a duel. God, he thought, not for the first time, what a mess. What an idiot I've been.

He stared out over the straits towards the dark, looming mountains of Calabria. 'I will lift up mine eyes unto the hills, from whence cometh my help' Wilkins thought, remembering the words of the psalm. He turned to look to the north, towards the narrows at Faro, to Scylla and Charybdis. He was confronting his own Scylla and Charybdis now: the rock of military discipline and the Adjutant-General's orders, facing the whirlpool of dishonour and disgrace. Fight and be damned or ditch the duel and be dishonoured? It was not much of a choice.

In Falcone's chambers, Luigi was telling his master about the abortive attack on George Warne in the alleyway the previous evening.

'You mean to tell me the idiot you hired didn't even land a blow on the *inglese*?' said Falcone.

'Yes, *signore*, I am afraid so. He ended up on the floor. The

Englishman was quick and hit hard. We did get his sketchbook and his hat, *eccellenza*.'

'I know,' replied Falcone, with a rueful smile. 'I've seen it. He's not much of an artist, our English friend, is he?'

'Still,' said Luigi, 'even if we failed to give him a good hiding, it seems to have scared him away. I can't see him out there anywhere keeping a watch on the building.'

'No,' said Falcone, scanning the piazza from the window, 'you do seem to have frightened him off, for the time being.'

The church clocks had just struck midday when George saw Falcone and another man emerge from the front door of the building. Watching them cross the piazza and turn left onto the Corso, on the spur of the moment he decided to follow them. Quickly, he left his post by the window and slipped out of the building into the street. It took George nearly a minute, threading through the crowd, to catch up with the two men, but once he had them in his sights, he hung back, following at a discreet distance.

The two men were heading north in the direction of the Porta Reale, Falcone carrying a small leather dispatch case tucked under his arm. They could not be going very far as, presumably, for a journey of any distance in this heat, Falcone would ride or take a carriage. It was not long before they passed through the great gate in the city walls and joined the coast road towards Faro. Here there was less traffic to obscure his view of the lawyer and his man as they strode along the road.

As George followed them, he began to think that the tall, slightly lumbering man beside Falcone looked familiar. There was something about his rolling gait; hadn't he seen it before somewhere? Then, as they were crossing the *fiumara* di Saddeo, it dawned on George that he was the fellow who had been hanging back while his sidekick attacked him last night. He's the man I've seen coming and going from Falcone's chambers – that's it, thought George, now I've got it. I was attacked at Falcone's orders. It was nothing to do with the moneylender: that, at least, is some relief. Falcone must have discovered that I burgled his office. But how? Had he spotted me watching them from the piazza posing as an artist? Possibly. Had I been seen entering the building that day? Equally possible. If Falcone is up to no good with the French, then he might well be aware of people spying on him.

The two Sicilians had only walked about half a mile along the coast road from the city gates when they turned off the road through a pair of marble gates. Beyond the gates, a magnificent confection of different-coloured marble bearing the date 1646, lay the monastery of San Francesco di Paola. George had passed it many times on his way to and from Faro but he had never seen anyone other than monks entering or leaving the monastery. What business could Falcone conceivably have with the friars?

He watched as the two men walked up to the door in the facade, knocked and, a moment later, were admitted. George could see an elderly, stooped friar in his distinctive pointed cowl opening the door to the two visitors. The door closed behind them. George scrambled up the bank on the landward side of the road and settled down in the shade of an ancient, gnarled olive tree to watch and wait.

The monastery of San Francesco di Paola sat between the road and the shoreline. Its buildings formed two sides of a square, although to the north of the site there were the ruins of a third wing, now abandoned. To the rear of the building and extending round to the north were the gardens, lush and shaded. George could see orange, lemon and olive trees as well as tomato plants, vegetables and other fruit trees. The friars were evidently industrious gardeners, although at present there was no one to be seen outside. George shifted on the hard, stony ground. How long would Falcone and his man be closeted with the earthly representatives of St Francis, he wondered?

At about the same time as Warne was watching the monastery, in the Citadel the five most senior British officers were meeting in Sir John Stuart's room. Gathered round the table with Sir John were his second in command, Lieutenant-General Lord Forbes, Major-General Campbell, Major-General Cockburn, commanding the southern division and Colonel Donkin, the Quartermaster-General.

'I know you all have many duties to attend to, so I will be brief,' Sir John began, looking round the small group of men. 'My Lord,' he continued, inclining his head in Forbes's direction, 'perhaps you would be kind enough to give us a brief report of the present situation?'

'Indeed, Sir John.' The eighteenth Baron Forbes was now in his late forties with thinning hair. His somewhat heavy, jowly features were lightened by a warm smile, twinkling, humorous eyes and quizzical, arched eyebrows that gave his face a look of perpetual surprise.

'As you all know, it looks as if the enemy is planning to launch an attack across the straits. It may come at any moment. The enemy has been very active lately moving his flotilla along the coast, marching his troops to and fro and firing almost daily across the straits. The day before yesterday,' he continued, 'General Cockburn and I rode up to Faro to inspect the defences. I am pleased to report that everything is in good order and the men appeared in good heart. I'd say, Sir John, that were Murat to attack there he would get a bloody nose.' There were nods of approval round the table.

'Thank you, My Lord. General Cockburn?'

'Well, Sir John,' Cockburn started slowly, 'it was my first visit to Faro and I was very impressed by the state of the defences. Our batteries are well sited, commanding all possible landing places and, indeed, the crossing itself. The visit brought home to me how close the enemy is: from the hill above Faro, every object in the French camp – even Murat himself – can be clearly seen. It would be hazardous for the enemy to attempt a daytime attack between here and Faro. Not only is the coast well protected by our batteries, we have a strong force waiting to repel any landing and the navy guards the coast in strength to prevent the French getting ashore. Nor, given the ease with which we can observe the enemy's every move, can he make a surprise attack.'

'I agree with General Cockburn,' said the Adjutant-General. 'We have fourteen thousand men on the island, the majority of which are stationed around Messina and Faro, with some at Milazzo. They are at high alert: every morning they are under arms from an hour before dawn. Our best intelligence is that Murat has somewhere between twenty and thirty thousand men in Lower Calabria, not all of them reliable troops or encamped near the straits ready to embark for Sicily. We think he has about five hundred transports in various anchorages along this part of the coast.'

'So what do you think he will do, My Lord?' asked Stuart, looking at Forbes.

'In my view, Murat is most likely to try to attack to the south of here, towards Taormina, where our defences are lighter and our troops more thinly spread.' Forbes paused. 'But it would be a much riskier undertaking. And, as the season advances, he must strike soon or postpone the attempt until next year. It may also be that the concentration of troops over there' – he pointed in the general direction of Calabria – 'is intended to prevent us from sending some of our regiments here to the peninsula.'

'Thank you, gentlemen,' said Stuart. 'I think we can safely conclude that if an attack is going to come, it will come before the end of the present month. Now, could we move to other matters. Colonel Donkin, I believe you have a report to make?'

It was becoming very warm, even in the dappled shade of the old olive tree. George had removed his coat but was still sweating in the afternoon heat. Earlier, a light breeze had been wafting off the sea but even that had now dropped away. He had been sitting here for an hour and a half but had seen no activity across the road in the monastery. He was beginning to wonder how much longer he should wait when a small knot of figures emerged from behind the buildings and began to stroll in the garden. George sat up.

Even at this distance, he could make out Falcone, a small, neat figure dressed in black, and his oafish sidekick who was slightly detached from the main group. Much more interesting were the three other men in the group. Who were they? They were definitely not monks as they were wearing ordinary clothes, coats, breeches and stockings, rather than habits. What were they doing in the monastery? And why were they meeting Falcone there? It was difficult to be sure at this distance but one of the men might have been the blonde Frenchman, Armand Jardel, whom George had seen with Falcone earlier in the week.

The four men strolled in the shade of the trees, deep in conversation, while Falcone's man inspected the vegetable plot. At one point, George saw him help himself to a tomato. After about twenty minutes Falcone shook hands with the other three men and, waving to his sidekick, turned for the gate and the road. George hurriedly scrambled in behind the broad trunk of the olive tree. He watched as Falcone and his man emerged onto the road before turning left back towards the city. Behind them, in the garden, the other three men disappeared from view behind the monastery. Once Falcone and his man had gone a hundred yards along the road, George stood up rather stiffly from behind the tree, shrugged on his coat, slid down the bank and set off after the two Sicilians.

About halfway along the Marina, in one of the remaining habitable blocks of the *Palazzata*, was the office that served as the headquarters of the Royal Navy in Messina. This outpost of the Admiralty was the administrative hub of the squadron, which patrolled the straits and the seas off Sicily, Calabria and Apulia. It was here that orders were laboriously written out in a flowing copperplate, that indents were made for the myriad supplies that a seagoing squadron required, everything from uniform buttons to replacement masts, and from here that a constant flow of reports, on operations, on individuals, on the state of the squadron's ships, their crews and a host of other matters were dispatched to Their Lordships in Whitehall. Outside the front door stood two scarlet-clad Royal Marines on sentry duty.

It was here that Frank Younge came – as he did most days – at about the time that George Warne was settling into his new observation post of the Piazza dei Quattro Cavallucci. Saluting the sentries, he strode up the steps into the building. The hall was a popular meeting place for naval officers, where they could see their friends, catch up on news and gossip, angle for appointments, favours and promotion. Today, however, it was empty; perhaps it was too early in the morning for his brother officers. He walked through into the clerk's room.

'Good morning, Johns, is there anything for me?'

'Yes, Mr Younge, sir,' replied the duty clerk, 'there's this.' He picked up a letter and gave it to Frank. It was folded into an envelope of thick, creamy paper and sealed with a blob of red wax impressed with the Admiralty's fouled anchor device. Younge nodded his thanks as he broke the seal and opened the letter.

It has come to my attention that you have offered to give satisfaction in a matter of honour to Lieutenant Wilkins of His Majesty's 27th Regiment of Foot. I hereby expressly forbid, on pain of severe sanction, that any such meeting shall take place. You should be aware that Lieutenant Wilkins has been similarly ordered.

This brief but explicit note was signed by the commodore, the grand, distant figure who commanded the Messina squadron. Younge stuffed the letter into his pocket before making his way out of the building. He crossed the quay and stood at the water's edge between two small fishing vessels. He watched distractedly as the crews made the final preparations for setting sail. Out in the harbour, *Sprite* rode at anchor. Frank could see sailors busy on her deck, mopping, scrubbing and polishing in the morning sun. From the quarterdeck rail a substantial figure was supervising this activity: was that David Plumb? If so, what would he have to say about this letter – this order – from the commodore? There's no point in speculating, Frank realised, I should go and ask him in person.

A few minutes later, Frank Younge was being rowed out to the *Sprite*. As the gig approached Younge could hear the officer of the watch ordering a rope ladder to be put over the side. As the little boat heaved to, *Sprite*'s wooden hull towered over Younge. He pulled the rope ladder towards him and started climbing the yellow-painted side, between the black squares of two gun ports. As Frank swung nimbly over the rail onto the deck, Plumb stepped forward to greet him.

'Good morning,' he said, clapping Frank on the shoulder. 'Just in time for some breakfast.'

The two men went below to Plumb's cabin where they were greeted by the drifting aroma of fresh coffee. Once they were seated at the table, Protheroe, the steward, brought in two plates of scrambled eggs and toast. They ate in silence as Protheroe hovered. Once they had finished, he gathered up the plates.

'Will that be all, sir?'

'Yes, thank you, Protheroe, and very good it was, too.' The steward left the cabin, shutting the door behind him. Plumb took an orange from the bowl on the table.

'I take it you have some news for me?' asked Plumb as soon as the door was closed.

'Yes,' replied Frank, taking the letter from his pocket before passing it across the table. There was a brief pause.

'Hmm,' said Plumb thoughtfully, peeling the orange. 'A very similar order was brought out to me earlier this morning.'

'What do you think I should do?' asked Frank.

'Well,' said Plumb, 'you're in a tight corner. I don't envy you.' He poured them both some more coffee.

'The commodore's orders apply to you, too, sir, don't forget.'

'Yes, but you're the principal, you're the one who's got to apologise. I'm just the second; it's my job to try to settle the thing. If you apologise men will say, rightly or wrongly, that you ducked the fight, perhaps even that you were running scared. And a lot of men witnessed the argument between you and Wilkins. They may even suspect that we somehow let the authorities into the secret so that they would put a stop to the duel. But if you let matters take their course, you will incur the commodore's displeasure – to put it mildly. You could be on half-pay, languishing in lodgings in Portsmouth for years . . .' Plumb's voice tailed off.

He began eating the orange, segment by segment. While he ate, he thought of the damage this duel – even as a second – might do to his career. He had a command for which every commander on the Navy List would give his eye teeth and, as he well knew, more than half of them were unemployed. There would be no shortage of keen, brave, competent officers to take his place should he fall foul of the Admiralty. Younge stared gloomily into space.

After a full minute of brooding silence, Plumb spoke.

'I think I might have the answer.'

Younge looked at him, suddenly hopeful.

'The duel could, I think, be postponed without dishonour.'

'What do you mean?' asked Frank.

'Simply that you undertake to give Lieutenant Wilkins satisfaction for the insult at some date in the future when a meeting can be arranged beyond the Admiralty's – and the army's – jurisdiction. You can let it be known that you were both explicitly ordered not to fight but that, as a gentleman, you wished to afford Wilkins the opportunity to defend his honour. It also means that you don't have to offer him an apology. The whole business is simply deferred. It's been done before, I know. What say you?'

'It might work, yes,' said Frank, cheering up visibly. 'It would at least allow me to hold my head up in the service *and* obey the commodore.'

'Good,' said Plumb. 'I'll write a note to Parsons immediately.'

Robert Thring flicked his whip at the chestnut horse between the cabriolet's shafts. Beside him was his sister Emma. They had had an enjoyable day's sightseeing along the coast between Messina and Faro and were now, the cabriolet's hood down in the late afternoon sunshine, on their way home. He had shown Emma the villages of Paradiso, Grotto di Paci and Sant' Agata; they had watched the fishermen repairing their nets on the beaches and they had walked round one of the saltwater lakes at Ganzirri. Once they had reached Faro, Robert had taken Emma around the fort and introduced her to John O'Connell. Emma had climbed up onto the ramparts to look across the straits to the castle at Scylla and the French encampment. All in all, it had been a most enjoyable and interesting day. Dear Robert, he was so sweet to have made the effort to do something to distract her from her recent troubles. She glanced fondly at him as he drove the cabriolet, reins in hand.

They were approaching the village of Grotto di Paci, the cabriolet bowling merrily along the coast road when there was a terrifying howl overhead. A moment later, a shot crashed into the hillside above the road, perhaps forty yards from the Things. It cut a swathe through the prickly pear covering the hillside, throwing up a cloud of dust and stones. The horse shied and bucked between the shafts.

'What the hell was that, Robert?' she asked, anxiety in her voice.

Before her brother could answer, another shot smashed in the ground just beside the road. This one was much closer to the cabriolet, perhaps only twenty yards away. A shower of dust, small stones and fleshy chunks of prickly pear rained down on the carriage. The horse, terrified, reared up in the shafts, tipping the cabriolet alarmingly backwards. Then a third shot came howling over, crashing a second later in the hillside to their left. Another shot fell into the sea, just beyond the narrow beach, throwing up a great plume of spray.

'It's the Frogs,' said Robert, fighting to control the horse. 'They've been firing at us across the straits for months now. Generally, they don't hit anything but occasionally they're lucky. We must get out of here, now.' He cracked the whip at the horse, which jumped immediately into a canter, sending the cabriolet speeding away.

'Are they shooting at us?' asked Emma.

'It's possible, yes. They might have seen our carriage and thought that it contained someone important. But they could also have been firing at our camp and battery up on the ridge above Grotto. It's hard to tell.'

'Either way, they are not making a very good fist of it,' said Emma with a smile.

Before long the cabriolet was half a mile further along the road and the firing had ceased.

'Perhaps the French were firing at us,' said Emma, brushing the dust and greyish-green fragments of prickly pear off her dress.

'Yes, maybe they were,' replied her brother.

'It's rather flattering in an odd way, don't you think?'

'I suppose so,' he replied, laughing.

'If only they knew,' said Emma with a smile.

'What business would Signor Falcone have with the Franciscan friars?' asked George Airey.

'Well, sir, it seems that his business was not with the friars themselves, rather that the monastery is being used as a rendezvous.'

George had tailed Falcone and his man back to the Piazza dei Quattro Cavallucci, where he had seen them into the building before returning to his observation point. He waited, concealed in his shadowy window, until Falcone left the building for the day, then followed him the short distance home. He had then walked briskly through the streets to the Citadel to report to the colonel.

'Are you sure that you saw the blonde French spy, Jardel?' asked Airey. 'It would be a tempting conclusion to make, would it not?'

'At that distance, sir, no, I cannot say that it was definitely Jardel with Falcone in the garden, but it did look like him.'

Airey stood up from his chair and paced across the room, deep in thought.

'So, George, what do you make of what you've seen today?'

'To start with,' he began carefully, 'I think we can now say for certain that I was attacked on Falcone's orders. I am pretty sure that the man with Falcone today was one of the two men in the alley yesterday. The question is, why, and what, if anything, does it prove?'

'It might show,' Airey replied, 'that Falcone is up to no good. After all, if he had nothing to hide, why not simply report the burglary – *your* burglary – to the authorities instead of taking the law into his own hands? And what of the meeting at San Francesco di Paola?'

'I suppose it could be innocent,' said George. 'Falcone could have been summoned to discuss the monastery's legal affairs but, if so, why was he not meeting the friars themselves? Who were the laymen he was talking to? And if the blonde man *was* Armand Jardel, then it all starts to look very suspicious indeed.'

'It seems unlikely that a monastery could be the headquarters of a conspiracy, don't you think?'

'Perhaps,' replied George, 'but it is secluded and might provide plausible cover for any conspirators. It's also worth remembering that its gardens run down to the shoreline, so it could be used as a dropping-off point by boats coming over from the mainland.'

'Yes, George, you may well be right,' said Airey. 'Taking everything we now know about Falcone together, it does look as if he's up to something. Keep watching him. Oh, and George, one last thing before you go.'

'Yes, sir?' said George, turning to face Airey who was now back at his desk.

'Do you know anything about a duel between Lieutenant Wilkins of your regiment and Frank Younge?'

'Well, I know them both, sir, and I've heard rumours that they had a rather public argument in the mess the other night but not much more than that. I'm a bit detached from the day-to-day goings-on of the army at the moment. I was out on a boat with both of them and Miss Thring a few days ago and there did seem to be a bit of competition between them for her attention. I thought Younge was making more of an impression than Wilkins. But I'm surprised that it's come to a duel. Wilkins has always seemed a mild-mannered fellow, not the fighting sort at all. Younge is quite a drinker, I know, so perhaps more likely to get caught up in all that nonsense.'

'She must be quite something, our Miss Thring,' said Airey. 'After all, she's only been here for a few days and she's causing a stir already.'

'She's certainly lively,' said George.

'But you've got other fish to fry, George,' said the colonel with the wisp of a smile.

'Indeed, sir.'

At that moment there was a knock on the door.

'Come in,' said Airey.

A tall, spare figure walked across the room towards the desk, his heels clicking on the stone floor. He was neatly but soberly dressed in civilian clothes, his dark hair close-cropped and slicked down. He had bony, hawk-like features and intelligent, questioning eyes. George stood up.

'Good afternoon, Sandro, what a pleasant surprise,' said Airey. 'Now,' he continued, turning to George, 'I would like to introduce you to the most important man in Messina, Colonel Carboni.'

'A pleasure to meet you, Capitano Warne,' said Carboni. His English was good, but heavily accented. 'I have heard much about you from the colonel here.'

'I hope it's not all bad, sir,' said George, with a smile.

'The colonel,' said Airey, 'is our eyes and ears in Sicily. He plays a vital part in keeping us informed about what is going on here politically, militarily and in every other respect. It is no exaggeration to say that without the colonel we would be living in almost total ignorance of local affairs. He is a fount of knowledge and I hardly need add that he is totally trustworthy. I am sure you will come to value him as much as I do.'

A few minutes later George was standing in front of the clerk's desk in the hall.

'Tell me, Mr Rogers,' he said, 'how often does Colonel Carboni come in?'

'Quite frequently, sir, to see Colonel Airey,' replied Rogers, looking at George curiously.

'Oh, that's strange, as I've never clapped eyes on him in the five years I've been here.'

'Well, he often comes in at odd times of the day, sir.'

As George was quizzing Mr Rogers about Colonel Carboni, Peter Wilkins and Charles Parsons were taking the air on the Citadel's ramparts. The heat of the day was receding as the shadows lengthened into the balmy Mediterranean evening. They could see the *passeggiata* beginning across the harbour on the Marina. Messina was relaxing, casting aside the cares of the day, slipping into the fun, laughter and gossip of the evening.

'I had a note from Commander Plumb an hour ago,' started Parsons, as the two men walked side by side around the Citadel's great bastions.

'What did it say, Charles?' asked Wilkins, trying to sound unconcerned. 'Are we meeting tomorrow morning?'

'It looks as if Plumb has found a way out of our difficulty.' Wilkins turned to Parsons, suddenly hopeful.

'Really?'

'Yes, but you'd have to agree to it. He suggests that we simply postpone the duel to a time when the meeting can be arranged without attracting the attention of the military and naval authorities. You will get the chance to defend your honour, to clear your name and it allows Younge to avoid having to apologise. You can both let it be known that as a result of the public nature of the row, it was almost inevitable that the matter would come to the notice of the powers-that-be and equally inevitable that they would prevent the duel. That way, you avoid any suspicion of collusion or cowardice. Does that appeal to you?'

There was a long silence. Eventually Wilkins, who did not want to appear too eager – even to his own second – to avoid the encounter with Younge, replied.

'Yes, I suppose it does make sense. We do have most specific orders *not* to fight, from very senior officers. General Campbell made it abundantly clear to me that I would be putting myself in serious jeopardy were the meeting to take place.'

'Good. I'll let Plumb know.'

CHAPTER ELEVEN

Messina, 15th September 1810

Peter Wilkins was riding north along the coast road from Messina on his way to visit John O'Connell at Faro. John was a year or two younger than Wilkins but they got on well. He had a gentle Irish charm and irreverent humour which appealed to Wilkins, a refreshing change from some of the touchy, pompous army types he rubbed shoulders with from day to day.

Wilkins was looking forward to going walking in the hills above Faro. The wild mountain landscape was breathtakingly beautiful and the views of the mainland spectacular. After a steep climb Wilkins liked to find a sheltered spot where he could sit, read, contemplate the view or snooze in the shade. John O'Connell would be a good companion, too. Above all, though, Wilkins was desperate to escape for a few hours from the Citadel. After recent events, he was acutely conscious that everyone was watching him and talking about him. It seemed as if his whole character was being publicly examined. Yes, a day away, some time immersed in the peace and sublime beauty of the mountains would be good for the soul.

Back in Messina, George was lounging in bed, listening to the church bells striking nine o'clock. Carlotta had just got up and was filling herself a bath. Earlier they had made love, slowly at first, then with increasing energy and abandon until orgasm overtook them both, almost simultaneously, releasing their bodies into a state of utter calm and contentment.

George was looking forward to the weekend. Colonel Airey had excused him his duties so, as Carlotta was visiting her family, George had decided to go shooting with Charles Parsons. They would set off during the afternoon in order to reach the hamlet in the hills where they would stay the night so that they could be out at first light the following morning. It would be less fun without Boney chasing round putting up birds and retrieving the dead ones but there was still good sport to be had at this time of the year with abundant partridge and quail. It would also be a chance to stretch his legs and enjoy the scenery after a week spent keeping an eye on Signor Falcone. Until then, he decided, he would start the first volume of Mr Gibbon's *Decline and Fall*, borrowed from the Citadel's library. He stretched luxuriantly, listening to Carlotta singing as she lay in the bath.

'Gentlemen,' Sir John Stuart began, 'I've asked you here this morning to hear some recent and, I think, important intelligence. Yesterday we heard assessments from Lord Forbes and General Cockburn as to the state of our defences here.' There were nods of agreement around the table in Sir John's room in the Citadel. On Stuart's immediate right was James Campbell, the Adjutant-General; beyond him was Colonel Airey, with a stack of papers on the table in front of him. On Sir John's left was Colonel Donkin, the Army's Quartermaster-General whose department was, formally, responsible for the troops' quarters and transport. Informally, Donkin had an important role in the gathering and analysis of intelligence, a responsibility that gave him oversight of Colonel Airey's activities.

Rufane Donkin was in his late thirties. A slight man, with a cool, rational gaze, his small mouth gave him a reserved, almost pinched, air. Burdened with a reputation among his contemporaries as an intellectual, he had served in the Quartermaster-General's department since 1805 but he nevertheless had a fine record as a fighting soldier. The previous year he had been decorated for his part in the Battle of Talavera, where he had commanded a brigade.

'Today, the Quartermaster, Colonel Donkin, will give us the latest intelligence from Calabria.'

'Thank you, Sir John,' said Donkin in his reedy voice. 'I have, gentlemen, some interesting intelligence, which may have a bearing on whether Murat will attack us this year or not.' The three officers round the table looked at Donkin with renewed interest.

'I have it on good authority that relations between the Emperor and Murat are as bad as they have ever been. Rumours to this effect have, as we all know, been circulating for a while but I have reliable intelligence that casts more light on the matter. My source tells me that Murat's journey north in the spring to attend Napoleon's wedding to Princess Marie-Louise was not a success. Murat was against the marriage as he worried that it

240

might undermine his grip on the Kingdom of Naples by making the Emperor more pro-Austrian and therefore less violently opposed to Maria Carolina's ambitions.'

'Yes, yes, Colonel Donkin,' Stuart interrupted impatiently, 'we know this. What does the *new* intelligence have to say?'

'That when the Emperor and Murat met at Compiègne in April they had a violent argument, during which the Emperor threatened to cut off Murat's head!'

'Really?' exclaimed Campbell, with a big grin on his face. 'Is this how the Emperor treats his brother-in-law now?'

'So I am reliably informed,' replied Donkin. 'We now know for sure that in early June one of the Emperor's ADCs brought orders to Murat that no attempt should be made to invade Sicily unless it is certain to succeed. The same informant also assures us that as a result of the Emperor's order that French troops shall be commanded by French generals, Murat has to convince General Grenier that any attempt at invasion will be successful. In other words, there are considerable constraints on Murat's freedom of action.'

'What does this mean in practice?' asked Sir John.

'In practice,' Donkin said, 'it means that he may wish to throw his army across the straits today but he can't do so without the say-so of the senior French generals, who have no particular desire to risk men, transports and materiel in an attempt to conquer Sicily. Which is to say, that the French are more likely to flunk the attempt than make it, in my view.'

'Thank you, Colonel,' said Stuart. 'Now, Colonel Airey, I believe you have something for us?'

The three men round the table looked inquisitively at Airey.

'Yes, sir,' Airey began. 'You will recall that last week's raids on various enemy anchorages across the straits did not achieve what had been hoped. We lost quite a number of men. One of the commanding officers, Captain Kendall, was killed and two others, Captains Coker and Entwhistle, are still unaccounted for. The only one to make it back was Captain Warne. I have, for various reasons, become suspicious that the operations were betrayed to the enemy; it explains why he was waiting for us in the dead of night in four separate places.'

'Are you sure about this, Colonel? It's a very serious allegation,' said Stuart sharply.

'Well, Sir John, we may have uncovered a spy operating here in Messina. At the moment there is nothing linking him directly to last week's raids, but we are digging hard.'

Airey then outlined the evidence unearthed by George Warne's observations of Fabrizio Falcone: the meeting with Armand Jardel, the information garnered from the Count of Pelorito, the attack in the street and the previous day's incident at the monastery of San Francesco. As he did so, the three others around the table listened intently. The Adjutant-General stroked his chin with the back of his hand as Airey spoke, while Stuart stared fixedly into space watching the motes of dust floating in a thin shaft of sunlight. When he had finished, there was a long silence in the room.

The Adjutant-General was the first to speak.

'How reliable is Warne?'

'I should say very,' answered Airey. 'He has a personal interest in unmasking this spy – he lost some good men in the raid. Indeed, it was Warne himself who first suggested to me that the raids might have been betrayed but I don't think he would allow this to cloud his judgement. He's taken well to intelligence work' – adding as the memory of George's break-in at Falcone's chambers came back to him – 'and although he can be impetuous, he's learning fast.'

'Sir John,' began the Adjutant-General, 'I have two disciplinary matters I would like to raise. The first concerns a recent argument between a young officer of the 27th and an officer of the Royal Navy. Arrangements were in train for a duel, but I've seen the young officer in question, one Wilkins, and ordered him not to proceed. The commodore has issued similar orders to the naval officer.'

'Good, General Campbell,' said Stuart. 'We can ill afford to have our officers fighting each other when the enemy is poised to cross the straits. I trust you have made it clear to the officer in question that no infraction of your order will be tolerated?'

'Yes, sir, I have,' replied Campbell. 'The other matter concerns a soldier also, as it happens, serving in the 27th, Michael Kelly. It's an unhappy case, I'm afraid. Kelly and his brother were both in Captain Warne's raiding party last week but, sadly, the brother, John, was killed on the beach during the raid. Once Kelly returned, he got drunk and was later arrested by the provost marshal's men following a brawl in an inn in the city. He'd been demanding money at the point of his bayonet. As we all know, this sort of incident is regrettably common, but Kelly has a good record and is, according to Warne, a solid, reliable soldier. Yesterday he was tried by a court martial and sentenced to two hundred lashes. I ordered that the court's sentence be suspended for a day so that I could bring the matter to your attention.'

'Yes, thank you, General Campbell.' Stuart paused, looking round the table. 'You all know how much I deplore the practice of flogging in the army. It is cruel and brutalises the men. In this instance, I order that Kelly's sentence be commuted to a month's imprisonment in the Citadel. His pay shall be stopped for the month of his imprisonment and halved for three months thereafter. Please ensure that this order is published in the next General Orders.'

It was mid-morning by the time Peter Wilkins and John O'Connell left the fort. Now, after more than an hour's climb they had reached the ridge above Faro. Thankfully, it was not as hot as it had been recently; the sky was milky, opalescent, under the thin layer of high cloud which screened the sun. They sat down on a rock to gather their breath. Spread out beneath them were the Straits of Messina and the Calabrian coastline. They could see, in miniature as in a diorama, Murat's headquarters and camp at Punta di Pezzo. Even at this distance they could pick out Murat's pavilion and the mass of smaller tents, no more than white dots on the dun-coloured ground, radiating out from it in well-ordered rows. To the north and west they could see the Lipari Islands, hazily indistinct on the deep, smooth blue of the sea. Far away to their left was Milazzo. On a clearer day they might have been able to see the long, thin promontory that extended like a beckoning finger out into the Tyrrhenian Sea but today it was hiding in the haze.

'Shall we eat our picnic here,' asked O'Connell, 'or would you prefer to press on?'

They had brought two bread rolls each filled with dried ham and local cheese.

'Why don't we walk on for half an hour?' replied Wilkins.

'I'm not hungry after that excellent breakfast you gave me!'

'Good. Let's keep going.'

The only sounds in the room were the noises drifting up from the streets through the open windows. Carlotta had gone out, smartly dressed in hat and bustle, to call on her many relations around the city. She would not be back until evening. George was sitting at the table, the first volume of *Decline and Fall* open in front of him. His father had been encouraging him to start reading Mr Gibbon's history for a long while. George knew – because he frequently referred to it in his letters – that his father admired the books even if, as a man of the cloth, he found Gibbon's unrepentant anti-clericalism shocking.

As he read on, he smiled at Gibbon's description of Scotland: 'gloomy hills assailed by the winter tempest, from lakes concealed in a blue mist, and from cold and lonely heaths, over which the deer of the forest were chased by a troop of naked barbarians'. What, he wondered, would his Scottish friends make of that? Two paragraphs later, reading Gibbon's opinion that 'the thirst of military glory shall ever be the vice of the most exalted characters', George found himself nodding in agreement. It was ever thus, he thought. He read on, drawn into the book by Gibbon's stately, sonorous prose.

O'Connell and Wilkins had enjoyed a peaceful afternoon up in the mountains. They found a flat, smooth rock in the shade of an ancient, stooped oak where they ate their picnic. After their stiff climb, the cheese, bread and ham tasted even better than it usually did. As they sat taking in the stupendous view of the

Straits of Messina and Calabria laid out before them, Wilkins raised the subject of his spat with Frank Younge.

'What have you heard about it, John?' he asked.

'Not that much, beyond the fact that it took place in the mess in front of a number of other officers. News travels slowly up the coast to Faro, you know,' replied O'Connell in his Irish lilt.

'Do you think I was foolish to challenge Younge?'

'Well, where I come from duelling is very common. The country squires and half-mounted men are hot for it and are forever shooting at each other.' He paused, looking at Wilkins. 'But I can't see that any good has ever come from it. They talk about honour, but it's more about bloodlust and revenge, if you ask me. Having said that, I don't think you were wrong, in the circumstances, to challenge Younge, no. He has, I've heard, something of a reputation as a hothead and a drinker. After all, almost all the other men in the room would have done the same thing.'

'Thank you,' said Wilkins. 'I'm glad to hear I've got someone sensible on my side.' With that, he rolled up his coat and, laying it on the warm stone as a pillow, stretched out on his back and closed his eyes. Within a minute, he was sound asleep.

It was late afternoon as the two men picked their way carefully down the last ridge above Faro. Suddenly, John O'Connell stopped.

'Look over there, Peter!' he exclaimed, pointing in the direction of Scylla on the far side of the straits. Wilkins followed O'Connell's finger.

'It looks like a ship's in trouble,' said Wilkins. 'Is it one of ours?'

As he spoke, O'Connell snapped open his pocket spyglass. He put it to his eye.

'I think she's flying the red ensign,' said O'Connell, 'and she looks more like a merchantman or a transport than a naval vessel. But she's definitely in trouble, by the look of it.'

Half an hour later, O'Connell and Wilkins were standing on the tower of the fort at Faro. Wilkins was scanning the far shore through a long telescope while O'Connell waited impatiently beside him.

'What can you see, Peter?' he demanded.

'I can't make out her name, but she does seem to be drifting down the coast, away from the castle. I can't see any crew on deck or aloft – I wonder what they're up to?'

At that moment, there was a commotion in the courtyard below. O'Connell looked down.

'Ah,' he said, 'the navy's arrived. I'd better go down.'

Two minutes later, O'Connell was back up on the top platform, making the introductions.

'Do you know Lieutenant Huxtable?' he asked. 'He's been sent up by the commodore to find out what's going on over there.'

'No, I haven't had the pleasure,' said Wilkins, inclining his head. 'Good evening to you, Mr Huxtable.'

'And to you, too, Mr Wilkins. Now, would you be kind enough to lend me your telescope so that I can see what the devil's going on over there?' Wilkins handed him the long, brass instrument. Huxtable raised the telescope to his right eye, balancing it with practised ease between the base of his left thumb and forefinger as he focussed on the ship stranded on the Calabrian shore.

'I'm pretty sure,' he said, returning the telescope to Wilkins, 'she's the *Harlech Castle*, one of our transports that plies the coast between Palermo and Messina. She's got into trouble in the currents over there, by the look of it, and drifted along the coast and is now grounded. As far as I can see there's no crew on board. Either they've already abandoned ship or the French have captured her and taken the crew prisoner. I must return to Messina at once to report to the commodore.'

With that Huxtable turned and clattered off down the stairs to the courtyard. He mounted his waiting horse and trotted out of the fort towards the road.

For the next couple of hours, Wilkins kept watch on the *Harlech Castle* through the telescope while O'Connell busied himself with his evening rounds. Having drifted along the coast from Scylla, she was probably no more than two miles from Faro so with the evening sun illuminating the far shore, Wilkins had an excellent view of the stranded ship.

It was mid afternoon when George and Parsons set off from the Citadel. It was not the first time that the two men had been on a shooting expedition together in the island's mountainous interior. The previous winter they'd been on a highly enjoyable four-day trip on the lower reaches of Mount Etna. This time they had decided that, with only a day to spare, they would stay closer to home. They knew a farm up in the mountains behind Messina where they could spend the night, ready for an early start in the morning.

They were both carrying a double-barrelled, flintlock shotgun, taken apart and packed into its wooden case. These weapons were a relatively new invention and, although still muzzle-loading, a great improvement on the single-shot guns on which earlier generations of sportsmen had relied. The wooden cases also contained a powder flask, shot, wadding and flints as well as cleaning equipment.

They'd got some bread and cold meat for supper that night and breakfast in the morning, along with some coffee. Wine, milk and vegetables would be provided by their host.

Having picked their way cautiously up the tracks into the mountains it was dusk by the time the two men arrived at the farm. As they dismounted, a short, wiry man emerged from a cottage. He was wearing a tatty smock and clogs.

He greeted them in the local dialect. 'I hope you've had a good journey.'

'Yes, thank you,' replied George. The Sicilian he had learnt from Carlotta enabled him to make himself understood in the hinterland. 'We are tired and hungry and we'll be starting out very early tomorrow.'

'You know where you are sleeping, I think,' he said, pointing to a small barn. 'Why don't you unload your bags and I'll stable the horses for you?'

Inside the barn there was still just enough light to make out the interior. On one side was a heap of fresh straw, piled in stooks. This year's, thought George. On the other side, against a brick wall, there was a fireplace. Here they could cook and although there was no chimney there were sufficient holes in the barn's roof to let the smoke out. All in all, it was a comfortable, dry, warm and quiet place to spend the night. Nor did the owner ask more than a few *carlini* for the pleasure. While Parsons unloaded the saddlebags, George busied himself laying and, with flint and oil rag, lighting the fire.

By now the light was fading, making it increasingly difficult for Wilkins to see the stranded *Harlech Castle* across the straits.

Then, in the gloaming, he heard a voice at his elbow.

'Good evening, Lieutenant Wilkins.' It was Michael Baldwin, one of the 27th's senior captains. Baldwin was a tall man, with a flat, bulldog-like face under a shock of ginger hair. He was a jovial fellow with a chuckling laugh and a ready smile, a popular officer who had been in Sicily since the regiment had arrived.

'I thought I'd come down from the camp to join the fun. We could see that there was some excitement in the offing. I thought I might lead a party out into the straits to see if we can help, although I've had explicit orders not to put ourselves in danger. I've brought a dozen good men with me. Would you care to come along for the ride?' Baldwin sounded as if he was suggesting a picnicking excursion on an English summer's day, rather than a hazardous sortie at night in dangerous waters against an unknown enemy.

'Yes, sir, I'll join you. I'd love to go and have a look over there.'

'Good man,' said Baldwin, clapping him on the shoulder. 'Why don't you go and put your uniform on?'

'I'm afraid to say that as I have been off duty today, it's back in my quarters in the Citadel.'

'Never mind. But get yourself armed: a cutlass or a sword and a pistol would be useful and be quick about it because we'll be going in a few minutes.' Baldwin nodded at the rising moon. 'I'm going down to the beach to get the boat organised.' With that he turned on his heel and cantered down the stairs to the courtyard.

Wilkins went in search of John O'Connell. He found him in the guardroom inside the fort gate, with Boney at his heel.

'So you need a weapon or two, eh? Well, I've got just the thing for this kind of operation,' said O'Connell, with a grin.

'I'll be back in a minute. In the meantime, ask the armourer to find you a cutlass.'

A few minutes later, O'Connell was back.

'I think you might find this useful,' he said. 'I was given it by an uncle just before I left Ireland. He said it had saved his life on at least one occasion and that, one day, I might be glad of it.'

He handed Wilkins an unusual-looking, short-barrelled gun. The walnut stock was the same size, approximately, as the stock of a standard-issue infantry musket, but the barrel was only two feet long, with a bulbous, flared muzzle. It was a blunderbuss, but a blunderbuss with a difference, for along the top of the barrel was its bayonet, spring loaded and secured by a catch next to the firing lock. This allowed the bayonet to be permanently attached without increasing the gun's length: once the blunderbuss had been fired there might well not be time to reload, so the bayonet could be released for close-quarters fighting. Wilkins released the catch holding the bayonet, whereupon the sharp blade sprang forward. It reminded him of a swordfish he'd once seen on the Marina quayside.

'It's quite a weapon, isn't it!' said Wilkins.

'Yes,' replied O'Connell. 'My uncle called it a coaching blunderbuss, the sort of thing you took with you on journeys in Ireland to fight off highwaymen and footpads. And, knowing my uncle, I shouldn't be surprised if he's used it more than once.' He handed Wilkins a leather pouch and a powder horn.

'Thank you, John, let's hope it'll come in useful. See you later.'

'Good luck, Peter.'

With that Wilkins left the fort and made his way round to the beach. He could just make out in the half-light Baldwin's men heaving the boat down to the water. In the coarse, holding sand pushing the heavy, clinker-built skiff back down to the sea took considerable effort. Wilkins could hear the men chuntering and cursing as they struggled to get purchase in the deep sand.

As Wilkins approached the skiff, he saw Michael Baldwin standing alongside while his men strained and heaved at the boat. He was carrying two oars, one in each hand.

'We're being joined by a detachment of the 58th in their own skiff,' said Baldwin, 'commanded by my old friend Captain Hibbert, a fire-eater if ever there was one. Two companies of the 58th are in camp just round the point where they are being shelled by the French almost every day. Hibbert thought this might be a good chance to get back at the enemy.'

Glancing round, Wilkins recognised Sergeant Fitt – his short, slight but powerful frame was instantly identifiable, even in the half-light – but only knew the names of a couple of the men as, although they were in the same regiment, they were not in his company. The only familiar figure was Michael Hughes who, as one of the tallest men in the regiment, always stood out. Hughes and Fitt, Wilkins knew, had both been on Warne's raid across the straits the previous week.

Once the skiff was afloat, Baldwin ordered his men to embark. One by one, they splashed through the shallow water and into the boat.

'Right, Mr Wilkins, will you push her off, please?'

'Yes, sir,' answered Wilkins, handing the blunderbuss to Baldwin in the boat's stern. Wilkins pushed the boat out from the beach until the water was up to his knees. He then jumped nimbly over the counter into the skiff. Baldwin was seated in the stern, with six of the soldiers manning the oars in the boat's waist while the others sat in the bows. Right at the front, acting as lookout, was Fitt, the sergeant. The wind had died down, so the sea was smooth and as the oarsmen picked up a rhythm, the skiff began to glide across the water.

'Keep those muskets up, boys, don't let the water get at them,' said Baldwin to the men in the bows. As Wilkins sat down next to him, Baldwin handed him the blunderbuss.

'That's an interesting piece of kit,' said Baldwin, 'not exactly regulation issue.'

'No, sir, O'Connell lent it to me. It's the sort of thing they carry on coaches in Ireland, he tells me.'

The skiff was now within half a mile of the *Harlech Castle* and as the moon appeared from behind a cloud she was suddenly illuminated, a pale, deathly white against the black shore. Wilkins glanced to his left, where the skiff carrying the men from the 58th was gliding smoothly across the water. In the moonlight, he could see the reassuringly bulky form of Captain Hibbert sitting calmly in the stern. Most of the men in the 58th's skiff had removed their shakos except for the man in the bows. He was leaning forward over the bow, where his outline beneath the distinctive cylindrical, peaked shako with its cockade picked out in the moonlight made him look like the boat's figurehead.

As the skiffs moved steadily closer to the *Harlech Castle*, Baldwin and Wilkins could see that her guns were still on board. Normally, a crew that found itself stranded on a hostile lee shore would make some attempt to throw the ship's cannon overboard to deny them to the enemy. They might also attempt to set fire to the ship. It was obvious to Baldwin and Wilkins, even at this distance, that the *Harlech Castle*'s crew had not attempted either course of action.

'They've left the bloody ship to the French, guns and all, by the look of it,' said Baldwin, glancing at Wilkins.

'What do you think we should do, sir?' asked Wilkins.

'Well,' Baldwin lowered his voice, 'I have orders not to put any lives at risk, but I can't help thinking that if we can do anything to save the ship from falling intact into enemy hands then we should attempt it. What do you think, Lieutenant?'

'I agree, sir. Once we get a bit closer, we should have a good idea whether there is anyone on board or not. And, in these skiffs, we can get away pretty quickly if need be.' Wilkins was suddenly excited at the prospect of action. Images of a swift, glorious success, spontaneous, brave and dashing, flashed through his head. Now *that* would stop the wagging tongues in the Citadel mess, putting an end for ever to any whispers, any doubts about his courage.

Baldwin turned to his left and signalled to Captain Hibbert in the stern of the other skiff to steer towards him. When the two boats were close enough that their oars were almost touching, Baldwin and Hibbert had a conversation in a loud stage whisper. As they talked, the water coursed with the current, rushing and gurgling against the oars and the wooden sides of the boats.

'William,' said Baldwin to Hibbert, 'I say we go closer in to see if there's any chance of landing a stroke. Wilkins here agrees.'

'Well, Michael,' replied Hibbert, 'it looks as if the crew scarpered at the first whiff of trouble, abandoning the ship, guns, cargo and all to the enemy. I think we're duty-bound to try something.'

'Good. I suggest we go ashore and board the ship from the beach. Let's make for the stern of the ship and beach there. Good luck.'

As the two skiffs pulled away, Baldwin passed instructions along the boat. The men in the bows loaded their muskets. As Fitt drew his cutlass, its long, curved blade glinted in the moonlight. The skiffs were gliding in towards the *Harlech Castle*, which was looming ever larger, massive and dark against the moonlit sea. All was quiet, serenely peaceful. The only sounds were the hollow creak of the oars in the rowlocks, the gentle whoosh of the blades pulling through the water and the more distant murmur of the sea on the shore.

By now the skiffs were within two hundred yards of the beached *Harlech Castle*. In the moonlight, Peter Wilkins could now make out the intricacies of the ship's rigging, the cannonades on her quarterdeck, the red ensign hanging limply from the flagstaff over her stern and the Union flag at her masthead. The ship's gun ports were closed, at least on the seaward side. The ship was dark; there were no lights showing on deck, her navigation lights had been doused, nor could Wilkins see any light emanating from the stern cabin windows or from the portholes in the fo'csle. There was no one on deck, no sign of movement. In the moonlight, she looked forlorn, abandoned. It reminded Wilkins momentarily of the moonlit ship of the dead in *The Rime of the Ancient Mariner* and Coleridge's description of the moonbeams as 'April hoar-frost', cold and scaly.

'She looks completely deserted, sir,' Wilkins whispered to Michael Baldwin.

'Yes, I think you might be right,' replied Baldwin.

The skiff was within a hundred yards of the ship now, with the beach just beyond her looming bulk.

'Get ready, men,' said Baldwin, 'we're nearly there now. When I give the word, disembark and get round to the landward side of the ship as quickly as you can. Sergeant Fitt will lead you ashore, Lieutenant Wilkins and I will be right with you.'

Wilkins could sense the men's nerves tightening as the skiff glided towards the stranded ship and the beach beyond. Where were the enemy? Where was the ship's crew? It all seemed very quiet. Wilkins's throat was dry and he noticed that his hands were shaking as they held the blunderbuss. The moon had come out from behind a cloud, illuminating the ship and the shore once again, deepening the shadows. He could see the rocks at the back of the narrow beach.

'I hope 'em bloody Frogs aren't waiting for us,' whispered the man in front of Baldwin to his neighbour.

'Shhhh,' hissed Baldwin. Up in the bows, Fitt picked up the painter, ready to jump out and pull the boat ashore. The skiff was turning round the stern of the *Harlech Castle*, about thirty yards from the ship, coming into the beach. The second skiff was a few yards behind and to starboard.

Then, suddenly, to their left, up on the stern of the *Harlech Castle*, there was the sound of movement, boots on wood, then an abrupt order followed almost at once by the thunderous crash of a volley of muskets. At such short range in the moonlight, even the little boats presented an excellent target. Some of the musket balls whined over the heads of the men in the skiff, some hit the water with a fizzing splash while one or two others clunked woodenly into the hull. Sergeant Fitt, in the bows, was hit several times and pitched forward into the water. Two of the soldiers manning the oars were hit; one slumped forward over his oar, killed instantly by a shot to the head; the other screamed as a bullet smashed his upper arm just below the shoulder.

'Jesus Christ,' exclaimed Baldwin. 'What the hell is going on? Look, boys, the beach.' He pointed to the beach where about twenty men were forming up in a rough line in front of the rocks. 'Fire!'

But as he spoke, there was a crash of musketry from the shore and the two skiffs were engulfed in a fizzing hail of bullets. Several more men were hit. Michael Hughes's tall figure was slumped over his oar. One man was moaning in agony, his elbow shattered; several others were also wounded.

'Quick, men, to the oars,' roared Baldwin. 'Pull.'

But it was too late. There was hardly a man in the skiff unwounded. Two volleys at close range had wreaked havoc. Baldwin himself had been hit, in the fleshy part of the thigh. He could feel the warm ooze of blood on his leg. He glanced across at the other skiff, which had drifted away towards the rocks to the right. From the dead bodies in the boat it looked as if the enemy's volleys had caused carnage among her crew, too.

By now the skiff was aground on the beach, confronted by a semicircle of French infantrymen, their muskets levelled at the men in the boat. An officer stepped forward, his sword drawn.

'*Qui est l'officier supérieur ici?*' he demanded.

Michael Baldwin stood up slowly and turned to face the Frenchman.

'I am,' he said calmly.

'*Il vous faut se rendre, monsieur.*'

'Yes, yes,' said Baldwin to the Frenchman. 'Wilkins. Wilkins?' There was no reply, so Baldwin looked behind him. There, slumped motionless in the stern of the skiff was Peter Wilkins, his head thrown back at an awkward angle. His hat was floating upside down on the water. A thin trail of blood ran down his cheek. In the side of his head was a neat bullet hole.

George Warne and Charles Parsons had enjoyed an excellent dinner. Their host had produced two chicken legs, a large handful of green beans, a flagon of red wine and two glasses. They had succeeded, with a good deal of juggling, in frying the chicken limbs and boiling the beans over the fire. Once they'd finished, they lay back on the stooks of corn, glasses in hand, watching the fire smoke curling up to the roof, talking, as the embers slowly died. They were both Herefordshire men so had some acquaintances and a deep love of the county in common. George was telling Charles the news of Harriet's recent engagement.

'He's a parson with a parish in Gloucestershire and he's ancient – even my mother says he's "of middling years".' George laughed.

'You shouldn't be too rude about clergymen, George,' said Parsons. 'After all, we're both sons of the cloth.'

'Yes, yes, I know, but Harriet was so lively, such a free spirit, you'd think she might have chosen a younger man.'

'Like you, you mean?' replied Parsons mischievously.

'Well, there was a time . . .' George's voice trailed off.

'I reckon you're better off with your Sicilian friend,' said Parsons. 'She has much to recommend her.'

'Might you marry her?'

'Well,' George replied, 'I confess that I have thought about it and I could certainly do a lot worse for myself.'

'But would she accept you?' asked Parsons with a grin.

'Who knows?' replied George. 'For all I know, she's got admirers all over Messina.'

'Ah, but you're different.'

'Umm,' grunted George.

As the wine went down the conversation turned to military gossip and then, at length, to memories of home, of the green fields, woods and rolling hills of Herefordshire, the repeating round of the seasons, all different, all beautiful, of the carefree days of their childhoods. It all seemed, at that moment, very far away. By and by, only a few embers remained of the fire and the wine was finished. George yawned.

'I'm going to sleep. We've got an early start tomorrow, Charles.' He reached for a blanket. 'Goodnight.'

'Goodnight.'

Michael Baldwin's left leg was painfully sore although, thankfully, the wound seemed to have stopped bleeding. Baldwin knew that it was not too serious, just a flesh wound. If the bullet had severed one of the main arteries in the thigh, or broken the bone, he would have lost a lot of blood and be very weak. He had seen too many thigh wounds prove fatal in the past.

It was now half an hour since he had surrendered to the supercilious French captain. With fifteen muskets trained on him and his men at point-blank range, he had had little alternative. Since then, he had been attending to his men. For such a brief engagement, Baldwin's detachment had suffered appalling casualties: of the eleven men, plus himself, Peter Wilkins and Sergeant Fitt, who had rowed out from Faro, only two had survived the French volleys unscathed.

Six of them were dead and a further six wounded, four of them gravely. To make matters worse, they had come out from Faro ill-equipped, without any medical supplies let alone a surgeon.

Private Burns had taken a shot to the abdomen and was now propped up against a rock, fading fast from loss of blood. He was groaning pitifully but there was little that could be done for the poor man. Nicholson's upper arm had been smashed by a shot from the first volley fired from the *Harlech Castle*; Baldwin had ripped off the man's tunic to bind the arm in an attempt to staunch the flow of blood. Private Harris had had his elbow badly damaged; now his forearm was hanging, useless. If he survived until they found a surgeon, it would have to be amputated. Gerry Byrne, a cousin of Dick Byrne who had been killed on George Warne's raid, had had a miraculous escape when a musket ball hit him in the chest, up towards the shoulder, but missed both heart and lungs. There was, Baldwin hoped, a good chance that he might survive his injury. The other wounded man, Holmes, had a slight wound in the fleshy part of the shoulder.

'I'm damn'd lucky, sir,' said Holmes with characteristic understatement, 'but it's still fuckin' sore.'

Michael Baldwin, now that the adrenalin of the moment had receded, felt overwhelmingly tired. He also felt shame, sorrow and guilt in equal measure. He had had explicit orders not to put the lives of his men at risk yet, in a gung-ho, foolhardy moment, he'd decided to ignore them, a decision which had cost six good men their lives and maimed several others. And for what? He looked at the six bodies laid out on the sand at the top of the beach. They were all, with the exception of Fitt, very young men with their whole lives ahead of them. To make matters worse, Burns had lapsed into unconsciousness a few minutes ago and would, no doubt, be joining the sad little line sooner rather than later.

His reflections were interrupted by the appearance at his elbow of William Hibbert. Baldwin looked at this friend. Half-naked, he was wearing only his breeches and had clearly been in the water.

'Good God, man, what's happened to you?' he asked.

'While you got beached, our boat was taken off by the current and got into the rocks down there,' he jerked his thumb over his right shoulder, 'and capsized. The waves were bashing us against the rocks. It was quite a struggle to get to the beach. Once we got onto the beach, we were set upon by some French soldiers who robbed us. They took my tunic and went through the pockets and demanded my boots – and did the same to the men.'

'How disgraceful,' said Baldwin. 'Bloody Frogs. Where was their officer?'

'He appeared after a short while and order was restored, but as you can see,' he laughed, 'I haven't got my kit back yet.'

At that moment, the French captain to whom Baldwin had surrendered came up to the two British officers and saluted.

'*J'ai trouvé une chaumière ou vous pouvez passer la nuit, vous et vos soldats ensemble. Allez.*'

Baldwin and Hibbert gathered up their remaining men and followed the Frenchman up the beach and along a rough track. The small, bedraggled column of men made a sorry sight as it wound its way up the beach.

'We'll come back in the morning to bury the dead,' said Baldwin quietly.

CHAPTER TWELVE

Messina, 16th September 1810

It was first light when Warne awoke. The gaps in the roof left by the slipped tiles stood out against the lightening sky. It was time to get going.

'Morning, Charles,' he called. Parsons's prostrate form shifted slightly and groaned. 'Shake a leg.'

Half an hour later, the two men were climbing steadily up the hill behind the barn where they had spent the night. They were carrying their guns; each had a bag containing powder, shot, wadding and spare flints hanging from his shoulder. George was carrying the game bag. This part of Sicily, Messina's hinterland, was wild, rugged, mountainous country, the lower reaches of Mount Pelorus. Tiny villages cowered in the steep-sided valleys or clung to the ridges; deep ravines gouged through the landscape. At this time of the year, the countryside was parched after the long, hot Sicilian summer. What grass there was covering the thin, stony soil had been scorched brown by the sun. Apart from the olive groves around the villages, there were very few trees; here the prickly pear was king.

After a while, the two men came to a plateau where the ground was flatter, slightly bowled. Here, thanks to an underground spring, the vegetation was thicker, lusher and greener: a clump of broom, bushes of myrtle and oleander and an ancient fig tree laden with fruit. It was here that they hoped to find some game, quail, partridge or maybe even the odd hare.

'Let's start at the far end,' said George quietly, pointing to his left, 'and walk through. If there are any birds in here, we'll have some chance of putting them up.'

'Good idea,' said Parsons. 'It's a pity we haven't got Boney or either of those dogs I used to have. Still, we'll do what we can.'

They loaded their guns, carefully measuring out the powder for each barrel and pouring in the shot before pushing the wadding home with the ramrod. Once in position, about ten yards apart, the two men started to walk slowly up the plateau, their guns cocked and at the ready, Parsons making loud clucking noises as they went. They had gone about thirty yards when there was a sudden flurry of flapping wings, virtually under George's feet, as a small covey of partridge, sitting tight until the last minute, got up, shrieking with alarmed surprise.

George raised his gun into his shoulder and, picking out one of the birds, squeezed the trigger. The pan flashed and then, a split second later, the gun fired.

'Bugger, missed,' George swore aloud as the powder smoke enveloped him. He would have liked to have fired the second barrel but the smoke from the first shot often made it difficult to aim a second. By the time the smoke had dispersed, the covey was out of range.

Parsons waited a second or two longer before firing, bringing down one bird.

'Good shot, Charles,' said George as the rest of the covey glided to ground, seventy yards ahead of them. Parsons walked over and, picking the plump, warm bird up from the tufty grass, handed it to George.

'First blood to you,' said George with a grin.

'Let's reload and see if we can catch up with them,' said Parsons.

Michael Baldwin's wounded leg throbbed painfully. After a night on the damp floor of the cottage he was stiff and cold. The pitiful groans of the wounded men had continued all night, turning the cramped, claustrophobic cottage into a foetid chamber of horrors. It reeked of blood, pain and impending death. The French military surgeon – a short, swarthy man with, Baldwin had noticed, dirty fingernails – had done what he could to treat the wounded men, but their agonised distress was heart-wrenching. Poor Burns had died before they had left the beach. Perhaps, thought Baldwin, he was the lucky one; at least he had been spared the protracted agony.

Harris, with his badly wounded elbow, had whimpered piteously for several hours before lapsing into a coma, poor man. Nicholson, his upper arm smashed by a musket ball, was still conscious but now very weak from loss of blood. Gerry Byrne, wounded in the chest, was in pain but otherwise cheerful. Holmes had suffered a flesh wound in the shoulder. They all urgently needed proper medical assistance. The French officer in charge had announced late the previous evening that Baldwin, Hibbert and their men, wounded and unwounded, would be returned to Messina in the morning under a flag of truce. We do not, he said, have the medical facilities here to treat the wounded men.

William Hibbert returned to the beach to relieve the sentries posted to prevent the foxes attacking the bodies of the casualties left out overnight. The three soldiers had made a hollow in the sand in which they had lit a driftwood fire.

'Good morning, Jenkins,' said Hibbert to the soldier who was poking the fire with a stick. The other two men were asleep, wrapped in their cloaks, in the shelter of the dunes. 'Any trouble?'

'No, sir, none that I know of. And the, eh, the lads,' he pointed at the sad row of corpses lying at the top of the beach, 'are fine.' At the left-hand end of the row, as if in command of this detachment of the dead, was the body of Peter Wilkins. His face was the colour of pale candle wax, his eyes closed, but he looked serenely peaceful.

'We're being returned to Sicily under a flag of truce this morning, so we'll take the dead with us for a proper burial in Messina,' said Hibbert. 'The bodies must be wrapped for the crossing.'

By the time George and Charles had finished walking the plateau and had repeated the process in the reverse direction, they had shot three partridge, George's one to Charles's two. George's bird had, if the truth be known, been rather a fluke. They then decided to continue up the mountain to a ravine they knew. Like the plateau they had just shot, they hoped that the lusher vegetation in the bottom of the ravine would be alive with game. Certainly, it had been on various occasions in the past. Once they reached the lower end of the ravine, the two men spread out, loaded and cocked their guns and began walking slowly uphill.

'Absolutely nothing,' said George, turning to sit on a flat rock. It had taken about ten minutes to reach the top of the ravine, but they had not seen a single bird. 'Not even a sparrow.' He gently pushed his gun's hammers forward, uncocking it.

'Look, there's a hare,' said Parsons, who was still standing up. The hare, alarmed, was bouncing away down the slope through the long, yellow grass. Parsons swung to his left, bringing his gun into his shoulder and firing in one, smooth movement. The sound of the shot rebounded percussively off the steep, rocky sides of the ravine as the smoke eddied around Parsons.

'Missed, damn it.'

Eighty yards away, George could still just see the hare. He – for he was a fine buck – had stopped and was sitting up alertly, ears pricked, looking warily round. Parsons leant his gun against the rock and sat down next to George. From the top of the ravine the two men had a magnificent view across the valley to the ridge opposite, beyond which the hills started to fall away down to the coast. The folds of the ridges were picked out in the morning sun; lower down, the deep valleys were still in shade. They sat in companionable silence for a few minutes, gazing at the view. Eventually, George spoke.

'Charles, what happened between Frank Younge and young Peter Wilkins? I've been a bit out of things lately so when Colonel Airey asked me about it two days ago I couldn't really help him.'

'Well,' began Parsons slowly, rubbing his stubbly chin, 'I'd been having dinner in the mess at the Citadel with Wilkins and

Alexander Hay of the 31st. We'd had a fair amount to drink, certainly, but nothing excessive. There had been some gentle banter about Wilkins and Miss Thring, and we'd drunk a couple of toasts. It was all very good-humoured, as far as I remember.' He paused, flexing his fingers together.

'The trouble started when Frank Younge came past our table on his way out of the mess. I did, I'm afraid to say, make a remark about Miss Thring as Younge was passing, which he overheard, something about him and Wilkins being rivals for her affections, but nothing provocative. There were three others who'd been having dinner with Younge, all naval officers David Plumb, Ned Huxtable and young Davidson. Plumb and Younge both looked a bit tight, but it was still all very friendly at this point.'

'So what happened?' asked George.

'I don't really know,' replied Parsons. 'A row just blew up from nowhere. It all happened so quickly. Suddenly, Plumb and I were trying to calm things down and others were turning to see what was going on. Then, before we knew it, Younge had in as many words accused Wilkins of cowardice and, as you know, there's no going back from there.'

'God,' said George. 'It's so easy to get into trouble, isn't it?' He lobbed a pebble into the air, catching it in his other hand.

'Yes, it is,' replied Parsons. 'Wilkins asked me to stand as his second and I agreed – rather against my better judgement, I have to say – I suppose, because I'd seen what happened and I like him and felt sorry for him being confronted by a man like Younge, who's older, knows the ropes and can be a bit wild. I didn't get the impression he relished the prospect of fighting a duel. Who would?'

'Very noble of you, Charles,' said George, turning to his friend with a grin. 'I hope I'd have done the same.'

'Well, in the end, thanks to Plumb's good sense, we managed to avert disaster.'

'Thank the Lord. That's what seconds are for. Let's hope that young Wilkins learns his lesson and, who knows, perhaps Frank Younge might be less touchy in future.'

'There's always the hope,' said Parsons. 'I'm glad that Wilkins has a second chance. He's a nice young fellow and I think could grow into a good, thoughtful officer, just what the regiment needs. Come on, let's get back.'

Sandro Carboni was late for Mass. The single bell, summoning latecomers, had stopped striking; the service was now starting. He hurried past the grand marble gates of San Francesco di Paola and on towards the church.

The main door of the church had been closed, so Carboni, who was a tall man, ducked in through the wicket gate. Inside, the church was cool and dark, sweetly spiced with incense and half-lit by shafts of sunlight slanting through the clerestory windows. The large congregation stood in respectful, expectant silence as the swelling sound of the choir began to fill the nave. At the east end, in front of the altar, the priest, resplendent in his robes, turned to face his flock. Carboni bowed his head and crossed himself.

Turning to his right, Carboni walked past a monument of a warrior reclining on his sarcophagus. He had been coming to this church since he was a boy and had always been fascinated by this statue. He wondered occasionally whether it had subliminally encouraged him to join the army. As he passed it, he ran his hand along the warrior's cold, marble arm before slipping into a pew towards the back of the nave. He knelt down to say a prayer.

Once he had finished, he sat up and looked around. The body of the church was divided into three parts by two rows of massive Doric columns of black Sicilian basalt. High above him, in the penumbra, was the panelled, carved wooden roof. He loved this church, it reminded him of his parents and the seemingly interminable services he had sat through as a boy. Despite those memories, Carboni was a devout man; he derived great comfort from the unchanging ritual, moving music and eternal certainties of the Church. Carboni had a powerfully theatrical imagination to which the carefully choreographed rituals of the Mass appealed strongly. As the service proceeded, its rites, the ringing Latin phrases, the choral flourishes, the chanting of the priests, all so familiar to Carboni, lapped over him, washing away the anxieties of his everyday existence.

Carboni attended Mass at San Francesco di Paola every Sunday, missing a service only rarely. As well as being a devout Catholic he was deeply attached to the church and monastery of San Francesco itself, giving generously to support its monks and its charitable works. This was why he had been so disturbed by what Colonel Airey had told him on Friday. The colonel and young Captain Warne told Carboni of their suspicions that the monastery was being used as the base for an anti-British conspiracy. They told Carboni about Armand Jardel, the French intelligence officer, about Fabrizio Falcone and about the meeting at the monastery. They revealed their fears that the plans for the attacks across the straits the previous week had been betrayed to the enemy.

He had left Airey's office in the Citadel in a state of mental turmoil and had spent much of the subsequent thirty-six hours trying to make sense of the colonel's revelations. Carboni was a bachelor and something of a loner – characteristics which perhaps suited him to his job – so had ample time to ponder what the colonel had told him. He had spent much of Saturday walking the streets of Messina, deep in thought.

Why would the monks allow their monastery to be used for this subversive purpose, if indeed that was what was happening? Surely, they could not be plotting against the British – or allowing such a plot to take shape under their roof? Everyone knew the strength of anticlerical feeling in the French army; the monks of San Francesco could expect little sympathy from invading French soldiers. The secularism of the Revolution ran deep. They would, in all probability, be turfed out of their monastery, deprived of their lands and endowments and left to fend for themselves on the streets. To a devout Catholic like Carboni, this was a distressing thought.

It was possible that the plot – if plot there was – was aimed at getting rid of the godless, Protestant British and restoring Sicily's rightful rulers, King Ferdinand and his Queen, Maria Carolina, to their full inheritance, which included, of course, the mainland portion of their kingdom, now ruled by Murat. Perhaps the monks had been persuaded that this was a just cause, an opportunity to strike a blow for the true Mother Church. Was it possible that the monks were being hoodwinked, that the monastery was being used by the conspirators without them being aware of what was going on? That they had been given some innocent explanation of the comings and goings? Yes, Carboni admitted to himself, that was *possible* but the monks, although almost by definition otherworldly, were neither stupid nor unobservant. They would soon realise if something untoward was going on in their midst.

Airey, knowing that Carboni regularly attended Mass at San Francesco, had suggested that he go to the service that Sunday and keep his eyes open. To Carboni the notion that he should in any way be spying upon the monks was distasteful, but he squared his conscience by reminding himself of the trouble into which the monks could, perhaps unwittingly, be getting themselves.

Mass was now coming to an end. The choir had processed out, followed by the altar boys, two of whom were vigorously swinging censers, trailing fragrant clouds of incense as they made their way down the nave. Behind them came the clergy, sedate and dignified. Once the procession had departed, there was a general stirring as the congregation started to file out of the pews into the aisles. Carboni stood up – being right at the back, he was in a pew on his own – and looked around him. Many of the faces were, of course, well known to him. He nodded a greeting to some old family friends in the aisle. He smiled at a childhood friend, now married with an ever-growing family. And over there, bent with age, were two of his parents' dearest friends. It was a familiar scene, and a comforting one.

As he watched his parents' old friends hobble slowly down the aisle, arm in arm, he noticed another, unexpected face in the crowd. It was Finbarr Rogers, the chief clerk from the Citadel, who sat, unmoving and all-seeing, outside Colonel Airey's office. He knew that Rogers was Irish and might therefore very well be Catholic but had never previously seen him at a service here. He had heard the rumours about Rogers' unorthodox – some might say licentious, thought Carboni – domestic arrangements but didn't know where Rogers lived or where he usually worshipped, even assuming he was a regular churchgoer. Why was he now attending a service here, all of a sudden? There was no particular reason to come to San Francesco today; it was neither an important saint's day nor some other red-letter day.

While the congregation filed out of the church, Carboni stood against one of the great basalt columns at the west end of the nave. He hoped it might look to a casual observer as if he was waiting for a friend. Rogers seemed to be on his own. Then a verger emerged from a side door in the aisle. He and Rogers exchanged a few words before going back through the door together and closing it behind them.

'Go easy there, they're not sacks of potatoes.'

Michael Baldwin was supervising the unloading on the quayside in Messina harbour of the bodies of the men killed in the attack on the *Harlech Castle*. Nicholson and Harris had both died during the morning, adding to the toll. Of the twelve men who embarked with Baldwin and Wilkins at Faro the previous evening, nine were now dead, their bodies wrapped in shrouds. The three wounded men stood some chance of survival but now faced the agonising prospect of treatment at the hands of the army surgeons. Only two men, Michael Fitzgerald – who had also survived George Warne's attack at Reggio – and Patrick Deary, had come through unscathed. The men of the 58th in Hibbert's skiff had suffered less badly but nonetheless four had been killed and several more wounded. Hibbert himself was unharmed.

It had taken the French the whole morning to organise a

suitable vessel to take the little group of British soldiers back to Messina. Eventually, at around midday, a ship hove to near the *Harlech Castle* and the shrouded corpses, the wounded men and the survivors were rowed out to her as she rode at anchor in the swirling current. At her masthead, fluttering in the breeze above the French tricolour was a plain white flag. The short passage back across the straits to Messina plunged Michael Baldwin, not generally a man given to introspection, into deep melancholy.

He stood alone at the stern rail, staring blankly at the Calabrian shore as the ship forged towards Sicily. Why had he disobeyed his orders – and, God knows, they had been specific enough – not to put the lives of his men at risk? A rush of blood to the head? Perhaps. The accumulated frustration of months, years even, of watching from across the straits as the French went about their business with impunity? Probably. The simple impulse to do something, anything, to rescue the *Harlech Castle* or deny her to the enemy? Almost certainly. It was little comfort to remember that both Wilkins and Hibbert had unequivocally supported his plan.

As a result of his recklessness and flagrant disobedience to orders, eight good men were now dead, wrapped in shrouds, lying on the deck. Three of them were married, Baldwin knew, which condemned three young women to early widowhood and made an unknown number of children fatherless. At least some of the others almost certainly had dependents too: aged parents, women and children, now suddenly cast adrift in an unfriendly world.

All eight of them had been solid, reliable men. They had their occasional lapses, a drunken spree in the taverns of Messina, throwing the odd punch and, when temptation became too much, a spot of petty larceny but basically they were as good a group of men as any officer could want. They were brave and unquestioningly loyal. Baldwin felt terrible about Fitt, too. He was too good, too valuable, to be thrown away in a futile action.

And then there was young Peter Wilkins. He had wholeheartedly endorsed, or so it had seemed at the time, Baldwin's reckless plan of attack. But given his youth and inexperience, Wilkins could scarcely have been expected to raise a note of caution against his superior's plan. A promising career that had barely begun had been cut short. His parents would be distraught; that he was not married was small consolation. And, to cap it all, he would soon be summoned by the colonel to explain why, precisely, he had felt at liberty to disobey express orders in launching an attack on the *Harlech Castle*. His hot-headed action last night could well permanently blight his career.

His gloomy reverie interrupted by the captain shouting orders in French, he buttoned up his coat and turned away from the stern rail. They were approaching Messina.

It was mid afternoon by the time Warne and Parsons walked in through the Citadel's great gate and, dismounting, handed their horses to a waiting groom. George felt grimy after two days out in the mountains and a night in a barn. He intended to report to Colonel Airey before going home to Carlotta's – odd, he realised, that he now thought of her apartment as home – for a bath and dinner. The Citadel was quiet, enjoying its day of rest. The armourer's workshop was closed and the farrier's forge idle, but high on the ramparts the sentries patrolled their sections, pacing and turning metronomically. That, at least, never ceased.

'That was great fun, Charles,' said George. 'I hope you enjoyed it, too.'

'Yes, I did. I'll hang the birds,' Parsons replied, raising the game bag, 'and we'll have them for dinner in a few days' time. See you next week.' He wandered off across the courtyard, his gun case tucked under his arm, his hat at a jaunty angle.

As George stepped in through the door of the staff headquarters building the two sentries snapped to attention. He walked over the stone-slabbed floor to the clerks' desks. Mr Rogers was not in today, the junior duty clerk informed him. George imagined Rogers surrounded by the brood of children he was widely rumoured to have fathered with his Messinese mistress, very much the family man. Somehow, it was difficult to reconcile that image with the hard-working, taciturn bureaucrat who sat for twelve hours a day, six days a week toiling away at his returns and his ledgers. The junior clerk was a younger, English version of Rogers, pale, bespectacled and slightly stooped.

'Is Colonel Airey in, Allsop?' asked George.

'I'm afraid to say that he's not, sir. He was here earlier but left not long after noon.' William Allsop had a London accent with a nasal twang.

'Thank you, Allsop,' said George, turning towards the door.

'Captain Warne.' George looked round. There, standing in a door behind Allsop, was the Quartermaster-General, Colonel Donkin. 'Do you have a moment?'

'Yes, sir, of course, by all means,' said George, hoping he didn't sound too flustered by the sudden appearance of one of the most important British officers in Messina.

'Good. Come in, then.' Donkin led the way into his office and closed the door.

'Please take a seat, Captain Warne,' said Donkin. His high, reedy voice seemed, George thought, in keeping with his slight figure; a *basso profundo* voice in such a man would be incongruous. George sat down on the hard upright chair that faced the desk.

'Captain Warne,' Donkin began, 'I am interested in what Colonel Airey had to say yesterday about a conspiracy against us here in Messina. As I gather that you have uncovered some of the evidence for this conspiracy, seeing you here, I thought I would ask you about it. Get it from the horse's mouth, so to speak.'

'I'll do what I can to help, sir.'

'Good.' Donkin sat down at his desk, lowering himself precisely into the crimson cushion on his chair. 'So tell me about this lawyer fellow, Signor, er,' he looked at the papers on his desk, 'Falcone.'

George collected himself before launching into the story. He told Donkin about his surveillance of Falcone's office, about the discovery of the gold *napoleons* (glossing over the exact circumstances of the find and the precise number taken), about the meeting between Falcone and the French intelligence officer, about the attack on him in the street, and about the strange goings-on in the grounds of San Francesco di Paola. Once he had finished, Donkin sat in silence, staring at the ceiling, deep in thought.

'But, Captain Warne, what do *you* think this all means?'

'It strongly suggests to me that Falcone is up to something. I am also convinced, as Colonel Airey has explained, that last week's raids across the straits were betrayed. What we are missing is evidence connecting the two, linking Falcone to the betrayal of the plans for the raids. It's hard to see that the plans could have been betrayed without some inside help.'

Donkin raised an eyebrow.

'You mean, by someone here, on the Citadel staff?'

'Yes, sir. I know it's a very serious allegation but, as I said, it's hard to see how the plans could have been betrayed without some inside assistance. The question is, who is it?'

'Indeed.' Donkin paused, shuffling the papers on his desk into a neat pile. 'So how do you suggest we find the traitor in our midst?'

'All we can do, sir, is keep watching and listening in the hope that he – or they – give themselves away.'

'Yes,' replied Donkin, ruminatively. 'Yes.' He stroked his chin. 'Tell me about Signora Fanelli, Captain Warne,' said Donkin, breaking the silence.

'What would you like to know about her, sir?' replied George, jolted by this change of tack.

'I don't give a damn what you get up to behind closed doors, that's your business and good luck to you. You're a grown man and you're not married. But it is my business to make sure that British officers, especially ones privy to important intelligence, do not pose a risk to our security here. What I'm asking you is, is she reliable?'

'Well, sir,' said George, 'I've known her for more than two years now and I'd say she's completely reliable. Her late husband was an officer in the Sicilian service who was very much on our side. I've no reason to think that Carlotta – Signora Fanelli,' George corrected himself hurriedly, 'isn't too. People like her have little to gain and much to lose from the French, especially now that, because of me, she's known to favour us.' Donkin nodded.

'Yes, I can see that.'

'Added to which, sir, she comes from a prominent family here, one with a certain amount of influence, and knows a lot of people. She could be useful to us.' George did not tell the Quartermaster-General that Carlotta had already been making enquiries on his behalf. 'And she's taught me the local dialect.'

'I've no doubt of that, Captain Warne,' said Donkin with a smile.

Airey had assured the meeting yesterday that Warne was reliable. Now, having listened to him make his case, Donkin agreed. This was a man who was level-headed, one who could be trusted.

That was the end of the interview and a minute later George was out in the bright, sunlit courtyard.

'Ah, George, good afternoon,' boomed a familiar voice. 'What a pleasant surprise!'

George looked to his left to see Michael Baldwin hobbling heavily on a stick towards him across the courtyard. He was out of uniform, wearing a charcoal-grey coat, dark breeches and white silk stockings. Against the sober subfusc of his clothes his shock of ginger hair stood out all the more prominently.

'Good God,' said George, walking towards Baldwin, 'what on earth have you been up to?'

'Haven't you heard the news?' asked Baldwin.

'No,' said George. 'Parsons and I have been shooting up in the mountains.'

'Oh, I see. Well, yesterday one of our transports, the *Harlech Castle*, got into trouble near Scylla and was taken by the French.

Hibbert and I, thinking we might be able to rescue her or, failing that, destroy her took a couple of skiffs across the straits last night. Unfortunately, we ran into a spot of bother.'

'What happened?'

'It turned out that the Frogs were on *Harlech* waiting for us, which, of course, in the dark, we couldn't see. As we were coming in towards the ship they opened fire. We didn't stand much of a chance.' Baldwin winced at the memory. 'I lost eight men, including Fitt.'

'Oh God,' said George. 'Fitt was an excellent soldier and a good man.'

'I am sorry to say that Peter Wilkins was killed, too.'

'Bloody hell. How?'

'A bullet in the head. I don't think he knew much about it, thank the Lord.'

The two men stood in silence, heads hung. From the ramparts above, they could hear the grating of nailed boots on stone as a sentry turned at the end of his beat.

'It seems unkind that he should be killed so soon after avoiding a duel, don't you think?' said Baldwin.

'Yes,' said George, 'it does, but I wonder whether the two might be connected?'

'Do you think so?' asked Baldwin.

'Stranger things have happened,' said George.

'Well, come to think of it, he did seem very keen to attack the *Harlech*. Perhaps there was more to it than I realised.'

'Maybe, but we'll never know. More to the point,' said George, brightening up, 'what happened to you?' He looked at Baldwin's left leg.

'I got one in the thigh,' he replied, rubbing his leg tenderly. 'I was bloody lucky. The ball went straight through, missing the bone and the main arteries. It's damn'd sore but the surgeon told me it'll heal well. I won't be out of action for long.'

'Well, at least there is some good news,' said George, clapping Baldwin on the shoulder.

'Mind you,' said Baldwin, 'Murat's ruined a perfectly decent pair of my breeches.'

'Send him the bill,' said George, laughing, 'he might buy you a new pair. It's the least he can do and I'm sure he can afford it.'

The church of San Francesco di Paola was now almost deserted. The vergers had finished snuffing out the candles. The congregation had departed; most of them were on their way home, but a few remained, in small knots, talking quietly outside the great door. Sandro Carboni had sat down in a pew but now, in the empty church, there was too great a risk that Rogers, should he re-emerge through the door, would see him. If the Irishman caught sight of Carboni, he would certainly recognise him: they had met too often for there to be any possibility of a mistake. He needed to conceal himself.

Leaving the church, he walked towards the road, where there was a row of tall, obelisk-like cypress trees along the edge of the monastery grounds. Leaning against the trunk of one of the cypress trees, Carboni had a good view of the doors of the church and the churchyard to his right and much of the sweep of the monastery's gardens ahead and to his left. He was partially concealed by the shade and the dark hues of the tree's trunk and foliage. It was not perfect but might protect him from a casual glance. As he stood close into the trunk, he caught the tree's fresh, resinous smell.

To his right, there was no longer anyone standing outside the church. Two vergers were closing the great west doors. In the garden, two monks were strolling side by side, deep in conversation, one of them fiddling the beads of a rosary as he walked. It was a peaceful scene. Treachery and conspiracy seemed far away.

His thoughts turned to Finbarr Rogers. What was he doing here at San Francesco? Of course, it was possible that he was, quite innocently, attending Mass. The fact that Carboni had never previously seen him here was strange but not everyone worshipped at the same church all the time. On the other hand, the fact that he had slipped off behind the scenes after the service suggested that he had some other business here than simply purging his soul. Could it be that Rogers was in some way implicated in the conspiracy that the British suspected centred on the monastery? But why would Rogers risk exposure, humiliation and incarceration – or worse, the destruction of everything he'd worked for? It was hard to believe that Rogers would conspire with the French but anything was possible, Carboni acknowledged wearily. A decade and more of intelligence work had taught him that, if nothing else. He ran his finger across his forehead, wiping away a filmy slick of sweat.

Emma Thring was sitting in the salon of her brother's lodgings, sipping tea and reading. It was now early evening; outside the tall, half-open window, the day was beginning to fade away. In the street below people hurried to vespers or strolled the streets, arm in arm, greeting friends. Emma was engrossed in Patrick Brydone's *A Tour through Sicily and Malta*, which she had been given by her father before she left home.

She had read the book during the voyage from England but was now rereading the sections covering Taormina and Etna. Brydone's account of his climb up the volcano contained some of the most memorable passages in the entire book. She and Robert had put the finishing touches to their plans for a trip to Taormina, although, rather to her disappointment, Robert would not even consider taking her up Etna. 'What,' he had asked, 'would Mama say, if she discovered I'd allowed you to climb an active volcano?' 'She might erupt,' Emma had replied.

Nevertheless, she was looking forward to the expedition. She had enjoyed the sights of Messina and the pretty villages up the coast towards Faro – even the occasion on which they had come under enemy fire had now been dressed up into an anecdote and would no doubt, in time, be embroidered into a full-blown traveller's tale – but she was eager to move on. It would also be a relief to escape the close-knit British community in Messina for a week or so. Although the gossip about the aborted duel between Frank Younge and Peter Wilkins had subsided, Emma was aware that people still looked at her differently – and not wholly favourably – as a result of the rumours. No, a few days away would do her a power of good.

At that moment, the door opened and Robert Thring came striding in, tossing his hat down on a chair as he crossed the room.

'Good news and bad news from the Citadel, I'm afraid, my dear,' he said. 'Is there any tea left?'

'Yes,' said Emma, picking up the silver teapot. 'What's the good news?'

'The colonel has just told me I can have a week's leave starting on Friday.'

'Oh, Robert,' cried Emma excitedly, standing up and holding her brother's hands in hers. 'That's wonderful. It means we can be off earlier than we'd hoped. I'm so excited.'

'The colonel said that I could be spared for a week as it's now unlikely that the French will attempt an invasion this year. In a few days we'll be wandering among the Greek ruins like proper English milords.' He laughed before taking a sip of tea.

'And what,' asked Emma, after a slight pause, 'is the bad news?'

Robert's expression clouded. 'I'm afraid to have to tell you that Lieutenant Wilkins has been killed.'

'How . . . did it happen?'

'He took part in an operation last night to rescue one of our ships, which had run aground at Scylla. It seems that the enemy was waiting for them. They fired several volleys at close range. We lost, I am sad to say, at least a dozen men and several more wounded. If it's any consolation, Wilkins was shot in the head and would have died more or less instantly. He wouldn't have known anything about it.'

'How awful,' said Emma. 'The poor man. He was so young, so sweet, so kind. That wretched business with Mr Younge is behind it, I am sure.' She paused, gazing out the window. 'I blame myself for causing the argument and driving him to his death.'

'Emma, my dear, please don't blame yourself. It's not your fault. Wilkins took part in a military operation that went wrong. He was simply doing his duty. What could you have done to prevent that? Nothing. Nothing at all.'

Sandro Carboni climbed the tight, stone spiral staircase to the narrow landing at the top, where he knocked on the door.

'Come in,' said an English voice from inside. He opened the door and went in. There, seated at a table, was George Airey, reading. Beside him was a decanter of wine. The room was dark apart from the yellow light cast by the candles on the table, which formed a luminous tent around Airey.

'Good evening, Colonel Airey,' said Carboni. Despite the fact that he had worked closely with Airey for nearly three years, Carboni was unable to address him as anything but 'Colonel Airey'. Anything less formal would have been anathema to Carboni. That Airey might have a Christian name was unthinkable. 'I do hope I am not disturbing you.'

'No, no, of course not, Signor Carboni. I was just reading some frivolous book.' He closed the small leather-bound volume and put it down. He had grown accustomed to Carboni's late-night visits. 'And what, dear Colonel, can I do for you?'

Carboni sat down, waved away the proffered glass of wine and began telling Airey what he had witnessed at San Francesco di Paola earlier in the day. Airey listened intently, gazing into the gloom. After a while, he interrupted Carboni's flow.

'You're sure it was Rogers, our chief clerk? Absolutely sure?'

'Yes,' replied Carboni, 'definitely. There can be no doubt it was him. Don't forget how often I've seen him here in the Citadel.'

'Yes, indeed. Sorry to interrupt. Do please carry on.'

'Well,' continued Carboni, 'after about two hours' – he

pronounced it 'ow-errs' – 'so at about three o'clock, Mr Rogers came out into the garden with a monk. They walked together in the garden for perhaps twenty minutes, talking. Rogers seemed at ease. He wasn't looking around. Then they both disappeared back inside and, about five minutes later, Rogers came out of the front door of the monastery.'

'Which is not the same as the big west door of the church?'

'No,' replied Carboni. 'It's to the right of it. I had to hide properly, but I could just see Rogers leaving the monastery through the gates and turning onto the road back to the city.'

'Was he carrying anything?'

'Not that I could see but he could have had something small, documents, money, concealed under his clothes.'

'And he didn't see you?'

'No, he didn't.'

Both men fell silent. Airey refilled his glass of wine and sat back in his chair. Carboni stood up and paced slowly across the room to the window. Airey's quarters were on the second floor, immediately under the ramparts, overlooking the Citadel's central courtyard. He stood at the open window, looking out.

'Do you think,' Airey said at length, 'this means that Rogers is conspiring with the enemy?'

'I don't know.' Carboni paused. 'But I do think that we should definitely keep an eye on your Mr Rogers.'

'I agree.'

Once Carboni had left, Airey stood at the open window, gazing blankly out, wrapped in thought. Could Rogers be a traitor? Could he be plotting with the French? Did he betray the plans for the attacks on the anchorages to the enemy? He certainly had access to the information, so he could have done. But why, oh why, would he do that? Rogers seemed so loyal, so reliable. Perhaps we have all misjudged him. Perhaps he is a traitor, a man with a powerful, well-concealed grievance, a grievance against God knows what, against King, against Country, against the Church, against the army, the list could be bloody endless. Or maybe it was more mundane. Perhaps Rogers was simply passing intelligence to the enemy for money. His wife, mistress, whatever she was, and family were costing him a lot more than he earned as a clerk, so he was obliged to make up the difference in any way he could. No doubt treachery pays handsomely, thought Airey ruefully. He yawned. It was time for bed.

CHAPTER THIRTEEN

Messina, 17th September 1810

Commander David Plumb was a happy man. He was standing on the quarterdeck of the *Sprite* watching as a party of men scrubbed the main deck. Two head pumps rigged over the side into the harbour were sending streams of water splashing across the decks while the sailors, their trousers rolled up to the knee, methodically scrubbed the planks. In truth, Plumb knew, it was hardly necessary as the decks had been scoured clean the previous day using a holystone, but scrubbing decks was an indivisible element of the navy's soul, part of the discipline of life aboard ship.

He found the navy's routines comforting; they demonstrated morale and efficiency in the ship's company, and the pride it took in the ship. But the main reason for his good humour was that the previous evening he had, at long last, received his sailing orders: *Sprite* was to leave Messina this morning. Plumb was looking forward to being at sea again; it brought him fully to life: every sense was tuned to the slightest change of wind, of weather, of current. Everything that happened in the ship was his responsibility: its discipline, its efficiency as a sailing and fighting unit and the well-being of the men. It all reflected on him, for better or for worse.

Periods in port were, of course, unavoidable and often enjoyable. They enabled ships to take on fresh water and revictual. It also gave the crew an opportunity to clean the ship and repair any damage suffered at sea. After a week in port, *Sprite*'s brass work was buffed to a lustrous shine, the guns had been blacked and her sides freshly painted. Sutcliffe, the bo'sun, had worked ceaselessly to repair the rigging; on a three-masted sailing vessel such as *Sprite*, there was an enormous length of cordage to be kept in working trim. Likewise, the carpenter and the sailmaker had been busy since the ship had arrived in Messina. *Sprite* was now ready for whatever the Mediterranean autumn might throw at her.

Similarly, a week in harbour allowed the men to go ashore – not always an unmixed blessing as the ship's disciplinary log recorded – to do what sailors do when in port. Plumb himself had had an enjoyable week. He had seen some friends, been to the opera, dined in the mess at the Citadel, attended a reception given by the commodore, given a couple of dinners aboard and enjoyed a day's shooting in the hills.

Less enjoyable, he reflected as he watched the sailors manning the head pumps hauling the hoses out of the water, was the spat between Frank Younge and young Wilkins. Thank God he'd found a compromise that allowed both parties to walk away with their honour intact and their careers unblemished. He had known Frank Younge for a good while and was fond of him, but he could be hot-headed on occasions. Nor did his penchant for the drink help. Whatever the rights and wrongs of the contretemps with Wilkins, there was no doubt in his mind that it was Younge's fault.

As the scrubbing party finished, the bo'sun was piping all hands to breakfast. It was now half past seven and Plumb himself was feeling peckish. Protheroe would have his breakfast ready in his cabin. Plumb went below.

The King of the Two Sicilies was sitting, impatiently still, swathed in a purple silk dressing gown, while his batman shaved him. Joachim Murat was in a foul temper. Yet another week had passed without the planned invasion of Sicily going ahead. It was a week since a detachment of his personal guard had crossed the straits and taken a British fort, tying up the garrison and running up the tricolour before returning to the mainland. The operation had been designed to demonstrate to General Grenier, the senior French commander in Calabria, that an invasion could succeed, despite the British defences. Moreover, as it was already the middle of September, time was now running out to launch an invasion before the autumn storms brought the campaigning season to a close. At most, there were two or three weeks left in which an invasion could be launched this year.

The main cause of Murat's exasperation was the Emperor's order that no attempt should be made to invade Sicily unless success could be guaranteed. This, when combined with the Emperor's insistence that French troops could only be commanded by a French general, rendered him, in effect, powerless. General Grenier had been given a veto over any plans Murat might make.

He had been hobbled by the Emperor, his own brother-in-law, for God's sake. It was, frankly, intolerable.

To make matters worse, Murat suspected that the Emperor had an ulterior motive in keeping the French and Neapolitan forces in position along the Calabrian coast. Far from wanting to invade Sicily, his real purpose was to deter the British from sending reinforcements from Sicily to Spain and to keep the Royal Navy occupied in the Straits of Messina while the French garrison of Corfu was resupplied. To a proud man like Murat this was a standing slight on his honour.

And then, on top of all this, there was his wife Caroline, now back in Naples after a prolonged stay in France. A few days ago, he had received the sad news that she had miscarried the baby she had been expecting. His grief at the loss of the baby was tempered, however, by his irritation at Caroline's behaviour. She taken to sending him long, nagging letters, most recently about the favours he had conferred on General Cavaignac and his family and the unpopularity of his reforms at court. How could he be expected to rule as king if his own wife was constantly undermining him? Her complaints about his reforms sounded suspiciously as if she was defending the old, corrupt system. What, thought Murat contemptuously, had the Revolution been for?

'*Voilà, sire, c'est ça, j'ai terminé.*' Jacques le Blon had been a barber in civilian life before joining Murat's entourage as his batman, so always did a good job shaving his master. Murat stroked his chin. It was smooth, soft and lightly scented.

'Thank you, le Blon,' said Murat, rising from the chair. 'I'll get dressed now.'

* * *

While Murat was being shaved in his tented pavilion, a few miles along the coast, immured high in the castle at Scylla, William Coker and John Entwhistle were finishing breakfast. This was their eleventh day in captivity; Entwhistle had that morning started the third group of five lines – four straight with the fifth striking through the others – with which he had been marking off the days since their capture. Time hung heavily on their hands. Coker had finished reading *L'Avare* and was about to embark on *Le Malade Imaginaire*, a copy of which he had found in the castle library.

'You should try it, John,' said Coker. 'I rather enjoyed it.'

'I've never bothered to learn French, I'm afraid.'

After this brief exchange they lapsed into silence.

Three-quarters of an hour later, Coker and Entwhistle were taking their morning exercise, lapping the castle's courtyard, as they had done every morning and every afternoon for the last ten days. As they came round to the gatehouse, Major Lafite strolled towards them.

'Good morning, gentlemen,' he said in his excellent English. 'I have some news for you.' Lafite looked rather pleased with himself.

'Oh yes, what is it?' asked Coker. They had realised by now that Major Lafite only liked passing on news of British reverses or French successes.

'Did you hear the night before last some gunfire from just along the coast?' he asked.

Coker and Entwhistle looked at each other. They had heard a brief burst of heavy musketry on Saturday evening and had speculated about it intermittently ever since.

'Yes, *monsieur*, we did hear some gunfire on Saturday evening,' said Entwhistle, raising an eyebrow.

Lafite told Coker and Entwhistle the story of the botched rescue of the *Harlech Castle*, of the capture of the boat party sent across from Faro and of the casualties it suffered.

'So where are Captain Baldwin and his men now?' asked Coker.

'They have been sent back to Messina under a flag of truce,' said Lafite with more than a hint of sadistic glee. 'Good day to you, gentlemen. Enjoy your walk.' He waved his arm expansively round the courtyard.

Just before eight o'clock, George Warne strode through the gate into the Citadel. He and Carlotta had been asleep, curled up next to one another, when they were woken by an insistent knocking. Bleary-eyed, George got out of bed, pulled on a pair of breeches and went to the door.

'Who's there?' he asked, in the local dialect.

'It's me, Mr Warne, sir, John Farrell, with a message for you from headquarters.'

George recognised Farrell's voice; he was one of the junior clerks on the generals' staff, one of Rogers' underlings.

'Yes, Farrell, yes, wait a moment,' said George, unlocking the door. Farrell was a fresh-faced young man, neatly dressed in a dark coat and breeches. He looked surprised and mildly embarrassed to find George half-naked. 'What is it?'

'I've got a message for you from Colonel Airey, sir.' Farrell handed George a small, sealed envelope.

'The colonel's up early,' said George, breaking the seal and unfolding the paper.

'He usually is, sir,' replied Farrell.

George read the note: *Please report to the Citadel at 8 o'clock. Urgent matter to discuss. Airey.*

'Farrell,' said George, 'please tell the colonel that I will be with him as he asks by eight.'

George closed the door, wondering why Airey required his presence so urgently.

George crossed the courtyard before entering the staff headquarters building. John Farrell was back at his desk at the far end of the room. Next to him, bent over a ledger, was Rogers. Allsop, the other clerk, had not yet arrived.

'Good morning, Mr Rogers,' George cheerily. 'Glad to see you're keeping the army going.'

'That's my job, sir,' replied Rogers evenly. He didn't have much of a sense of humour, did Rogers, thought George. 'The colonel's in his office, sir.'

'Sorry I'm late, sir,' said George looking round Colonel Airey's office. Standing in the middle of the room while Airey gathered some papers up off his desk were Sandro Carboni and Colonel Donkin, the Quartermaster-General.

'Don't worry, you're not late, Captain Warne. I'm sorry I disturbed you so early.' He turned and grinned at Warne. 'Young Farrell told me he found you half-dressed. I hope he didn't interrupt anything.'

'No, sir. He woke me up.'

'Well, I'm glad to see you're dressed now. Gentlemen, shall we repair to Sir John's room?'

Two minutes later, the four men were sitting at the long table in Sir John Stuart's office. At this early hour, it was cool and quiet. Airey checked that the door was firmly closed, resumed his seat, shuffled his papers and looked round the table.

'I have asked you here this morning to hear some important new intelligence from Colonel Carboni.' He paused, before nodding at Carboni. 'Colonel.'

'Gentlemen,' Carboni began slowly. Donkin and Warne turned to look at the tall, dark, spare Sicilian as he spoke. 'Yesterday I attended Mass at San Francesco di Paola, as I do most Sundays. Everything was normal, as it is every Sunday and has been for years and years. I was a little late, so took a seat at the back of the church. At the end of the service, when people were leaving, I noticed an unfamiliar face at the front.' He paused, briefly. 'It was Mr Rogers, your chief clerk.' He nodded towards the door, in the direction of the clerks' room.

'What was Rogers doing at San Francesco? Is he a Roman Catholic?' asked Donkin, his voice tinged with mild disapproval. 'He's Irish, so he could be, I suppose.'

'It was not, Colonel Donkin, seeing him there that caught my attention so much as what happened next.'

'Yes . . .' said Donkin.

'While I was watching him, a verger came out of a side door in the aisle and started talking to your Mr Rogers. And then after a short time, they went together through the door.' Carboni then recounted the rest of the story, of his vigil under the cypress trees and his sighting of Rogers walking in the monastery gardens. When he finished, there was silence.

'Clearly, this must be investigated,' said Donkin eventually. 'It could, I suppose, be entirely innocent but it is my responsibility as Quartermaster to ensure our security here. We all know,' he waved a hand round the table, 'of the suspicions that there is an enemy spy ring operating here, that last week's raids were betrayed. Rogers has the knowledge and the means to do so. The activities Colonel Carboni observed at the monastery are, to put it mildly, open to misinterpretation. The question is, how do we go about it? If Rogers is in league with the enemy, I don't want to move too soon and frighten him off. We should bide our time until we can collect enough evidence against him to send him to the gallows.'

'We can try to dig around in his background,' said Airey, 'without risking him finding out, but it's tricky. The problem is that he knows everything that goes on here. It would be difficult, I suspect, to dig too deeply in the files here without him getting wind of it. Apart from anything else, only he knows where most of the records are, so we might end up asking him to find files on himself.'

'I can see that makes things tricky,' said Donkin with a rueful smile. 'But we could have him followed.'

'Yes, we could,' said Airey, looking at George.

'We could search his house' said Donkin.

'Yes, we could,' replied Airey, 'but it might be difficult to do so without alerting Rogers. I believe he has,' here Airey cleared his throat, 'a wife and children who live with him, so we might not get a clear run.'

Less than a quarter of a mile from where the four officers were pondering how best to investigate their own chief clerk, David Plumb was cocking a worried eye at the jack fluttering energetically at the head of the *Sprite*'s mainmast. He had noticed over the last half hour that the wind seemed to be strengthening from the south. With orders to sail for Malta, this was not what he wanted; after a week in port, Plumb was anxious to get to sea. At the daily ten o'clock divisions – when the ship's company paraded on the main deck – Plumb had announced that they would be sailing later that morning, although he did not give out the intended destination.

'Mr Roscoe,' said Plumb turning towards his first lieutenant, 'would you send a man up to see how the wind is bearing out in the straits?'

'Aye aye, sir.' Roscoe hailed a midshipman who was standing at the foot of the mainmast.

'Mr Heffer, if you please, up to the maintop to report on the wind, and take a glass with you.'

'Aye aye, sir,' said the midshipman, tucking a telescope under his arm before swinging onto the starboard ratlines. As Plumb watched, he climbed rapidly and with great agility. Once the midshipman, who was no more than fifteen years old, reached the maintop, he turned and, bracing himself against the ratlines, looked out across the straits.

'Strong from the south, sir,' shouted the midshipman, his voice shredding in the wind. The remainder of his message was lost as a gust hummed through the rigging.

'What was he saying, Mr Roscoe?' asked Plumb.

'I lost it, I'm afraid, sir. The wind's getting up, I'd say, sir.'

'Yes, damn it, it is,' replied Plumb. 'I'd hoped we might be away before noon but it's not looking too promising at the moment.'

* * *

George Warne was striding across the Terra Nova in the direction of Finbarr Rogers' house. The meeting in the commander-in-chief's room had debated what to do about Carboni's disturbing intelligence concerning Rogers. In the end, it was decided that George should pay a visit to his house. Once there, he should find a position from which he could keep watch on the place. Then, having seen the lie of the land, he could decide what, if anything, he should do; he was to use his initiative, discreetly, Colonel Airey emphasised heavily. Later on, in the early evening, once the clerks had gone home, it was agreed that George would return to the Citadel and start the long process of going through the files to see if he could find anything that might incriminate Rogers.

George had been given an address in a street in the south-western angle of the city walls, not far from the Porta Imperiale. He passed the southern end of the strada Candines and walked beneath the imposing wall of the city's main hospital. Passing the hospital, he crossed the Corso, dodging the traffic as he did so. To his right, the wide, open channel that contained the *fiumara* di Porta di Legna – now, at the end of summer, dry – ran under the street.

To his left, along the Corso, was the Porta Imperiale, the northernmost of the three gates in the southern range of the city walls. The gateway itself was a ponderous piece of architecture, flanked by heavily rusticated Tuscan columns. It had been built to commemorate the Emperor Charles V's visit to Messina in the 1530s. The Emperor and his gateway suited each other, he thought: heavy, pompous and lacking in charm. Turning away, he plunged into the shadows of a narrow side street.

About fifty yards in from the Corso this narrow, dirty street widened marginally. The resulting space was too small, too irregular and too insignificant to be given a name let alone be dignified with the title piazza. Nor did it boast a fountain, a marble wellhead or even a small statue of a minor saint. The houses were narrow-fronted with two upper storeys. Washing draped on lines hung between windows. Scruffy children played in the dusty, litter-strewn street, while mangey dogs sniffed hopefully at refuse in the gutters. Rogers and his family occupied, according to the note in George's hand, No. 4, in the far-left corner close to where the wider space narrowed again into a street.

George leant against a wall and took in the scene. One thing was certain: the army gossips had got Rogers wrong. This was a far cry from the wing of an obscure royal palace in which he was popularly supposed to live in lascivious bliss. This was backstreet Messina, cramped, smelly and disease-ridden. It was close enough to the Citadel, no more than twenty minutes' walk to work for Rogers, so it was at least convenient.

On the other hand, George realised, it was the far side of the city from San Francesco di Paola. Rogers must have had some very good reason for attending Mass there. It must be forty, fifty minutes' walk from there. How many nearer, more convenient churches were there? In a city as devout as Messina, perhaps as many as thirty, certainly fifteen.

George looked round for somewhere he could conceal himself while keeping an eye on *casa* Rogers.

Emma Thring was clinging to her brother's arm. Six feet in front of them was the open grave in which Peter Wilkins's mortal remains were about to be interred. There was a small knot of mourners: Emma recognised Charles Parsons among them and, standing apart, Frank Younge. On the far side of the grave was the priest, his surplice and clerical bands flapping in the breeze.

The British cemetery in Messina was a quiet, solemn place, shaded by short, flat-topped Mediterranean pines. From it there was a fine view of the sea and the Calabrian mountains over the city's rooftops. It was a peaceful resting place for those who had died far from home. To Emma's left was a new gravestone, its pale surface as yet unweathered, bearing the inscription:

To Captain Thomas Hunter and Captain Angus Cameron of his Britannick Majesty's 21st Regt of Foot Killed in the Service of Their Country 1809
Their Brother Officers have Erected this Monument

Emma wondered how they had met their death. Robert would probably know – he probably knew both of them; she would ask him later. But now six soldiers of the 27th, Wilkins's regiment, had arrived at the graveside, bearing the coffin. The service was about to begin.

'I am the resurrection and the life, saith the Lord,' intoned the priest, his voice a fine rolling English baritone. Emma bowed her head. 'He that believeth in me, though he were dead, yet shall he live: and whosoever liveth and believeth in me shall never die.'

'I know that my Redeemer liveth . . .' Emma was staring blankly at the coffin, trying not to cry. 'We brought nothing into this world, and it is certain that we can carry nothing out.' Poor Peter, he didn't want to die. He loved this world and what it offered, gently but wholeheartedly, with curiosity and wonder. 'The Lord gave, and the Lord hath taken away; blessed be the name of the Lord.'

Emma was jolted out of her tearful reverie by the soldiers lowering the coffin into the grave. She watched as they straightened up, stepped back and stood to attention in a line.

'For as much as it had pleased Almighty God of his great mercy to take unto himself the soul of our dear brother Peter here departed; we therefore commit his body to the ground; earth to earth, ashes to ashes, dust to dust; in sure and certain hope of the Resurrection to eternal life . . .'

Charles Parsons stepped forward and, reaching down, scooped up a handful of earth and dropped it onto the coffin. Emma squeezed her brother's arm and dabbed her eyes with a handkerchief.

It was now noon, but David Plumb was still on the quarterdeck as he had been all morning, pacing, watching, waiting. *Sprite* was still in harbour, unable to get under way. As the forenoon watch had just gone off duty, the entire morning had now vanished and the southerly wind had strengthened to almost gale force. Until the wind relents or swings round to the north or the west, thought Plumb, we're stuck here.

At that moment Heffer, the young midshipman, appeared at his side.

'Captain Plumb, sir, if you please,' he bleated nervously, for young midshipmen did not often address the captain directly.

'Yes, Mr Heffer, what is it?' asked Plumb kindly.

'Well, sir,' said Heffer, 'I've just come down from the maintop, sir, and it looks as if our ships off Faro are being blown out to sea, to the north, sir.'

'Are you sure?' asked Plumb.

'Yes, so far as I can see, sir.'

'Thank you, Mr Heffer.'

Damn it, thought Plumb. If the ships patrolling the straits can't hold their station in this wind, there's no chance of *Sprite* being able to beat to the south against it. We'll have to wait until the gale blows itself out.

As the clock in the map room at Punta di Pezzo struck two, Murat was standing over the big table morosely examining, for the umpteenth time, the map of Calabria and the near parts of Sicily. The dispositions of the French and British forces were marked on the map by an array of different-coloured pins. In his right hand was a cane with which he was tracing the Sicilian coastline on the map, deep in thought.

Murat's mood had not improved since he had been shaved by le Blon earlier that morning. Once he had dressed in his riding clothes – white breeches, and a loose shirt – he went out with two of his ADCs. As befitted a celebrated cavalryman, Murat was a magnificent horseman, fearless and intuitively at one with his mount. He rode for an hour every morning; it kept him fit and was a good way to clear his head for the day ahead. Once they had returned to camp, Murat dressed, putting on the grandiose, dark blue uniform of a Neapolitan general before eating breakfast – good coffee sent from France and fresh bread from the camp bakery.

Normally, his morning ride improved Murat's mood. He

found the exercise and the fresh air bracing and relished the sense of freedom that came from being mounted on a big, lively horse. But today, he could not shake off the creeping realisation that his prospects of taking Sicily, of completing his kingdom, were fading as the days shortened and the leaves turned. There was also the nagging thought that he was being duped by the Emperor. Nor did the gale, which had blown up during the morning, do anything to improve his temper. Wind had always irritated Murat but now it seemed to mock his plans to cross the straits. It was as if even the gods were conspiring against him.

Once he had dressed, Murat had retreated to his study where he read the latest government dispatches from Naples. Although he had been away from his capital since early June, he worked diligently to keep abreast of government business. As King, his decision was required in a multitude of matters, great and small. Every morning he spent at least two hours closeted with his civil secretary, an intelligent, hard-working young man called Jean Albertini, dealing with the contents of the dispatch cases. Murat would sit at his desk, the portrait of the Emperor brooding on its easel behind him, with Albertini facing him across the tooled leather surface as they worked their way through official memoranda, cabinet papers, notes from ministers, and endless, pleading letters begging favours. Murat would read the document and tell Albertini how to reply before moving on to the next one. Such, he sometimes thought, was the majesty of kingship.

Murat's reverie was interrupted by the appearance at his elbow of the gaudy figure of Lieutenant Henri Peyronnet, one of the three *adjoints* attached to his staff. Peyronnet, despite being an infantryman, had adopted the fashion current among young staff officers of wearing a hussar uniform, an affectation much derided by older, more conservative officers. He was sporting a maroon dolman, the short, tight, elaborately braided hussar jacket; hanging from his left shoulder was a lemon-yellow *pelisse*. His get-up was completed by tight sky-blue breeches and a dark green sash. To Murat's eye, he looked peacockish, ridiculous even. Peyronnet saluted smartly.

'Sire, the gale has blown all the English ships from their stations off Faro. The straits are undefended, sire.'

'That's all very well, Peyronnet, *mon brave*,' replied Murat, putting the cane down on the table, 'but presumably the same gale would prevent us putting to sea, *n'est-ce pas?*'

'Yes, sire, but it shows that even the famous English navy cannot control the winds.'

'*Vous avez raison*,' replied Murat in his nasal southern twang, 'but if we cannot get our soldiers across what does it matter?'

George Warne was in a narrow alley opposite the house in which Rogers and his family lived. He had been standing here for the best part of two hours now but had not seen anything of any note. No one had gone in or come out of the house. He had not even noticed any movement at the windows. Rogers' house was every bit as dilapidated as the other houses in the street. The paint on the front door was faded and peeling at the edges. The stucco on the facade was dirty and showing signs of damp and age. A couple of the windowpanes were cracked, and George could see weeds growing in the guttering under the eaves. The central window on the first floor opened onto a small balcony with rusty iron railings. It was the only window in the front of the house which had an awning instead of shutters to keep out the midday sun. If Rogers was taking bribes from the French, he wasn't spending the money on his living accommodation.

He was beginning to wonder what he should do. Should he perhaps see if he could get in and have a look around? That was risky. If there was someone at home, he might be able to bluff his way out but if it was Rogers' wife, mistress, whatever she was, she would realise he was English and would certainly tell Rogers. Then he would know that he was under suspicion and the game would be up. On the other hand, almost anything was better than standing in this dark, smelly, rubbish-strewn alley for another two hours.

Out in the street two young boys were throwing stones at a skeletally thin cat, which scurried away screeching its disapproval. A dog dozing in the shade, disturbed by the noise, lifted its head momentarily.

David Plumb was sitting in the *Sprite*'s cabin reading his sealed orders for the third time. The window and the skylight were both open and, as he read, Plumb sensed that the gale that had delayed his departure might be abating. The noise made by the rigging slapping against the masts, especially the mizzen mast closest to his cabin, was noticeably less insistent than it had been an hour ago. At that moment, as if to confirm his intuition, there was a knock on the door and Heffer, the young midshipman, stepped into the cabin.

'Mr Roscoe presents his compliments, sir, and begs to inform you that the wind has died away, sir.'

'Thank you, Mr Heffer. Will you please tell Mr Roscoe that I'll be on deck in a minute.'

'Aye aye, sir,' said Heffer, closing the door.

Plumb folded up the thick sheets of cream paper on which his orders were written and, locking them into the drawer of his desk, stood up.

A moment later, Plumb was standing on his quarterdeck looking up at the jack at the head of the mainmast.

'Very strange, Mr Roscoe, how quickly the wind has died away. Generally, a gale like that lasts twelve hours before blowing itself out. It's time to weigh anchor and get to sea.'

'Aye aye, sir.'

There were three figures standing together on the wide expanse of baked mud in front of Murat's tented pavilion. Behind them, above the grand entrance, the Imperial eagle glinted in the sun. The outsized tricolour hung limply on its pole, as if exhausted by its energetic flapping and fluttering in the recent gale.

In the middle of the group was Murat, scanning the Straits of Messina through a telescope. On his left was General Cavaignac, a tall, spare man with prematurely thinning dark hair, and to his right the *adjoint* Peyronnet in his *opera buffa* hussar uniform. After a while, Murat lowered the telescope and turned towards Cavaignac.

'Well, *mon general*,' he said, with a smile, 'it must have been a powerful gale; the English ships are still out at sea. The straits are undefended. If we could launch an invasion now, we might have a chance to get across.' He looked at Cavaignac. 'And if we can land our best troops in good numbers, who knows what might happen? The peasants are ready to rise against *les Anglais* and Sir John Stuart's troops lack fighting spirit. The day will be ours, *mon general*. My kingdom will be complete and the Bourbons forced to flee with their British lackeys to Malta or Egypt.' He paused, savouring this glorious prospect. 'What do you think, Cavaignac?'

Cavaignac was a young and ambitious general, a man on the make. Murat had recently appointed him his first aide-de-camp, a singular honour. As a further mark of favour, the King had obtained the Grand Cordon of Westphalia for him from Jerome, the Emperor's brother, a rare distinction for a mere major-general. For this and for future advancement, Cavaignac was deeply in the King's debt – jealous tongues whispered that he was the King's creature, overpromoted and overfavoured. He was determined to do everything in his power to show himself – and his family – to be worthy of the royal bounty. He was certainly not going to pour cold water on plans that might achieve his sovereign's greatest ambition, the conquest of Sicily.

'I think, sire,' said Cavaignac smoothly, 'that if the sea is calm, you should launch an attack while the enemy is out of position.' He could see that Murat was torn, torn between not taking a risk, playing safe, thereby avoiding failure, and risking all to achieve a great and longed-for goal. 'It might be the last chance we get this season, sire. Once the autumn storms begin, any invasion will have to be postponed until next year. And who can know,' he added rhetorically, 'what next year will bring?'

There was a pause of about ten seconds while Murat looked at the ground, scuffing the dust with the sole of his boot.

'*Mon cher general*,' he said, looking Cavaignac in the eye, all doubt now gone, 'please send someone down to the coast to get information about the state of the sea.'

'Je le fais tout de suite, sire,' said Caviagnac saluting smartly. He turned on his heel and strode back to the pavilion.

George had made up his mind. It was now past four o'clock in the afternoon. Rogers would not be back until at least six, so the coast was clear. Despite watching the house for more than three hours, he'd seen no one enter or leave nor anyone in the window under the awning. If there was anyone inside, he or she was lying low. George was wary now of exceeding his orders, but Colonel Airey had explicitly permitted him to use his initiative. And this seemed, to George, the perfect opportunity. He would tread carefully and if challenged, he would make his excuses and leave.

Having left the welcome if malodorous cover of the alley, George crossed the street towards Rogers' house with all the sangfroid he could muster. 'Look as if you belong here,' he kept repeating to himself. As he turned the handle he noticed that under the peeling paint the door had once been blue. The latch clanked up. He pushed the door open and stepped in, closing it behind him. Once inside, he was almost knocked backwards by the smell. Three hours in the alley had done nothing to prepare him for this assault on the senses. Rotting vegetables, human excrement, uncleared rubbish, blocked drains and God knows what else. Christ, thought George, small wonder Rogers spends such long days in the Citadel if this is his alternative.

By the light that filtered through the small, dirty window above the door, George could see that he was in a narrow stairwell. According to the note he'd been given, Rogers lived on the first floor. As George climbed the narrow wooden stairs, he noticed how rickety they were underfoot. On the first-floor landing there were two doors, both of which bore a painted wooden sign. The one on the right-hand door, in plain black capitals, read simply 'Rogers'. George took two paces across the dark, grimy landing, grasped the handle, twisted and pushed. Rather to his surprise, the door opened.

Once inside, George quickly closed the door behind him. He leant against the inside of the door, listening. He could not hear any sound emanating from inside the apartment. The shutters were half-closed but he could see that the room was furnished with a gate-legged table, some chairs and a settee whose stuffing was bursting out of a hole in the worn covering. On the table were two empty glasses. On a shelf opposite the window was a small statue of the Virgin in blue-and-white china. On the far wall was a large cupboard. George opened it: it contained some crockery and a basket of cutlery but nothing else. There were no books in the room, no desk and no sign of any documents. There was nothing to detain him here, George realised.

He walked across the room, through the door and into the next room. This was the room behind the main window that opened onto the balcony. The shutters were open, but the sun was kept out of the room by the awning. Judging by the three cots, this was where the children slept. In the middle of the floor was a tatty rug and opposite the window a large chest of drawers. George opened it: inside were a few children's clothes.

Then, just as George was beginning to wonder whether he would find anything interesting let alone incriminating in the apartment, he heard a noise from the stairwell. It sounded like a crying child. He stiffened. Damn, he thought, is that someone coming home? Quickly he moved towards the window. The child was still crying, but now he could hear footsteps on the stairs as well. He couldn't risk being caught here. Not knowing the layout of the place, the window was his only escape route. As the door of the far room opened, George stepped out onto the balcony and flattened himself against the wall beside the window. He could hear a woman's voice and the sounds of two or three children. He could only pray that whoever she was, she didn't decide to come out onto the balcony. Equally, George realised, he could be seen, as clear as day, from the street below, on the balcony hugging the wall outside the window. He looked down. It was about twelve feet to the ground, he reckoned. There was nothing else for it.

So, gingerly, he climbed over the balcony railings. They were about waist-high and although rusty they felt, thank God, solid enough. On the far side of the railings there was a lip about three inches wide. Once over the railings, George perched precariously on this lip while he squatted down, both hands grasping the railings, and lowered himself off the edge of the balcony. Once he was hanging at full length he looked down. It was a drop of about five feet to the ground. Bracing himself, he let go.

George landed with a heavy thump, rolling onto his backside in the gutter. Picking up his hat, he stood up, dusted himself off, straightened his coat and strolled off with as much nonchalance as he could muster. The two urchins who had been stoning the cat looked at him in blank amazement.

'The boatmen and fishermen at Scylla all say, sir, that the sea is calm enough for the transports to use oars as well as sails.' The young ADC had just returned to Murat's headquarters and was reporting breathlessly to General Cavaignac.

'Are you sure?' asked Cavaignac.

'Yes, sir, and I could see with my own eyes that the sea is calm.'

'Good. Thank you.' Cavaignac turned away with a smile. Now, he thought, we can finally set the invasion in motion.

A few minutes later Cavaignac and Murat were standing at the map table giving orders for the invasion. It was an operation that had been planned – and repeatedly postponed – over several months so the detailed troop movements had already been thoroughly worked out. Murat and Cavaignac rattled off the orders while the ADCs made notes, which were then passed to the clerks to write up. Once fair copies had been made in looping copperplate, they were given to messengers to be distributed to brigade and regimental headquarters all along the coast.

The plan was simple. Cavaignac would command three thousand men, two battalions of Corsicans and two of Neapolitans, who would embark at Reggio and cross the straits landing several miles south of Messina near San Stefano to create a diversion. Cavaignac's men would then move up into the hills and, making their way by mountain paths towards Messina, descend into the city from the west. The main attack was to be launched across the undefended straits from the army's bases between Scylla and Punto di Pezzo. A force of around ten thousand men would cross the straits in five hundred transports escorted by one hundred gunboats. These men would land on the beaches between Faro and Messina and push towards the city. It was widely expected that the peasantry would welcome the French troops as liberators and rise against the English.

'*Mon cher Cavaignac*,' said Murat, 'the Fates have given us this chance. We must take it. A good general will seize an opportunity, however slight, whenever it arises. This is what we are doing now. The Emperor would approve, I have no doubt.'

'Will you be going across with the troops, sire?' asked Cavaignac.

'*Naturellement, mon general*,' replied Murat. 'I didn't charge at the head of ten thousand troopers against the Russians in the snow at Eylau to sit on my arse at headquarters while a few regiments land on a beach in Sicily. You know I like to be in the thick of it. Think of Egypt or Austerlitz. I shall be there, *monsieur*.'

Over the next hour messengers streamed out from Punta di Pezzo taking orders for the invasion to commanding officers at headquarters from Scylla to Reggio. The orders, torn open and read, pitched the army into a frenzy of organised activity.

'*Mon Dieu*,' exclaimed one regimental colonel, 'it's finally happening. King Joachim's plucked up his courage. We're going across.'

Officers roused sergeants who in turn roused men, turfing them out of their tents and billets. Soon the men were forming up in columns and marching out of their encampments down to the anchorages.

Cavaignac himself, once the orders had been dispatched, rode off with two ADCs to join his troops at Reggio. As he galloped along the coast in the late-afternoon sun he thought to himself 'This is my day, my chance' and spurred his horse towards Reggio.

The sun was going down over the sea. In half an hour the dazzling disc of red and gold would start gradually extinguishing itself in the ocean. John O'Connell stood on the tower at Faro scanning the Calabrian coast through a telescope. He had been standing out on the platform gazing at the view when some glinting movements in the evening sun on the far shore had caught his eye. Now, through the telescope, he could see that the glinting was troops on the march, hundreds of them, maybe thousands. Through the telescope he could just make out the individual men in the columns, tiny worker ants in white breeches and blue coats brilliantly lit in the low evening sun, which glinted off their shako plates and their bayonets.

This was not an unusual occurrence. In recent months the garrison at Faro had frequently observed troop movements along the Calabrian coast. These varied in size from a company to a regiment and, sometimes, even a brigade could be tracked as it marched along the coastal roads. Occasionally, such sightings had stiffened the defensive sinews around Faro, but nothing had yet come of these distant manoeuvres. As a result, they were not taken particularly seriously.

'Well, Boney,' said O'Connell to the spaniel sitting patiently at his feet, 'the French are on the move again.' The dog, hearing O'Connell's voice, looked up expectantly, thumping his tail on the flagstones. 'Shall we tell the major?'

A more experienced, more confident subaltern might not have bothered to alert his superior officer. But O'Connell was young and recently promoted; this was his first command and a temporary one at that. He'd better send a message to the major, he decided, although in all probability he was already fully aware of the enemy activity on the far shore.

The twilight was gathering as Murat stood on the jetty, watching as the royal barge was backed alongside. To left and to right, his troops were clambering aboard the transport vessels – each one took about twenty soldiers as well as its oarsmen – as they bobbed around in the shallow water. Up the beach, in patient lines, their comrades awaited their turn.

Murat was keyed up, that heightened sense of being, of awareness, which comes with the anticipation of action. He was about to take his rightful place at the head of his army to lead it into battle. The opportunity presented by the storm and the subsequent calm was wholly unexpected. Suddenly, out of the blue, he had a golden chance to strike at Sicily, to seize the island, unite his kingdom and show the Emperor, once and for all, that he was worthy of being King. He was confident that the invasion had a good chance of success: the plans were well rehearsed, his troops experienced and in good spirits. The indications were that the Sicilian peasantry would rise against the English and welcome his troops with open arms; it would be a modern Sicilian Vespers. He, Joachim Murat, would be the man who delivered to the Empire the last significant part of western Europe – Britain apart – it lacked.

The royal barge, its starboard-side oars shipped, was now alongside the jetty. Murat was about to step aboard when he heard a commotion behind him. He looked round. In the gloaming he saw General Grenier walking towards him, a posse of ADCs trailing behind him. He stopped in front of Murat and bowed.

'Good evening, sire,' said Grenier, who had a slight but noticeable German accent. He was, Murat thought, a plain-looking fellow, although his richly embroidered, high-collared general's uniform did invest him with a certain dignity. But whatever he thought of Grenier's appearance, the fact remained that Grenier was the senior French general in Calabria. He held the Emperor's veto.

'Good evening, General Grenier,' said Murat with elaborate politeness. 'To what do I owe the pleasure of your company?'

'I have come to see what my men are being asked to do.'

'Have you not seen my orders? I sent a copy to your headquarters, *mon general*.'

'Yes, I have seen them, sire. That is why I am here,' replied Grenier. 'I do not give my consent to my men, the French forces here, taking part in this ill-considered, reckless attack.'

'Sir,' said Murat drawing himself up to his full height, 'may I remind you that I am the King and commander-in-chief here? You will do as I ask, *monsieur*. You *will* permit your men to take part in this operation. I order it.'

Everyone, the ADCs, soldiers, deckhands and oarsmen, sailors and sergeants, around the two men were watching now, silent and expectant in the failing light. Two giants were squaring up to one another: there could only be one victor.

'Your Majesty,' replied Grenier evenly, 'I cannot give my consent.'

'I order it, General Grenier, I order it,' said Murat quietly, looking Grenier straight in the eye.

'Your Majesty, I cannot give my consent. I have here,' he reached into his inside pocket and produced a letter, 'the Emperor's written authority giving me sole command of all the French troops in your kingdom.'

'Damn you, damn you,' said Murat fiercely, snatching the letter from Grenier's hand and tearing it into pieces before tossing them into the air.

* * *

George Warne was sitting in his shirtsleeves at a table in Colonel Airey's office. To his left was a heap of files, pay sheets, disciplinary logs and staff records, which George was leafing through in search of information about Finbarr Rogers. It was well past eleven o'clock and the room was dark except for the pool of yellow light cast by the three candles on the desk.

He had returned to the Citadel in the late afternoon, following his ignominious retreat from Rogers' house. He had reported to Colonel Airey who was greatly amused when George told him the story of his escapade on the balcony. 'How are the mighty fallen,' laughed Airey. It had been agreed at the meeting that morning that George would start trawling through the files to see if he could find anything that might cast some light on Rogers. So, once the clerks had gone home – and, much to George's irritation, Rogers hung around until nearly seven o'clock – he started work. And, bar a brief visit to the mess for some supper, he had been there ever since.

Not that, in the best part of four hours, he had come across anything especially illuminating. From the staff records he had discovered that Rogers was indeed an Irish Roman Catholic, from County Kilkenny where he had been born in June 1773, making him thirty-seven years old. He had started in the army as a junior clerk in Ireland but had transferred to London before volunteering for overseas duties. He arrived in Sicily with the first British regiments in early 1806. Since then he had acquired an unrivalled reputation for efficiency and hard work. He had been promoted to chief clerk in May 1809 and – perhaps as a result – had married Maria Scafatti the following month. The record disclosed that Mr and Mrs Rogers had two children, born in 1807 and 1808, but there was, as George had discovered, probably now a third, although its existence had yet to be officially recognised.

From the pay sheets George saw that Rogers' salary was four shillings a day. By comparison, a private soldier in a line regiment received one shilling a day, while his colonel got twenty-two shillings and sixpence a day. George's pay, as a captain in a line infantry regiment, was ten shillings a day. Rogers could expect some allowances on top of his basic pay, but he probably didn't get more than five shillings a day. That was not a lot, George thought, to maintain the wife and three children that Rogers seemed to have. Also, George knew, the locals tended to raise their prices when selling anything to the British: it was assumed that they could afford it. His house spoke volumes for the straitened circumstances in which Rogers and his family lived. Certainly, money – or rather, a lack of it – could be a motive for Rogers to sell secrets to the enemy.

George yawned and closed the file in front of him, placing it on the pile to his right before picking up the next one.

Finbarr Rogers was restless. The city's many clocks had just finished striking midnight but he still could not sleep. Maria, his wife, was now snoring softly beside him, although when he'd arrived home earlier she'd been very distressed.

'Finbarr,' she had said, before he'd even had time to give her and the children a kiss, 'Finbarr,' she pronounced it 'Fin-e-barr', '*i ragazzi* told me that they saw someone, a tall man, falling from the balcony this afternoon, just after we got home. There was someone, a thief, a villain. in our house.' She became almost hysterical but Rogers managed to calm her down and establish that nothing was missing. He found the boys in the street, but they couldn't say more than that the man was tall and that he fell from the balcony.

In the dark, he stared at the ceiling. Nothing had been taken – not that there was anything of any value to take – so what had the mysterious intruder been looking for? Was it a random, opportunist burglar who, finding the door open, went in, only to be disturbed, or was it something more sinister? He'd have to keep his eyes open. Eventually, he drifted off to sleep and dreamt of a giant seabird, with a golden beak, emerald eyes and enormous wings of fire, swooping low over Messina, plucking British soldiers off the Citadel's ramparts in its talons.

CHAPTER FOURTEEN

Messina, 18th September 1810

'George, George,' said the voice, 'wake up, there's something I want you to see.' George sat up in the chair with a jerk. He was stiff and cold. How long had he been asleep here? The voice belonged to his regimental commanding officer, Lieutenant-Colonel Warren. 'There's something going on down the coast. Come and have a look.' George got to his feet.

'What's the time, sir?'

'Not long after four,' replied Warren who was the duty officer at the Citadel that night. George grunted. He had stopped working on the files in Colonel Airey's office sometime after one o'clock, and, not having quarters in the Citadel, had repaired to the mess where he found an armchair and promptly fell asleep.

Warren led the way up onto the Citadel's southern bastion from where the two men stared into the night to the south. It was warm, with a breeze coming off the sea.

'Do you see, there?' said Warren, pointing.

'Yes, I see,' said George. 'It looks like gunfire, don't you think?'

'Yes,' said Warren, 'it does, but if it is, what the hell's going on?'

'Do you think the Frogs have landed? It looks as if it's somewhere beyond Contesse, maybe five miles away.'

'Well, if the bloody Frogs have landed, why the hell hasn't someone fired a warning gun?' asked Warren.

'God knows, sir,' answered George.

'Anyway, we should tell the Adjutant-General. I don't want to wake Sir John in the middle of the night.'

The two men clattered down the steps from the bastion. Major-General Campbell's quarters were on the harbour side of the Citadel, on the first floor overlooking the central courtyard. They knocked on the door and, after a minute or so, a sleepy-looking Campbell appeared in his nightshirt.

'Colonel Warren, Captain Warne,' he said. 'What can I do for you at this ungodly hour?'

'I am sorry to disturb you, sir, but I thought you should know that we've seen flashes of musketry from the south, somewhere on the coast beyond Contesse.'

'Are you sure, Colonel?' asked Campbell, rubbing his chin.

'Yes, sir. And Warne here,' he put his hand on George's shoulder, 'can confirm it.' George nodded.

'Right, I'd better get dressed,' said Campbell, opening the door to let the two men in. 'Come in, I won't be a minute.'

Five minutes later, Campbell, Warren and George were up on the southern bastion again watching the distant flashes.

'Yes,' said Campbell, staring into the night, 'it's musketry all right. The question is, what do we think it is?'

At that moment, there was a commotion down in the

courtyard near the gatehouse, urgent voices and the sound of a horse's hooves on stone. Two figures came out of the guardroom; one of them was carrying a lantern.

'What the hell's that?' said Campbell. They filed down the steps to the courtyard and walked towards the gatehouse where a trooper of dragoons was dismounting. His horse was streaked with sweat across its withers and blowing hard. He was wearing the blue jacket and yellow facings of the 20th Light Dragoons and the regiment's bell-topped shako.

'General Campbell, sir,' said the trooper, flustered and out of breath, saluting hurriedly. 'Capt'n Jaris sent me to tell you that the Frenchies 'as landed. Ride quick, 'e said, to the Citadel an' find the general even if you 'as to wake 'im up.'

'Yes, thank you, Trooper,' said Campbell calmly. 'Take a moment and tell me slowly where you've come from and what happened.'

'We was stationed at Mili,' the trooper began, having composed himself, 'an' the Capt'n put out a patrol to the south of the town, as he always does, but it sent a messenger back in sayin' that it had been fired at by French soldiers. That was when he sent me to you, sir, to warn you, sir.'

'Thank you, Trooper, and well done,' said Campbell. Then, turning to Warren and George, he continued, 'I think I'd better get down there as soon as possible. Colonel, your place is here. Captain Warne, you will accompany me. Find yourself a horse and some pistols and meet me here in five minutes.'

Ten minutes later, George and General Campbell were trotting along the road that led out of Messina to the south. Riding at night, even when, as now, it was not especially dark, was a hazardous occupation on Sicily's roads: to canter or gallop would be risking their necks.

George had roused the armourer and once he had unlocked the armoury, equipped himself with a cavalry sabre, a carbine and a pistol. The pistol, the nine-inch 'Light Dragoon' weapon, was stowed in the saddle holster to his right, while the sabre hung from his belt in its scabbard. George had selected a light cavalry sabre, which had a gently curved blade with a very slightly splayed end. In the right hands it was a lethally effective weapon. The carbine, carried on a shoulder strap, was the standard British sixteen-inch cavalry issue, nicknamed the 'Paget' after its designer. Its ramrod was fitted to the barrel with a stirrup swivel to prevent it being dropped while loading on horseback.

As Contesse was only three miles from the Citadel, it wasn't long before the Adjutant-General and George were leaving the town behind them, heading for Mili. The beach with the sea beyond it was only a few yards to their left as they rode along. George could hear the waves hissing softly in the sand and smell the fresh, iodine tang of the sea in the warm night air.

Then, as they rode on, Campbell suddenly pulled his horse up.

'Shhhhh. Can you hear that, up ahead? What is it?' In the distance there was a continuous, rhythmic crunching.

George had stopped his horse and was listening.

'It sounds like marching troops,' he said. 'What do you think, sir?'

'I agree. But whose troops are they? Ours? Or the enemy's?' General and captain looked at each other through the darkness. Neither of them voiced it, but they were both hoping to God that they were not about to run into a column of French infantry. They sat still and listened intently.

After a while George spoke. 'They don't seem to be getting any closer, sir.'

'If you're right, they're our troops not the enemy's.'

'Yes, very likely, sir.'

'Good. Let's press on and catch up with them.' Kicking their horses forward, they trotted off.

After five minutes, the noise ahead resolved itself into the tramp of marching men. As the road came over a low rise, George and the General could make out, up ahead through the semi-darkness, a solid block of moving shadow. It was a column of troops and it was heading south along the coast. Here, still to the north of Mili, they could only be British troops. A few minutes later, the two men reached the rear of the marching column.

'What regiment are you?' Campbell shouted over the crunch of marching boots.

'Twenty-first Foot, Colonel Adam, sir,' came back the reply.

'Come on,' said Campbell, 'let's pay Colonel Adam a visit.' They trotted up the marching column, counting four companies of the regiment as they did so, perhaps three hundred men in all. At the head of the column, mounted on a fine grey horse, was Colonel Adam. He looked surprised to see the Adjutant-General out here on the coast road in the middle of the night.

'Good morning, sir,' he said to Campbell, touching his hat in salute. 'And a good morning to you, too, Captain Warne.'

'So, Colonel, what's going on here?' asked Campbell.

'Well, sir,' said Adam, turning in his saddle, 'the regiment was parading as usual, an hour before dawn, at the camp at Contesse. I was about to dismiss the men when a dragoon orderly arrived at the gallop to tell me that the enemy had landed down the coast between Mili and San Stefano.'

'Didn't you see the flashes of musketry?' asked Campbell. 'We could see them clearly from the Citadel.'

'No, I didn't. Contesse lies in a fold in the ground, so there's no view south along the coast. The first I knew of it was when the orderly arrived. I decided at once to march against the enemy with three companies of the regiment and the light company, leaving the other three companies and the grenadier company to defend Contesse.'

'Very good, Colonel Adam,' said Campbell. From their mounts at the head of the column, the three men could now see the flashes of gunfire up ahead and hear the shots. From here, the fighting seemed more desultory than it had appeared from the Citadel earlier. Was the landing being pushed back? Or perhaps it had overcome any resistance and was moving inland. They would find out soon enough.

To the east, George could see the very first signs of the coming dawn, the first flecks of day.

It was still dark as the first transport vessel approached the beach. The man in the bows jumped into the shallow water with the painter, pulling the boat up the beach until she grounded in the sand.

'*Avancez, avancez, vite, vite,*' said the sergeant in a hoarse stage whisper. The rest of the men stepped over the side into the shallows. The beach was an ideal landing place: sandy, wide and not too steep. There was a half-moon but as it was now low in the sky and partially obscured by clouds it was too dark to be able to make out much beyond the immediate vicinity of the landing area.

On either side, other landing craft were coming in, grinding softly into the sand. Once the men were out of the boats, the officers and sergeants led them up the beach at the trot, muskets at the ready, bayonets fixed. By the time the advance parties reached the scrub at the top of the beach it was clear that they had landed unopposed and, perhaps, unobserved. The British were nowhere to be seen.

Within a few minutes General Cavaignac was stepping from his boat into the shallow water, accompanied by his *chef de bataillon*, Major Robert Levieux, and two *adjoints*, both lieutenants. Cavaignac was resplendent in his full general's uniform: the dark blue jacket trimmed with oak leaves in gilt thread at the cuffs and down the front, gilt epaulettes on the shoulders and a golden sash around his waist, the get-up completed by white breeches and high cavalry boots. On his head was a cocked hat, worn fore and aft, edged in gold braid and topped off with a white plume and a sky-blue *panache* of ostrich feathers. He looked every inch the Imperial Napoleonic general.

Cavaignac's four infantry battalions, three thousand men in all, had crossed the straits from Reggio in about forty-five transports, escorted by a number of gunboats. One of Cavaignac's battalions was a regiment of Corsican light infantry. The Corsicans were good soldiers, tough and independent, traits well illustrated by the fact that Corsican regiments fought for both the British and the French throughout the Revolutionary and Napoleonic Wars. The one major weakness of Cavaignac's little army was its complete lack of field artillery.

The general and his staff gathered in a cluster at the top of the beach. One of the *adjoints* set up a small portable table and unfolded a map onto it, smoothing out the creases. Meanwhile, an orderly lit a storm lantern. Cavaignac was conscious of his force's role as a diversion for the main attack to the north, between Messina and Faro. His job was to create the impression of a landing in strength, in the hope that the British would detach part of their army from the north to counter it.

'*Messieurs,*' said Cavaignac, '*nous sommes arrivés à l'heure.* Now we must move quickly.' He turned to the *chef de bataillon*. 'Levieux, the Corsicans should be moving off inland now. They are to make for this hill here.' He pointed at the map in the glow of the lantern. 'Once they are established, they should hold it until further orders, is that clear?'

'*Oui, mon general,* I will make sure that their colonel understands your order.' He turned away and strode briskly off along the beach to find the Corsicans.

Cavaignac then busied himself giving orders to the young *adjoints* for the other three regiments. The two Neapolitan battalions were to move inland while the second Corsican battalion was to remain behind, to defend the beach.

There was still no sign of the British. So far, thought Cavaignac to himself, so good.

William Coker pressed his head against the iron bar that bisected his cell's tiny window. Now that the dawn was coming up, he and John Entwhistle were desperate to see what, if anything, was going on outside.

The previous evening as the sun went down and for hours after dark, they could hear the unmistakable sounds of military activity: shouted orders, the tramp of marching men, the creaking, clanking and grinding of wheeled vehicles, wagons, and artillery limbers, the whinnying and clip-clopping of horses, all the myriad sounds of a large body of soldiers on the move. It was obvious that something was afoot. Was this the long-awaited invasion that Murat had boasted about? Perhaps. Had the British landed in Calabria? Maybe. But, from their cell, in the dark, they could see nothing. It was very frustrating.

Now, with the sun coming up, they were none the wiser. There was no unusual shipping out in the straits. The castle was asleep. Perhaps last night's great stirrings had been a figment of their imagination. It had seemed real enough at the time, but maybe after twelve days locked up in this cell they were losing their grip on reality.

The Adjutant-General, as the senior officer present, took command. As he, Colonel Adam and George Warne trotted along at the head of the column, Campbell mentally ran through his options before coming to a decision.

'Colonel Adam, march your regiment along the coast until you come to the enemy's landing beach near San Stefano. Once you've arrived do your best to disrupt their departure. We want to make sure that this attack is a costly failure, to discourage future attempts to invade. You've brought some field pieces with you, which should be useful.' Two six-pounder field guns were rumbling along at the back of the column. 'Captain Warne and I are going inland to see if we can find the fighting.' He pointed to the right and ahead towards the popping, cracking and flashing of gunfire.

A few hundred yards along the road, the column came to a *fiumara* cutting through the rugged landscape from the mountains to the sea.

'Right, Colonel,' said Campbell, 'this is where we part company. Stick on the coast road and you're bound to find where the French've landed. And when you do, give 'em a bloody nose. Today's the 21st's chance to throw the enemy back into the sea. You'll be the toast of the army. Good luck!'

With that, Campbell and Warne turned their horses off the road into the dry, flat, stony bottom of the *fiumara*.

After fifteen minutes of picking their way up the *fiumara*, Campbell and Warne had climbed well above the coast. Dawn was now coming up on the eastern horizon. Sunrise was not until about twenty minutes to six but it was getting lighter all the time. It would not be long before they would be able to see all along the coast in both directions. In the meanwhile, they were now no more than a few hundred yards from the gunfire.

'Let's dismount and continue on foot,' said Campbell.

'Right, sir,' said George.

Once the horses had climbed up out of the *fiumara*, they tethered them to a gnarled oak tree. George took the pistol from its holster in the saddle and shoved it into his waistband, leaving the carbine slung over his back. He drew his sabre, running his thumb along the blade; that was sharp enough, he thought approvingly. Campbell likewise had armed himself with a pair of pistols and a sword, the pistols shoved piratically into the scarlet sash around his waist.

'Right, let's go,' said Campbell quietly.

They began walking towards the sound of the gunfire. It was slow going as they were forever slipping on the steep, gravelly, boulder-strewn ground. The big, spiky grey-green lobes of prickly pear were constantly getting in the way, too, further impeding their progress. As the light gradually improved, they could make out a low but steep-sided hill about one hundred and fifty yards ahead. From the top of the hill, a standard fluttered in the breeze. Beneath the standard, George could make out movements of men darting between rocks, trees and other cover. Whoever was occupying the hill was keeping up a good rate of fire. Up ahead, George could see soldiers in British uniform ducking from rock to rock as they crept closer to the bottom of the hill.

Thirty yards ahead of them Campbell and George could see a group of soldiers taking cover behind a large outcrop of rock. With them were three men in peasant dress, billowing shirts, sashes, loose trousers and clogs, armed with muskets.

'Let's join 'em,' said Campbell. 'Be careful, Warne, we're in range of the hill now.' They ran, jinking between the rocks and the prickly pears. A musket ball smacked into a prickly pear to George's right; another brought up a puff of dust and pebbles as it hit the ground. As they sprinted towards the outcrop, one of the soldiers looked round and, seeing two figures running towards them, raised his musket to his shoulder.

'Shit,' exclaimed George aloud, 'he's going to shoot.'

'Don't shoot, we're English officers!' bawled Campbell.

'General Campbell here. Don't shoot! Don't shoot!' The man slowly lowered his musket.

A few seconds later the two men threw themselves down behind the outcrop. As they did so, two bullets hit the rock, zinging viciously away. They crouched panting as they recovered their breath. Looking round, George recognised the uniform of the King's German Legion.

'*Guten Morgen*,' said the man next to George. 'And who are you?' He spoke English with a heavy German accent.

'I am Captain Warne of the 27th Foot and this,' he said, pointing to his right, 'is Major-General Campbell, the Adjutant-General of His Majesty's forces in Sicily.'

The man hurriedly saluted.

'Who is in command here?'

'Lieutenant Heise, sir. He's over there,' the man replied, pointing towards another rocky outcrop to the right.

'I'd better go and see him,' said Campbell. 'George, you stay here.' With that he was off, keeping low and dodging behind rocks as he went.

Campbell slipped behind the large rock, out of breath after his weaving dash across open ground. He had been aware as he ran of several near misses; one bullet had hit a prickly pear right by his hand, another had hit, glancingly, the blade of his sabre, which now had a dent in it.

'Lieutenant Heise?'

'Yes, sir, that's me,' said a young man busily reloading a musket. He was tall and sparely built with a shock of blonde hair, blue eyes and a fair complexion, the epitome, Campbell thought, of a German officer. He didn't look at all unnerved to find himself suddenly confronted by one of the most senior officers in Sicily. With him were three riflemen, taking it in turns to reload and fire, rising from the cover of the rock and immediately ducking back again.

'What are your orders, Lieutenant?' asked Campbell.

'Colonel Fischer ordered me to engage the enemy, to do my best to keep them from moving too far inland. Half the battalion was sent along the beach from San Placido to engage the enemy. We were ordered to circle round inland to turn the enemy's advance.' Heise's English was good, only lightly accented.

Campbell nodded his approval. Colonel Fischer was an experienced officer who commanded the 2nd Foreign Light Infantry. He knew what he was doing.

'Do you know who they are?' asked Campbell, pointing to the hill as a volley of shots, aimed at the rifleman who had just ducked, ricocheted off the rock just above their heads.

'I think they're a Corsican regiment. One of our boys thinks he recognises the uniform.'

'Now it's getting light we should be able to make out the colour flying over their position,' said Campbell.

'If you're willing to stand up for long enough, sir,' said Heise with a grin.

George watched as General Campbell raced across the open ground to the next outcrop. Once he'd disappeared to safety, George moved, bent double, towards the three Sicilians who were sharing the cover with the Germans. Their colourful dress, darkly stubbled cheeks, wide-brimmed, low-crowned straw hats and the pistols and daggers shoved into their sashes gave them a raffish, bandit-like look. Like the German riflemen at the next-door outcrop, they were taking turns at firing and reloading, bobbing up and down from behind the rock to get a shot at the enemy.

'*Buon giorno*,' said one of the Sicilians, 'are you enjoying yourself?' A bullet zinged off the rock, throwing up a shower of fragments.

'What are you doing here?' asked George in the local dialect. The Sicilian looked surprised to hear a British officer speaking his language.

'I hate the French,' he replied. 'They fuck our women, steal our cattle and rob our churches. In the middle of the night, they' – he gestured towards the French infantry on the hill – 'came to our village. They broke into our cottages with the butts of their guns and stole our food.' He swung his musket as if battering down a door. 'I saw one of them rip the earrings from the ear of my neighbour's wife. There was a lot of blood. She screamed and sobbed with pain, but he just laughed and said, "You Sicilian bitch, you're the lucky one." Then they looted the church. They're pigs, these people, savages.'

'God,' said George, 'that's terrible. So you joined our troops?'

'Well, we chased the French from the village – we have a lot of guns,' he brandished his musket proudly, 'and down the hill. Then we met the Germans as they were advancing, so we joined them.'

He craned out round the side of the rock, raised his musket to his shoulder, aimed quickly and fired. The crash of the gun going off so close to him momentarily deafened George as the acrid smoke billowed around them.

'We must show the French that they cannot treat us like

animals,' he said, grinning wildly through the smoke, showing George his dirty, snaggled teeth.

'We should try to get closer,' said George to the man, pointing towards the hill, 'to get a better shot at the enemy.'

'*Si, si, signore,*' said the Sicilian, waving to his two comrades.

George ducked out from behind the rock, peering ahead.

'There's a big rock about twenty yards in front of us, just to the left,' he said pointing. 'Can you see it?'

'*Si, si.*'

George picked up his carbine in his left hand and gripped the sabre in his right. Crouching, he looked behind him. The three Sicilians were all waiting, muskets in hand.

'Right, let's make a run for it. Go!'

The four men sprinted across the stony open ground, sidestepping the prickly pears as they went. George was aware of several bullets coming too close to him for comfort. Just as he slid down behind the rock, he heard a yelp and an oath from behind him. One of the Sicilians, the oldest of the three, slid in beside George.

'Are you hit?' asked George.

'Yes, in the shoulder,' he gasped, dropping his musket and tenderly feeling his shoulder. He flexed the joint gently. 'It hurts like hell, but I don't think it's broken,' he said, wincing. George could see a tear in the man's shirt and around it a rapidly expanding patch of fresh, scarlet blood.

'Get one of your mates to bind the wound to stop the bleeding.'

While the wound was being bound, George edged to one side of the rock and gingerly stuck his head into the open to see what lay ahead. Immediately two bullets zipped past him, one of them smacking into the rock a few inches from his face, throwing up several shards of stone, which hit him stingingly on the cheek. The enemy has spotted our run, he thought; we're marked men here. In the few seconds he had had to look forward, George had seen that their new position was no more than thirty yards from the front line of the enemy's makeshift defences. He wished he had some grenades here; they would be the ideal weapon. From thirty yards he could lob them into the enemy lines without having to break cover.

George checked the priming of his carbine and, counting to three under his breath, swayed out from behind the rock and taking rapid aim, fired. This time he was too quick for the enemy and was back behind the rock before the inevitable shots came. Reloading, he turned to the Sicilians. They had finished binding the shoulder wound and were loading their muskets. In the distance, George could hear church bells ringing, as if to welcome the new day.

'Why are the bells ringing? Is there an early service?' he asked.

'No, I think they are summoning the men from the villages to fight the French.'

'Right, *amici*,' said George, 'let's help them. Get shooting.'

General Cavaignac, Major Levieux, his *chef de bataillon* and one of the *adjoints*, Lieutenant Folard, were standing on higher ground inland from the beach. Now that the sun had risen, they had a good view of the coast to the north towards Faro. What Cavaignac could see through his eyeglass confirmed his worst fears: the straits to the north were empty – the main invading force had not put to sea. The attack planned against the British between Faro and Messina had not taken place. That much was abundantly clear to all three officers. Cavaignac and Levieux looked at each other in astonishment.

'*Messieurs*,' said Cavaignac slowly, 'we have been abandoned. For some reason, the main attack to the north did not take place. Therefore our diversionary attack is futile. I – we – and the men have been badly let down.' He was now fizzing with anger. 'I always knew that Grenier was an old woman. He wouldn't attack a bloody chicken coop for fear of finding a fox. What do you suggest we do now, Major?' he asked, turning to Levieux.

At that moment the second *adjoint*, Lieutenant Cailloux, arrived at a run. Halting in front of Cavaignac, he saluted.

'The Corsican regiment, sir, is cut off,' he announced breathlessly. 'It is surrounded by British troops and a large number of armed local men and more are arriving all the time, called to the fight by the church bells, it seems.'

'Is that it?' asked Cavaignac.

'No, sir. I also have reliable reports that a large body of British troops, possibly a whole battalion, has been seen on the coast road, marching in this direction,' said the *adjoint*.

'What about the other two battalions?' asked Levieux.

'They are less heavily engaged and keeping the enemy at bay, sir,' replied the *adjoint*.

'Thank you, Cailloux,' said Cavaignac. 'Right, Major, we must decide what to do.'

'I can see little point, sir, in fighting on. The main attack has not taken place so our operation is pointless. The Corsicans are surrounded. The British are sending reinforcements and the peasants have risen against us. I would advise, sir, that we re-embark as many of our men as we can and return to the mainland.'

Cavaignac listened to his *chef de bataillon* in silence. Once Levieux had finished, the general turned to face the sea, his hands clasped behind his back, deep in thought. So much for my ambition, my hopes of delivering Sicily to the King. The operation is a fiasco. It is not my fault, we have been abandoned, he thought bitterly, but that would be of little account during the recriminations that would inevitably follow. But now was not the time to dwell on his misfortunes.

'*Alors*,' said Cavaignac, suddenly decisive. 'We will retire in an orderly fashion to the beach and re-embark. Get a message,' Cavaignac turned to Cailloux, the *adjoint*, 'if you can, to the Corsicans. Tell them that we are re-embarking. They are to cover the retreat of the Neapolitan battalions before doing their best to fight their way back to the beach.'

Major Levieux took a notepad from his pocket and began scribbling orders with a pencil. He tore the sheets off the pad and gave them to two waiting orderlies.

'*Allez vite, tous les deux*,' said Levieux, '*et bonne chance*.'

Behind their rock, George and the three Sicilians had been firing away at the half-concealed enemy for twenty minutes. The barrel of his carbine was too hot to touch, his eyes were stinging from the smoke and George was almost out of powder. He now knew that they were facing a Corsican regiment. He was beginning to wonder what action to take when, in a slew of dust and pebbles, General Campbell and a small posse of German riflemen slid in beside him. One of the Germans tugged George's sleeve.

'Sir, look, look, white flag, white flag,' pointing towards the enemy position on the hill. George craned warily round the edge of the rock.

'Bloody hell, sir,' he said to Campbell, 'it looks as if the Corsicans have surrendered.'

Up on the hill, a large white flag was being waved above the Corsican position. All was suddenly quiet. George could see that some of the soldiers on the hill had started to stand up. Cautiously, George stood up to his full height and stepped away from the cover of the rock.

'They've stopped shooting, sir,' he said to Campbell. 'It looks as if they are laying down their arms.'

'Keep the hill covered, lads,' he shouted, 'in case they try any tricks.'

Then, from the top of the hill, several men started making their way down towards the British lines. One of them was carrying a pole with a white flag hanging limply from it. George and Campbell watched the small party as it picked its way across the rocky ground towards them.

'George,' said Campbell quietly, 'you speak French, challenge them.'

'*Qui va là?*' shouted George at the top of his voice.

'*Colonel Franceschetti du neuvième regiment corse,*' came the reply. 'I want to see the senior English officer here, please.'

'*C'est le General Campbell,*' George shouted back. '*Avancez, monsieur, avancez, mais doucement, s'il vous plaît.*'

As the small party of Corsicans, the white flag of surrender above them, came down the hillside, the Sicilians began to emerge from their cover. They watched the Corsicans closely as they approached; when they were ten yards away, the Sicilians burst into a great cheer, '*Viva il Re Giorgio! Viva il Re Giorgio!*'

Two minutes later Colonel Franceschetti, with a party of three junior officers and a handful of soldiers trailing in his wake, strode up towards General Campbell, stopped six feet away, stood to attention and saluted. Campbell returned the salute.

'*Dominique-César Franceschetti, colonel du neuvième regiment corse, à votre service, monsieur.*'

'James Campbell, Major-General and Adjutant-General of His Majesty's Forces in Sicily,' he replied. 'You wanted to see me.'

'*Oui, monsieur le general.* I wish to surrender my battalion to you. We have been abandoned, we are surrounded and we have seen your reinforcements arriving.' He drew his sword from its scabbard and, taking it by the blade, offered the hilt to Campbell.

The men of the 21st Foot were swinging steadily along the coast road in the pale morning light. The eastern horizon was flecked with thin wisps of pink-tinged cloud against the luminous sky. To their left out in the straits, they could see a shoal of transport vessels, like small aquatic beetles, heading back to Calabria.

'Damn it,' exclaimed Colonel Adam, pointing out to sea, 'it looks as if they've turned tail already.' Spurring his horse on from the head of the column, he cantered up the road. Coming over a rise, Adam saw, three hundred yards ahead, the beach of San Stefano laid out in front of him. All along the waterline, men were scrambling into the landing craft as they pulled away from the beach. Only the French rearguard was still ashore; most of Cavaignac's troops were already on their way back to Calabria. If he was to inflict any damage on the enemy, there was not a moment to be lost. He turned his horse's head and cantered back to the column.

'The French are on the beach,' he shouted. 'Deploy the front company into line. Bring up the six-pounders. At the double, now!'

A subaltern scurried down the column to pass the order to the gun crews. Soon the two field guns were passing the head of the column.

'Quick as you can there, Lieutenant Boyd,' shouted Adam to the artillery subaltern over the grinding of the gun carriages' wheels on the road. 'You've only got a few minutes to get some rounds off.'

Once the two six-pounders had been dragged into position in the dunes, Boyd watched as the two five-man gun crews went through their well-rehearsed routine.

'Range four hundred yards,' shouted Boyd, 'load with spherical case shot.'

The loader placed the shell in the muzzle of the gun for the sponge man to ram it home. The vents man then punctured the cartridge with a spike, placed the fuse in the vent and stood clear while the firer lit the fuse with his linstock – a pike holding a piece of slow-burning match.

The two guns fired almost simultaneously, recoiling into the soft sand. One of the shells exploded in the air more or less above the waterline – Adam could see the musket balls hitting the water like a deadly rain shower – one man was hit, pitching forward into the surf. The other one, with a longer fuse, exploded further out to sea, beyond where the men were embarking the boats. So far as Boyd could see, no one was injured.

'Reload,' shouted Boyd. 'Trim that fuse, number two.'

By now the regiment's leading company was advancing at a trot in a ragged line across the beach towards the departing enemy. The two six-pounders, their barrels screwed to maximum elevation, fired over the heads of the advancing infantry. Once again the fuses were too long, so the shells exploded too far out over the sea to cause any casualties among the retreating French. By the time the leading men of the advancing 21st were within fifty yards of the sea there were no more than a hundred French soldiers still on the beach. Two of them, seeing the oncoming English, raised their muskets to their shoulder and fired. The bullets flew harmlessly overhead.

'Halt!' shouted the captain. The panting soldiers stopped, taking deep breaths to steady themselves. 'Take aim! Wait for it! Wait!'

Then, as the English line took aim, the French soldiers looked at one another and, one by one, raised their arms in the air. Trapped between the sea and the enemy, they had little alternative. Resistance was futile: they had no time to board the few remaining transports and put out into the straits to safety. They would have been shot down where they stood in the shallow water.

'Right, lads,' said the captain, 'fix bayonets and forward at the walk.' All along the line, the men fixed bayonets, the thin, bright blades glittering menacingly in the morning sun.

'Look, sir, look,' shouted the British sergeant, pointing out to sea. 'There's a couple of 'em swimming for it.' William Ball, the captain, followed his sergeant's finger. There, perhaps thirty yards off the beach were two men in the sea. One of them was bobbing up and down as if he was afloat but the other was only up to his chest in the water. They were making for the nearest of the transport vessels, which was already at least a hundred yards further out to sea.

'So there are, by God. Who's a strong swimmer and fancies a dip?'

Two men put up their hands.

'Right, Wilson, Hall, in you go and see if you can catch them up and bring them back.'

The two men stripped off their packs, tunics, breeches and boots and, each holding a knife in their teeth, waded into the sea, to a barrage of wolf-whistles from their mates on the beach. Both men were powerful swimmers, so it was not long before they were gaining visibly on the heads in the water. All the while, the last transport vessels were getting further and further out to sea, far enough out now that they were momentarily hidden by the roll of a big wave. On the beach, the sergeant and a party of redcoats were disarming the French prisoners, stacking their muskets like stooks of corn and piling their sidearms in a heap on the sand.

Offshore, meanwhile, the slow-motion race between the heads in the water was continuing. The pursuing heads of Wilson and Hall were almost upon the nearer of the two fleeing heads. The hounds were gaining on the fox. A few minutes later, to much ribald cheering, Wilson and Hall waded naked out of the sea; between them, pinioned by the arms, was their prisoner.

They marched him up to Captain Ball. He was a big, paunchy man and his soaking uniform clung to him, although he had lost one of his boots. With all the dignity he could muster he came to attention in front of Captain Ball and saluted.

'Colonel Ambrosio, of His Neapolitan Majesty's service.'

Ball, trying not to laugh, returned the salute.

General Campbell and George Warne were standing in the middle of what had been the Corsican position looking on as Franceschetti's men surrendered their weapons under the watchful eyes – and fixed bayonets – of the German riflemen. The Corsicans placed their muskets in a big pile with their powder horns and ammunition pouches. As they laid down their arms, the Sicilians circled like vultures, helping themselves liberally to the booty.

'Well, Captain Warne,' said Campbell, 'so much for King Joachim's plan to conquer Sicily. The invasion, or this part of it, doesn't seem to have been pushed with any great vigour. There have been hardly any casualties on either side.'

'Yes, sir,' said George, 'it's like shadow-boxing.'

'I wonder if Murat attacked to the north, between Messina and Faro?' mused Campbell.

'I don't know, sir, but I'm sure we'll find out.'

'Well, after this, he won't try again this year, so we're safe until the spring, I'd say.'

'I'd agree with that, sir,' said George, wiping the blood from his cheek with the back of his hand.

On the beach at San Stefano, Colonel Adam's men were marshalling the hundred or so prisoners they had captured, marching them up to the dunes beside the road. The colonel himself was talking to Frank Berry, his second in command.

'I wonder what's happening up there,' he nodded inland towards the hills.

'Well,' replied Berry, 'there was quite a lot of shooting, but it's stopped now. Perhaps the enemy has surrendered.'

'Ah, look who's arriving now.' The two men looked up the beach towards the road. Threading his way through the dunes on a horse was General Cockburn.

'Good morning, gentlemen,' he said. 'I'm sorry to see that I've missed the excitement, but General Campbell seems to have dealt with the situation very efficiently. I wasn't woken until five o'clock. I met Brooke and the 44th just as they were getting under way, so joined them.' He paused. 'I gather that a Corsican regiment has surrendered,' said Cockburn.

'We had noticed that the firing had stopped, sir,' said Berry, 'so wondered what was happening.'

'After all that,' said Cockburn, 'it's been rather a damp squib, I should say.'

'*D'accord, monsieur,*' said Colonel Carboni to the Corsican major. Carboni had already spent several hours interrogating officers captured after Cavaignac's ignominious retreat that morning. Once the prisoners, about eight hundred of them made up of Franceschetti's Corsican battalion and the hundred or so stragglers caught on the beach, had been corralled, they were marched up the coast to Messina, guarded and occasionally goaded by the men of the 21st. The captured soldiers were then confined in the *lazaretto* – the building on the harbour in which sick sailors were quarantined – and in Fort Salvador. The captured officers were separated from their men and taken to the Citadel. Among the forty-five captured officers was the Corsican colonel Franceschetti, a French colonel, a brigade major, one of

Cavaignac's ADCs and several other senior field officers. It was, thought Carboni, a good catch, one he was determined to trawl for information while he had the chance.

George Warne was exhausted. He'd been in action since four o'clock in the morning but the adrenalin that had fired him up during the march down the coast, the skirmish with the Corsicans and its aftermath had drained completely away. Now, as he walked his horse towards the gates of the Citadel, he felt as tired as he'd ever been, almost falling asleep in the saddle. His whole body was stiff and aching; his clothes were filthy and torn and his cheek throbbed where he had been hit by the splinters of rock. He had also, he remembered, somehow, somewhere lost his carbine. The armourer would be after him but that could wait. For now, he longed for Carlotta's bed and her warm embrace.

CHAPTER FIFTEEN

Punta di Pezzo, Calabria, 19th September 1810

'Ask General Cavaignac to come in the moment he arrives,' said Murat to the orderly as he disappeared into his study.

'Yes, Your Majesty,' said the orderly, bowing.

Murat went into his study and sat down at the desk. Thirty-six hours had passed since his humiliation at the hands of General Grenier but time had done nothing to calm his anger or heal his bruised amour-propre. Even his morning ride had failed to improve his mood. He, the King, had been publicly humiliated by a mere general, a man who was nominally under his command. It was an intolerable insult and a public demonstration of the limits of his power. Whatever his subjects had thought of him, they would think less of him now. To add insult to injury, his long-cherished plan to reunify his kingdom by conquering Sicily lay in ruins. There could be no further attempt this year and who knew what 1811 would bring? He stared gloomily at the white canvas ceiling. Where the hell was Albertini? There was work to be done.

Half an hour later, by which time King and secretary had started ploughing through the daily mountain of paperwork, the orderly announced General Cavaignac. As he entered the room, Murat stood up.

'*Bonjour, mon general*,' said Murat. Cavaignac tucked his hat under his arm and bowed. 'I would like a full report of your operation. I've had some news, but I want to hear your account of what happened. Please, sit down,' said Murat indicating the chair next to Albertini. There was a pause while Cavaignac composed his thoughts. Then, at length, he began, in the precise French of the Loire Valley.

'The embarkation from the beaches near Reggio went smoothly, as did the crossing to Sicily. We came ashore at about three in the morning without encountering any opposition. The British were nowhere to be seen. I gathered my staff at the top of the beach from where we directed the movements inland.'

'When was the first contact with the enemy?' asked Murat.

'It was sometime after half past three, once the troops had moved inland. It's not clear which came first but the leading elements of one of the Neapolitan battalions ran into a patrol of British dragoons to the south of Mili. There was an exchange of fire, but the dragoons disengaged and, I assume, raised the alarm. At about the same time the Corsican battalion encountered enemy skirmishers – Germans, I think.'

Cavaignac explained to Murat how the operation had unwound once the dawn had come up, revealing that the main invasion to the north between Faro and Messina had not taken place.

'Once it was clear that the main invasion force had not sailed,' said Cavaignac resignedly, 'there was little point in wasting my men's lives in fighting on. I ordered Colonel Franceschetti's Corsican battalion to hold its position to cover the withdrawal, which they did admirably.'

'But Franceschetti surrendered, *n'est-ce pas?*' said Murat.

'Yes, sire. I can only assume that he was surrounded. The British were bringing up reinforcements and the peasants were fighting us in large numbers. Franceschetti would, I imagine, have been anxious to surrender to the British rather than to the Sicilians . . .' Cavaignac's voice trailed off.

'Yes, I can understand that,' replied Murat. 'Incidentally, why do you think that the peasantry failed to rise against the British as we expected?'

'I don't know for sure, but I have heard reports of looting and violence on the part of our troops, which may be to blame.' There was a silence before Murat spoke.

'How many men did we lose, *mon general?*'

'I don't know how many casualties, killed or wounded, Franceschetti's Corsicans suffered but his battalion numbered around seven hundred and none of them have returned. In the battalions that did get home, the roll-call returns show that we suffered around a hundred casualties. For what it is worth, sire, I believe that almost all of that hundred were captured by the British on the beach. I saw very few wounded or dead men.'

'So we lost around eight hundred men, *mon general.* That's a high proportion from a force of three thousand, more than one man in four.' Murat paused and looked at Cavaignac. 'I will do my utmost to ensure that you are not blamed for this debacle. It is not your fault that the main attack was called off. The responsibility for that,' he continued, his voice rising with anger, 'lies with General Grenier and, ultimately, with the Emperor. It is they who are responsible for the fact that eight hundred of my troops are now either dead or languishing in a British prison. It is they who are responsible for the fact that French arms – and I – are now a laughing stock. Sir John Stuart will be making jokes about it for weeks.' Cavaignac and Albertini exchanged glances and fidgeted. Then, like a storm which has blown itself out, he stopped and stood up.

'Look at this,' he said, placing his right hand on the hilt of the sword that hung from his belt. Cavaignac and Albertini watched as Murat drew the sword from its scabbard and held it up over the desk. 'Look at it,' he commanded. They looked.

'*C'est une épée magnifique*,' said Cavaignac. The pommel was a gilded lion's head, with the curved handguard emerging from its open jaws. The gilding on the lion's neck, the top of the handle and the handguard were richly decorated with embossed steel, faceted and polished to resemble precious stones. It glinted in the light as Murat held it up. The long, bright, menacing steel blade was richly engraved with palms and scrolls of vine leaves. It was a weapon fit for a King.

'I commissioned it from the royal armoury in Naples and it was delivered three days ago. It's a beautiful, deadly thing.' Murat made an imaginary pass with the sword in the air. 'But if I can't even order my own soldiers into battle, what, gentlemen, is the point? I might as well give it to my gardener to hoe the beans.'

At about the same time as Murat was showing off his new sword, across the straits Sir John Stuart was welcoming his staff officers to his office in the Citadel.

347

'The Adjutant-General will be with us shortly, I dare say,' said Sir John, 'so let's begin.'

At that moment, the door opened.

'Good morning, Sir John,' said Campbell as he entered the room. 'I've brought you a trophy, a souvenir of our victory over the King of Naples.' He turned the regimental standard he was carrying horizontally so that the flag could be seen.

'This,' Campbell announced as he walked across the room, 'is a colour captured when the Corsican ninth infantry surrendered.' The red, white and blue silk standard, which was about three foot square, bore Murat's cypher in each corner and was inscribed as a gift to The Royal Corsican Corps from 'Giachino Napoleone'.

'Thank you, General Campbell,' said Stuart. 'As you say, it is a splendid trophy, a fitting reminder of my victory over the invading enemy, of how I turned Murat's forces back into the sea.' Forbes and Donkin exchanged amused glances across the table. 'It will, gentlemen, stand alongside my victory at the battle of Maida as a triumph of British arms.' He paused, looking round the table. 'General Campbell, if you would be so kind?'

Campbell cleared his throat and began his report of the French invasion. 'I was woken by Colonel Warren at about four o'clock on Tuesday morning . . .' He told of his night ride along the coast to San Stefano, of his encounter with Colonel Adam and the 21st, of his and George Warne's joining the German riflemen in the fight with the Corsicans and of the enemy's surrender.

'The invading force, I estimate, numbered three and a half thousand men of which, gentlemen, more than eight hundred have fallen into our hands, including forty-five officers of varying ranks. This represents a considerable reverse for the enemy.'

'How many casualties did we suffer, General Campbell?'

'Well, Sir John,' replied Campbell, 'remarkably, we lost not a single man killed and only one rifleman was slightly wounded. Given the amount of shooting, it is extraordinary that we should lose no men at all. I am sad to say that two Sicilians were killed in the fighting and three more have since died of their wounds.' He paused. 'I would like to single out two officers whose prompt and decisive action did much to repel the invasion. One of them, Colonel Fischer, is well known to us all. The other, Lieutenant Heise, of the King's German Legion, is a young officer whose conduct yesterday morning deserves the highest praise.'

'Please make sure that your commendations of these officers are published in the army orders, General Campbell,' said Stuart.

'I would also like to bring to your attention the exemplary conduct of Captain Warne of the 27th Foot. His coolness under fire and his knowledge of the local dialect did much to keep the peasants in the fight against the enemy. This was, in my opinion, a major factor in the defeat of the invasion.'

'I was under the impression,' said Colonel Donkin, 'that Captain Warne had been seconded to intelligence duties under Colonel Airey.'

'That's right, Colonel,' replied Campbell. 'He had.'

'So what was he doing in the front line fighting the French in the middle of the night seven miles from Messina?'

'He happened to be at a loose end in the Citadel when we realised what was going on, so I ordered him to join me, which he did eagerly.'

'Where would we be without the ever-present, ever-busy Captain Warne?' asked Donkin, mischievously.

'Where indeed,' replied Campbell.

There was a brief silence around the table before General Cockburn caught Stuart's eye.

'I wonder if I might add a couple of things, Sir John?'

'By all means, General Cockburn,' replied Stuart amiably.

'I am convinced,' Cockburn began in his Irish lilt, 'that General Cavaignac's force was ordered to retreat to the mainland by telegraph. In other words, it was Murat's decision – or possibly Grenier's – not to continue the fight. Having said that, I do think that Cavaignac could have made more of a fight of it.'

'Shouldn't we be glad that he didn't, General?' asked Stuart.

'Yes, of course, but I think he allowed himself to be gulled by the size of our forces. We only had two battalions advancing on the enemy, yet one captured French officer said to me, "*De quoi se battre contre toute l'armée Anglaise!*" It looks as if they gave up rather easily.'

'Well, General,' said Campbell, 'your idea is certainly backed up by the fact that we found only two enemy corpses. One was a drummer and the other an infantryman, killed on the beach. These are scarcely the casualties of an army fighting in earnest.'

'Which begs the question,' said Cockburn, 'of what the object of the landing was? Could it have been simply to demonstrate to General Grenier and the Emperor that it is possible to ferry troops in large numbers across the straits and land in Sicily? That would certainly explain the enemy's lack of fight and his early flight.'

George Warne was slowly coming to life as Carlotta wriggled gently against his back, nuzzling his neck and nibbling his ear. Before long, her fingers grasped his penis and began lovingly to stroke it. George, now fully awake, turned to face his lover.

'Oh, my darling, you were so tired last night,' said Carlotta softly, 'you fell straight asleep.'

'I'll make it up to you now, *carissima*,' said George, lifting her onto his stomach and pulling her forward so that her breasts hung almost to his face. 'I was exhausted last night, so tired even you could not get me going,' he said with a laugh. 'But I'm ready now.'

'Yes, my darling, yes, so I see.'

'There is something I have to tell you,' said Carboni.

Sandro Carboni and Colonel Airey were standing on the Citadel's northern bastion, looking across the harbour towards Fort Salvador. As it was mid morning, the port was abuzz with activity: fishing boats disgorging the daily catch at the Marina, slithy and silvery in the sun, coasters loading and unloading their cargoes and everywhere men springing nimbly between deck and quay. Out in the harbour a Royal Navy frigate was being painted, sailors suspended like monkeys from ropes over her side, paint pots and brushes in hand. All the noises and smells of the harbour floated up to the two men on the breeze. Up here on the bastion they would not be overheard: their secrets would be lost in the ether, entrusted to the sea and the sky.

'I interrogated around thirty captured officers yesterday,' said Carboni, 'mostly Corsicans taken when their regiment surrendered. I was up half the night.' He did look tired, baggy-eyed.

'Did you discover anything useful?' asked Airey.

'Most of them had little to say but one officer, Signor Cattaneo, a captain aged about thirty-five, says he has something to offer.'

'Oh, yes?' said Airey, raising an eyebrow.

'*Il capitano* Cattaneo says he has a bargain for us,' Carboni said slowly. 'He says that he has some useful intelligence for us, information we would be very keen to have.'

'What's his price?' asked Airey immediately.

'Ha, ha,' said Carboni, with a smile, 'you're quick this morning, Colonel.'

'I try, I try,' said Airey, laughing.

'Well, I don't know. He won't tell me. He says that he will only discuss it with a senior British officer.'

'Well, I never,' said Airey. 'He must be confident that his intelligence is valuable.' He paused. 'And trusting that we won't extract it by other means . . .' His voice trailed off.

'I think you ought to talk to him, Colonel. It will give you a chance to judge for yourself how reliable he is and so on.' He paused. 'Whether we can trust him.'

'Yes, that's a good idea.'

'He speaks good English, too, by the way,' added Carboni.

Half an hour later, Airey and Carboni were sitting at a table in a room in the bowels of the Citadel. High above them was a window through which, at a steep angle, a broad shaft of sunlight lit up a rectangular patch of stonework on the opposite wall. Across the table sat a slim, wiry man of medium height, with black thinning hair and dark, alert eyes. At his temples, Airey could see the first traces of grey. He was wearing a standard French infantry officer's dark blue tunic, unhooked at the neck, cut away at the front to reveal a white waistcoat with a single row of brass buttons. On his left shoulder was a tarnished pinchbeck epaulette.

'So, Captain Cattaneo, I gather that you have some intelligence which you think we might like?'

'Yes,' replied Cattaneo. 'I do.'

'Colonel Carboni tells me that you will only discuss the matter with a senior British officer.'

'That is so, yes,' replied Cattaneo.

'Well, my name is Airey,' he said, looking Cattaneo straight in the eye. 'I am a colonel on Sir John Stuart's staff, so you can talk to me.'

There was a pause while Cattaneo considered this. Then he put his hands together on the table and began.

'Colonel Airey, if you promise me that I will be granted a commission in the Royal Corsican Rangers, then I will tell you what I know.' He paused, looking intently at Airey. 'But not before.'

Airey paused, straightening his back in his chair.

'Tell me, Captain, why do you want to leave the French service and join His Majesty's army?'

'Colonel, like some of the other officers in my regiment – Colonel Franceschetti is one of them – I have served with your Corsican Rangers in the past. I was with them in Egypt and fought at the Battle of Alexandria.'

'I see,' said Airey, glancing at Carboni. That, thought Airey, accounts for the man's excellent English. The British Corsican regiment had been temporarily disbanded following the Peace of Amiens in 1802 so presumably Cattaneo had switched allegiances at that point.

'I have friends and relations serving with the British. Two of my cousins are in the Royal Corsican Rangers and several friends also.' Cattaneo paused. 'I admire Colonel Lowe greatly. He is a fine officer and leader of men. I have served under him and would like to do so again.'

Airey glanced at Carboni again. Hudson Lowe had commanded the Corsican Rangers since before the expedition to Egypt nine years earlier and was, Airey knew, lionised by his men.

'But, Captain Cattaneo, why are you so keen to leave the French service after so long?'

'Serving in a Corsican regiment, I feel a second-class officer. The French regiments look down on us. We get all the bad, dangerous jobs, like hunting down the insurgents in the mountains of Calabria in the winter. Our pay is always in arrears – I am owed a lot of money – and we are left to find our own food where we can. This makes the soldiers angry and, sometimes, violent. How do you say it in English?' He paused and looked down. 'I've had enough.'

'Good,' said Airey. 'The colonel and I are going to leave you now so that we can put your proposition to the Adjutant-General. We will be back soon.'

With that the two men stood up and left the room, locking the door behind them.

'I am so bloody bored,' said John Entwhistle. 'We've been in this hole for thirteen days now, rotting away.'

Neither he nor William Coker was any the wiser as to the cause of the commotion two nights earlier. Lacking an explanation, their excitement and curiosity quickly faded as the tedium of their daily routine reasserted itself.

Then, they heard footsteps on the stone stairs that led up to their cell. These were not the careful tread of their gaoler, with his tray of food. These steps were brisker, more purposeful. The key turned in the lock and the door swung open.

'*Bonjour, messieurs.*' It was Major Lafite, as always immaculately turned out: his tunic freshly pressed, his breeches crisply laundered, his boots buffed to a dark gleam and his fine, walrus moustache neatly trimmed. 'I have some good news for you both.'

Coker and Entwhistle looked quizzically at the Major.

'You are to be exchanged with some French officers. The exchange will happen today, so by this evening you will be back in Sicily.' Coker and Entwhistle looked at each other incredulously. Suddenly, wholly unexpectedly, a gap had opened in the clouds.

'Are you sure, Major Lafite?' asked Coker. 'Are you sure?'

'*Oui, messieurs, c'est vrai.*'

'But what has brought this about so suddenly, *monsieur*?' asked Entwhistle.

'One or two French officers had the misfortune to fall into the English hands and we've agreed an exchange. You are pleased to be going back to Sicily, *n'est-ce pas*?'

'Yes, of course, it's a very pleasant surprise.'

'*Bon.* I will send the guard for you in half an hour so pack your things,' he gestured around the cell, 'so that you are ready to leave when they come for you. *Au revoir, messieurs.*' He saluted, turned on his heel and walked out of the cell, locking the door as he went.

'Good God,' said Entwhistle as Lafite's footsteps receded down the stairs. 'Well I never.'

'A bolt from the blue, I'd say,' said Coker. 'Just think of it, John, tonight we'll be having dinner in the Citadel.' They laughed.

Finbarr Rogers was at his desk in the Citadel. Beside him at a large table his junior clerks, John Farrell and William Allsop, were beavering away at their ledgers. Yesterday had been a hectic day. From the moment he'd arrived in the office at quarter past seven in the morning until he left after eight o'clock in the evening, he had worked flat out, drafting orders for the generals, gathering information, compiling returns, answering endless questions. The habitually ordered calm of the staff offices had descended into organised chaos. By the time he had arrived home, exhausted at nine o'clock, he realised that he hadn't thought about the break-in at his house the previous day for a single moment.

Things were now quieter, so Rogers had a chance to consider the implications of the break-in. If it was the work of a casual thief, then no harm had been done as nothing had been stolen. On the other hand, if it wasn't a run-of-the-mill burglary, what was it and who was behind it? Rogers knew he was playing a dangerous game, but he had no indication that anyone in the Citadel had any idea what he was up to. He had been very discreet, both in how he conducted the business and in what he did with the proceeds.

Throughout the day he tried to see if anyone important – Colonel Airey, the Quartermaster, the AG, any of the generals – was looking at him or speaking to him differently but try as he might, he could detect no change in tone or attitude towards him. Maybe he was worrying unnecessarily. Better to keep his head down and not say anything to the men at San Francesco di Paola. They were not, he suspected, forgiving types.

'It's not entirely surprising that Cattaneo wants to rejoin our Corsican regiment. After all, he's got friends and relations serving in it.' Colonel Airey paused. 'It's happened before. Do you remember after the fall of Capri two years ago, one officer and about eighty men from our Corsican Rangers deserted to one of the French Corsican regiments?'

'Yes, I do remember,' said Carboni. 'Colonel Lowe was very upset and defensive about it, too.'

The two men were walking across the Citadel's courtyard. They had just come from the Adjutant-General's office where they had secured his consent to offer Cattaneo a commission in the Corsican Rangers – but if, and only if, his information proved valuable. He was not, Campbell stressed, going to be granted a King's commission in return for some second-hand military gossip.

Airey unlocked and opened the door of Captain Cattaneo's cell. As the two British officers entered, he stood up.

'Please sit down,' said Airey as he and Carboni pulled up chairs opposite the Corsican. Then Airey began.

'You will be glad to hear, Captain Cattaneo, that the Adjutant-General has authorised me to offer you a commission in the Corsican Rangers on condition that the intelligence you have to offer us is new and important.'

'I think you will find, Colonel, that it is both of those things,' said Cattaneo calmly. In the circumstances, he looked remarkably composed. 'How can I be sure that you will keep your side of the bargain if I tell you what I know?'

'You will have to trust me as a British officer and as a gentleman,' replied Airey. 'And, of course, you have Colonel Carboni here as a witness.'

'Yes, of course,' said Cattaneo.

'So, what is it you have to tell us?' asked Airey, looking the Corsican straight in the eye across the table.

'I know about a French spy ring in Messina.'

'Tell us more,' said Airey.

'It is widely rumoured that there are many French spies in Sicily, especially in Messina, but very few men in the French army have any precise knowledge of what is going on. I've been stationed in Calabria for three years, but until recently I knew no more than anyone else. I'd heard the gossip and the rumours but that was it.' He spread his hands.

'So what happened?'

'About two weeks ago I was ordered to take my company to Catona, a little harbour not far along the coast from San Giovanni. I thought nothing of it at the time. Just another posting. However, on my first evening there, the garrison commander – there is a small fort guarding the anchorage – invited me to dinner.' He paused.

'Yes?' said Airey.

'He wasn't a Corsican but we got on well. During the course of the evening – and there were only the two of us – he drank a lot of wine and became increasingly talkative. He let slip that he had been told to expect a night attack on his anchorage in the next few days. This, he assured me, was why I had been ordered there with my company, to strengthen the defences. The information, he said, came from our spies in Messina.' Cattaneo leant back in his chair and rubbed his chin. It made a slight rasping sound in the silence of the cell.

'At first I assumed it was nothing more than drunken speculation on his part, the wine talking, trying to impress me. But when, the following night, the raid happened I wondered whether there was something to it. I then heard that three other raids had taken place on anchorages along the coast on the same night. In each case extra troops had been sent to their defence, which made me think perhaps my drunken friend had revealed something he shouldn't have done.'

'Carry on, Captain Cattaneo, please,' said Airey. Carboni was scribbling notes on a piece of paper.

'Two days later, I was ordered to return, with my company, to camp at Melia. There I began to ask around, to make enquiries, very discreetly, using the story of the raid as cover.'

'And what did you find out?' asked Airey.

'Well, as I said, I've been in Calabria for three years, so I've got friends – some of them have important jobs on the staff. Also, I have my Corsican contacts. To cut a long story short, as you English like to say, I discovered that the French had received a warning about the raids from their agents in Messina.'

The two colonels looked at each other for a moment before Airey continued.

'What else do you know about this conspiracy?'

'My sources agree that the spies use a monastery as their headquarters, which seems odd.'

'Which one? There are many monasteries in and around Messina,' said Airey, stifling his rising excitement.

'The monastery of San Francesco di Paola, not far from the Porta Reale.'

'And Captain Cattaneo, do you have a name – any name – which might help us identify the conspirators? Without a name, our job is much more difficult . . .' Airey let the implied threat hang in the air. There was a long silence, while Cattaneo stared at the ceiling, deep in thought, before eventually, he spoke.

'There was one name I kept hearing.'

'Oh, yes?'

'I think he's a French intelligence officer.'

'What's his name?'

'Armand Jardel.'

It is not a long crossing from Scylla to Messina. William Coker and John Entwhistle stood side by side at the port rail of the fishing smack watching the ramparts of the castle, their prison for the last fortnight, slip astern. By the time the vessel had passed the point at Faro, the castle at Scylla was no bigger than the nail of a man's little finger. Now, ahead on the starboard side, Messina was gradually revealing herself.

Entwhistle's soldiers were gathered in the vessel's bows, talking, laughing or just gazing out to sea. Of the twenty men who had left Messina for San Giovanni with Entwhistle nearly a fortnight ago, only six were returning. Twelve had been killed in the raid and of the three who had been wounded, one had since died and one returned to Messina under a flag of truce. This left just six men, plus Sergeant Warwick and Entwhistle himself, of the original raiding party, a stark reminder of the cost of the operation.

Entwhistle had been separated from his men during

the fortnight at Scylla so when they marched into the castle courtyard he was pleased to see them. They looked healthy enough – clearly they had been adequately fed and allowed a decent amount of exercise – but their uniforms were torn and dirty. Some of them had lost their boots and most of them their kit, canteens, packs and so on. None of them, of course, had their muskets, bayonets or any ammunition.

'It'll be nice to see our friends again,' said Coker, gazing absent-mindedly at the view.

'Yes, it will,' said Entwhistle, adding, more forcefully, 'and to find out what happened to the other raiding parties. I particularly want to know what that knave Warne got up to.' A fortnight languishing in a cell had done nothing to diminish Entwhistle's animus against George Warne.

'Do be careful, John,' said Coker. 'Don't get yourself into trouble the moment you get home. That would be a pity.'

'That's kind of you, William, but I can look after myself, thank you.'

It was approaching midday as Emma Thring turned out of a side street onto the Marina. She had walked the short distance from her brother's lodgings off the Corso, picking her way carefully through Messina's busy streets. At first, she had found the city's seething traffic daunting, even frightening, but over the last fortnight she had become accustomed to it. Two weeks ago, she wouldn't have dared to venture out without her brother but now she felt perfectly safe on her own in the thronging crowds. Indeed, yesterday she had brushed off three urchins who had been pestering her for money, something she would never have done a week ago. She enjoyed strolling along the Marina watching the ships loading and unloading their cargoes, the fishermen landing their catches, vessels putting off and coming in, all the noise, colour and activity of a large port. Out in the middle of the harbour, a Royal Navy frigate was at anchor, her sails furled neatly on the yardarms. On her quarterdeck, Emma could see two figures, pacing to and fro. It was hot. She twirled her parasol.

'Miss Thring.'

Emma turned. It was the tall figure of Frank Younge, dashing in his naval uniform.

'Mr Younge, to what do I owe this unexpected pleasure?'

'I've just been in the Admiralty office,' he nodded in the direction of the *Palazzata*, 'to see if there were any letters for me.' He paused. 'Do you often come here on your own?'

'I've taken to it in the last few days. I rather enjoy the harbour. There's a lot going on, don't you think?'

'Yes, indeed there is. Which way are you going?'

'This way.' Emma pointed in the direction of Fort Salvador.

'Allow me to accompany you, Miss Thring.'

'That would be a pleasure, Mr Younge.'

'I was surprised to see you at poor Mr Wilkins's funeral the day before yesterday,' said Emma after a few minutes. 'I thought that with all that had passed between you, you might have stayed away.'

'No, I didn't know him particularly well but didn't dislike him at all. Fighting a duel with someone doesn't necessarily mean you hate them. Indeed,' Younge continued, 'regrettably, many duels are fought between friends.' Emma looked surprised.

'Really?'

'Yes. I had a cousin who was killed in a duel by one of his best friends as a result of an argument over cards. It was a terrible business.' He paused. 'I suppose I felt in some way responsible for Wilkins's death. If I hadn't been drunk that night in the mess, I wouldn't have accused him of being a coward and, who knows, he might not have joined that attack on the *Harlech Castle*.'

'I don't think you should blame yourself, Mr Younge,' said Emma. 'Peter could have been killed in any operation.'

'Speaking of operations,' said Young brightly, changing the subject, 'did you hear about the French landing yesterday?'

'Yes, dear Robert gave me a brief account of it. He said that Captain Warne distinguished himself.'

'Yes,' replied Younge, 'it seems from the reports that Captain Warne threw the French back into the sea almost single-handed.' He turned to Emma and smiled.

'Robert said it was remarkable that we captured so many French soldiers and suffered so few losses ourselves.'

'Yes, we gave Murat a good hiding. He won't be trying again this year, at any rate.'

They stopped to watch a naval cutter, the white ensign flapping gently at her stern, negotiate the entrance to the harbour under the ramparts of Fort Salvador.

'Shall we retrace our steps?'

George Warne reached for his glass of wine and leant back in his chair. On the table were the remains of a first-rate dinner, probably the best George had eaten in the four years he had been in Sicily. The Count of Pelorito was known for keeping one of the best tables in Messina, if not all of Sicily. His servants, immaculate in their green livery, had brought a seemingly endless series of courses to the table in the high-ceilinged dining room. They had started with a fragrant lemony broth before moving on to a dish of stewed beef – or *stoffata* as George thought it might be known in Sicily. This was followed by fresh, grilled tuna, a deliciously fluffy omelette, some macaroni and a selection of delicious local salami. The dinner had been washed down with the excellent white wine from the count's estate on the lower slopes of Mount Etna.

George was sitting next to a prominent Sicilian general, weighed down with stars and orders, who was pontificating about the failure of the French invasion.

'I can't imagine,' the general was saying in the Sicilian dialect, 'how they were allowed to get ashore. If I'd been in command, they wouldn't have left their boats before they were blown out of the water.' George listened politely, saying 'Yes' from time to time. At that moment the general was stopped in mid flow by the count's voice from the far end of the table.

'*Signore e signori,*' he intoned as he stood up, 'before we have dessert, I would like to propose a toast to our loyal allies with whom we stand united against the Corsican tyrant.' He raised his glass. '*Il Re Giorgio.*'

'*Il Re Giorgio,*' rippled round the table as the guests all raised their glasses and drank.

'*La Regina Carlotta.*'

'*La Regina Carlotta,*' Glasses were raised again.

'*E finalmente, il Principe di Gallia,*' said the count.

'*Il Principe di Gallia.*'

The count sat down and, with a wave of the hand, set the footmen clearing the table. Within a minute or so great bowls of *granita* and dishes of fruit, grapes, apples, pears, oranges and figs had been placed on the table. As George reached for the fruit, he noticed the count lean towards Carlotta and say something to her. She laughed, prettily.

George and Carlotta had been invited to dine with the count a few days earlier. The invitation – a singular, if not quite unique, honour for a junior British officer – had been delivered to Carlotta's house by a liveried footman. That morning, having fucked rapturously, they bathed before dressing in their best clothes. Carlotta looked ravishing in a pale blue dress and hat; George wore white breeches, a cream shirt, a yellow coat and a tricorn hat with a blue cockade.

'Who do you think will be there?' he asked Carlotta, glancing in the mirror as he tied his stock.

'I have no idea, *Giorgio mio*, but the count knows everyone so he's sure to have invited interesting people. And we will be given a very good dinner.'

They had arrived to be greeted by the count, who was wearing a pale silk coat embroidered at the cuffs and collar with flowers. He inclined his head to kiss Carlotta's hand.

'What a pleasure to see you, my dear,' he purred, looking her directly in the eye. After a moment – slightly too long a moment, George felt – he turned to George to shake his hand.

The other guests were Madame Signotti, the count's mistress – 'My wife spends the summer in the country' – the Sicilian general and his wife, a wealthy local landowner and a prominent Messinese merchant with their wives.

Before dinner the count's guests discussed the prospects for the vintage – three of the five men present owned vineyards

– chatted about the political situation in Sicily and gossiped merrily about friends. But the conversation was dominated by the failure of the French landing at San Stefano.

'I can't understand why they attacked there rather than further north, between Faro and Messina,' said the general, fiddling ostentatiously with an enamel cross hanging from a silk ribbon round his neck. 'And why they had such a small force.'

'My theory,' said the count, twiddling his glass, 'is that Murat planned the main attack in the north with a diversion in the south but, for some reason, failed to press it.'

'Certainly,' said George, 'the San Stefano attack was launched using only Neapolitan and Corsican troops. It is widely rumoured that Murat and General Grenier have . . .' he paused momentarily, 'their differences about the use of French regiments so maybe this accounts for the failure to attack in the north.'

'Yes, Captain Warne, you may well be right,' said the count. 'Shall we go in?' He held out his arm to Carlotta.

'Do you think he's telling the truth?' asked Airey.

'How could he know that we know about Monsieur Jardel?' asked Carboni.

They had left Cattaneo's cell shortly after his revelation and were now up on the Citadel's ramparts again, away from inquisitive ears. In the far corner of the harbour, between Fort Salvador and the *lazaretto*, they could see the mastless hulks of two old Spanish ships of the line, captured and scuttled by Admiral Byng after his victory at the Battle of Cape Passaro in 1718. After nearly a century in the waters of Messina harbour, the *Harmonia* and the *San Fernando* were rapidly rotting away.

'So what should we do now?' asked Airey.

'Well,' replied Carboni, 'it seems to me that we should investigate San Francesco.'

'How can we do that without alerting the conspirators?'

'I've worshipped there regularly all my life, so I know many of the priests and monks.' He paused and turned to lean against the warm stonework. 'I could make enquiries.'

'If they do know what's going on under their roof, will they tell you?'

'They might,' Carboni replied. 'And if they don't, I can remind them where their interests lie.'

'Let's hope they listen to you,' said Airey. 'When can you go?'

'There will be vespers this evening.'

'Good luck,' said Airey, turning for the stairs.

'It's splendid to see you looking so well, John.'

'I'm very glad to be back, I can tell you,' said Entwhistle. 'Coker is a charming fellow, but two weeks is a long time to be locked in a cell with him.'

The news of Entwhistle's exchange had spread rapidly and a gaggle of seven or eight young officers of the 44th Foot had converged on the Citadel to welcome him home. They were now crowded round Entwhistle in the anteroom of the officers' mess, eager to stand the returning hero a drink. Entwhistle was happy to knock back everything put in front of him while he told his story and listened to news of what had been happening in his absence.

'Poor George,' one of the captains was saying, 'ran into a hornets' nest at Scylla.'

'What happened?' asked Entwhistle. He and Kendall were close friends, having joined the regiment in the same week.

'It's not all that clear but it seems that they were attacked almost the moment they landed. George was killed, as were a good number of his men. The rest managed, just about, to escape out to sea.'

'Good God,' said Entwhistle. 'It sounds pretty much like my attack and, for that matter, Coker's at Catona.' He drank the rest of his wine and held out the empty glass. 'Is there any more?'

'What did happen at San Giovanni, John?' asked another of the circle, filling Entwhistle's glass.

'Well,' he replied, 'we came into the beach as planned and managed to get ashore but very soon came under attack. I had only just reached the dunes when I heard firing *behind* me, down by the water.'

'Bloody hell.'

'It quickly became clear that we were in a hopeless position,' he continued. 'Most of the men were killed or wounded and the galley was wrecked. So when I was summoned to surrender I had little alternative. We were surrounded with no means of escape; to fight on would have been pointless,' he said, looking defiantly at the other man.

'We would all have done the same thing. There's nothing to be gained by pointless sacrifice.' He gave Entwhistle a sympathetic pat on the shoulder.

'Do you know what happened to George Warne's attack at Reggio?' asked Entwhistle.

'From what I've heard he ran into the same sort of reception as you and the others and had little option but to withdraw.'

'I've heard,' said Entwhistle, 'that Captain Warne turned tail and ran for it at the first sign of trouble.'

'Where did you hear that?'

'From none other than the King of Naples himself.'

'Well, well, well,' said the other man. 'George Warne has, they say, been relieved of his duties at Faro since the attack on Reggio. By all accounts he has been spending a lot of time here at headquarters, God knows why. More wine, John?'

Dusk was falling as Warne strode towards the gates of the Citadel. After he and Carlotta had left the Count of Pelorito's house in the strada Candines, he walked her home before returning to the Citadel to report to Colonel Airey.

As he walked through the familiar streets he reran the afternoon's events in his mind. The count's dinner had been a memorable and enjoyable occasion. Listening to what the prominent Sicilians present made of the French attack at San Stefano had been instructive. It was difficult to know precisely where people's loyalties lay, but the count was strongly pro-British so it was reasonable to assume that his friends would be that way inclined too. Certainly, he hadn't detected any undercurrents of anti-British sentiment around the table. The count had entertained them royally; Carlotta – who was knowledgeable in such matters – could find no fault with the food or the wine. All in all, George reflected, it had been one of the high points of his time in Sicily, a dash of *la dolce vita*.

But there had been one false note. George couldn't help noticing how attentive the count had been to Carlotta. There was the ever-so-slightly lingering kiss of the hand when he greeted her and then the fact that he put her next to him at table. Then there was the odd quiet aside during the meal and Carlotta's lovely laugh. After dinner he showed her the paintings in the salon, guiding her from picture to picture, his hand on her arm. The count was a wealthy and influential man of considerable charm, with a reputation as something of a Lothario. Moreover, George knew that he had given her money after her husband's death. Certainly, Carlotta seemed to enjoy the attention. And who wouldn't? George wondered as he emerged on to the Marina whether the count had decided to make a play for her, to call in his investment, as it were. He already had a wife and a beautiful, commanding mistress – was that not enough?

George was not by nature a jealous man but, he had to admit, the count's attentions to Carlotta during dinner had piqued him. Maybe he was fonder of Carlotta than he cared to admit. Perhaps he should adopt the magnificent indifference affected by Madame Signotti to the count's flirtation. She must have noticed what was happening but remained, outwardly at least, wholly unruffled.

Walking in through the gates of the Citadel, George saluted the guard and crossed the courtyard towards the staff headquarters. Now that night was falling, the Citadel was quieter; the stable lads and grooms had done their evening rounds; the armourer had dampened down his forge and closed his workshop. An orderly was lighting the lanterns around the courtyard.

'George,' said Colonel Airey, 'it's good of you to come in so late. Do sit down.'

George sat and waited, expectantly, while the colonel closed one file on his desk and opened another.

'While you were dining in state with the count,' he said, 'there have been some interesting developments here.' He told George about the deal he and Sandro Carboni had reached with Captain Cattaneo and about the intelligence the Corsican had given them revealing the spy ring. As he listened, George raised an eyebrow.

'So what, sir,' he asked when Airey had finished, 'are we going to do about it?'

'We will investigate Cattaneo's story. On the face of it, it seems plausible. It fits with what we already know and seems to corroborate our suspicions that the raids were betrayed. Colonel Carboni is attending vespers at the monastery this evening.'

'Does this mean that we are going to raid the monastery?'

'Yes,' replied Airey.

'When, sir?' asked George.

'If all goes well, tomorrow,' said Airey.

It must have been nearly an hour later that George walked across the courtyard from the staff offices to the officers' mess. Airey had told him that William Coker had been exchanged that day, so George went to the mess in the hope of finding his old friend. As he opened the door a wave of noisy, boozy bonhomie swept over him.

On the far side of the anteroom was a group of about ten or twelve men round a table, some sitting, some standing. The table was thickly strewn with bottles, many empty, some still to be drunk. Several of the men were smoking cigars. In the middle of this raucous group, talking loudly and waving his glass around, was John Entwhistle.

As there was no sign of Coker in the mess, George thought he ought to greet Entwhistle. They had, after all, been together on the same operation. He walked across the room.

'Aha,' said Entwhistle loudly, seeing George approaching, 'here's Captain Warne of the mighty Irish.'

'Good evening, John,' said George evenly. 'Nice to have you back.' It was obvious that Entwhistle was very drunk.

'What's happened to your uniform?' asked Entwhistle glaring at George's yellow coat. 'Been a-kissing with your Sicilian whore, have you? Broderick here,' he waved his glass in the direction of another officer in the group, 'tells me you've been relieved of your command at Faro. P'raps that's why you're dressed for the tart's boudoir.'

Entwhistle took two paces towards George. He could smell the wine on Entwhistle's breath. His face was flushed and the scar on his left cheek stood out, lividly pink. His uniform was dirty and smelt rancid. Clearly, thought George, he had come straight in here off the boat from Scylla and had been drinking ever since. It was time to beat a tactful retreat.

'I'll be off, then, John,' said George, turning towards the door.

'Yes,' replied Entwhistle, 'I dare say you will be. That's what you're good at, Warne, running, like you did at Reggio once the shooting started. You're a disgrace to the King's commission, you fucking coward.'

CHAPTER SIXTEEN

The Citadel, Messina, 20th September 1810

The early morning light was seeping through the curtains into the officers' mess. The air was thick and still, heavy with cigar smoke and the sweet, cloying smell of last night's wine. The table at one side of the room was crowded with bottles and glasses, one or two tipped over. All the candles had burnt down to the end, the wax hanging in smooth, pale stalactites from the candelabra. On the stone floor was a broken glass. Over in one corner, a figure was sprawled in an armchair, snoring peacefully, his tunic unbuttoned and his waistband loosened. John Entwhistle was sleeping it off.

The door to the mess swung open and Winch, the orderly, came in. He shuffled over to the windows and began drawing the curtains. As he did so, Entwhistle started in his chair.

'What the hell's that?'

Winch, surprised, turned towards the voice.

'Oh, good morning, sir. I'm sorry to disturb you.'

Entwhistle grunted and sat up.

'What's the time?'

'Just past seven, sir,' replied Winch.

'Hmmm. I'd better go and have a bath. It was quite an evening last night.' Entwhistle did not feel well. Indeed, that was an understatement. His head was thick; his whole body felt grey and lifeless. There was a foetid, acidic taste in his mouth. He slumped back in the chair. Winch went to the table where he started to clear empty bottles and dirty glasses onto a tray. The clinking and clanking decided Entwhistle; he heaved himself out of the chair, fastened his breeches and made his way, stiffly, out of the mess.

It was only then that the events of the previous evening began to drift back to his hungover, addled brain. He climbed the stone stairs to his quarters – pausing halfway up to allow a sudden wave of nausea to pass – and, shouting for his servant, opened the door. Once inside the room he slumped on the bed and began to piece together the events of the previous evening.

'What the bloody hell did I think I was doing?' he asked aloud. He couldn't exactly remember what he had said to George Warne – he'd have to ask someone. Alcoholic amnesia, the drunk's bane and his boon. He was pretty sure that Warne had challenged him to a duel – so whatever he'd said must have been damning. Christ, why had he got so fucking drunk? The moment, the excitement of release from captivity, of returning to his friends and the regiment, all had played a part, he supposed. Once he'd bathed and put on a clean uniform, he'd have to go and find someone for a full account of what had happened.

As Entwistle was stirring in his chair in the officers' mess, Warne was walking briskly along the Marina in the direction of the Citadel.

It was a bright, cool morning. He'd just passed the Royal Navy's Messina headquarters, its two marine sentries in their flat-topped shakos standing guard by the entrance. To his right, men were lifting the boards from the front of their shops and putting out their wares, groceries, fruit and vegetables, meat, ironmongery. To his left, the fishmongers were crowding round the sterns of the vessels along the quay, competing for the day's catch, haggling loudly.

He had been summoned by Colonel Airey to attend an intelligence briefing. As he strode along the Marina, George thought about the events of the previous evening. What Entwhistle had said had left him no alternative but to challenge him to a duel. You can't, George reflected, go around calling brother officers cowards. It was asking for trouble. If only Entwhistle hadn't been so drunk. Thank God he'd left when he did, avoiding things getting any more heated.

By chance, as he was leaving the mess, George had run into Charles Parsons. He had told him what had just happened.

'I'll be your second, if you'd like,' said Parsons without a moment's hesitation. 'I've become quite an expert lately, you know.' He laughed.

They had agreed that Parsons would approach whoever Entwhistle had appointed as his second in the morning, once everyone had sobered up. In the meantime, all he could do was hope that Parsons would achieve a compromise. George had no wish whatsoever to fight a duel, with John Entwistle or anyone else.

'Signora Fanelli?' asked the green-liveried footman standing in the doorway.

'*Si*,' said Carlotta, 'that's me.'

He handed her an envelope and bowed.

'*Grazie.*' She took the envelope and closed the door as the footman disappeared down the stairs.

She looked at the envelope. It was addressed in a firm hand to *La Signora Fanelli* and sealed with a blob of scarlet wax impressed with an eagle. Breaking the seal Carlotta unfolded the thick paper. At the top of the sheet was a cypher, a green '*P*'. Carlotta thought she had recognised the green livery; now she realised exactly where this note came from. Written in Italian, it read: *I have something for you which might be to your advantage. Please come to my house at six this evening. I will be glad to see you.*

It was signed *Luciano Pelorito.*

'My visit to San Francesco last night was partly successful. After the service I spoke to one or two of the priests who I have known for a long time – I have been going there since I was a boy, do not forget.' Sandro Carboni looked round the table, where George Warne, Colonel Airey and the Quartermaster-General, Colonel Donkin, were listening attentively. 'One of the priests told me that he has been worried about the unusual activity at the monastery for some time: comings and goings at night, men landing from the sea, that kind of thing.'

'Did your priest have any idea what these nocturnal comings and goings might be?' asked Colonel Airey.

'If he did, he was reluctant to say. I got the impression that he was afraid. I should not be surprised if these men are ruffians, who don't take kindly to being informed upon.'

'Colonel Carboni,' said Donkin, 'that's fine so far as it goes but we need more precise information, details of who's involved, what they're doing and where in the monastery they are hiding. We'll need to keep the place under close surveillance before we can risk launching a raid.'

Airey nodded. 'We can't just go wading in, it's a house of God. You know what store Sir John sets by behaving properly towards the Sicilians – and that definitely includes their monasteries.'

'There is one more thing,' said Carboni. The three men round the table looked at him. 'The priest I spoke to pointed out a gardener to me, a man who he said might be happy to speak to me for a . . . a payment. According to the priest, this man is also employed as nightwatchman, so sees a lot of what goes on there . . .' Carboni's voice trailed off.

'And . . .' said Donkin, drumming his fingers on the table.

'He was reluctant to speak to me – out of fear, I suppose – but keen on any money I might offer him in exchange for information. Eventually, he agreed to speak to me for a few minutes in a dark corner of the church, but only if we entered and left the building separately. He was frightened, that was clear to see.'

'What did he tell you?' asked Airey.

'He says that there are secret rooms in the monastery that the conspirators use. They come in at night by boat, landing on the beach at the bottom of the monastery gardens. Sometimes they have packages, parcels, with them, sometimes they collect packages and leave again soon. Sometimes they disappear into the monastery. But, he says, you never see anything during the day. They hide in the secret rooms.'

'Does he know where they are, these secret rooms?' asked

Airey. 'San Francesco is a big building and we need to take these men – if they are hiding there – by surprise. We won't be able to search the whole monastery from top to bottom.'

'Can we trust this man?' asked Donkin.

'I don't really know,' replied Carboni. 'He's very keen to get his hands on our money, that's for certain.' He paused. 'But I'm not really sure that we have much alternative. At the moment he's our only chance of finding where these men are hiding. The worst that can happen is we don't find anyone or anything incriminating.'

'We could end up with egg on our faces,' said Donkin.

'Yes, we could,' said Airey, 'but it's a chance worth taking if it leads us to the spies. I say we raid the monastery and damn the consequences. We'll surround the place with armed men at dusk, go in, and hope that your man can lead us to the conspirators.'

Donkin nodded. 'I agree.'

John Entwhistle was feeling better. A long soak in a warm bath and a careful shave followed by a hearty breakfast had done something to banish the shadows of his hangover. He was about to leave the mess – now returned to its usual state of lived-in clubbishness after the previous evening's excesses – when Arthur Broderick strolled in.

'Ah, John,' he said, 'there you are. Banks said I'd find you here.' Banks was Entwhistle's servant. 'Wanted to make sure you're still in one piece after last night.' Broderick was a tall man, with auburn hair and a busy manner. He and Entwhistle had joined the 44th within a month of each other and had been firm

378

friends ever since. He looked fresh and alert. Why hasn't he got a hangover? wondered Entwhistle.

'Come and sit down, Arthur. Coffee?' He waved at Winch. 'Now tell me exactly what happened last night. Did I make a fool of myself?'

Winch brought another pot of coffee and poured a cup for each of them. Broderick waited until he was out of earshot.

'Yes, I'm afraid you were a little abrupt.'

'What do you mean by "abrupt"?' Entwhistle asked.

'To put not too fine a point on it, John, you called George Warne "a fucking coward".'

'Christ,' said Entwhistle, taking a sip of coffee. 'What the hell did I do that for? Did he say something?'

'No, I don't think so. I think he came into the mess to find William Coker. He wasn't even drunk, so far as I could see.' He paused. 'But he did challenge you to a duel.'

'Yes,' said Entwhistle, 'that I do remember, just about, through the haze.' He buried his face in his hands, rubbing his cheeks in his palms. 'What am I going to do, Arthur?' he asked.

'Will Warne accept an apology?' asked Broderick.

'I don't know,' replied Entwhistle. 'I haven't asked.'

'Have you got a second?'

'No, not yet. I've only just got up.' Entwhistle paused, looking at Broderick. 'Arthur, would you do it?'

'Of course I will, John. I've done it before, you know.'

'What, you've been a second for someone?'

'No, fought a duel,' replied Broderick.

'Against who?' asked Entwhistle, surprised. Broderick seemed such a calm, practical man, not the duelling type at all.

'It was about a girl, but it's a long story. I'll tell you one day.' Broderick drank his coffee. 'Right, then, first things first. Are you prepared to apologise?'

At Faro, John O'Connell was finishing his breakfast. All was well with the world. The morning parade had passed off without a hitch. There had been no defaulters to deal with: John found disciplining the drunks, the scrappers and the petty thieves a dispiriting process. It had to be done, of course, but it rarely made much difference and the punishments were disproportionately harsh. Fortunately, here at Faro, away from the temptations of Messina, there were fewer opportunities for the men to get themselves into trouble. He had a report to write this morning but then would have time to finish the letter home, which had been lying on his desk – and his conscience – for over a week now. Then, perhaps, there might be time for some reading.

He had been in command of the fort here at Faro for a fortnight and was beginning to feel as if he was getting the hang of it. Boney, who had been lying at O'Connell's feet, sat up and put his head on John's knee, looking up at him in that expectant, silently pleading way that spaniels have perfected. At that moment, Callaghan, who doubled as mess orderly and O'Connell's servant, came into the room.

'This arrived just now, sir,' he said, handing O'Connell a small package tied with tape. These were the army's daily orders, issued to all commanding officers, however lowly. Printed and distributed daily, they published dispatches, gave details of courts martial, promotions, issued general orders and amendments to standing instructions. Being handed the daily orders for the first time after he had taken over from George had given him a momentary thrill.

'Thank you, Callaghan,' he said, untying the tape and unfolding the package. On the front page was a message from the commander-in-chief, Sir John Stuart himself, about the French invasion. It gave details of the action before concluding that Sir John '*has only to regret the Dastardly Flight of the enemy at almost the first Sight of the British forces was so successfully pressed as to prevent their entire Number from becoming victims to the valour which pursued them.*'

The army rumour mill had been working overtime, but this was the first official word that had reached O'Connell about the events at San Stefano.

'Well, well, well, Boney,' he said, looking down at the spaniel, 'how about that?'

'Is Captain Entwhistle prepared to offer Captain Warne an apology?'

'No. He stands by what he said last night, drunk or not. To apologise would, in the circumstances, be dishonourable.' What Arthur Broderick did not tell Charles Parsons was that Entwhistle had said that he was happy to fight 'that fucking charlatan Warne, with his airs and graces' and 'was damned if he was going to apologise to him'. Nor did he tell Parsons that Warne owed him more than sixty pounds in accumulated winnings from cards.

Parsons and Broderick, respectively seconds for Warne and Entwhistle, made a contrasting pair: both about the same height, just shy of six foot tall, but Parsons was heavily built with a ruddy complexion whereas Broderick was slim and fair-skinned. It was a clear, sunny morning, fresh and promising, the antithesis,

Parsons thought, of the ugly matter they were discussing.

'If Captain Entwhistle is not prepared to apologise, a meeting is unavoidable. I suggest we arrange it as soon as possible, to prevent the authorities intervening as they did in Younge and Wilkins's case.'

'Parsons, you've been here much longer than I have, do you know somewhere the duel can be fought?'

'Yes, I believe I do.' He told Broderick about the orange grove along the coast where he had taken Peter Wilkins for target practice. 'Sunrise is at about quarter to seven at the moment, so I suggest that we meet at the Porta Chiara at six o'clock tomorrow morning. That will give us time to ride to the orange grove and conduct the duel before too many people are up and about.' Given what he was proposing, it sounded so matter-of-fact, so bloodless.

'That sounds fine,' said Broderick. 'Do you have a set of pistols?'

'No, I don't, but I do know a man who does, so I'll ask him if I can borrow them.'

'Steady there,' shouted Sergeant Burchfield. The cart grinding along in front of him through the traffic on the strada Ferdinanda had stopped abruptly. A barrel, dislodged by the sudden movement, slid off the back of the cart, crashing onto the black paving stones. The impact of the fall dislodged the barrel's bung so, as it rolled towards the gutter, red wine belched out onto the street, flecking the bottom of Burchfield's trousers. Bloody fools, he said to himself, sidestepping the barrel.

Burchfield was, with Lieutenant Fowler in command, taking a detachment of twelve men from their regiment, the 31st Foot, on a special operation. They had not yet been given any details of what was in store for them but they had been told that they would be back in the Citadel that night. When the colonel had detailed off the detachment, William Coker had volunteered to command it but was forced to admit that his broken collarbone was not yet sufficiently healed. As a result, Fowler, a keen if callow young officer, had been placed in command of the detachment.

His orders were to march the men to a spot about three-quarters of a mile outside the city walls at Porta Reale, beyond the monastery at San Francesco di Paola, where they would find a small patch of scrubby woodland in which they were to conceal themselves and await further instructions. Fowler had been told that Colonel Airey, one of the commander-in-chief's staff officers, no less, would join them there at sunset. As he marched at the head of his men, he touched his brightly polished gorget. This was an important job.

'Who's that?'

'John, it's me, Arthur,' came the reply through the door.

'Come in.'

Broderick came into the room, closing the door behind him.

'John, I saw Charles Parsons, Warne's second, this morning.'

'Oh, yes,' said Entwhistle, standing up and stretching.

'I told him that you were not willing to apologise so he suggested that we get the whole bloody thing out of the way as quickly as possible.'

'What does he mean by that?' asked Entwhistle.

'That you and Warne meet tomorrow morning,' replied Broderick.

'Tomorrow morning?' said Entwhistle. This was sooner than

he'd expected. He tried not to sound shaken. 'Why so soon?'

'If t'were done, best t'were done quickly, don't you think?'

'Yes, I s'pose so,' replied Entwhistle. 'Where are we meeting?'

'Parsons knows an orange grove somewhere along the coast towards Mili. Apparently, it fits the bill.' Broderick paused. 'And he can lay his hands on some pistols.'

Entwhistle walked across the room and looked out of the window. Below in the courtyard, men were going about their business, as they did every day, running errands, moving stores, mounting guard, doing evening stables. The rhythms of daily life in the Citadel were comfortingly familiar, but by this time tomorrow, he realised, he might be dead, shot through the chest, drowned in his own blood. Or, worse, wounded in the abdomen or thigh, condemned to a painful, lingering death. And all because he'd had too much to drink. It was a high price to pay for an evening's revelry.

'John.' Hearing Broderick's voice, Entwhistle turned away from the window.

'Yes, Arthur?'

'I hate to say this, but you'd be well advised to spend the next two hours putting your affairs in order.' He looked sympathetically at Entwhistle. 'You never know what might happen tomorrow, although part of me hopes you don't kill Warne.'

'Why on earth not?'

'He owes me quite a lot of money from the tables.'

Entwhistle grunted contemptuously.

'I made a will before I left England, but I'll write a letter to my parents, explaining everything.'

'Good,' said Broderick. 'I've got to go now but will you let me treat you to supper in the mess later?'

'Yes, Arthur, thank you,' said Entwhistle. 'That would be very kind. Take my mind off things.'

'Till later, then,' said Broderick as he left, closing the door behind him.

John Roper swished his hand for the umpteenth time at the flies, which buzzed irritatingly around him. He was leaning against the trunk of an old olive tree, his backside on a flat stone. Private Roper was one of the twelve men of the 31st Foot who had been marched out of Messina by Lieutenant Fowler to this hot, fly-blown olive grove for some purpose as yet unexplained. Roper was a member of his regiment's light company, something of which he was immensely proud. Known affectionately as 'light bobs', these men were the best shots in the battalion, in action deployed as skirmishers, ahead of the main body of the regiment. They regarded themselves as crack troops, a cut above the plodders of the battalion line companies.

Roper stopped swishing at the flies and looked around. The ancient olive trees offered only partial shade from the afternoon sun but did screen them from passers-by on the coast road. The other eleven men were also from the light company, good, reliable fellows. Babcock, over there, his skew-whiff nose the result of many a tavern brawl, was Roper's best mate in the company. Rose, leaning back-to-back against the same tree as Babcock, was a brawny, athletic country lad, fair and tough. Then there was Cowan, sucking ruminatively on his pipe, who was probably the best shot in the battalion. Roper had seen Cowan hit a shako plate at seventy yards with a musket shot, and then do it again to prove it was no fluke. Roper loosened his collar and picked up his water bottle. It was still hot, despite it being late afternoon.

About fifteen minutes later, Roper's snooze was interrupted by Sergeant Burchfield.

'On your feet, you lot, now, and form up! Look smart there!' There was nothing that riled a sergeant more than being caught unawares by the arrival of an officer.

Roper woke up abruptly, got to his feet, fastening his collar as he did so and took his place in the line. As they formed up and came to attention, the two new arrivals halted in front of them. Lieutenant Fowler saluted.

'At ease,' said one of them. 'I'm Colonel Airey.' He was wearing a plain dark blue tunic and white breeches but no hat. His immaculately polished half-boots were covered in a film of white dust, Roper noticed. 'This,' he continued, 'is Captain Warne. We will be joined by Colonel Carboni shortly.'

'Just over there,' Airey pointed to his right through the olive trees, 'is the monastery of San Francesco di Paola. We suspect that it is being used as the headquarters of a French spy ring. The monastery's grounds extend down to the beach, so it is perfect for coming and going across the straits to Calabria.' He paused, looking at the two ranks of men before him.

'The plan is to surround the monastery to stop anyone getting away. Lieutenant Fowler will be in command of that party. Is that clear?'

'Yes, sir,' said Fowler, nodding.

'Good. Meanwhile Colonel Carboni and Captain Warne will enter the building to flush the spies from their hiding places. I need two volunteers to accompany them.'

'Anyone?' asked Fowler, looking at his men.

Roper raised his hand. 'I'll go, sir.'

'Good man, Roper,' said Fowler. 'And another?'

'If Private Roper's going to mix with the monks, sir,' said Babcock, 'I'd better go to 'elp 'im out.'

'Right, Babcock, you'd better keep your wits about you in there,' said Fowler.

'Thank you, Lieutenant Fowler,' said Airey. 'Now listen carefully. We will move into the monastery grounds by climbing the broken-down wall over there through the trees. Three men will cover the main door of the monastery, which is on the road side, to the right. Almost next to it is the main door of the church. These are, so far as we know, the only ways out of the building at the front. A high wall runs along the entire length of the far end of the grounds, preventing any escape south towards Messina. That leaves seven men plus Lieutenant Fowler and Sergeant Burchfield to cover the other side of the building, the garden front. We think it's likely that if anyone attempts to escape, they will run towards the beach in the hope of being able to board a boat and get out to sea. So it's important that you're all alert. Any questions?'

'Sir?' It was Cowan.

'Yes,' said Airey.

'If we see someone from the monastery coming towards us, should we shoot?'

'Order them to stop and if they don't, shoot,' said Airey.

'Even if it's a monk, sir?'

'If it really is a monk coming towards you, he'll stop. So if he doesn't stop, you can safely assume he's not a proper monk and open fire.'

'Thank you, sir,' said Cowan, uncertainly.

The light was now fading rapidly. It was time for Fowler's little force to take up its position in the monastery grounds. There was a rustling in the trees to their right; one or two of the men raised their muskets.

'It's all right, men' said Airey. 'Lower your weapons.' Out of the gloom came Sandro Carboni. Behind him was the short, slight figure of the nightwatchman, Carboni's informant.

'Right,' said Carboni, 'we're all here now, so shall we get on with it?'

Outside, in the strada Candines dusk was gathering. Inside, beneath one of the tall windows on the *piano nobile*, Carlotta Fanelli was perched on an upright chair eating lemon *granita* with a silver spoon from a silver-gilt bowl. Next to her on a settee was the Count of Pelorito. They were alone in the grand salon, the count having dismissed the footmen who normally hovered in the background.

After the count's note had been delivered that morning, Carlotta had thought carefully about what she should do. Why did he want to see her? What could be so important that he had a note delivered by hand to her apartment? And why this evening? Why the urgency? Could it be something to do with the raids, with the questions she had asked him when they'd met ten days ago? Perhaps. On the other hand, the count had been very attentive towards her when she and George had dined with him the previous day. Time would tell.

'Right, my dear,' said the count in the local dialect, 'now that you've finished your *granita*, allow me to show you my collection of engravings. They are said – even by my enemies,' he laughed, 'to be the finest in the Two Sicilies.' He stood up, offering Carlotta his arm as he did so.

Colonel Airey stopped and extended his right arm.

'Halt,' said Fowler quietly. Behind him the men stopped.

They had scrambled over the collapsed stone wall at the northern end of San Francesco di Paola's gardens without making much noise and were now fifty yards inside the grounds, standing among the fruit trees. Ahead and slightly to the right of them in the gathering dusk was the looming mass of the monastery building.

'Right,' said Airey in a stage whisper. 'We split up here.' He looked at Carboni. 'Sandro, you and George take your informant,' he gestured at the young Sicilian, 'Babcock, Roper and the three men detailed to watch the two doors at the front of the monastery. Lieutenant Fowler, you and I and the remainder of your men are going to fan out to cover this side of the building. Let's go.'

Three minutes later, Warne and Carboni were standing under the old ilex tree facing the main door of the monastery. The place was deserted, thank God. George had posted the three soldiers detailed to watch the door. Now he checked the priming of his two pistols; satisfied, he pushed them into the waistband of his breeches and drew his sword. He turned towards Roper and Babcock to ensure that they had fixed their bayonets. There might not be time for that later.

Carboni was speaking to the young gardener–nightwatchman who was acting as their guide. The operation depended on him.

If he did not, or could not, lead them to the conspirators' hiding places, the entire operation would be an embarrassing failure. It was obvious that the young Sicilian was scared out his wits.

'*Allora*,' whispered Carboni, '*avanti*. I'll go first and open the door. You two,' he gestured at Roper and Babcock, 'make sure you're right behind me. George, you keep hold of our friend, please.'

On the other side of the monastery, Fowler's men were spreading out in a line from the north-eastern corner of the monastery building across the gardens to the point where the high southern boundary wall reached the beach. With ten men – including Colonel Airey standing in the middle of the line, Sergeant Burchfield at its left-hand end, and Lieutenant Fowler next to the beach – there was no more than fifteen yards between each man. Even in the dark, it should be easy to see anyone escaping from the monastery building.

'Who's the best shot among your men, Lieutenant?' asked Airey.

'Cowan, sir, without a doubt,' replied Fowler.

'Good,' said Airey. 'I want him next to me in the line so that he can bring down anyone who gets through. A backstop, if you like.'

Sandro Carboni walked up to the double door in the facade. He took the iron handle, lifted, turned it and pushed. The heavy door opened slowly, creaking on its hinges as it did so. Inside was a dimly lit hall. The air was musty, as if it had been there for too long, unstirred. Babcock and Roper stepped through the door, their muskets at the ready and advanced two paces, followed by George and the Sicilian. Carboni pushed the door shut.

'Right, Guilio,' whispered Carboni to the Sicilian, 'which way now?'

'*A destra, a destra*,' he replied. 'The church is to the left.'
Carboni nodded: that much he did know.

Carboni, flanked by Babcock and Roper, led the way across the hall to where a passage opened to the right, stretching away into the shadows.

'There's nobody around,' said George, relieved.

'No,' replied Carboni in a whisper, 'after vespers all the monks return to their cells on the first floor. Down here it's just cellars and storerooms.'

They started walking along the wide, half-lit passage, trying to make as little noise as possible on the stone flags. The five men were an incongruous sight in a monastery: two soldiers in their scarlet tunics, white cross-belts and shakos, holding muskets with bayonets fixed; the tall, dark figure of Sandro Carboni, anonymous in civilian clothes; George Warne, the blonde Englishman in his uniform; and the diminutive Guilio, the Sicilian informant, barefoot and scruffily dressed.

Stealing along, they soon reached the turn in the passage where the two ranges of the monastery, the north and the east, met at right angles.

'The hiding places,' Guilio whispered to Carboni, 'are just around this corner.'

Carboni raised his hand in a halt signal and peered cautiously round the corner. The passage stretching away into the gloom was empty.

'*Avanti.*'

About five yards along the passage beyond the angle was a door in the wall to their left.

'That's it,' said Guilio, pointing. Carboni tried the handle.

'It's locked,' he said. He reached into his pocket, pulled out a jemmy and handed it to Roper. 'Break it in, please.'

As Roper wrenched the lock of the door open, Carboni turned to George with a smile, 'I thought it might come in useful.'

'I didn't know you were a burglar in your spare time, Colonel,' grinned George.

The lock gave way with a crunch and Roper swung the door open. On the other side, separated from the first door by the thickness of the wall, was another door.

'Come on,' said George. 'This one opens inwards.' He turned half-sideways and gave the door a powerful kick with his right boot. The lock broke with a snap and as the door burst open into the room beyond, George bounded forward.

A man jumped towards George, thrusting a stiletto towards his stomach. George reacted instantly, slashing down at the man with his sword. The blade cut into the flesh of the man's upper arm. He grunted but stabbed again at George with his stiletto. George raised his sword and brought it down hard on the man's forearm, slicing through the tendons. He grabbed his wounded arm, dropping the stiletto as he did so.

A second man, holding a stiletto in his right hand, leapt at Babcock as he entered the room a pace behind George. Babcock parried the blow with his musket, thrusting through with the bayonet, but failed to connect. Seeing the man momentarily off balance, he dropped his gun with a clatter and grabbed his adversary's right wrist with his left hand and punched, hard, up under the man's chin. He swayed back and Babcock hit him again, hard, square in the solar plexus. The man doubled up in pain and as he did so Babcock smashed his knee into the man's face. He staggered backwards, dropping the stiletto as he went, and pitched sideways onto the floor, where he lay groaning, spitting blood and broken teeth onto the stone. Babcock stood over him, about to give him a final kick for good measure.

'Leave him,' said Carboni. 'He's not going to trouble us any more.'

'Over there! Stop him!' shouted George. There was a door in the far corner of the room, which a third man was opening. Beyond it was the garden. Roper lunged across the room with his bayonet but was too late to stop the man escaping, slamming the door as he went.

'Bloody 'ell,' exclaimed Roper, kicking at the door. As he did so, there were two shots outside in the garden, then some voices shouting.

George looked round the room, panting from the sudden, ferocious exertion. His hands were shaking. The room was about fifteen feet square, poorly lit by two lanterns, with a single, demilune window high in the outside wall. The walls were panelled to waist height. Opposite the door they had broken down was a circular table, strewn with playing cards and gaming chips, and two chairs. Against the wall to George's right was a long trestle table, covered with dirty plates, half-eaten packets of food, a crust of bread and three bottles of wine. To one side, on the floor, was a heap of mattresses and blankets. It was obvious from looking round and from the smell and the stale atmosphere that the men had been in this room for some time.

'Roper,' said George. 'Make sure that the wounded man,' he pointed to the man with the slashed forearm, 'can't go anywhere.'

Roper turned away from the door and thrust his bayonet menacingly in his direction.

'You sit down there, sonny,' said Roper, pointing him to one of the chairs. The wounded man was now in considerable pain and holding his arm up in an attempt to stop the bleeding. The man flattened by Babcock was getting groggily to his feet.

'You sit there, you,' said Babcock, half-lifting the man onto the second chair.

Meanwhile, Carboni was looking round the room for any evidence of a conspiracy: letters, maps, money, weapons, anything that might give a clue as to what was afoot. He rifled through the cards on the table.

'Not much here, I'm afraid,' he said to George. 'We'll question these idiots later,' he jerked his thumb at the two prisoners, 'but I'd like to find some evidence, something that will make heads roll.'

'What's that, over there?' said George. He had noticed a small trapdoor in the panelling in the left-hand corner of the room, opposite the door to the garden.

'Well spotted, George,' said Carboni. He walked towards it. 'What do we have here, I wonder?'

Carboni then put his fingers under the edges of the trapdoor and gently prised it open. As he did so, Babcock thrust his bayonet into the void.

'No shoot, no shoot,' came a frightened voice from inside in heavily accented English.

'All right, come out slowly, and we won't shoot,' said Carboni in the local dialect. After a moment or two, a man crawled out of the trapdoor head first. He was young, no more than twenty-five, with dark hair and a straggly beard. His skin had a greyish pallor which suggested that he had been confined in this room for weeks, if not months. There was a hunted, nervous look in his eyes.

While Carboni was talking to his new prisoner, George took one of the lanterns and leant in through the trapdoor. Inside was a chamber about twelve feet long but no more than four feet high. Once inside, a man could only crawl on all fours. Three or four men could hide in here for a short while, George thought, but it wouldn't be very comfortable. From the outside, apart from the trapdoor cut into the panelling, there was no trace of the chamber's existence. It reeked of sweat and stale breath.

As George was extricating himself from the trapdoor, he noticed, to his right on the floor of the chamber, a leather dispatch case with a brass lock. He picked it up and, twisting out of the trapdoor, held up his trophy in triumph.

'Look what I've got here.'

The count's engravings were hung in a room with heavy blinds to prevent the Sicilian sun from damaging the pictures. In the middle of the room was a tall glazed cabinet displaying the count's collection of *objets trouvés*: Greek and Roman coins, a few pieces of antique jewellery and some early weaponry, spearheads, arrow tips and the like. The count was proud of his collection because all the pieces had been found on his estates – testament, he liked to think, to Sicily's rich history and his family's part in it. But proud as he was of his antiquities, it was his collection of engravings that was the apple of the count's eye.

It was to this room that the count escorted Carlotta. When he opened the door, she saw at once that the room was barely half-lit. The reason for the count's unexpected invitation was now apparent: he was trying to seduce her. Part of Carlotta was flattered by the count's attentions; he was, after all, an attractive man and, let it not be forgotten, a rich and influential one, too. On the other hand, she was keenly aware that in allowing herself to be seduced by the count, she was betraying George.

'Now, my dear,' he said, pulling the blinds up to halfway, 'let me show you the pictures. I think you will enjoy them.'

The count's engravings were indeed magnificent. He was particularly keen on Piranesi's work.

'I love his engravings of the views of Rome. As you can see, I have quite a number of them. I put it down to the fact that my mother was from a Roman family.' He laughed.

'They are very beautiful,' said Carlotta.

'I'm glad you like them,' said the count. 'What do you think of *I Carceri*?' He was standing very close to her now.

'They lack the beauty of the views, but they are interesting pictures. You would never get bored owning them.'

At this moment, the count put one hand on her crinoline and the other on her shoulder, turning her gently into his arms. 'You know, *signora*,' he said, 'that I would never get bored with you.' He kissed her on the lips, drawing her closer.

Carlotta tilted her head backwards and looked into the count's eyes.

'You are rich, you are powerful, you are a friend of the King. Why do you want me, a lowly widow, when you can have any woman in the Two Sicilies?'

'I have observed you from afar for a long time, *signora*.' He stroked her cheek with his forefinger and traced gently around her mouth. 'And I have always liked what I have seen, very much.'

He bent to kiss her again. This time, Carlotta parted her lips a little, letting the count's tongue snake into her mouth, searching for her.

'Why the hell did you drop your musket when that fellow came at you?' George asked Private Babcock.

'Well, sir,' he replied in his slow English country accent, 'I couldn't really shoot him in that little room an' I couldn't swing it either, so I decided I'd use my fists on 'im. I'm good at that, sir.'

'Yes, Babcock, that much was obvious. Anyway, well done. You put him out of action, good and proper.'

Carboni's little party was now out in the gardens, where they had rejoined Colonel Airey and the rest of the detachment. Roper and Babcock were standing guard over the three prisoners. The man who escaped through the door had been shot.

'I saw him coming out through the door,' said Airey, 'and make a run for it. I ordered him to stop. When he didn't, I told the nearest man to shoot. He missed but Cowan got him after he'd passed through the line.'

'Did you find anything on him, Colonel?' asked Carboni.

'Yes, I searched his pockets and found these.' He held up a small packet of letters tied together with string. 'It's time to get back to Messina. It's getting late and we want to be out of here before the monks start investigating. Sergeant, form the men up, if you please.'

My dear mother and father,
By the time you read this letter I shall have been dead for

at least a month, killed by my own recklessness. Two nights ago, shortly after my return to Messina after a fortnight in captivity in Scylla, I insulted a fellow officer – not of my own regiment – and he challenged me to a duel. I am ashamed to say that I was in a state of advanced intoxication at the time.

John Entwhistle was sitting at the table in his quarters. He and Arthur Broderick had eaten supper in the mess and played two rubbers of whist, which Entwhistle had lost by a wide margin. Broderick had made a marked effort to be merry, but the impending duel hung over proceedings like a storm cloud.

Now John was struggling to write to his parents. He had never found writing letters easy but this one – only to be posted to England in the event of his death – would have taxed a more literary man than he. The mere act of writing the letter brought home the full imbecility of his behaviour. How could he have been such an idiot? He might well be killed for one crass, drunken remark. His parents would be mortified and ashamed. They had made great sacrifices to buy him his commission – Entwhistle knew that his father had borrowed much of the purchase price from a moneylender, no doubt at a usurious rate of interest – and this was how he thanked them.

Nor was it the first time he'd got himself into trouble like this, as the scar on his left cheek proved. That was the result of an argument arising from a game of cards. They had fought with swords, Entwhistle suffering a bad cut to his cheek. The seconds had stopped the fight at that point; he had been lucky not to have been blinded in the left eye. In military circles, the risk of a challenge was an ever-present danger but there was no excuse for a sensible officer to be challenged more than once. One should, Entwhistle reflected, learn from one's mistakes. He had failed to do so and for that, if nothing else, he was ashamed of himself. He dipped his quill into the inkwell.

I feel deeply ashamed that I have let you down in this manner. Some men will tell you that I died preserving my good name and my honour – and by extension, that of the family – but you will know that this is a fiction, a convenient and widespread lie to justify a cruel, violent and irrational custom.

Fortunately, I am not by my recklessness creating a widow and orphans but I shall, I fear, leave my dear parents bereft of the succour they should be entitled to expect of a son in their dotage.

I have left a will with Mr Rolls, the solicitor. In it, I bequeath all my worldly goods to you.

Adieu, my dearest parents,

Your loving son,

John

Some men passed the night before fighting a duel by reading some work of literature, but John was not a great reader. He read through the letter to his parents before folding the paper into a neat square. He picked up the stick of sealing wax from the table and held it into the flame of the candle, over the folds of his letter. He'd always liked the smell of sealing wax – it reminded him of sitting as a boy on his father's knee while he sealed letters – and watched as the top of the stick melted and fell onto the paper in small, glistening scarlet drops. Once the drops had coalesced into a patch about the size of a waistcoat button, Entwhistle pressed the metal seal into the soft wax. It was a phoenix, rising from the flames. Having done that, Entwhistle walked across the room and lay down on his bed. Broderick was coming for him at five. He'd better get some sleep.

In the excitement of the raid on San Francesco di Paola, George Warne had almost forgotten what the morning had in store for him. Once they had returned to the Citadel the two colonels, Carboni and Airey, retired to the staff offices to read through the dispatches captured at the monastery. Lieutenant Fowler had his soldiers to deal with, so George was left in charge of the three prisoners. They were each locked up in the cell while he found a surgeon to treat their wounds. Feeling immensely weary, George then wandered into the mess in search of some supper. As he entered the room, Winch, the mess orderly, hobbled up to him.

'Captain Warne, sir, I've got a note for you from Captain Parsons. He says it's important.' He handed Warne a folded and sealed letter. George tore it open.

Dear Warne. We have an engagement early tomorrow morning. I will come for you at five o'clock. When you get this note, come to my quarters if you wish. CP

So it was that having eaten a plate of beef stew and pasta, George found himself knocking on the door of Charles Parsons's quarters in the Citadel. Parsons was in his shirtsleeves reading a book, a decanter of wine and two glasses on the table in front of him.

'Ah, George, good evening. Would you like a glass of Marsala?'

'Yes, thank you, I suppose a glass won't do me any harm.'

'Busy day?' asked Parsons.

George told him about the raid on the monastery and the fight in the cell. Parsons laughed when George recounted how Babcock had preferred to use his fists rather than his musket.

'I don't know why the War Office wastes money on supplying these men with weapons.'

After a while, the conversation moved on to the duel with Entwhistle. Parsons ran quickly through the practical arrangements while George listened carefully.

'What are you going to wear?' asked Parsons.

'Isn't it thought best that one should wear dark clothes? Something to do with presenting a less obvious target?'

'Yes, I think that's it, although I did hear of one fellow who fought his duel in the buff.'

'Really?' said George.

'He had been a surgeon in the East India service where he had seen too many injuries complicated by fragments of cloth carried into the wound by bullets, so when it came to his turn to fight a duel, he decided to face his opponent as the day he was born.'

'Is that true?' laughed George.

'Yes, I believe so. It wasn't that long ago, either. I seem to remember that the fellow in question was a Member of Parliament.'

'Good for him,' said George, 'but I have no intention whatever of standing in front of John Entwhistle with no clothes on.'

The two men chatted away amiably for half an hour before George got up.

'I must go to bed. I'm falling asleep and we've got an early start.'

An hour later, George was lying on the bed in the room he'd been lent for the night. He'd tried but failed to write to his parents. He was too tired; the words simply wouldn't come. He had not made a will but in truth he had little enough to leave. As he lay in the dark, longing for sleep, he thought about Carlotta. He felt guilty that he hadn't told her about the duel, although he had scarcely had the chance to do so. It would be a terrible shock to her nor would she understand why he had exposed himself needlessly – as she would see it – to the risk. God, what a bloody mess. His thoughts turned to his parents. His father was a good, wise man, his mother a kind, gentle soul; they would do their best, he supposed, to sympathise with his dilemma but they would never understand it nor approve of it. Honour, to a clergyman, was synonymous with pride and pride was one of the Seven Deadly Sins. With these thoughts running round his head, George eventually fell asleep.

CHAPTER SEVENTEEN

Mili, near Messina, 21st September 1810

They met, as arranged, at the Porta Chiara just after six o'clock in the morning, five anonymous, shadowy figures on horseback, wrapped in riding cloaks. It was dawn and the streets of Messina were deserted. Although Warne, Parsons, Entwhistle and Broderick had all come from the Citadel they left separately to avoid arousing suspicion and met at the Porta Chiara before riding along the coast road to the orange grove near Mili. The fifth man was a naval surgeon, an acquaintance of Parsons', who had agreed to accompany the duellists in a professional capacity. In his saddlebag was his box of surgical instruments. The guard opened the gate for them and they trotted off towards the coast road.

As they rode along, George's mind was a blank. He had slept poorly and despite several cups of strong coffee he was still half asleep. No doubt he would perk up once they arrived at the duelling ground. He wondered what Entwhistle was thinking as they rode towards their fate. Was he calm or nervous? Was he regretting his drunken outburst? Perhaps Entwhistle had 'been out', as the saying went, before, so was calmer than a novice duellist might be.

Trotting along to George's left was Charles Parsons. He was, George decided, the ideal second, calm and reassuringly solid; if one was foolish enough to get entangled in a duel, then Charles was the man to have by your side. In his saddlebag was the case containing the pair of duelling pistols, which might, all too soon, kill him or Entwhistle. George shivered.

After about two miles, Parsons turned his horse off the road into the orange grove, waving for the others to follow.

'Here we are,' he said. The five men walked their horses well into the grove, away from the road, dismounted and tethered them to the trees. In the middle of the grove there was an open space between the trees, perhaps thirty yards long and ten wide. This was where Warne and Entwhistle would face one another.

'Right, gentlemen,' said Parsons looking up at the sky, 'it'll soon be light enough for the business to get under way.' Across the straits, the eastern sky above the dark mass of the Calabrian mountains was clear and pale. 'Broderick and I will make the necessary arrangements.'

Entwhistle, wrapped in his black riding cloak, nodded and walked away. He looks composed enough, thought George. It was bad form for a duellist to display nerves before the fight; cool insouciance was what was required. George, too, turned and walked away with as much indifference as he could muster.

'Right, Parsons,' said Broderick, 'let's mark out the distance.' One of the seconds' most important duties was agreeing and then marking the distance at which the combatants would shoot. A pistol duel fought at less than ten paces was likely to be lethal; it was difficult to miss at that range. He and Parsons had agreed that Warne and Entwhistle would fire from twenty paces, Broderick adding that as he was a tall man, he had a long stride.

'Let's start here,' said Broderick. Parsons picked up a flat stone and placed it on the ground. Broderick then started walking with slow, deliberate strides up the middle of the open ground, with Parsons alongside him counting the paces.

'. . . seventeen, eighteen, nineteen, and twenty.' He placed another marker stone.

Parsons retrieved the case of pistols from his saddlebag. Putting the case on the ground, he squatted down and opened it.

'They are magnificent weapons,' said Broderick.

'Yes, they are,' replied Parsons, 'the best money can buy. Shall we load?' Standing up he held the case out to Broderick.

'You choose.'

Parsons put the case back on the ground picking out the second pistol as he did so. He flicked up the cover of the priming pan to check that the touch hole – through which the spark from the pan passed to detonate the main charge – was clear. Any blockage could cause the pistol to misfire. He then carefully poured gunpowder from the powder horn into the muzzle followed by the round lead shot and the wadding to keep it firmly in place. He then tamped the charge down with the miniature ramrod. Beside him, Broderick was loading Entwhistle's pistol with equal care. It was now past seven o'clock, so the sun had come up; the duel could take place.

'Right, gentlemen, we're nearly ready,' Parsons called out. Entwhistle and Warne both strolled back to the spot where the seconds were standing. 'You will be facing each other at twenty paces. Captain Broderick and I have agreed that once you are both in position, I will give the command to fire. I will be standing between you, back to one side.' Warne and Entwhistle nodded. 'I will say, "Are you ready? Fire." There will be no second shots. Prepare yourselves, please, gentlemen.'

Entwhistle took his hat off, unbuttoned his riding cloak and dropped them on the ground. Underneath, he was wearing a black, close-fitting tunic, which he took off, revealing a waistcoat and white sleeves. George likewise discarded his riding cloak but decided to keep his coat on: it was a chilly morning and he didn't want to risk shivering. It might disrupt his aim and betray his inner fears to the world. He was a bad enough shot as it was. His hat he kept firmly on his head.

'Right, then, please take up your positions,' said Broderick. 'There's no difference between the ends as they've both got the same dark background of the orange trees.'

'I'll go to the right,' said Warne.

'That's fine,' said Entwhistle, taking his pistol from Broderick. Parsons handed Warne his loaded pistol. Both men walked to their markers.

As George walked towards the stone he was breathing deeply, trying to calm himself. Breathing, he knew, was one of the secrets of good marksmanship. He tried not to think about the ball from Entwhistle's pistol ripping agonisingly into his chest, tearing tissue and vital organ, perhaps splintering his spine. He was holding the pistol upright, so close to his cheek that he could smell the gun oil. The walnut butt felt smooth, perfectly balanced in his hand. The steel-blue of the barrel gleamed in the sun.

When he reached the stone, George turned. At the far end of the marked ground, Entwhistle still had his back to him. Twenty paces seemed hardly any distance at all. Over to his left Parsons and Broderick were standing, still in their hats and riding cloaks, chatting nonchalantly. George took up his firing position, turning side on facing to his left, with his right foot pointing down the ground towards Entwhistle. In the distance he could see his opponent taking up position. His heart was pumping, the blood pounding in his ears. He took a deep breath, in through the nose and out through the mouth. And again. Entwhistle was facing him now, his pistol held up in his right hand. Out of the corner of his eye, George could see that Parsons had stepped forward a pace or two. It wouldn't be long now. He blinked several times and focussed intently on his target. He extended his right arm so that the upper arm and elbow were parallel to the ground and the forearm pointing upwards.

'Are you ready?' Parsons's voice was firm, decisive. George took a deep breath. 'Fire!'

He lowered his forearm smoothly so that his eyeline ran along the top of the barrel of his pistol. He could see Entwhistle's black-and-white form beyond the pimple sight at the end of the pistol's barrel. He squeezed the trigger. The powder in the pan flashed with a gout of smoke, followed a fraction of a second later by the crash of the main charge firing, jolting his hand upwards. Just as he fired, George heard, far away, Entwhistle's pistol firing. Then nothing.

George stepped out of the cloud of smoke that hung around him. There, at the far end of the duelling ground, also emerging from a pall of smoke, was John Entwistle. He was unharmed. Charles Parsons was saying loudly, 'That's it, gentlemen.'

Warne and Parsons walked their horses through the gates of the Citadel. The others had split off at the Porta Chiara: Broderick and Entwistle to visit a friend for breakfast and the surgeon to return to his ship. Despite the fact that it was not yet eight o'clock in the morning, George was exhausted. The adrenalin and tension generated by the duel had long since drained away.

Both men had missed and as Parsons and Broderick would not permit a second shot that was the end of the matter. The two adversaries had shaken hands before stowing the pistols back in their case, getting dressed and mounting their horses to ride back to Messina. It had been, George reflected, an extraordinary experience, terrifyingly real – at least at the moment of engagement – yet utterly banal.

As they came through the gates into the Citadel, George could see Colonel Airey standing in the middle of the courtyard. In front of him was a small detachment of troops: six men, a sergeant and a man in plain clothes. George dismounted and, handing his horse to a groom, walked over to Airey.

'Good morning, sir.'

'Good morning, Captain Warne,' replied Airey, looking quizzically at George's riding cloak. 'Look what we have here.' He pointed at the man in plain clothes between the soldiers. It was Finbarr Rogers, looking dishevelled in scruffy clothes. Round his wrists was a pair of iron manacles. George, from force of habit, nearly said 'Good morning, Mr Rogers' but stopped himself in the nick of time. Airey, seeing the look of surprise on George's face, took him to one side.

'After we returned from San Francesco last night, Colonel Carboni and I read the dispatches we'd seized and interrogated the three men you captured in the raid. From the correspondence and what the prisoners had to say, it was as plain as a pikestaff what had been going on. The dispatch case you found was full of incriminating letters. Rogers has been supplying information about our plans to French agents based at the monastery. From there it had been passed to the French military authorities in Calabria. That's how they knew about the raids and were able to organise detailed defence in four different places at once at the dead of night. You were right in your suspicions that the raids were betrayed. We decided to act at once so went with some soldiers to Rogers' house early this morning.'

'Good God, why did he do it?' asked George, inclining his head in Rogers' direction.

'Heaven alone knows,' replied Airey, 'but he may tell us. He'll face trial for treason, of course, and may hang.'

'Did the letters incriminate anyone else?'

'They show that Signor Falcone was in cahoots with the French, as a link between them and their spies here. That certainly would account for the gold you found in his chambers. We paid him an early morning call, too, but his butler told us that he'd left for the mainland at dawn. Most unexpected it was, he said. We searched the house but there was no sign of him. He must have got wind of the raid on the monastery because it looks as if we only just missed him.'

'Well, well, well,' said George.

'And last but by no means least is the Count of Pelorito. The correspondence makes it abundantly clear that he was, at the very least, playing a double game between us and the French, hedging his bets by keeping in with them and us. He fed the French information, some of it through the conduit of San Francesco, and corresponded with the Queen about her plans to eject us and reclaim her kingdom.'

'Bloody hell,' said George. 'What a shit.'

'Yes,' said Airey, 'but I fear he's beyond our reach, he's too well connected, too powerful. We'll just have to keep a close eye on him from now on.'

Ten minutes later George was riding out of the Citadel once more. This time he was returning to his military duties. Now that he was no longer needed as an intelligence officer, Colonel Airey had released him to resume command of the fort at Faro. As he walked his horse out onto the Terra Nova, George decided to pay Carlotta an early morning visit. He would surprise her with the news of his duel. He might get a hero's welcome. Or, alternatively, perhaps not. But it would be lovely to see her.

Leaping off his horse outside Carlotta's house in the strada Ferdinanda, George handed the reins to the shopkeeper's son. He went in through the front door and climbed the stairs two at a time. He tried the door of Carlotta's apartment. It was locked but George had a key. He unlocked the door and went inside. The salon was empty and the shutters still closed. He looked into the bedroom. It too was empty. Nor had the bed been slept in.

'Carlotta?' he said, loudly. There was no reply. It didn't take long to check the rest of the apartment but Carlotta was nowhere to be found. She'll be at her parents' house, thought George. On the table was some paper so he wrote a note and dated it 'Friday 1/2 past 8'.

C, I've gone to Faro. All well. Looking forward to seeing you. Get in touch. Love, G.

Leaving the note on the table, George went into the far corner of the salon and, crouching down, rolled back the rug. Underneath, a section of the floorboard had been sawn through to create a hiding place; it fitted snugly but George, with the help of a knife, levered it up. Inside, pushed along the joist, was a small canvas packet, tied with string. He reached in and, retrieving the packet, placed it on the floor where he opened it: inside were the fourteen gold *napoleons* he'd taken from Falcone's office. George picked one up; it was cool to the touch, weighty. Replacing it, he folded the canvas again and retied the strings. Now that he was returning to Faro, the *napoleons* would come with him. He trusted Carlotta implicitly, of course, but they would be much safer hidden away in the fort at Faro, beyond the reach of Messina's burglars, thieves and petty criminals.

George replaced the floorboard, rolled the rug back and stood up, putting the packet in his pocket. Then with a last look around, he locked the apartment and went downstairs. Giving the boy a coin, he mounted his horse and turned for Faro.

As George walked into the little fort at Faro, he was greeted by Boney, who had been lying in the shade by the water trough. The spaniel bounded up to George, wagging his tail and jumping round him with delight.

'Good boy, Boney, good boy,' said George as he knelt down to stroke the dog and riffle his long brown ears.

At that moment, O'Connell emerged from a door into the courtyard.

'Good morning, sir,' he said. 'To what do we owe the pleasure?'

'I'm afraid, John, it's bad news. My secondment at the Citadel has come to an end, so I'm back in command here. I'm sorry, because you've done a good job in my absence.' Certainly, from what George could see, the fort was immaculately tidy and the men seemed busy, always a good sign.

'Well, sir, I've done my best, but it'll be nice to have you back at the helm. There are one or two things you should know about, sir, now that you're back.'

An hour later, having listened to O'Connell's report and eaten a good breakfast, George strolled out into the courtyard with Boney at his heels. As he did so he heard a carriage drawing up outside the fort, the noise of horse and harness and the crunch of wheels on the rough surface of the road. George walked towards the gate.

'Good morning, Captain Warne,' shouted Robert Thring as he brought the cabriolet to a halt. Sitting next to him in the two-wheeled carriage was Emma, in a dark coaching cloak, her hair tied back in a ponytail. Robert jumped down from the driving seat and held out his hand to his sister as she stepped out of the carriage and ran towards George.

'I'm so relieved to see that you are unharmed,' she said, taking his hands in hers. 'When I heard about you and Captain

Entwhistle, I was worried sick. After poor Peter's death I couldn't bear to lose another friend.' She squeezed George's hands and smiled. 'I'm so happy.'

Robert cleared his throat. 'I've brought Emma here as she wanted to say goodbye.'

'You're leaving already?' said George turning to Emma. 'You've only been here for a few days.'

'Well,' said Emma, 'Robert has got some leave and he's taking me to Taormina and on to Syracuse. He's promised,' she glanced at her brother, 'to show me Etna on the way.'

'Are you not returning to Messina?'

'Almost certainly not,' replied Emma. 'My parents have some friends who live in Syracuse who have invited me to stay, and I may well take my passage home from there with them, perhaps stopping at Trapani and Palermo along the way.'

'You will be greatly missed here in Messina, Miss Thring,' said George, stepping back. 'I hope you have enjoyed yourself during your stay in our little outpost.'

'I shall never forget my time here, dear Captain Warne. You have been most kind to me.'

'I hope you enjoy Taormina and Syracuse.'

'I will write to tell you how I get on.'

'We should be going back now, my dear,' said Robert, jumping up into the cabriolet, 'as our felucca leaves for Taormina at midday.'

'Goodbye,' said Emma.

'Goodbye,' said George. 'I look forward to hearing of your adventures. Do write to me.' With that he kissed her hand and helped her up into the carriage. Robert flicked the reins at the horse, which started forward. George watched as the cabriolet swung round towards the road and picked up speed. As it did so, Emma turned, her face just visible over the folded hood, and waved. George waved back.

Once the carriage had disappeared out of sight, George walked round to the seaward side of the fort and onto the beach. He stood in the rough, gritty sand and stared out over the ruffled surface of the straits towards Calabria. A merchantman was beating up towards Scylla against the wind. Boney picked up a piece of driftwood and trotted over to George to drop it at his feet. He looked up expectantly.

RICHARD HOPTON is an author, historian and journalist. He graduated from the University of Oxford with an MA in Modern History and has previously published three works of non-fiction. His interests include architecture, the British countryside, art, politics, cricket, racing and springer spaniels. He lives in Dorset with his wife and two children. *The Straits of Treachery* is his first novel.

richardhopton.co.uk   *@richard_hopton*